Blue Pages

Blue Pages

A NOVEL BY *Eleanor Perry*

J. B. LIPPINCOTT COMPANY / PHILADELPHIA AND NEW YORK

For their encouragement and belief the writer wishes to thank her children, Ann Bayer and William Bayer, and her friends, Rodney Pelter, Yael Woll, Nathaniel Shapiro, Ron Taft, Jack Guise, Erika Freeman, Max Palevsky, Mickey Watson—and special gratitude to Gene Young, Ed Burlingame and Janet Baker of the J. B. Lippincott Company.

U.S. Library of Congress Cataloging in Publication Data

Perry, Eleanor.
    Blue pages.

    I. Title.
PZ4.P462 5B [PS3566.E696] 813'.5'4 78–13503
ISBN-0-397-01254-3

For Hilda Lindley and Alan Shayne
and for Geneviève

*Is life a director's medium
or a writer's medium?*
—DANA FRADON

Writers are the women of the film industry.
—OVERHEARD IN THE BEVERLY HILLS HOTEL

Blue Pages

Final cut

Is this a scene from a movie?

"I like you very much," the man says, "but I don't love you any more. It's as simple as that."

Nothing about the man in the more than ten years the woman has been married to him has ever been simple. She doesn't believe his leaving is simple.

"Are you in love with someone else?" A futile question that will never get a straight answer. Anyway, she knows the answer.

"No."

He's always been a bad liar and he's lying now. He is staring into her eyes so determinedly the woman feels an impulse to laugh. He actually believes that idiotic myth—if you can look the other person in the eye it proves you're telling the truth.

"Please don't leave me," she says.

I'd cut my throat before I'd write a line like that!

"Please don't," she says again. "I need you now."

Has she no pride? This dialogue has got to be rewritten.

"I want to be free," the man says.

"Why now? Why not last year? Or the year before?"

The man shrugs as if there is no particular reason. She knows the reason. The year before she was writing the script of *Somersault* for him, and last year he shot it. It was their biggest hit.

"There is someone else, isn't there?"

The man puts his finger in the glass and stirs the ice cubes around. "We said if it didn't work out we'd get a divorce. We said that when we got married, didn't we?"

Oh, yes, they had said that. The woman nods. It had made them sound flippant and cool, helped to handle their embarrassment at being so crazy about each other.

"Well, there you are then," the man says. He takes a long drink.

This whole scene is wrong. If I were writing it I'd stop and ask myself, what have I got here? What I've got here is a man and a woman in a half-furnished living room. The man is a film director. The woman is a film writer. There is also a dog in the room. I would never write a dog into a scene like this. Nevertheless, there's a dog in the room.

"Please stay," the woman says.

This scene isn't going anywhere! What is the intention of this scene? The man's intention is to leave forever. The woman realizes that things can never get better between them but she wants him to stay until they finish their next film. She has been working on the script for a long time.

"At least until after we make the picture," the woman adds.

"I'm not going to make the picture."

This rocks the woman. It is not cold in the room but she feels cold. "You can't mean that!" she exclaims. She tries to hide her shivering. "We've already made the deal. A fantastic deal. Best we ever had!"

He knows that! I'd flunk my film writing students for those lines! How many times have I explained exposition—told them they must find a way to let the audience in on a situation without allowing the characters to tell each other what they already know?

The dog, a large black poodle, has dropped a saliva-dampened ball at the man's feet. She is looking up at him and wagging her tail.

The man ignores the dog. "I don't want to be the Wades any more," he says. "I don't want to be Vincent-and-Lucia Wade." He runs their names together as if they're one name.

"Why not? We haven't done so badly."

"I want to be Vincent Wade from now on." He avoids looking at her. "I've renegotiated our deal for a different picture that I'm going to do alone."

"Let me get this straight," the woman says. "You've turned our deal into another deal that doesn't include me? When did you do that?"

"There're phones in Dublin, you know."

So he'd arranged the whole thing from the set while she sat in a room a few blocks away writing the script for a picture he knew he wasn't going to make.

"What about the studio? That sleight of hand was all right with them?"

12

"They don't like your script anyway."

"Why not?"

"They just don't like it." He lifts his glass and takes a long drink of scotch. "The ending—they think the ending's too downbeat."

The woman suspects he's improvising. "It's the same ending as the book's. They didn't object when they read the book."

"I'm bringing them a terrifically commercial property. A best seller."

"Oh? What?" The woman is still shivering, but now it's from anger, not cold.

The man names the novel he's bought.

Remarkable how much one can do over the telephone from Dublin to Los Angeles.

He tells her how many top-notch directors were after it. He lists their names triumphantly. It sounds as if he's prouder of beating them out than he is of the novel.

For God's sake don't let her ask who's going to do the adaptation.

"Who's going to do the adaptation?" she asks.

"The author." He gives the woman a sharp accusatory look over the rim of his glass. "You didn't even like the book!"

"I admired the writing—I didn't like the heroine. She seemed so paralyzed, so numb. . . ."

"She's numb because she's in pain," the man says defensively. "She suffers more than ordinary people."

"How come?"

"Because she's more sensitive."

"I didn't understand her."

"How could you? You're a *survivor.*" He has called her a survivor before, with the same edge of contempt to his voice. He is denouncing her for not being sensitive enough, not fragile enough. He implies that she is ordinary, because when she's in pain she isn't paralyzed. Is he perhaps remembering that night in the Beverly Hills Hotel a couple of years ago, the night she turned into a howling maniac and almost killed him? If there hadn't been a short cord on that lamp she threw she might have killed him.

"Well," the man says, "I've told you what I came over to tell you." He drains his glass.

"Are you going back to the hotel?"

He nods.

"It's ridiculous. This is your apartment, your home. That's your dog. I'm your wife."

13

Another ghastly line. Why is she cataloging herself as one of his possessions?

Suddenly she realizes he isn't wearing his gold wedding band. Vacant, the third finger of his left hand looks broader and pudgier than ever. He looks fatter, too, since she last saw him two weeks ago in Dublin. He had been shooting a picture there, his first by another writer. She'd wanted that. When they needed money she'd written scripts for other directors. She knew it was good for them both to work with different people. This particular writer was a journalist friend whom they themselves had paid to write a first draft. After that, Vincent made a deal with a studio. The woman had been in Dublin during most of the shooting but left early to come home and finish the apartment. After the wrap, the man unexpectedly (to her) went to Paris. When he returned to New York he went directly to a hotel.

"How come you went to Paris?"

"I—felt like it."

"Did you see Claude and Monique? Did you scc Nelly?"

"I—I just enjoyed my own company."

He's such a bad liar. He's never been able to bear his own company, bear being alone. After a very few years he couldn't bear being alone with her.

"Where's your ring? At the bottom of the Seine?"

"What're you talking about?"

He has always had a selective memory. Now he stands up and glances around at the newly delivered furniture they had selected together.

"This room looks terrible without a rug," he says. He says it with disdain as if that's why he couldn't possibly stay.

"I didn't want to choose one without you. I was waiting for you to . . ." Her voice trails off as the man crosses toward the foyer. The poodle accompanies him eagerly, her ball in her mouth. Finally the woman rises and follows them.

At the door the man says, "I hope we'll be friends. I'll always consider you one of my best friends." He doesn't ask her what she hopes or how she'll consider him.

He leaves. The poodle's tail droops. She gives the door an indignant look.

"C'est la vie," the woman tells the poodle.

They go into the living room and play ball. The poodle's paws slide and scratch as she scrambles over the bare floor. After a while she gets tired of the game and sprints into the kitchen toward her water dish.

14

The woman crosses to the coffee table, which still has padding laced up around its legs. There is nothing on the table but a leaflet of instructions for the care of the new suede chairs and a shallow silver bowl with a single cigarette in it. The bowl is a baby's porringer, monogrammed *V. W.*, dents in its side from baby teeth. The woman picks up the cigarette, lights it and stands there smoking. At least I'll no longer be living an adaptation of his life, she thinks; from now on my life will have its own script. After a moment she stabs the cigarette out in the silver bowl.

She leaves the room and starts down a hall hung with posters of the films she and the man made together. Their two names are above each title except on the poster for their last film—although she found the novel and adapted it and worked with the man the way she always had. Her name is nowhere on it at all, nor is the name of the author of the book. Above a photograph of the star is the title SOMER-SAULT and below the photograph, in large letters, A Vincent Wade Film. That's all. The man had pointed out how handsome the design was—no clutter.

The woman goes into her study and sits down at her desk. Along the windowsill beside it there is a row of mementos: a small poodle made of black wool, a little ivory bust of Nefertiti bought in Cairo, an antique perfume bottle, gift from a young actress in one of their pictures, a framed invitation to the White House, a framed quote from Jean Renoir, a drawing of Balzac, photographs of her daughter and her son, a unit photographer's shot of the man riding a dolly, a snapshot the man took of her and their dog on the Croisette in Cannes and a sterling-silver oversized brandy snifter holding pens and pencils. The man had presented it to her at the wrap party for *Somersault*. It is engraved with her name and, under that, *Your vision, your talent, your guts, my love always.* Below is the man's name and the date. The date is eleven months ago.

The dog comes to the door of the study with her ball in her mouth. The woman begins to cry. The dog stands in the doorway wagging her tail.

That dog has got to be cut out of this movie!
But it isn't a movie.

1

Oh, well, it's only a movie, I thought.

The Southern California sun beat on the window, scorching my neck, and sweat dripped off my face onto the open script, onto the scribbled rewrites between the lines and in the margins. For a moment I watched the dumb words insisted on by Ernie and Grant melt away into inkblots. Good riddance. I swiveled my chair around and banged on the air conditioner. If Maintenance couldn't get it to run, maybe my fists could. They couldn't.

I opened the venetian blind and peered out at the lot. Heat waves were rising from the hoods of the cars parked in front of the bungalow so that everything that lay beyond was fragmented and quivering. A man on a bicycle, a strapped box of film under his arm, pedaled toward me down the alley. He looked like Peter O'Toole riding across the desert in *Lawrence of Arabia*. At the end of the alley a limp pennant was strung between the second floors of two mud-puddle-colored buildings. It said WELCOME BETTE DAVIS in huge letters. Bette Davis had come out to guest-star in some television sit-com, finished shooting and gone away months ago, but the greeting still hung there, grimy and faded.

It's only a movie, I thought again. What the hell do I care? But I did care. Desperately. I had been a "hot" writer after *Somersault*, and after Vincent split I'd written on assignment, five scripts, one right after the other. Now more than two years had gone by and none of them had reached the screen. In a town where you're only as good as your last picture I was becoming lukewarm. I needed a screen credit. I absolutely had to get this picture made. Anyway, no movie was "only a movie" to me. Writing screenplays was my work, how I spent the time of my life. My self-image was involved, my principles and, in a

16

sense, if the word isn't too archaic, my honor. Professional honor, at least.

"So where does he fuck her?" The question boomed through my office.

I whirled around. Ernie had opened my door and stuck his head in. I was surprised to see him because for the last couple of weeks only Indians had stuck their heads in.

"Can you gimme where he fucks her?" Ernie shouted.

I squinted at him through the smoke of my cigarette. God, he was unattractive. His bald scalp was toasted from his daily jog on the beach at Malibu, speckled with darker brown spots and spanned by a few lonely hairs he combed up from the sides.

"I warned you there'll be fuckin' snow in Utah when we shoot. He can't fuck her on the riverbank so where does he fuck her?"

The sun shining between the slats striped the lower part of his face —that mingy red-lipped mouth through which no puff of nicotine or rare steak or graceful word has ever passed.

"I've got to think about it," I said. "This room's a sweatbox and—"

"We'd all better think about it! My office. Twenty minutes."

"I have a lunch date."

"Break it. I'll give you lunch." Ernie withdrew his head and slammed the door.

My stomach lurched. Ernie's idea of food was a mixed-up mess of granola, blackstrap molasses, wheat germ and yogurt. It was torment enough to work on a film with that idiot without having to eat his health-food crap. I grabbed a handful of script pages and fanned myself.

The door opened. An Indian stuck his head in. He was in full regalia—feathers, braids, deerskins. All the Indians wore their gear when they came to see the casting director.

"Toilet?" The Indian's voice was guttural the way Indian's voices are supposed to be in movies.

"Next room." I gestured. "Where the sign says 'Convenience.' "

The Indian glowered at me. I shrugged. He slammed the door.

For about the sixth time in two days I dialed Maintenance to beg them to do something about my air conditioner. Maintenance was busy. As I put the phone down, Bill Curtis, a screenwriter friend of mine, knocked and walked in.

"Jesus!" he said. "Feels like Death Valley in here."

"I can't have lunch with you," I told him. "Story conference."

He was staring around the room—at the broken-down chaise longue without cushions, the cracks in the stained plaster walls, the splintery floor with my splintery wooden desk to match, a battered old Remington on a metal typing table.

"I worked in this bungalow once," he said. "I never even *saw* this room. What *is* this room?"

"My office."

Bill burst out laughing, his usual gallows laugh. Along with his pale hollow-cheeked face it gave him the air of a prisoner newly released from a dungeon. He was currently working on a television pilot in the television building, so he *had* come from a dungeon.

"Sit down a minute." I indicated a lopsided chair, rubber tips missing from two of its legs. When Bill sat on it, it slanted perilously sideways. He had to put out a foot to brace himself, which made him laugh all over again.

"And you're the co-producer of this film?"

"That's right."

"This isn't a *producer's* office."

I fanned myself again. "Ernie moved onto the lot a week before I got in from New York. He assigned the offices."

"Uh-huh. Where's your secretary?"

"I use the receptionist when she's free."

"Uh-huh. Where's your car?"

"In the parking lot."

"That's half a mile from here, isn't it?"

Bill's chuckles irritated me. "Listen," I said, "I don't care about all the phony status symbols you guys out here care about."

"No shit?"

"I want to write a good script, make a good movie. That's what counts."

"Where'd you get that droll idea? In film school?"

"You know I never went to film school."

Bill took out his handkerchief and mopped his face. "Bet Ernie's in the suite to the right of the entrance."

I nodded.

"Paneled walls, leather couches, oriental rugs, bathroom, kitchen, secretary's office, right? What about the conference room?"

"Grant Ames is in there."

"*Grant Ames?* Is he directing this picture?" I nodded again. "You're in more trouble than I thought. What about the big room to the left of the entrance? That's the one I had."

"Ernie's aunt's in there."

"His *aunt?*"

"She's the set decorator. Ernie got her into the union." More snickers from Bill. "I guess it is kind of funny."

"It's a goddamned farce! Didn't you say anything when Ernie stuck you in here?"

"Why waste energy squabbling over an office?"

"You made a big mistake, kid. You should've turned around and gone straight back to the hotel and stayed there until you got an office as good as Ernie's."

"Would it've worked?"

"That's the way it *does* work!" He stuck out his lower lip and blew a whiff of breath up over his face. "What you call phony status symbols are *real* phony status symbols. When you have a producer's office, you're a producer. When you're in a hole next to the john you're a Little Match Girl." Bill coughed, a hacking sound that came from his chest. "You optioned the book, didn't you?"

"Sure did."

"How'd Ernie get into it?"

"My agent put us together."

"Didn't you know about all the stinking pictures Ernie's made?"

"What about *The Castle?*"

"He had nothing to do with it—the director wouldn't allow him on the set. They gave him a producer credit for bringing in the star."

"My agent said he's the best deal-maker in the business. He got us a deal in a week."

"Yeah? Who'd he pay off?"

"Pay off?"

"Don't you know about kickbacks, kid?" Bill laughed. "Works both ways. I heard Ernie demanded a kickback from his chauffeur when he was making that last stinker in Madrid."

"God!"

Bill took a cigarette from the pack on my desk.

I tossed him my lighter. "Thought you'd quit."

"A writer can't quit without cracking up. It's the producers who can stop smoking."

"Every time I'm in Ernie's office I chain-smoke. He goes bananas. It's worth it even if I lose a lung."

"You got the right values, kid. So how's he screwing you?"

"Ruining the script. Messing around with every line—"

"That's called giving the writer 'creative input.' "

"I'm on the third rewrite and it's worse every time."

"You ain't seen nothin'. Wait till he starts getting in other writers!"

"Over my dead body."

"You were dead the day you signed a contract with Ernie Kaplan." He stood up. "I'll pass out if I stay in here. Call me when you're free for lunch. Old Father William'll tell you the facts of life."

I gave him a glum look. "Okay."

"Upset you, huh? You should be upset." He put his hands on my desk and leaned toward me. "You're no kid, kid. You got a lotta gray in your hair."

"Why not? I'm about to be forty-seven years old."

"You should've learned by this time that if you let people treat you like shit, you'll *be* shit."

When he got to the door, he grinned back at me.

"Your name isn't even on the goddamned building."

As soon as Bill was out the door I dialed Maintenance.

"Oh, yes, Mrs. Wade," Maintenance said. "My man can't repair your air conditioner. We'll have to requisition a new one, but the studio's in an economic downturn so I don't know when—"

"Never mind the air conditioner!" I interrupted. "I want someone over here on the double to put my name on the building right next to Ernest Kaplan's."

"Can't do that, Mrs. Wade. Not unless Mr. Kaplan requests it."

"*I'm* requesting it. Mr. Kaplan and I are *co-producers*. We're *equal! He is not my boss!*"

I heard a rattle of papers. "Bungalow Five. It says here you're only the writer. . . ."

"What do you mean *only the writer?*" I screamed. "There wouldn't *be* any picture without me! None of these people over here would be working without me! You might not have your job without me!"

"I had you pegged for a lady, Mrs. Wade," Maintenance said sadly. "That's not a very ladylike tone you're taking."

"I'm sorry, but—"

"What's more, I've been here thirty-two years," Maintenance added with firm dignity. "I had my job before you came, Mrs. Wade, and I'll have my job after you go."

"I apologize. I shouldn't have said that."

"It says here: 'Bungalow Five, *The Lady and the Robber*, Ernest Kaplan, producer.' That's all it says."

20

"Okay, thanks anyway," I said. "I'll take care of it."

I snatched up an armload of scripts and started out of my office. Before I reached the door the phone rang. It was Ernie's secretary, to tell me Mr. Ames had been delayed. Our meeting was postponed for another half hour. I knew Grant was late for the same reason he was always late. "Delayed" was a euphemism for overslept. Grant Ames, our director, The Sleeping Prick.

The first half dozen "bankable" directors we'd tried had turned the project down. Word came to me from Ernie, who said it came to him from their agents. Their reasons were various: preparing another picture, not available, doesn't want to direct a period picture, hates the script, hates the script, hates the script.

"Did all three of them use the word hate?" I asked Ernie.

"Gives you the feeling something's wrong with the fuckin' script, huh?"

"No."

"Writers!" Ernie opened his desk drawer and took out a little box of raisins. "Writers are always right and everyone else is always wrong!" He popped a raisin into his mouth. "You think you know more than three bankable directors know?"

"We've got to send the script to Marshall Macklin, Ernie."

He shook his head.

"Why not? He's the best director on the list."

"Stop bugging me about Macklin. You fuckin' him or what?"

"I love his pictures. I'd like to work with him."

"I don't want him. I don't need him. An Ernest Kaplan Production doesn't need a director because it's an Ernest Kaplan Production."

"Tell that to the studio."

Ernie poured a pile of raisins onto his palm and stuffed them in his mouth.

"I'm sending Macklin the script today." I marched out leaving him there flooding his system with potassium, which, I feared, would not be fatal.

Twenty-four hours after the script went to Macklin's agent, Ernie called me into his office.

"Just heard from your big crush," he said.

"That was quick." I knew it was bad news from the smirk on his face.

"He hates it."

"Did he say why?"

"Maybe because it's no good."

"Didn't he even want to talk to me about it? He's a friend of mine."

Ernie snorted. "Nobody has any fuckin' friends in this business!"

"Is he out here? I want to call him—"

"Forget it." He got very busy tearing at a cellophane pack of dried apricots. "I got Grant Ames."

"Grant Ames? He's a terrible director!"

"Picture he made with me could of been a smash!" He chewed on an apricot for a moment. "Asshole spaced-out star fucked it up. Actors." He groaned. "If you're so smart, figure out a way to do without actors. If I could do without actors and writers, I'd be a happy man!"

"I won't accept Grant Ames."

"Trust me," Ernie said. Next to "fuckin'," "trust" was his favorite word. "Grant'll bring the picture in on time and budget. What's more, I can control him—he'll do exactly what I say." He read the apprehension on my face and narrowed his eyes. "I'm not your corner-candy-store producer, you know. I'm a *creative* producer."

"The studio won't accept Grant Ames."

"They'll take anyone I want. They trust me."

"What about somebody I want?"

"You should get down on your knees and thank God Grant likes your script, if you . . ." He stopped to dig a piece of apricot out from between his back teeth.

"If I what?"

"If you want to get this picture made. No director—no picture."

He knew exactly which of my buttons to press.

Grant Ames was an American who had been living in London trying to hustle himself a British picture. He flew out to the coast and was installed in the conference room in Bungalow Five. He brought with him either one black turtleneck sweater or, I hoped, seven black turtleneck sweaters, since he never wore any other shirt. He also brought a filthy denim crew cap which he removed only to scratch his head. From under the cap his stringy unwashed hair hung almost to his shoulders. Very Carnaby Street, ten years out of date. Cindy, his English girl friend, came along too and they rented an expensive house in Brentwood.

Cindy usually called three or four times an hour when Grant and I were working. Grant never refused the calls or apologized to me for taking them. "Cindy's homesick," he told me. "And now she's developed this psychotic hang-up that I'm cheating on her."

"Are you?"

"For Chrissake when do I have the *time?* This bloody script takes all my *time!*" He opened the script in the middle and read for a minute. "Bullshit!" He grabbed a felt-tipped pen and crossed out the page.

I leaned over to look at it. "Hey!" I said. "Why're you cutting that?"

"It's bullshit."

"It's one of the few times they really talk to each other."

"It just lays there."

He turned another few pages and Xed out again.

"*Why?*"

"Nothing's happening."

"Plenty's happening between the two people!"

He glanced at me. "What've you got that long face on for?" He tossed his pen down. "Women don't belong in this business."

"I'm going to put back that dialogue."

"Not if I'm gonna shoot this picture."

After a couple of weeks Cindy's calls got longer and more hysterical, and we did less and less "work." One day they got into an argument when Grant told her he'd be late getting home. He began to shout at her.

"I don't give a damn what you do! Jerk off! Watch TV! Fuck the pool boy! . . . I don't *know* what time. . . . I may be here all night! I'll put the writer on if you don't believe me!" He put his hand over the mouthpiece. "Come on, luv, tell her we've got to work all night."

"I will not!"

Suddenly he shouted into the phone. "Oh, that again! You promised if I brought you out here you wouldn't start that again. . . . All right, luv, do it and get it over with! Got enough pills? Hope it's a full bottle so you don't fuck up the way you fucked up last time!" He slammed down the phone. "Some chicks get off on vibrators," he said. "That one gets off on stomach pumps."

I was worried. "Do you think she'll really do it?"

"She'd do *anything* for attention."

"You'd better give her some."

"I'll give her a kick in the ass. Masochistic bitch!"

"That's for sure. Why else would she stay with *you?*"

Grant smiled and bent over the script again.

"Why don't you send her home?"

"Uh-uh," he said. "I like her around." He looked up at me from under the brim of his cap. "She gives good head."

At a quarter past one, scripts in my arms, I hurried down the long corridor toward Ernie's office. An Indian was coming toward me, naked except for a loincloth and about twenty pounds of turquoise and silver jangling around his neck. He was peering tentatively at each office door.

You're on your own, Buster, I thought, as I rushed past him. I, who had signed petitions for water rights for the Pima Indians and donated money to the American Indian Development Association and written furious letters to the Bureau of Indian Affairs about schools on the Sioux reservation, wouldn't even tell a Red Brother where he could pee. The monsters in this place were turning *me* into a monster.

A blast of icy air-conditioned air hit me as I flung open the door to Ernie's office. Grant Ames was already there, stretched out on one of the leather couches, his cap pulled down over his eyes. The door to the little kitchen was open and I could hear Ernie rattling around at the refrigerator. I slammed my scripts down on the coffee table. Grant didn't move.

Ernie came in carrying a tray. On it were three glasses of white viscous liquid that looked like milk of magnesia.

"Listen here, Ernie." My voice was shaking with anger. "I want my name put on this building today."

Ernie glanced at Grant and chuckled. "Balls all night and sleeps all day."

"I want my name on this building!" I shouted.

Ernie set the tray down. Then he whipped off Grant's cap and slapped him with it hard across both cheeks. Grant opened his eyes and sat up. Blearily, he ran his fingers through his greasy hair.

Ernie thrust a glass into my hands.

"Taste it. You'll love it."

"Are you listening to me, Ernie?"

"What'd you say?"

"This is the third time I've said it! I want my name on this building! I want a reserved parking space in front!"

"Cool it, for Chrissake!" He gave me an outraged look. "We got big script problems and you're on some fuckin' ego trip!"

Grant tasted the white liquid and made a face. "Something's wrong with this milk."

"It's not milk. It's *kefir* milk!" Ernie tilted his glass and took a long

24

swallow. "Marco Polo got it from the Moslems in the thirteenth century."

"Shit, no wonder it's sour!"

"Not sour, *fermented*. Good for everything in the elimination track."

I slammed my glass down on the table. Lucky for the studio's economic downturn the glass didn't break.

"Aren't you gonna taste it?" Ernie asked. "It's good for hemorrhoids."

"I do not have hemorrhoids."

"All writers have hemorrhoids from sitting on their asses all day. Tolstoy had hemorrhoids."

"I am not Tolstoy."

"Better fuckin' believe it!"

Ernie sat down and drained his glass. I could hear the kefir milk plop noisily down his throat.

"So let's get to work," he said. "Where's he gonna fuck her?"

"Would you mind saying 'make love'?" I asked. "It's a love story."

"Our writer's a little uptight about your vocabulary." Grant winked at Ernie.

"Just trying to make her feel like one of the boys," Ernie said.

"What I think," Grant said, "is that Andrew fucks Cecelia in that cabin after Buck Barnes rapes her."

I stared at him. "You crazy? Buck Barnes does not rape her!"

"He's got to rape her," Ernie said.

"Absolutely not! This may be the first picture in ten years without a rape in it."

"The rape motivates the fight," Grant said.

"What fight?"

"Didn't we tell you?" Ernie put on an expression of fake surprise. "The star wants a kick-'im-in-the-nuts fight between him and Buck Barnes."

"Impossible. After Buck Barnes hops that freight we never see him again."

"If the star wants a kick-'im-in-the-nuts fight," Ernie said, "that's what the star's gonna get."

"I'll talk to him about that."

Ernie gave me a withering look. "He doesn't want to talk to *you*. He never talks to *writers.*"

"Then he can talk to me as co-producer."

"I promised him there'd be one line of communication. *Me.*

25

We'll get our fuckin' wires crossed if he has to talk to everybody."

"I'm going to talk to him anyway."

Ernie got red in the face. "You make him mad, he'll walk. You want this fuckin' picture made or don't you?"

I lighted a cigarette and puffed hard. "I can't imagine a woman wanting to make love after she's been raped or a man wanting to do it. It's a disgusting, sick idea."

"What do you know about it?" Ernie asked. "Rape turns men on."

"Turns broads on too." Grant stretched himself out on the couch again. "All broads have rape fantasies. Don't you?"

"No."

"There've been surveys," Ernie said. "You're a minority." He got up and went back into the kitchen.

Grant turned to me. "What about those sex books where they tell you how to tie up a chick before you fuck her? Why's that in the books if the chicks don't dig it?"

"That's not rape, that's bondage."

"One chick I had never went out without her ropes. Carried them around in her handbag."

Ernie came out of the kitchen with another tray. There were three bowls on it and a plate of flat dung-colored muffins.

"Kill that fuckin' cigarette," he told me. "We're gonna eat. We got kelp and bran and sesame seeds." He put a big spoonful of the stuff in his mouth and chomped his milk-white baby teeth up and down. He picked up the plate and offered it to Grant, "Have a triticale muffin. Invented by stone-age women. That oughta please our writer."

"Why should it please me?"

"Lookit what your sex accomplished without even a women's lib?"

When he thrust the plate at me I pushed it away.

"High in proteins. You're making a mistake."

"My mistake," I said, "was agreeing to do a picture with you."

Ernie laughed. "We're gonna have a big hit and then you'll love me to pieces!"

It was impossible to insult him. I lighted another cigarette.

When Ernie's bowl was empty he sat down at his desk and took a yellow studio memo out of a drawer.

"Here's what we're gonna do. Write this down," he told me. He consulted the memo. "Andrew and Cecelia find an abandoned cabin in the woods. Cecelia cleans it up while Andrew goes out to hunt for their supper."

26

"I want him to kill a deer," Grant said, "a fuckin' deer with big deer eyes."

"Then Buck Barnes sneaks into the cabin. He rapes Cecelia. Andrew comes back. He beats Buck up. Then he shoots him."

A faraway look had come into Grant's eyes. "I'll choreograph a fight like you've never seen!" He jumped up and started dancing around the office lashing the air with his fists. "One punch—he breaks Buck's nose. Another punch knocks his teeth out. One–two like this to the kidneys! Buck screams! Blood pours out his mouth!" Grant's foot shot out. "He kicks him in the crotch! Another vicious kick in the crotch! Buck screeches! He crumples to the ground. Andrew drags him up on his feet. He twists his arm like this. You hear the bone crack! Maybe he breaks his other arm. Buck's back on the ground. Andrew throws himself on top of him. His thumbs go for Buck's eyes. Then he stands up, takes out his gun. Bang! Bang! He shoots him in the balls! You'll see the impact! Those balls will *quiver*, man! They'll *leap!* Bang! Bang! Bang! He empties his gun into those balls!"

Grant's eyes were gleaming. He was gasping for breath as he slumped into his chair.

"I gotta talk to Special Effects. I wanna see those balls *leap*, man!"

Ernie frowned at me. "Why didn't you write it down?"

"I'll remember it," I said. "Vividly."

Another shuddering breath from Grant. Then he went limp.

"Look at him! He got off on it." Ernie put the memo away and waved his arms at the cigarette smoke. "Okay," he said to me. "Go and write it!"

"What's Cecelia doing during this fight?" I asked Grant.

"Watching it, for Chrissake!"

"I don't believe she'd watch it."

"Cecelia will eat that fight up," Grant said. "She's a strong woman. You're the one keeps telling us how liberated she is."

"By the way." Ernie shook his finger at me. "I got a memo from the studio about that quote in Army Archerd's column."

"What about it?"

"Where you said we're making the first Women's Lib Western. Pissed them off." He pulled another memo sheet and read it aloud. " 'Advise Wade that she is never under any circumstances to use the term Women's Lib Western about this picture in any publicity, interviews or statements to the press.' That's what the memo says."

I stood up and grabbed my scripts. "Up the memo!"

"Atta girl!" Ernie beamed at me. "Loosenin' up a little!"

"She's gonna be a real mellow broad time we finish this picture," Grant said.

"Go fly a kite!" I said.

I left my cigarette burning in the ashtray and walked out. Halfway down the hall I could still hear them laughing like hell.

Back in my office I picked up the phone to call my agent, Sidney Powker, in New York. I gave the studio switchboard operator his name and number and my name and extension. It was the first time I'd made a long-distance call from Bungalow Five.

"Who is calling New York?" the operator asked.

"I am."

"Whose secretary are you?"

"I'm not a secretary."

"You're required to give the name of the man who's going to speak on this call."

"*I* am going to speak on this call."

"I can't put the call through until I get the correct information," the operator said.

"Look here, I'm a producer. I'm producing a picture at this studio!"

There was a pause. "You'll have to have this call approved. I'll give you the supervisor."

The supervisor came on like a recruiter for the CIA. She asked for everything but a brain scan. Finally she agreed I was eligible not only to make a call but to speak on it.

"It confuses my girls when they hear your voice and you're not a secretary," she explained. "I'll warn them about you." She assigned me a charge number so the accounting department would know exactly who was bankrupting the studio. "Please refrain from making calls between ten and one and two and five," she said.

"Why?"

"The men here make heavy use of the lines during those periods."

"I'm surprised the way Ernie's acting," my agent said. "Especially to a nice lady like you."

"Nice ladies finish last, Sidney."

"What's that, honey? I didn't get that."

"You seem to be the only person on both coasts who doesn't know how Ernie operates. I was married to a shit and now you've married me to another shit."

28

"That hurts me, honey," Sidney wailed, "to hear you talk about Vincent like that."

"Because you're his agent? Or because it's true?"

"Because you're a lady."

"Cut out that lady stuff. Ladies can't even get their air conditioners fixed out here."

"Hey, I hear you're having a heat wave!" Sidney loved weather talk. "Freezing in New York—nineteen degrees! You don't know how lucky you are."

"Sidney, I want you to call Ernie. Tell him he's got to stop Ted Clayburn from changing the script—"

"Clayburn's a star, honey! Clayburn's box office! You can't argue with that."

"He's turning this picture into some other picture I've never heard of. I think we should replace him."

From three thousand miles away Sidney's terror was palpable. "My God, do you know what you got there when you got Clayburn? A gold mine is what you got! You don't know how lucky you are!"

I didn't answer.

"Honey?" Sidney said after a moment. "You there?"

"I'm here," I said. "I'm here because Ernie is your client too— so you put us together and got two commissions."

"That kind of talk hurts me," Sidney moaned over the wire. "When I made your deal with Ernie I felt I was doing the best thing for you, and I still do." He paused to let me hear him bleeding. Finally, he said, "Honey, call Maintenance and get your air conditioner fixed. You'll feel better. Don't forget it's nineteen degrees *here.*"

"You don't know how lucky you are."

After this conversation I wrote four lines into the script. I turned to the scene where Cecelia is cleaning up the abandoned cabin in the woods and I wrote:

Buck Barnes sneaks into the cabin and rapes Cecelia. Andrew returns dragging a deer with big deer eyes. He catches Buck Barnes zipping up his fly and beats him to a pulp before shooting him.

I stared at the page. Something was wrong. I crossed out "zipping" and wrote in "buttoning." Something was still terribly wrong. I stopped typing and looked out the window to see what the action was outside. As usual, not much. A studio security guard rode by in a little

29

electric cart. A bearded guy with a script under his arm was walking along with a little boy. The boy was wearing a T-shirt that said in large block letters IGNORE THIS PERSON. I recognized a skinny middle-aged woman in a green and white uniform. She was a waitress from the commissary probably heading for home. She dragged along, scuffing up dust, drinking a Coke from a bottle. She saw me as she passed and waved. "Have a nice day!" she called. I sat there squinting for a few minutes, aching to be back in New York where there were no palm trees and it *rained.* I wanted to take my dog, Tory, out to the park and watch her as, perfectly on point, she stalked the autumn squirrels. I wanted to walk along streets and look at people with pale skins who wore heavy coats and boots and were so unlaid-back they talked to themselves, crossed against the lights and never ever told each other to "have a nice day."

I closed the blind, turned around and put my head down on my arms on the desk. My sweaty face dampened the sleeves of my shirt. Sweat trickled down my back. It was difficult to breathe.

What am I doing in this room, on this lot, in this town?
How did I get here?

Take one

How did she get here?

In this cruddy Greenwich Village room with its stained walls and crumbling plaster, on this lumpy daybed, under this dirty blanket?

How did she get here, lying curled against the superabundant flesh of this stranger, this young man with the body of Rodin's Balzac, the same huge belly and broad chest? He looks like Balzac too—with his plumped-out cheeks and rolls of chin and shaggy hair and beard—except that the young man's hair and beard are ginger red, his eyes green. Moss-green now, at night.

The only light in the room is from the fireplace where the two logs they picked up at the corner grocery store flame and crackle. On the record player across the room Barenboim is playing Mozart's Twenty-fourth Piano Concerto accompanied by the occasional shouts of winos down in the street. Now and then the young man reaches to the floor for his scotch and soda. He offers her the glass first. After he drinks, he put the glass back on the floor.

How did she get here?

Every signpost in her life has pointed in another direction. She should be right now in the spacious Tudor house in a Middle Western suburb. She should be in the master bedroom with its rows of leaded glass windows and its fireplace (never used) and its oriental rug and its antique English furniture. She should be in her twin bed under a monogrammed satin comforter separated by a night table from her husband of seventeen years in his twin bed under his monogrammed satin comforter. Practically everything in the house—the linens, the shower curtains, the demitasse cups, the cigarette boxes, the matchbooks, the key rings, the dog's tag and she herself—bore her husband's initial.

31

That initial had been her destination. Some shadowy "they" had mapped out the journey for her and, without protest, she had followed all the arrows: the one to the wedding in white, the two to the delivery room, the one to the bigger house, the one to the summer house, the six to Good Works, the three to the women's committees of the orchestra and the museum and the community playhouse. "They" had even directed her dreams. This was the right dream, "they" said. And after this one there is another right dream: grandchildren. And after that one? They didn't have to answer. She knew the answer. Everyone did but it was considered vulgar to talk about it.

Her typewriter did not appear on their map but she found her way to it anyway, at odd times when there was nothing else she was supposed to do like have the antifreeze put into the cars or take her daughter to the orthodontist or cheer for her son in a track meet. Her husband didn't mind her typing until she began to get published, and then he grumbled that the money she earned gave him "a tax problem." Her third novel sold to the movies for a substantial sum which her husband "took care of" for her. He raised her personal allowance and made it clear that if she wanted anything more she had only to ask him. Everyone they knew said he was a fine man and a devoted father. At odd moments over the years she would snap to, fully awake. "I've been dreaming the wrong dream," she told herself, and she began to wonder how to get away from there.

She wrote herself away finally. She wrote a play that, like her others, got produced in community theatres around the country. But this one was optioned by a Broadway producer. She went to New York to meet the producer, and when she opened her hotel room door she found him on his knees in the corridor. "I adore you!" he cried. "I adore your play!" What wonderful people there are in the theatre, she thought, and she never went back to the Middle West. After half a year of adoration and rewrites, the producer dropped his option. He informed her of his decision in a letter signed "Sincerely yours."

Her play was optioned again by another producer, famous, powerful, with a long list of distinguished productions behind him. He put together a star, a director and a cast, and she went on the road with the play for the tryout tour. Frequently she got long-distance calls from the producer's assistant. She had seen him hurrying around the office like the rest of the staff, a very heavy, not very tall young man, but she barely remembered his face. What she did remember was a paper taped to the shade of the lamp on his desk. Printed in large letters across the paper were the words NO SINS OF OMISSION. The young man called to relay messages from the producer. Then he would ask if there was anything she needed, anything he could do for her. He was so polite, so *concerned.* What wonderful people there are in the theatre, she thought again.

During the week of the Broadway previews the young man was at the rear of the theatre every night, and every night, after the final curtain, he came backstage. After she was finished with the director's notes, he asked her out for a drink. She never could go because she had a previous engagement with one of the actors in the cast.

"I'm sorry," she said each time. "I'm really sorry."

Now she knew his face very well. It was large and full, framed by his curly red hair and beard, his eyes an extraordinary green. Sometimes when she was with the tall handsome actor in Sardi's, whose hair and eyes were gray, his face would be replaced by the young man's face and she'd have to blink to clear the illusion away. But the green eyes came back in her dreams. In the middle of the night she'd sit straight up in bed, wide awake.

Who me?

Her fingers are searching through the fleecy patch of red hair on the young man's chest for crumbs of the Fig Newtons they've been eating because there is nothing else in the apartment to eat. She hasn't tasted a Fig Newton since summer picnics on the beach at Martha's Vineyard when her children were little. Each time she finds a crumb she puts her mouth down to the young man's chest and scoops it up with her tongue. He laughs and tries to wriggle away. Finally, she lifts her head and props her chin on her elbow to look at him. His eyes are closed, the ginger lashes lying in thick crescents above his cheeks. His lips curve upward in the curly frame of his beard.

How did she get here?

"What're you doing?" he asks.

"Looking at you."

"What're you thinking?" He opens his eyes. "That I'm too fat?"

"You're beautiful."

"All your lovers were tall and lean, I presume."

"There weren't that many."

"You told me your ex-husband was tall and lean and crew-cut and Ivy League and sterling—"

"I didn't say sterling. I don't even know what it means applied to a person."

"Same thing it means applied to silver. Alloy's almost pure—a minimum of copper."

"He wasn't all that pure."

"What about that actor you've been shacking up with?"

"Lots of copper."

"How am I going to get you away from him?"

"You've done it a couple of times already."

"What'd you tell him tonight?"

"Old friends in town."

"Someday I suppose you'll be telling *me* you have old friends in town."

"It's over with him."

"Because of me?"

"Indeed not!"

"You're leaving him for me!"

"No I'm not."

"Why not?"

"You're too stuck-up already."

"I am?" His voice rises with interest. "What makes you think so?"

"Intuition." She flings the blanket aside. "I've got to go home."

"One more cigarette."

They lie together, smoking, listening to the music. When the record stops he says, "I wonder how soon you'll leave me."

"In a little while—when I get too old for you. I'm too old for you now."

"That's patronizing! Do you realize how *patronizing* you are? Don't ever say that again!"

"All right. Not tonight, anyway."

"I'll make you a bet. When you do leave me it'll have nothing to do with your age or my age."

"We're just beginning and you're talking about my leaving."

"You told me you've always been the one to leave. It's a habit with you. You'll leave me too."

"No, you'll leave me."

"Never."

"Well, I won't."

"You will."

They get up and dress. She goes into the bathroom to comb her hair in front of the mirror using only the reflection of light from the other room. She doesn't want to snap on the switch as she did on a previous night and get a clear look at the grimy, dirt-encrusted basin and floor.

On the street he flags down a taxi. He folds his arms around her fiercely for a long, long moment. His eyes have turned aquamarine in the headlights of passing cars. He smells of cigarettes and whiskey and of himself and of her.

The taxi speeds uptown and she is six years old again sitting beside her father who is driving her home from Sunday school. She is wearing white gloves and patent-leather Mary Janes and a round-brimmed hat with streamers down the back. She is a good girl and she knows that God is in his heaven for her and the people on the street are smiling for her and the traffic officer is beckoning "go" for her and her mother is waiting for her with roast beef and strawberries and cream.

Now she stares through the taxi window at the dark empty avenue, loose dirt and papers blowing along the gutters, an overturned trash can, plastic bags of garbage piled like sandbags against the window of a coffee shop, a lighted telephone booth covered with graffiti, its broken instrument askew on its cord. She is almost a middle-aged woman, neither good nor bad, who doesn't believe in God, her father and mother have long ago waged their wars and parted, and too many times these days the strawberries taste like damp cardboard. She is remembering how the young man looked heading toward his room, his broad back in the shabby raincoat, its belt flapping, his hair glinting orange-gold under the street lamp.

And the next morning when she wakes up the sun is shining for her.

Who me?

2

I spent the rest of the afternoon after the story conference moonlighting and therefore in violation of my contract with the studio. My contract stated in bossy legal language that I would devote my "services as long as needed and exclusively" to *The Lady and the Robber.* Except for a few of my red brothers looking for the john, I knew that no one would come near me, so I dug into the back of my file drawer and got out a script I was writing for Philip Rowan and me to produce.

Philip Rowan was a man who, I believed, was devoted to me and to whom, I believed, I was devoted. These fantasies, it turned out later, were on a level with believing in the Tooth Fairy. At the time, however, they made life pleasanter, not to say bearable—and I suppose the proof was that I forgot about the temperature in my office as I went to work on those pages.

Philip had dreamed all his life of becoming a producer but somehow he had never found the right script, at least not right enough to make him leave his various highly paid jobs in the film industry and their bountiful perks—the Mercedes, the lavish offices, the staff of assistants and secretaries, the generous expense accounts, the use of the company jet. At the moment he was Vice-President in Charge of Business Affairs at one of the big studios and one day perhaps, he confided to me, he might even get them to build a screening room onto his house in Bel Air. The fact that he had reached the age of fifty-three without having produced even a home movie didn't bother him. He was fond of pointing out that a friend of his hadn't produced a movie until he was fifty-six, at which time he had found "the right script" and made millions. Now Philip had found me and I was going to write this terrifically right script and we'd produce it together and make millions.

"It's all up to you," Philip said. He said this with his head on my breast and the rest of him stretched out beneath the sheets in the Beverly Hills Hotel while I played with his wavy hair, running my seasick but plucky fingers up and down the perfect peaks. When I promised I would make his lifelong dream come true by the time he was fifty-four, he sneezed a dozen times. He must be allergic, he told me, to the laundry soap they used at the hotel.

How to explain about Philip? *Is* there an explanation? I can't even say it was a *coup de foudre*, thus blaming heaven instead of myself. I didn't like him at all the first time we met at a dinner party in Bel Air. Philip was a perfect example of the affluent, middle-aged, permanently tanned boy-men in the "business," a type that usually gives me eye trouble. They glitter. Their silvery hair, shampooed with high-protein conditioner, glitters, the blinding caps on their teeth glitter, the gold bands on their Piaget watches glitter and their shoes, made by Lobbs in London, glitter.

I guessed a lot about Philip just by looking at him during drinks. I guessed he played super tennis and (they all do) suffered from tennis elbow. (Philip also, I learned later, suffered from deviated septum, migraine and susceptibility to food allergies.) I guessed he was a "collector"—impressionist paintings or African masks or Calder mobiles. (It turned out to be Ch'ing Dynasty porcelains.) I guessed he screwed actresses and secretaries and maybe his wife if it was an anniversary or he felt guilty enough. I guessed he had at least two children and, like most of the kids around there, the boy would be wacked out on rock and the girl would be nutty over horses.

At dinner, seated next to me, Philip told me all about his son, the fender-bass player, and his daughter, the equestrienne. There was also a nine-year-old son with a problem: bed-wetting. But they had hopes for a cure now that they were on to a new invention called Wee Alert Buzzer. Philip explained how it worked during the first course, and I, a writer always in search of material, listened avidly. I still haven't a clue under what circumstances I can use this information, but it is there to this day taking up room in my gray cells.

During the main course Philip's subject was EST. The first weekend he had spent being called an asshole and not being allowed to go to the bathroom for eight hours, and the second weekend he had spent no longer being called an asshole and not being allowed to go to the bathroom for eight hours. In some inscrutable way this experience had gotten his "head together."

"EST convinced me I've been living a pea-soup existence," he said as he passed me the salt. "Everyone is. You are too."

"I'm living a sassafras-broth existence," I said, thinking of Ernie.

"I understand what you're doing. What you're doing is confronting me and that's okay. EST taught me to welcome confrontations."

"Why?"

"They help me to actualize myself."

"How?"

"Werner doesn't like us to talk about it—but I'll tell you one thing." He flashed me a glittering smile. "For the first time in my life I'm ready for a balls-on relationship."

"A what?"

"A commitment no longer scares me," Philip said.

I saw his wife watching us from the far end of the table. She was extremely chic and extremely thin and she had a kind of thoughtfully smug expression on her face as if she knew a lot that I didn't know. Which indeed she did.

After the party they drove me back to the hotel. Philip's wife, whose name was Janice, sat between us, "because I'm a little thinner than you," she said tactfully. As we sped down Sunset Boulevard Janice talked about her recent stay at "the best fat farm in California." She offered to give me the name of the best fat farm in California if I wanted to lose five pounds.

"Why should she lose five pounds?" Philip demanded. "She looks fine to me."

"She *looks* fine," Janice said, "but she might want to live closer to the bone."

"I'd say her weight is just right for her height," Philip said.

"Height has *nothing* to do with it!" I could feel the tension in Janice's skinny thigh.

"Silly goose! That's what all the charts are based on."

"Charts are crap." Janice shot him a baleful glance. "It's a matter of living closer to the bone."

Anxious to divert them from each other, I announced that my husband was sixty pounds overweight.

"You should ship him off to a fat farm," Janice said.

"I'm afraid that's impossible. We're separated."

"*Somebody* should ship him off to a fat farm," she snapped.

"Maybe the woman he's living with will do it."

"I could never live with a fat man," Janice said.

We drove in silence for a while. I looked out at the huge houses, their doors and facades festooned with Christmas lights. In front of one of them was a giant cutout of Santa sitting in his sleigh driving his team of reindeer. They were galloping straight into a cluster of palm trees. I longed for New York, where if Santa Claus suffered a contusion it would be from an honest mugging.

Janice was staring at me. "What did you do to your husband," she asked suspiciously, "stuff him with starches?"

"No. He was very fat when I married him."

"Didn't it make you nervous—living with a man who was so far from the bone?"

"That was the least of it," I said.

At the hotel Philip got out of the car and walked me up the long walk to the lobby entrance. When we got there he impaled me with an intense blue-eyed stare. "Consider yourself kissed good night," he said.

The next day I left to spend the holidays in New York. The moment I got home from the airport Philip was on the phone. He called me the next day and the next. He called me every day—sometimes twice a day—until I returned to California. Can that be the explanation? Did I, like Amanda's husband in *The Glass Menagerie*, fall in love with Long Distance?

During the holidays my husband telephoned too (a local call from his office on Broadway) to inform me that he was now my ex-husband. He had flown to the Dominican Republic a couple of weeks before and divorced me. His friend had gone along and divorced her husband at the same time. Of the four of us, I gathered that I was the only one who hadn't known about this symmetrical little jaunt. All I had known up to then was that my husband had become one half of a Fun Couple. I should have realized, if only from reading gossip columns, that Fun Couples often flew to exotic places to get uncoupled—from other people, of course. After their suntans fade and the native straw baskets unravel, they each have a divorce as a permanent souvenir. As it happened, my ex-husband's souvenir wasn't permanent at all but I didn't find that out until a few months later.

I spend my days dreaming myself into the psyches of fictional characters and writing what I hope is appropriate dialogue for them. Faced with a real ex-husband, I couldn't think of anything to say.

39

"How is the Dominican Republic?" I asked, not that I gave a damn.

"Very small."

I recognized the inflection and accent and, as I always had, played straight man and cued him for the next line.

"And the beaches?"

"Very big."

I laughed. "Remember that night in Nassau when we walked through the hotel garden and you kept making loud obscene remarks with a Noel Coward accent?"

Today, I thought, is the end of our memories. We won't ever be doing anything together again.

"That wasn't a very classy thing to do," I said, "to divorce me without telling me."

"I'm telling you now."

"That's a fact," I said. "An indisputable fact."

We hung up.

After this call I began to think that Philip was remarkably sweet and nice on the phone. A little square, of course, but he made me laugh. I needed to laugh. Also, when I got back to Los Angeles and looked at him for the first time with my glasses on, I saw that his teeth weren't capped after all, which was a plus.

He sent me books and flowers and asked me out for drinks and dinners. (No lunch dates because our studios were too far apart.) Our dinner dates were in obscure Chinese restaurants in Hollywood with a stop at a Baskin-Robbins afterward for ice cream cones. After that we'd usually wander into Pickwick's to inspect the new books. During one of these evenings, Philip told me about his ambition to be a producer and his long search for a "property." He had found some novels that would make great movies, but while he was trying to negotiate the option figure downward someone else always came along and paid the asking price.

"Next time you want a book you'd better just write out a check," I said. It seemed a sensible thing to say. What I didn't know, but immediately found out, was that although he was an extremely rich man, Philip had become so used to perks he couldn't bear to spend a substantial amount of his own money on anything—not even a "life-long dream."

"It could get too expensive!" he told me in a shocked voice. "Don't forget I'd still have to pay for a script!" He was reading the jacket copy on a current best seller. "I could never afford *your* price, for example." He leafed through the best seller like a hungry waif.

I'm a pushover for waifs—one look at those famished eyes, that grubby little nose pressed yearningly against the showcase, and I get a knee-jerk mothering reaction. I knew I shouldn't have said it, let alone blurted it out.

"I'll write you a script for nothing!" I blurted out.

It was giving candy to a baby—a multimillionaire baby.

Philip was so excited he insisted we stop at the Polo Lounge for a nightcap. After all, we were legitimate now—working partners. In the spy-thriller shadows of a back booth where countless idiot deals have been made, we made ours. Philip would option a book and I'd write the script, as they say, "on spec." Once we got a studio to finance our project they'd buy the book, pay Philip back for what he'd laid out, and pay me my script fee. Then we'd produce the picture together, fifty-fifty partners all the way. The deal sounded good but it wasn't exactly as good (for me) as it sounded. Even while we sealed it with a stealthy kiss I realized that Philip would gamble a few thousand dollars and the minute it took to write a check. I would gamble, at the very least, three or four months of my increasingly shorter life.

Our deal was modified a couple of weeks later when Philip came up with an ingenious new angle. Why did two smart people like us need someone else's book? Why not gamble on an original story of our own? My romantic nature and gutless passivity when I even think I'm in love kept me from pointing out that in that case I'd be the only one who was gambling.

"Brilliant idea!" I said.

Frequently on weekends I was urged to drive out to Paradise Cove where the Rowans had a beach house, to watch Philip play tennis with three other movie moguls. While they were dashing and leaping about the court it was difficult to tell them apart—all in whites, all trim, all gray-haired and all the same shade of brown, as if that Master Baker in the Southern California sky had left them in the oven for the same amount of time.

After three sets with the moguls Philip would drop his style as a hard-hitter to play a patty-cake kind of set with me. This switch infuriated me but even so I kept myself from scoring many points—which says a lot about my (at the time) attitude toward men. Every time I played a shot well I called out an automatic and anxious "Sorry!"

When our set was over we'd go back to the house to work. Our discussions were interrupted by my constant trips to the kitchen faucet to refresh the hot-towel compresses for Philip's tennis elbow. (Clever Janice was away warming her bones on someone else's sun deck.) Toward sunset Philip and I would saunter over to the local Baskin-Robbins for ice cream cones and then I'd drive myself back to Beverly Hills. There was never any dinner at the Rowans because Sunday was Janice's fruit-juice day.

One Sunday the game was rained out and Philip came over to the hotel to work with me. And so began what I presume he thought of as a "balls-on relationship." I, in my bruised, newly divorced condition, thought of it as "a love affair." I hadn't had a love affair since I'd met Vincent all those years ago. Maybe it helped me to "actualize" myself —it was a lot jollier than going to EST. Also, it felt good. It felt almost as good not to spend any more Sundays in Paradise Cove because Philip couldn't "handle" his guilt. He'd been unfaithful to his wife for years but, until now, had drawn the line at women who were welcomed into the (flat) bosom of his family.

His first infidelity, he confided to me, was the day after he returned from his honeymoon.

"So soon?"

"It was my birthday and a guy I know sent me a present—lunch and champagne in a picnic hamper delivered by two gorgeous call girls."

"To your *office?*"

"He sent along the keys to his apartment."

"But . . . you could've just had lunch with them."

"Silly goose," he said.

Whatever it was called, what Philip and I were having helped break down some barriers between us. Eventually I felt able to tell him I hated ice cream and he felt able to tell me his fantasy while lovemaking.

"Does it upset you?" he asked.

"Um."

"It's fun, isn't it?"

"Um."

"I think sex should be fun, don't you?"

"Um."

A little later I asked, "What did you call her?"

"Addie."

"Short for Adeline?"

"Adele."

"Why? D'you think Adele is a sexy name?"

"Shhh. Don't ask so many questions."

Still later I asked, "What does she look like?"

"Never mind what she looks like. It's what she does."

At some point I started to giggle.

"What's so funny?" Philip sounded furious.

"She is! I can't help it! She breaks me up!"

"You're spoiling everything!"

A quick downward glance showed me I was.

"I'm sorry. But you just said sex should be fun."

That hot afternoon I wrote a long sequence for our script. At five thirty I hid the pages in my file drawer and left for the hotel.

I was dragging myself through the lobby when I ran right into Marshall Macklin. His short dark beard felt furry and reassuring as we hugged each other. He said he'd been at the hotel for a week but he hadn't known I was there and now we couldn't even have a drink together because he was that minute on his way to the airport—going home to New York.

I stood in line at the cashier's window with him while he waited to check out.

"Thought you were in New York," he said. "I was going to call you about your script—soon as I got back."

"Ernie told me you hated it."

"What?"

"Marshall, it's okay. I just wondered why, because—"

"Damn it!" Marshall said furiously. "I should've found out where you were and called you."

"It's *okay!* Honestly! But I thought that if—"

"Ernie's a goddamned liar! I never read it. I had it sent back immediately."

The cashier handed him his bill. After he'd signed it he took my hand and we hurried over to the bell desk to ask if his limo had arrived. The bell captain went outside to see.

"Listen to me," Marshall said. "I think you're one hell of a writer but I won't work with Ernie Kaplan if I never direct another picture in my life. He's not only a cretin, he's totally destructive to a project. I had an experience with the sonofabitch a couple of years ago—"

"I didn't know you ever—"

"I quit during preproduction."

The bell captain came over to us. Marshall's car was out in front, the luggage already in the trunk.

"I'm off to Austria next month scouting locations," Marshall said.

He put his hands on my shoulders. "You shouldn't be doing a picture with that creep. Watch yourself!" He gave me a quick hug and was out the door.

When I got up to my room I threw myself on the bed and closed my eyes. After a moment I heard the door next to mine being unlocked and the laughter and low voices of two men in the room. In a couple of minutes there was the sound of the shower rushing full force in the bathroom. When it stopped, the man in the bedroom shouted, "Hey! Know that fountain in the middle of Wilshire Boulevard?"

"Downtown on Wilshire? Sure!" the man in the bathroom shouted back.

"I fucked Sandy in it last night."

"In the fountain?"

"In the fucking fountain!"

"Jesus H. Christ! You could get busted for that!"

"It was two A.M. No cops around. Nobody around."

"What'd you do it for? I mean, in the *fountain?*"

"Always wanted to fuck somebody in that fountain."

"Why?"

"One of the things I always wanted to do."

"Was she . . . was she scared or anything?"

"You kidding? That cunt would fuck in Macy's window if I asked her."

"Is there a Macy's out here?"

"Put it this way—she'd fuck in I. Magnin's window if I asked her."

"How was it . . . I mean, in the fountain?"

I never did hear how it was. By this time the man in the bathroom was back in the bedroom and their voices dropped to a murmur again. In a few minutes the door opened and slammed behind them, and I listened to the sound of their footsteps going down the hall.

I opened my eyes and stared at the ceiling. After a while disjointed scenes in bits and pieces began flashing across it, and I had the bizarre notion I was watching rushes up there. I imagined each take numbered and slated. Title: *Today.* Director: Me. Oh, no, not me. God? I doubted it. The stars? Destiny? Fate? I left the space for director blank. A hand came into frame holding clapsticks. Clap!

EXTREME CLOSE-UP: Marshall's lips. "I never read it." EXTREME CLOSE-UP: Ernie's button eyes. "He hates it." MEDIUM SHOT: Grant's dirty fingernails splayed across the script. "It's bullshit." MEDIUM SHOT: Bill Curtis falling off his chair laughing. TRACKING SHOT: Naked Indian,

44

his necklaces rattling as he walks down the hall. CLOSE-UP: Grant's eyes. "I wanna see those balls *leap,* man!" CAMERA PANS LUCIA'S OFFICE: Bill Curtis (voice-over): "When you're in a hole next to the john, you're a Little Match Girl." CLOSE-UP: Lucia at the telephone. "I was married to a shit and now you've married me to another shit." LONG SHOT: Sidney Powker at the telephone. "Hurts me, honey, to hear you talk about Vincent like that. . . ."

I closed my eyes and changed reels.

Montage

They were on a high together.

They were happy together—whatever happy is.

Only movie moguls know for sure what happy is. Whenever the moguls make a love story they almost always order the wretched screenwriter to write in a "happy montage." Montage, in the non-Eisenstein and limited sense of the word, is a film term meaning a section of rapid images which can be spliced together to give a unified impression. A happy montage is supposed to give an impression of lovers being happy. The lovers must be *shown* doing loverlike things together because the moguls are convinced that the mouth breathers (a film term meaning audience) are too dopey to assume bliss. They must *see* bliss. (Film is a visual medium and don't you forget it!)

As a result one hardly ever sees a love story on the screen without a selection of RUNNING SHOTS: the lovers racing hand in hand through golden wheat fields or along sun-dappled beaches—her hair flying. Or, if it's winter, they skim over snowy meadows—more hair flying—and sometimes stop to fool around, falling flat in the snow and pumping their arms to make angels, or rubbing the cold stuff on each other's faces. There are also RIDING SHOTS—lovers on a whirling carousel or galloping horses down a country road or in a speeding open car, all very good for hair flying—DRINKING SHOTS—suggestive moments of eye-to-eye foreplay—and EATING SHOTS (important for symbolism)—licking ice cream cones or gnawing the thighs of Cornish game hens. Once Lucia wrote in a scene of lovers eating meat loaf and cottage fries. The moguls didn't get it. It was cut. Another time, after the lovers had an energetic romp in bed, she showed them eating a flat soufflé. The moguls got it but they didn't like it. It was cut too.

Shots that are never cut are (a) OLD FLOWER LADY SHOT—the

lovers stop at a flower stall; he picks out a bunch of violets for her; the Old Flower Lady turns out to be both a fool and a fool for love; she refuses to take his money—and (b) CHIN STUBBLE SHOT: the lovers are in the bathroom. He is shaving. She is sitting on the edge of the tub, her attention glued to this super-macho performance! He dabs her face with shaving cream. She screeches and chases him through the bedroom. They end up tumbling on the bed, suddenly solemn and aroused.

The reason for these clichés and juvenile high jinks is that most film writers have rarely been happy. If they had been happy people they wouldn't have become writers. As a result they have few memories of their own to tap for material. What they do is tap other movies, which is why happy montages seem to be all alike.

Vincent and Lucia weren't characters in a movie. In any case, Vincent was too heavy to race through fields and Lucia's hair was only two inches long all over her head. Carousels made them dizzy, they owned no horses and Vincent never bought flowers on the street. He ordered extravagant bouquets from a florist on Park Avenue. He had moved into Lucia's apartment so she might have seen him shave the small spaces above his beard, but it would never have occurred to her to watch him.

This is what they did.

They talked and talked.

They talked about the best times in their lives and the worst times. One of his best was when he was a small boy with what sounded like a hundred grown-up aunts who adored him and spoiled him. One of his worst was when he lived on a ranch and found, one Sunday, his pet chicken served up for dinner and his father ordered him to stay at the table until his plate was clean. She told him about the fifth-grade play she wrote to promote good nutrition. She starred as the Queen of Health and the boy she liked most played the Queen's favorite, a carrot, and the performance was a triumph. She told him how she fell madly in love with a man her mother was going to marry, and one day she came home from school to find his photograph torn from its frame and her mother burning his letters and she never saw him again.

On many nights they walked into Broadway theatres for free because Vincent knew all the house managers. During the first intermission they usually walked out again, gloomy about the bad plays.

They stood in long lines at movie houses to see the latest Godard or Fellini or Resnais or Truffaut. The films were marvelous and they discussed them for hours afterward.

He cooked dinner in their small kitchen. She peeled vegetables and tossed salads and wiped his brow when heat and exertion made him sweat. He sweated kneading pastry dough for a *boeuf en croûte*. When he brought it to the table, the crust perfectly browned and flaky, with her initials baked into it, she said it was the sexiest love offering she'd ever received.

She casually admired a cashmere trench coat in a magazine. He had it delivered to her by messenger the next day.

She wandered through shops buying him scarves and sweaters and looking for anything marked "extra-large." She bought him a robe and gloves and a half dozen pairs of shorts because his own were in tatters.

She paid the rent and the bills. He brought home presents for the apartment—two Limoges demitasse cups for their after-dinner coffee, a cachepot planted with ivy to put beside her typewriter, a pewter candlestick. He gave the apartment a silver porringer, a gift from his grandparents when he was born. His initials were on it and the marks of his baby teeth. She ran her fingers over the dented places and thought of her own children when they were infants and was moved in the same way she had been then. They put the porringer on a table and kept cigarettes in it.

She bemoaned the fact that their windows looked out on the monotonous facade of a building across the street. He went to an artist friend and bought her a "view" on installments—a huge abstract painting in misty flowery colors that made one end of the room into a garden.

They were robbed. When the cops came they opened a bottle of champagne and spent a convivial hour with them in the stripped-down apartment. But by the time they went to bed with another bottle of champagne she was despondent. Her typewriter and everything else could be replaced but not the antique gold locket, the first thing he had ever given her. Its value was merely sentimental, he told her. But that was the only value she cared about.

She sent his laundry out and took his suits to the cleaners and went to the market and kept the apartment dusted and hung up his clothes. He told her it was the first time since he was a little boy that anyone had ever hung up anything for him.

He plugged the percolator into the wall beside their bed and rigged up a timer so they woke to the smell of coffee and drank their first cup sleepily propped up on pillows.

He found plays she had never heard of and read them to her, acting out all the roles. Her favorite was by Giraudoux, in which a young woman, practicing how to speak to the man she loves, addresses a chandelier with such passionate admiration the chandelier lights up by itself. That is the way he made her feel, she thought, all radiance and sparkling prisms.

He longed to be a director in the theatre. She started to write another play. It was for him to direct, and one of the characters in it, flamboyant and charming, was based on him.

When her son and daughter brought school friends home for Christmas, they turned the apartment over to the kids and took a suite in a hotel on the park. They called Room Service often and ate and drank and watched the snow falling on the trees and the skating pond and listened to carols on the radio and made love.

They went to parties together. She loved to look at him across a room—the flaming beard, those stunning eyes. He was so *alive!* He was so *theatrical!* He had such an amusing way of telling anecdotes. Some of them hadn't happened quite as he said, but she knew he embellished them only to be more entertaining. And somehow whenever she needed a cigarette or a drink he was there beside her offering her both.

One evening on the street when she waved to signal a taxi, he told her never to do that—he would take care of getting taxis, he would take care of everything.

They bought a secondhand Jaguar together and spent winter weekends at country inns. At the most charming one they were given a room with a fireplace, logs already blazing when they arrived. They found a dozen matchbooks on the dresser; the printing on their covers read "Mr. and Mrs. Vincent Wade." That made her laugh but she noticed he didn't like her laughing.

Her play closed after half a season but she was too absorbed in their life together to grieve about it. On the last night he invited the cast to his favorite restaurant for supper. He hadn't paid his bill for months and the manager refused to let him sign the check. He was chagrined. She couldn't have cared less. She still had plenty of money from royalties. She signed the check.

In the spring they flew to Nassau, where he had worked a couple of winters in stock. They sailed and swam and browned themselves in the sun. He introduced her to his old friends and took her to his old hangouts, where native trios played romantic Bahamian songs. The days were glorious but at night he drank too much. It was still glorious. They went to bed in a massive mahogany four-poster with a flowered canopy and flowered sheets. She watched him—Vincent asleep on a field of daisies and bluebells.

When they went to his New York hangouts he would frequently

49

drink a lot too. He would become glazed and unfocused and fall into bed half undressed. He'd sleep deeply for a while and then restlessly, thrashing his legs, slinging his heavy arms across her body. In the mornings he was always apologetic when he realized her breast was bruised or her face.

But it didn't matter.

It was the right dream.

They were on a high.

And there were no sins of omission.

3

Grant rang me up and told me to come to the conference room right away because he had a great new idea for the script. When I walked in a couple of minutes later he was on the phone with Cindy. They were talking about the flowers she wanted the Mexican gardener to plant around their pool house. Grant winked at me as he spelled out some Spanish words for her. My Spanish was fairly good—those words had nothing to do with flowers. He hung up looking pleased.

"If your gardener's under eighty she could get into trouble."

"Cindy has a sense of humor." He lifted his cap and scratched his head. His nails were as black as his hair. "I'm not sure *you* have a sense of humor."

"Don't I laugh like a loon at everything you say?"

"There's a lot of subliminal hostility in that remark."

"Subliminal!"

He leaned way back in his swivel chair and gave me what I guess he thought of as a sincere stare. "I can't work with a writer who doesn't like me. Why don't you like me?"

"What's your great new idea, Grant?"

"Tell me something, luv, you getting it on with anybody?"

I smiled to show I had a sense of humor.

"You're in bloody good shape—very attractive. This flick has too many booby traps already or I'd make a pass at you."

"Is that your great new idea?"

"Benjamin Franklin said fucking older women was terriffic." He grinned at me. "He said they're always so *grateful!*"

I wanted to kill him. I wanted him dead there on the rug at my feet, his limp little organ never to rise again. It was not the first time in my life I had felt murderous and felt the same wave of nausea engulf me. I closed my eyes and took a deep breath waiting for it to pass.

"After I get an answer print, we'll fuck," Grant said. I opened my eyes. "What d'you say?"

"I say you'd have to take a long hot shower first. With soap."

He roared with laughter and slapped the table. "Funky's good, luv! I'll show you!"

"Not in a million years." I pushed his battered copy of the script over to him. "What is it you wanted to tell me?"

He always approached our work discussions reluctantly, but he seemed more unwilling than usual that day. His fingers drummed on the script.

He sighed loudly, opened it and studied the first page as if he had never seen it before. "What we got here is basically a story from Cecelia's point of view, right?"

"That's what we've got."

"Now don't go into shock—this story's gotta be told from Andrew's point of view."

"Are you kidding?" I thought he was.

"I know it's Cecelia's story in the book—"

"That's why I optioned the book! That's what it's got going for it—a Western from a woman's point of view for a change!"

"The broad who wrote the book was jerking herself off. It's Andrew's movie."

"Not the movie I'm writing."

"Cecelia doesn't know enough. She doesn't understand enough. She has to find out about Andrew gradually."

"That's the point! That's the suspense! He's a mystery to us too. We get hooked on figuring him out along with her. As she puts it all together—we put it all together."

"If we weren't stuck with her P.O.V. we could cross-cut and get a lot more action at the opening. The mouth breathers aren't going to sit still watching a chick in a long dress for ten minutes."

"Why not?"

At that moment Ernie walked in carrying a cup of yogurt and a plastic spoon. He pulled a chair up to the table. "Didja tell her?" he asked Grant.

"It's another movie if we change the P.O.V.," I said. "I won't even talk about it."

"For Chrissake, it's the same story no matter whose P.O.V. we tell it from." He pried the cardboard top off the cup. "It's a minor change."

52

"It's a *major* change!"

"That's what we need—a major change." He took an open packet of sesame seeds out of his pocket and shook it over his yogurt. "Just got a call from Rosalind Young's agent. Roz hates the script."

"I don't want her anyway."

"I do," Grant said. "She's the kind of uppity-lady type we need."

"You agreed we'd find an unknown," I reminded Ernie.

"Those chicks we saw film on stink. Ask Grant."

"They stink," Grant said.

"When'd you see film?"

Grant's eyes had misted over. He leaned back in his chair again, his arms behind his head. "That Rosalind Young is one cool cunt," he said dreamily.

Ernie put a spoonful of yogurt into his mouth and made a sucking sound. "Underneath that ice there's fuckin' fire," he said.

"What's going on, Ernie? How come you saw film on actresses without me?"

"Know what every stud in the house wants when that Rosalind Young is on the screen?" Grant asked. "He wants to knock her off her pedestal! Dirty her up! Bang her till her ears fall off!"

Ernie nodded. "She was dynamite in the picture I made with her."

"I saw that picture in Cannes," I said. "It got booed."

"Fuckin' hippies!"

"I saw it at the *night* screening. Everyone was in diamonds and dinner jackets."

"Old farts."

"It was a bomb. It never even got released in this country."

"It will." Ernie scraped the last globs of yogurt out of the cup. "Soon as people see Roz in this picture."

"They won't see her in this picture."

"Fuck her agent." Ernie stood up and crossed to the door. "I'll personally talk her into it—"

"Ernie!" I shouted. *"I don't want her!"*

Ernie looked back at me. It was the first time he'd looked at me since he'd come into the room. "Roz trusts me. I'll explain we're fixing the script."

I picked up the yogurt cup. It was too soft. I dropped it. I picked up the ashtray and threw it with all my might. Instead of piercing Ernie's skull it hit the door, already closed behind him.

"What's wrong with you?" Grant asked. "Menopausal?"

———

One afternoon I came back from lunch and stood in the blazing sun in front of the signboard on Bungalow Five. There was a change. Until then it had simply announced the title of our movie and Ernest Kaplan, producer. Now the names and titles of six more occupants had been added: associate producer, director, production manager, art director, casting director and, at the very bottom, writer. No indication that I was also co-producer.

Suddenly I felt a stab of nutty compassion for Ernie. What had happened to him that made him play such games? What old scores was he using me to settle? Had his mother snatched her breast away too soon and left him to cry in the dark? Had the little girls on the playground swiped his scooter and tripped him with their jump ropes? When they grew up did they spurn his invitations to the prom? Was it that no woman's eyes had ever lighted up when she awoke beside him? Had his ex-wife mismatched his socks and poured bottled dressing on his alfalfa sprouts?

"To understand all is to pardon all," said Madame de Staël. She was a more generous-hearted person than I and, besides, Ernie was no Talleyrand.

My name had not been painted on a parking space but I was parking my car outside the bungalow anyway. It was a Pyrrhic gesture because I had to arrive twenty minutes early every morning to grab someone else's space. Next to my car, blocking the entrance that day, was a gleaming brown Jaguar. I circled it and went inside. In the lobby area, Rita, the curvy young receptionist, was typing. Three bearded and booted actors were sitting on a bench, waiting for the casting director and staring at Rita's cleavage. A funereal-looking man in a black suit, white shirt and black tie was standing propped against the wall reading *The Hollywood Reporter.*

"Whose Jag?" I asked Rita.

She stopped typing and flung her mane of wavy black hair out of her face. "We have a visitation from royalty. Rosalind Young's inside with Ernie baby."

"What's she like?"

"She's like you feel she expects you to curtsy."

I laughed. "I'd like to meet her."

"He left orders not to disturb them, Mrs. Wade."

As soon as he heard my name the man in the black suit hurried over. "This is an unexpected pleasure!" He put out his hand. "I'm Brian Kohn's agent."

54

We shook hands. "Brian Kohn, the screenwriter?"

The agent nodded. "He liked your script a lot. Coming from Brian Kohn that's a real compliment!"

"I'm confused. How did Mr. Kohn happen to read my script?"

The agent looked confused too. "Mr. Kaplan sent it to him—you know, about doing a rewrite."

"I did *not* know."

His eyes clouded. "Anyway, Brian doesn't do rewrites. Only reason he read the script was because you wrote it."

"I see."

"Brian thinks it's just fine the way it is. That's good news, isn't it?"

"It's certainly *news.*"

"I was on the lot, so I dropped in to tell Mr. Kaplan—"

"I'll tell him for you."

He started to edge away from me. "It was a real pleasure, Mrs. Wade. Mean that sincerely. . . ."

Once he was outside, Rita rolled her eyes at me. I spun around, marched to Ernie's door and threw it open.

Ernie was startled but, as usual, not speechless. "Just about to see if you were back from lunch and here you are!" He jumped up beaming at this miraculous coincidence. "Want you to meet Rosalind Young. Roz, darling, this is my writer, Lucia Wade."

Either the expression on my face frightened her or, in deference to my age, Miss Young jumped up too.

"Won't she make a fantastic Cecelia?" Ernie demanded. "Rosalind Young and Ted Clayburn! That's fuckin' chemistry!"

"Ernie's getting a bit ahead of himself," Miss Young said as she bestowed her hand on mine. Her hand was narrow. All of her was narrow—her skull, her neck, her body in a skin-tight denim jump suit unzipped to her navel. Even her ponytail was a narrow hank of blond hair. Her voice was cool. So were her chiseled-out-of-white-marble features and her blue eyes.

My smile skated over their agate surfaces. "Ernie told me you hate my script."

Ernie gasped. "I told you no such thing!"

Miss Young sat down and curled her long legs under her. She presented me with her profile. "Hate is a big word," she proclaimed. "What I did say is that the script needs work."

"Ever see a script that didn't need work?" Ernie demanded.

"Could you be a little more precise?" I asked Miss Young.

55

Although I couldn't see it I assumed that a narrow frown had appeared between her brows. "Precise?"

"Less general."

She stayed in profile. I wondered if this avoidance of eye contact was her idea of the appropriate behavior of a princess. If I left first would I be expected to back out of the room?

"To be perfectly honest with you"—she addressed some undefined space between Ernie and me—"it's the character of Cecelia. Frankly, she doesn't seem . . . well, she doesn't seem . . . representational as . . . as a woman of the period."

My shrink had taught me to translate those prefaces "to be perfectly honest" and "frankly" into their opposites, and though I thought the theory simplistic, it had mostly turned out to be true. I was sure Miss Young would be along soon with "to tell you the truth" and "in all honesty." It was going to take time to find out what was really on her mind.

"That still seems pretty general," I said.

"To tell you the truth, it's a . . . a general feeling I have."

"Could you give me an example?"

"An example is that Cecelia is too ballsy," Ernie said. "Broads didn't act that way in the olden days."

"That's the way she acts in the book."

"The book's a piece of shit."

"You told Sidney Powker you were crazy about it."

"Because I could see how I could make it not a piece of shit." He turned to Miss Young. "You trust me to fix it, don't you, Roz, darling?"

Under this weighty question, Miss Young's head bent on its slender stalk. "Of course I trust you, Ernie, but . . ." She picked at the initial R worked in brilliants on the pocket of her suit. "In all honesty, I think it needs an objective point of view. It's so difficult. . . ." She lifted her hands and floated them downward to indicate her helplessness. "Perhaps it's the angle of vision. The script is a—a paradigm of a modernist approach." She turned to me at last with a princess-to-peasant smile. "It suffers from being filtered through a—a feminine sensibility. Or should I say a feminist sensibility?"

I put my chin in my hand and pretended to ponder which she should say. What I was pondering was who had taught her this English Lit 101 jargon.

"Keith Ryan!" Miss Young said suddenly, as if she had read my thoughts. "A man like Keith Ryan could explain to you!"

"Who's he?"

"Hot young writer," Ernie barked. "Just wrote a terrific sci-fi script."

"It isn't sold yet," Miss Young said, "but I was telling Ernie how fantastic it is. My agent doesn't handle writers, but she's handling this script because it's so fantastic!" She was back in profile again. "Keith could be an enormous help to both of you."

Ernie was nodding his head like one of those cuckoo-bird toys you balance on the rim of a glass.

"Keith ran the Film Society when he was at Princeton and, for instance, he saw *Gunfight at the O.K. Corral* eleven times!"

"Gee," I said, "I only saw it once."

"Keith's a real Western buff."

"We're not making a real Western, Miss Young. We're making a love story that happens to take place in the West."

"I let Keith read the script and he absolutely pinpointed everything that bothered me. You really ought to get him to come in and talk to you about it."

"Terrific idea!" Ernie said.

Miss Young leaned toward him eagerly. "Keith can tell you what my instinct tells me but I can't communicate." Ernie's eyes were fastened on her two little snowball breasts on either side of the unzipped zipper. "After all, I'm not a writer. Keith is a writer."

"So am I," I reminded her.

"We'll get the kid in here tomorrow," Ernie said.

"No we won't," I said.

The heat of his glare cut through the air conditioning but he restrained himself from asking me why because he knew I'd tell him.

"What a shame! I wanted you to hear what Keith thinks about Cecelia. I couldn't possibly play her the way she's written." Miss Young unfolded her legs and stood up. She smiled at me again—this one was more like princess to pygmy. "In all honesty, I'm an enormous fan of yours. Your work is so—so *heuristic!*" She put out her hand and allowed me to clasp it for an instant. "Best of luck with your Western."

For once I had to hand it to Grant Ames. She was one cool cunt.

Ernie left with her to take her out to her car. While I waited I lighted a cigarette. Ernie came back fuming. He slammed the door and waved his arms at the smoke.

"You sure as hell don't know how to handle a fuckin' star!"

"Who's fucking Keith Ryan, the hot young writer?"

"So what?"

"She may think his pen is as good as his cock, but I don't have to." Ernie started opening and closing drawers. "Anyway, it's academic. She's too cold for Cecelia. I don't want her."

"Okay, okay, take your fuckin' cigarette out of here. I got work to do."

I blew another long stream of smoke into the air. "I heard you sent my script to Brian Kohn."

"Yeah? Where'd you hear that?"

"Around."

"This town!" He banged a drawer shut. "A guy has a wet dream at three A.M. and everybody in the Polo Lounge is analyzing it at breakfast."

"I didn't hear it in the Polo Lounge. I heard it from Brian Kohn's agent."

"The schmuck!"

"He gave me a message for you. Brian Kohn likes the script—you sent him the old script, I assume. He thinks it's just fine the way it is."

"Brian Kohn ain't Tolstoy." Ernie began rifling through a pile of telephone slips.

"I have a message for you too. Forget your wet dream about getting any other writer on this script—or," I added sweetly, "I'll kill you."

This time Ernie raised his head. He gazed at me for about five seconds. Then he opened a folder, took out a yellow studio memo sheet and slid it across his desk toward me.

FROM: M.L.

TO: E.K.

RE: THE LADY AND THE ROBBER

Cal Jordan, the writer I spoke to you about, is available to do a new draft for us. He will be in your office at four today to go over the changes we discussed.

We've used this writer on several Westerns. He knows his oaters—which Wade obviously doesn't.

Perhaps we should have sent her out onto the range with a gang of illiterate lunatics who'd drink her saliva.

Drink my saliva? I didn't know what it meant but it sounded awfully unsanitary.

I called Sidney Powker.

"Honey," he said, "the studio has a right to do anything they want with your script. It's their property. It's spelled out in plain English in your contract. Didn't you read your contract?"

"I pay you to do that."

"It's the standard writer's contract. You've signed it every time you've worked."

"How the hell could you *let* me sign a contract like that?"

"You don't sign it, you don't work. We live in the real world, honey, and we're stuck with it."

"What about my producer's contract?"

"You've got mutual approvals with Ernie, but if the studio wants a certain writer neither of you can do anything about it. I never heard of Jordan—he may not pan out. Bet they'll come back to you."

"Don't serve me that chicken soup, Sidney."

When he started to tell me how much snow there was in New York, I said good-bye and hung up.

I called my lawyer. My lawyer is one of the most intelligent, most sharp-minded, cleverest and toughest men who has ever been admitted to the New York Bar. He speaks, however, with the melodious, comforting voice of an ideal member of the American Medical Association.

"Nothing you can do," he said gently. "Not if you want the picture made."

"I do. Desperately."

"Replacing writers is routine. Happens on almost every picture I ever heard of. You're taking it hard because it never happened to you before."

"It's that damn contract."

"Look at it this way," he advised soothingly. "If you hadn't signed the contract you wouldn't be doing the picture."

"I'm *not* doing the picture! I've got about as much to do with it as . . . as the busboy in the commissary! Maybe they'll get *him* in to rewrite!"

"It's not going to be as bad as you think," my lawyer said. "It'll probably turn out all right. Don't worry so much, take it easy, relax."

"You'd make a great obstetrician!" I said.

When I put the phone down it rang immediately. Philip's joshing baritone came over the wire. "Caught you! You don't work. All you do is talk!"

"What's on your mind, Philip?"

"I think I can finish up here around three. How about you?" He lowered his voice to a conspiratorial whisper. "We could make the four o'clock showing of *Deep Throat.*"

"I've got a meeting. Anyway, there's enough pornography around here already." I told him about Cal Jordan.

"What's pornographic about that?" he asked, literal as ever. "They're only doing what they think'll be good for the picture."

"That's what they think."

"I don't think they're deliberately trying to ruin your script."

"That's what you think."

"You're like every writer in town. Every word you put down is a rare jewel. Total perfection. You think no one can improve it."

"Now that we know what everybody thinks could we hang up? I've got to—"

"Just one minute! I'm going to tell you something for your own good. Like all so-called creative people you—"

"So-called?"

"Like all creative people you don't realize movies are first of all a business. The point is to make money."

"I *know* the point is to make money! *I pray this picture will make money!"* I shouted at him. "Will you tell me how a stupid, hacked-up, written-by-committee movie can make money?"

"That's your opinion. The studio's putting up millions of dollars. They've got to protect their investment."

"Christ! Would you please stop telling me things I know?" He's got an Establishment head, I reminded myself, he's the Enemy. Why was I, like some sneaky collaborationist, going to bed with the Enemy? Why couldn't I be strong like some of my sisters and give up men who were mostly all the Enemy?

"Anyway, if Jordan's going to work on that script, you'll have more time to work on *my* script." At what point, I wondered, had our script become his script? "It's an ill wind that blows nobody good," Philip said.

"Every cloud has a silver lining."

"Now *that's* the right attitude!"

"You're full of shit, Philip." I banged down the phone.

I called the Writers Guild. My story was so old it had sprouted a white beard down to the ground. They had heard it thousands of times from thousands of writers. There had never been anything they could do about it and there never would be. The Money has the clout, always has had and will have for all eternity. A guild for writers is like a benevolent association for hookers. No matter what kind acts it performs for its members, they must inevitably lie down on their backs and spread their legs. That's the nature of hooking. And if they get

60

their noses bloodied or their teeth knocked out that's the risk of hooking.

Philip called back. Since he had learned at EST not to be afraid of confrontations, he furiously confronted me with the fact that I had said something nasty to him and hung up on him. I apologized. I backtracked. I assumed guilt. I admitted fault. I murmured something tender. I murmured something sexy. I praised his whole persona. I agreed that there was no use brooding over a situation I couldn't do anything about. I acknowledged that the only healthy solution was to get it together and forge ahead. I swore I'd get it together and forge ahead. When we said good-bye, I waited for him to hang up first.

It was the typical behavior of the romantic young girl inside of me who unfailingly sprang to life, tremulous and starry-eyed, to call the shots whenever I was "in love." It was more than unbecoming, it was unsavory at my age to be taking orders from this pink-cheeked maiden —this whiz-bang masochist. My shrink, the good mother, had wrestled with her for years and a few times pinned her to the mat, but even black and blue and aching with contusions she would crawl to her corner and lurk there waiting for the next round. My shrink's real ambition was thoroughly and terminally to break her neck. One time she thought she had. But I put the poor girl in traction for a few months and soon she was as good as new. I'd have panicked without her. It was, after all, she who had married Vincent.

Voice-over

I want my name on the lease, Vincent said. I want my name on the mailbox. I want my name on the charge accounts. I want my name on the laundry. How would you feel if you had to put on your shorts every morning and see the name of the ex-husband of the woman you love stamped on the waistband?

I want my name on *you,* he said. When I send flowers I want to say, "Deliver them to Mrs. Vincent Wade." When I introduce you to friends I want to say, "This is my wife, Lucia Wade." I want to tell the waiter, "My wife would like it medium rare, please." I want to tell the bartender, "Extra-dry Tanqueray martini on the rocks for my wife." I want to tell Lionel that I can't run over to the theatre and check the box office every night because "my wife expects me home for dinner." I want to tell the salesman, "My wife will be in to see the jacket before I decide." I want to ask the doorman if "my wife's come in yet." I want, I want, I want, he said. I want to marry you.

Oh, what the hell are we even discussing it for? he asked. *I am going to marry you.* I told you so the opening night of your play, didn't I? Didn't I come over to your table at the party and crouch down between you and that creep actor you were sitting with, and having an affair with, and there on my knees, *on my goddam knees,* inform you that I was going to marry you? I remember you laughed like hell, which only shows how little you knew me then.

The way we're living now, he said, is dishonest. You've got your kids in those boarding schools learning how to be solid citizens, and then they come here on vacations and find you shacked up with a young man. *Shocking! Unhealthy!* Very bad for *my* health! Haven't you seen the statistics on single guys? We get sick more often than married men.

We commit suicide more often than married men. We die younger. *You've got to marry me to save my life!*

And don't give me any more of that jazz about your age. Age is for redwood trees. Your age may be of interest to the driver's license bureau or the passport office. It is of no interest to me whatsoever. Please don't keep reminding me that in ten years I'll be thirty-five and you'll be forty-seven. I can add. My math is superb. God, you're going to be dynamite at fifty! Beautiful, sexy, complicated, a lived-it-all, seen-it-all kind of woman—I'll love you even more at fifty! If you say another word about my marrying a young girl and having a baby, I'll hit you. Young girls bore me. I do not want a baby. I do not want to reproduce myself in some puking infant. I repeat, I do not want a baby.

It's you I want, he said.

Please marry me, he said.

He'd been saying it for months.

4

If we had called our casting director and told her we needed a man to play a screenwriter specializing in Westerns, she'd have sent us Cal Jordan. He was perfect, from the tips of his pointy-toed boots to the stained Stetson on his head. The sun had both browned him and bleached him. When he removed his hat his hair was almost colorless, and so were his jutting eyebrows and the pale eyes beneath. His face was cordovan leather, cross-hacked with as many lines as an L.A. County road map. He even had a gap between his front teeth through which he presumably spat tobacco juice. On one forearm, beneath the rolled-up sleeve of his checkered shirt, was a tattoo of a tootsie with a cupid's-bow mouth and the name Mary Sue. The only false note was his yellow canvas tote bag with the word SMILE in black letters on each side above a cartooned face with an upturned mouth.

He took the book out of his bag and leapt on it as if it were a bucking bronco. His big fists clutched both covers and forced them backward until the spine split. He grabbed a handful of red-ink-marked pages and ripped them out. The binding stitches fought him for a moment, then tore apart as he tugged at more clumps of marked pages. Action scenes, he announced, as he flourished them in the air. They should follow one another without the non-action scenes in between. The non-action scenes were el snorro. Most of the two-scenes between the lady and the dude were el snorro. The book writer had put them in for the surgical stocking set, and who else gives a hoot? The two-scenes had to go thataway. He pointed to Ernie's wastebasket. It was okay to have some yak-yak before the dude and the lady got down to it, but short yak-yak. All those wet lines at the end had to go. Wet lines were tearjerkers for the S.S.S. Matter of fact, the end had to go thataway. The popcorn munchers don't mind if the dude bleeds a case of catsup but, by golly, he has to be on his feet at the end! The popcorn munchers are losers. They groove on winners up there on the silver screen.

He dropped the disemboweled book on the floor and opened the script. Lawd-a-mercy! The script writer had been ambushed by the book writer into unreelin' the yarn from the lady's P.O.V. Only way to bear-trap the story was to switch to the dude's P.O.V. First off the switch would open up a whole new can of beans. Beans make you fart —excuse me, little lady—same as the dude's P.O.V. would let all the gas out of the script. In the openin' scene we should be on the dude settin' out dynamite under the train tracks. He looks up and darn if the lady ain't up there on her horse watchin' him. Bingo! The popcorn munchers fergit to munch. She's seen his face! Two minutes into the pitcher show and the dude's in big danger!

He turned some pages. On this here page fifty-six he had found a note for two dandy scenes that weren't in the book—a rape and a fight. These were not el snorro. He would write out these dandy scenes, but he would move them about twenty pages sooner where the drunk Indian raid is now. In this here other scene the lady shoots the Indian who's rasslin' her, cuz the dude's got his hands full with the other Indians. That's gotta be turned around so the dude whups the others and then *he* shoots the one who's rasslin' the lady. The lady's got too much action in this script. The dude's gotta have all the action. Look at the expression on this here little lady's face! She thinks I'm plumb loco!

Crazy or the biggest send-up artist I ever saw. The next day Ernie gave him a little room on the second floor and he was on the payroll for a "two-week rewrite."

A couple of times a week I left the lot at five thirty and drove to the Cedar Tree Country Club to meet Philip for drinks. It was Philip's unimaginative notion that if we were seen together at his own club people would assume we were meeting for professional reasons only. He was already in the bar when I arrived, talking and joking with a quartet of female golfers. He looked, as he would be the first to admit, great. He was wearing a custom-tailored denim suit. The jacket had more pockets than a herd of kangaroos, each one outlined with white stitching. Around his neck was a small-patterned scarf in white, yellow and blue to pick up the blue of the suit. (Philip was very big on picking up colors.)

When I got to his side he shook my hand sedately and introduced me around. Just to make sure, he added a little label after my name. "She's the screenwriter—you know, *Somersault.*" The golfers reacted with enthusiasm. "We've got to get to work," Philip announced significantly. And led me across the room to a table for two.

"How're you doing?" he asked while we waited for our drinks.

"I've seen some of Cal's stuff. It's awful."

"No, no, I mean how're you doing on my script?"

"I'm into the scene where Françoise goes to George's apartment for dinner."

"Got them in the sack yet?"

"I'm going to write that part tonight."

"So you're staying in for a change." He wagged his finger at me. "You go out too much. I want my writer at her typewriter!"

My instant reaction to the possessive case was to reach for a cigarette. Philip slapped my wrist. "Bad for you. Bad for my script." He gave my hand a furtive squeeze. "I've been having these fantasies about our production offices."

I tensed. "What kind of fantasies?"

"The decor—you know, furniture, colors . . ."

I relaxed. "Isn't it a little premature?"

"Ready for this? Walls a smooth, creamy—not taupe, exactly, a sort of cross between taupe and khaki. Brown suede furniture, beige rug. Draperies in a print of the taupe-khaki-brown and a touch of turquoise to pick up the color of the turquoise sofa pillows. Like it so far?" I nodded. "I plan to design my desk myself. Right now I'm thinking in terms of a free-form slab of beige marble set on a square of stainless steel."

He said his ideas for my office weren't crystallized yet. It was going to be very feminine—lots of wicker and plants and maybe Moroccan tiles on the floor. He didn't mention a ceiling fan but even so it sounded like a set from *Casablanca.* I imagined myself sitting in a peacock chair writing *Casablanca,* and my mind wandered to my long-ago idol, Claude Rains. Recently I had noticed my mind wandering a lot while Philip was talking. As he went on and on I began to wonder about his "lifelong dream." Maybe it had really been to be an interior decorator.

Four women in tennis dresses settled down at a table close by. Philip jumped up abruptly and hurried over to them. I watched him kissing cheeks, patting shoulders, laughing boisterously. Overdoing it. The women glanced toward me so I knew he was explaining my presence.

When he came back he said, "Janice's friends."

"What if Janice was with them?"

"What if she was? We're hardly having a secret rendezvous!"

You're the goose, I thought.

"By the way," Philip said, "I showed Janice that scene where Françoise is sitting on her bed watching George on TV."

"And?"

"Well—" He hesitated. "Janice doesn't understand why Françoise is naked."

"Does Janice come out of a shower in her clothes?"

"Janice thinks Françoise would've put on a robe."

"It says in the script that when Françoise hears George's voice on the TV set she grabs a towel and rushes out of the bathroom."

"She could grab a robe as fast as a towel."

I felt the familiar knot in my guts that I feel at story conferences. "A robe would ruin that shot where George stares straight out of the screen and suddenly Françoise tries to cover more of herself with the towel."

"Is that because she thinks he can see her?"

"For God's sake, Philip! She *knows* he can't see her!"

"Then why does she try to cover up?"

"It's a—an instinctive gesture. It's supposed to be funny."

"Janice didn't get it."

I exhaled a long deep breath. "She's got lots of bones but maybe she hasn't got a funny bone."

"If Janice didn't get it, will the audience get it?"

Deep breathing wasn't doing anything for me. "Could I have another drink, please?"

"Don't forget, Janice is pretty typical."

"Philip, will you please signal the waiter?"

"Janice says if Françoise is that attracted to George she'd have given herself plenty of time to take a shower before the broadcast so she wouldn't miss any of it."

The perfect marriage, I thought. Mr. and Mrs. Tunnel Vision.

"Janice says that's what she personally would do if she personally was that attracted to George." Upset by my stare he dropped his eyes and peered at the lemon twist floating in his glass. "Janice thinks it's more realistic if Françoise is an under-secretary instead of the ambassador."

I smiled at the waiter who put the second drink in front of me. After I gulped down half of it, I was even able to smile at Philip.

"Know what, Philip?" I said, louder than necessary, "I don't give a *shit* what Janice thinks!"

Alarmed, Philip glanced quickly around. Nobody was paying the least attention. "What're you so huffy about?" he demanded. "Like I told you the other day, you just can't take criticism!"

"I can't take peeing in it to make it better."

"What?"

"Nothing. Old joke my ex-husband used to tell."

"If you don't want me to show any pages to Janice, I won't."

"That's best. Let's wait till it's finished." I tapped the rim of my glass. "How about one more?"

"No. You won't work tonight if you're loaded." He reached under the table and pressed my knee. "I love what you've done so far," he said. "I'm mad for you."

Interesting, the way he put it. I whacked the starry-eyed maiden across each cheek until she cringed and backed away. But not far enough. Not yet.

At that moment a tanned middle-aged couple called to Philip as they passed our table. They were both wearing shirts and Bermuda shorts and visored caps with tees stuck in the bands. They looked amiable and healthy and as if they knew how to hit a golf ball. Philip waved and smiled. We watched as they hoisted themselves up on the high stools at the bar.

Philip lowered his voice. "That's Addie."

"Addie?"

"You know, Addie!"

"Addie who?"

"*Addie!*"

A three-hundred-watt bulb clicked on in my head.

"Don't stare," Philip said.

Addie looked like any affluent Beverly Hills matron you'd see picking over the asparagus at Jurgensen's or ordering T-shirts at Theodore's. Her blond hair was combed in a flip, little strands hung down and curled damply on her neck. She wore a golfer's leather wristband and brown and white golfer's shoes with studs. I could see the little pompoms on her socks peeking over the backs of her shoes. She was sipping a fancy rum drink through a straw. I tried to superimpose certain images over all of that but the opticals in my head didn't work.

"I thought Addie was a made-up person."

"There she is, big as life!" Philip chuckled. "Why don't we give her a call some night? It'd be fun, don't you think?"

"Who's the man with her?"

"Her husband."

"Does he know about her—uh, activities?"

Philip nodded. "He doesn't care."

"What kind of a marriage *is* that?"

Philip looked surprised. "It's just a marriage," he said.

Exposed footage

He bought two narrow gold bands at Cartier and they got a license at the city hall and went to see her doctor for their blood tests. Afterward they sat in a dark empty bar drinking Tanqueray martinis while she offered him any number of chances to call the whole thing off. He refused them.

"Oh, well," she said, "if it doesn't work out we can always get a divorce."

"Sure," he said, "we can always get a divorce."

They grinned at each other.

"I hate us to get married in that hideous city hall," she said. "Wish it could be in Paris."

"We'll get divorced in Paris."

"We'll stand on the Pont Neuf and toss our rings into the Seine!"

"A romantic divorce!" He took her hand in his, closing his fingers around it so tightly she winced. "What's bothering you?" he demanded.

"You. You look scared."

"It's my *first* marriage, for God's sake!"

"You're so pale."

"I've just lost blood!"

"Three drops. What a baby!"

"A baby and a hypochondriac and a fat man. Too fat. I'll die young."

"But I'm about to marry you to save your life!"

He shook his head. "I'll have a heart attack one of these days. You'll be a widow soon."

"Don't," she said. "Don't, *don't!*"

"Smoke too much, drink too much, weigh too much. . . ."

"You can do something about it."

"I've been on every diet in every diet book ever published—and some I made up myself."

"Darling, pounds would drop off you—if you cut down on the alcohol."

He laughed. "I saw a specialist about that. In her whole practice she'd had about a dozen failures. Guess who made it thirteen?" He lifted her hand to his lips and held it there for a moment. "What do you want with me? What do you want with a weak-willed, boozing fat man?"

"I want you."

"Just the way I am?"

"Just the way you are."

He leaned over and kissed her quickly. "So how about it?" He motioned the waiter to bring another round. "Will you wear widow's weeds after I'm gone?"

"Don't start that again."

"Will you? I want to know. Will you?"

"Oh, sure. I look wonderful in black."

"Will you come to the cemetery every Sunday and leave one perfect flower on my grave?"

"How about a black orchid bred from the heart of an Inca virgin? I'll have it flown in each week from Peru."

His eyes lighted. "You'll become a legend!" He gestured with both hands, directing the scene. "There you are—pale face under a floppy-brimmed black hat, two enormous mournful eyes, quivering mouth—this mysterious figure all in black! You fling yourself down on my grave, sobbing, convulsed with grief, black orchid clutched in your hand. Christ, I wish I could be there to see you! Everyone will point you out. 'So tragic! Her true love died in the first flush of youth.'"

"Don't let it happen till you're in your second flush, please."

"What will you put on my headstone?"

"What would you like?"

" 'He was *here*. He *mattered.*' Memorize that." He lighted her cigarette and his own. "How long will you grieve for me?"

"How long do you want me to?"

"Forever. How long will you stay without a man?"

"Not forever."

"How long?"

"I'm getting bored with this."

"You'll never find my like again," he warned her.

This time, along with their drinks, the waiter brought a bowl of peanuts. After Vincent had eaten a handful she picked up the bowl and put it on the next table.

"Dearest heart," he said, "please don't do that. You're the first woman I've ever been with who hasn't nagged me about eating too much. I have to do something about it—but *I* have to do it."

"Yes, you're right." She put the bowl back in front of him.

An hour later they walked tipsily home, their arms around each other. Vincent fixed supper and served it to Lucia in bed.

Perfectly scrambled eggs, crisp strips of bacon and beside them a sprig of parsley. When he put the plate down on her lap she looked up at him, her eyes suddenly wet.

"What's wrong?" he asked. "What's the matter?"

"The parsley . . ."

"The *parsley?*"

"It proves you care—you *care* about everything!"

He burst out laughing as the tears rolled down her cheeks.

5

So far I had hardly been permitted to function as a producer, but during this Cal Jordan period I was completely shut out of the film. Whenever I tried to talk to Ernie he was in a meeting or on his way out to a meeting or on the phone. He never called back. I knew casting was going on because actors came up to me at parties in Beverly Hills to tell me how thrilled they were to be in "my" film. I spent the time working on the script for Philip and looking out the window. Whenever I spotted Ernie and Grant walking along the alley to the projection room, I raced down the hall and out of the bungalow to catch up with them. In this way I managed to see some of the actresses being considered for Cecelia. The stuff we looked at—tests, clips from movies, television tapes—was discouraging. The ones who could act were too quirky; the ones who looked right canceled out when they opened their mouths. The only good actress we saw who also passed Grant's test—he wanted "to knock her off her pedestal and dirty her up"—came in to see Ernie after she'd read the script. She turned down the role because she was newly pregnant and didn't want to risk riding horses and being slung about. Ernie didn't tell me this, his secretary told me. She was surprised that Ernie hadn't tried to pressure the actress into having an abortion. I wasn't surprised. Ernie wanted Rosalind Young. And along with her I knew we'd get that ex-Princeton Western buff.

Quite often when Cal had to use the Convenience he would stop in my office to "yak." He was a real chatterbox. I figured it was a holdover from his cowboy days when he was out on the range for months—no one to talk to but cows. One day he came in, flopped down on my cushionless chaise longue and goggled at me. I felt like a cow. He seemed to be calculating whether I was "prime" beef or "utility."

He told me he knew how bad I felt when he was brought in on

73

the script. He was always bein' brought in on scripts and all the writers felt bad. I, fer instance, had yet to smile at him. If I was jist a plain little lady and not a writer we might have lighted a flash fire by this time! His fourth wife had thrown him out a month ago so he'd jist about given up on womanhood. Then he met me, and goldarn it, I turned out to be a writer. Could we beat the rap on this here bad start and have dinner at his favorite waterin' hole on the Strip? When I turned him down his pale eyes iced over. I wasn't prime, I was utility. He wasn't a cowboy, he was a rejected cowboy.

"Think yer too good for me? Yer one of them there double-domed writers and I'm jist a hack! Webster's Sixth New Collegiate Dictionary says a hack is a person who takes wages for kickin' his artistic self in the ass. That's what yer doing, ain'tcha? Yes, ma'am, yer a hack jist like me. We're both gittin' paid for bein' squashed like a bug between the caviar munchers and the popcorn munchers. That's what we're givin' em, little lady, bug juice!"

Ernie said it wasn't fair to Cal for me to read pages of his draft before it was finished. Naturally, though, it was fair for Ernie to read them as they drifted down from the second floor and were put through Rita's typewriter. When she could, Rita buzzed me, and if I was swift on my feet I got a look. There were no surprises in the new story line. Cal made the changes he said he'd make. The outlaws sounded no more illiterate than I'd written them—but they used more "cuss words" and they were certainly laconic. Entire exchanges consisted of:

"Bullshit."

"Ain't no bullshit."

"I say it's bullshit."

or:

"Good tits on'er."

"Gonna see them tits tonight!"

"Can't see tits at night, asshole!"

The dialogue sounded familiar, as if Cal were speaking all the lines. But even more familiar than that. He'd made the six members of the outlaw gang sound alike—they spoke in the same kind of crude shorthand, told identical sexual and scatological jokes. He'd cut all their character lines and transferred them to Andrew, even when they were totally inappropriate.

When I complained to him about this he was astonished. Didn't I know that the movie star hadda have all the lines? The movie star is the money. The P.M.s don't give a hoot about the minor characters,

74

so's it was wastin' time to make 'em different from each other. All the P.M.s wanna know is which is the bad guys and which is the good guys. That's what they plunk down their wampum fer.

One muggy afternoon Philip and I finally made it to *Deep Throat.* His disguise was an out-of-season tweed cap pulled down to his eyebrows. I had a scarf tied around my head babushka-fashion to obscure my profile. We both wore dark glasses. In spite of all this we were greeted boisterously in the lobby by a director we knew and his girl friend. There were many jock chuckles and slaps on the back between the director and Philip which reminded me that I was in L.A., where grown-up men spend a lot of time in locker rooms.

The picture had already started when we got inside and were ushered to two seats on the aisle. Several rows in front of us were empty except for one man so far slouched down that only his bald head showed, glimmering faintly against the seat back. After a few minutes, long enough for us to get bored with the mortar-and-pestle sex, we heard a small commotion in the back of the theatre. We looked back up the aisle. Three uniformed cops were standing there with the usher and the manager.

Philip and I gaped at each other.

"Raid!" he whispered, his eyes desperate.

"*Raid?* Is it illegal to be here?"

His face crumpled. "Oh, God, oh, God, oh, God!"

I knew what he was thinking—arrested, handcuffed, fingerprinted, locked in the slammer, a photograph of us in the papers ducking from the cameras as we climbed into the paddy wagon. Headlines flashed before my eyes: MARRIED STUDIO BOSS NABBED IN PORN MOVIE WITH SCREENWRITER PARAMOUR! PRODUCER INVOKES LITTLE-USED MORALITY CLAUSE TO FIRE SCREENWRITER! SCREENWRITER SAYS EXEC TOOK HER TO DEEP THROAT TO STUDY SCRIPT TECHNIQUES! Putting the blame on Philip like that, even in fantasy, wasn't being very loyal to him, but what had loyalty ever got me? I had been loyal to Vincent to the point of insanity and what it had got me was a sneer. "Loyalty is your *thing,* isn't it?" he'd sneered on several occasions.

We heard the thump of feet coming down the aisle toward us. Philip's fingers tightened around my arm. We sank down in our seats. Everything I had read about cold sweats proved to be true. I squeezed my eyes shut as the cops came abreast of us. They passed us—obviously going to the front of the theatre to announce a mass arrest. I opened

75

my eyes and looked back up the aisle. The third cop was still there. We couldn't even make a dash for it.

Two cops had edged into the bald man's row and were bending over him. The bald man didn't move. They were talking to him but we couldn't hear what they said because of the hullabaloo of orgasmic ecstasy on the sound track. One of the cops shook the bald man violently by the shoulder. The bald man's head flopped forward in utter humiliation. The other cop straightened up and signaled toward the back of the theatre. A moment later two men rushed down the aisle with a stretcher. We could see their silhouettes against a huge close-up of a glistening, wriggling tongue as they lifted the bald man onto a stretcher and shook out a blanket to cover him.

"Heart attack," Philip whispered. "Taking him to a hospital." When the stretcher passed us going up the aisle we saw that the bald man's face was covered by the blanket too. They'd be taking him to the morgue.

We waited for two minutes and hurried up the aisle ourselves. The manager was in the lobby eager to tell the story.

"I had guys sit through two shows, maybe three shows," he said. "I wouldn't lie to ya, this bald guy sat through *five* shows. I figure he got enough for his money so I go to throw him out. There he is, eyes open, but he ain't seein' nothin'. It hits me he'll never see nothin' no more." He shrugged. "I wouldn't lie to ya—that's the first one I had croak on me."

Philip grinned. "What a way to go!"

"It's kinda sad," the manager said. "I wouldn't lie to ya."

We drove over to Beverly Hills, where I had parked my car, and I went along with Philip on some errands. He picked up his slacks at the cleaners, a terry-cloth beach robe at Dorso's and an ice cream cone at Swensen's Ice Cream Shop. We walked over to Gucci's while he finished his cone. Then we went inside so he could price attaché cases.

"Pick out some little thing you like," he said. "I want to buy you a present to make up for that arm."

I looked down. Between my wrist and elbow was a dark purple ring of bruised flesh.

We separated and I looked at "little things" for a while. When the key cases and address books palled I wandered over to the jewelry case and watched a bald man buy a silver bikini chain for a girl with a sensational body. Most of the body was in view since she was wearing a bra top and low-cut jeans. She was about to fasten the chain just below her navel when the man snatched it away and fastened it himself. He

76

had a marvelous time doing it. He was such an *alive* bald man!

Philip came over to me later carrying a handsome leather-bound case in tan canvas with a red and a green stripe running diagonally across both sides.

"Understated," he said, "but anyone can tell where it's from."

"It screams Gucci's," I said.

"What've you found?"

I held up a thin gold wire bracelet marked $35.00. He didn't even look at the price tag. He was frowning at the bracelet.

"Can I afford that?" he asked.

"You can," I said. "I wouldn't lie to ya."

During his third week in Bungalow Five, Cal began to stop in at my office two or three times a day. When I asked him how he was getting any work done, he laughed.

"I'm too smart for 'em," he said. "Fast writin' makes 'em antsy. They think fast is easy so's it's gotta be bad. Slow is hard so's it's gotta be good. How come yer air conditioner's broke and I ain't even got one? The caviar munchers want us writers to *sweat*, that's why! Take a tip from this here old pro, little lady, never deliver on time."

I didn't need Cal's tip. I'd learned all that years before when Vincent and I worked for the greatest caviar muncher of them all —an aging and legendary producer, a Turk named Omar Lederman. During his long career he had produced some of the most fantastically expensive pictures in the history of Hollywood. Several of them were also fantastically successful. A couple became classics. A few bombed—grandly. Omar ran his projects with an iron hand in an iron glove. He was a devil to work with but a devil with brains, unlike Ernie Kaplan, who was only a nitwit dressed up in a Halloween costume of a devil. Omar deliberately contrived a hell for the creative people on his films—he believed conflict and brawling were as necessary to film-making as cameras and lights—but when he cast you into the flames at least you burned with a certain splendor. Scandals of infighting and intrigues, all the clamors of war, hung over his production. One read about the Oscar-winning writer who threatened to throw Omar from the fifth floor of the Hotel Ritz in Paris and had indeed shoved him as far as the window. One heard about the distinguished woman writer who had had nerves of steel during a nasty political investigation but was seen rushing from Omar's office in tears. Famous directors tried to get court orders to bar him from their sets and vowed they'd never

work with him again. But when he wanted them they came running—ulcer pills in their pockets.

Vincent and I sweated sweat and we sweated blood on the picture
we did with him. It was a heart-stopping experience—in Vincent's
case, literally. A couple of weeks after Omar fired him, Vincent had
a heart attack. Long before that happened, however, I was the one
Omar took on first. Although he had agreed to produce our picture
because the script was "brilliant," the script must, of course, be rewritten. ("Scripts, my dear Lucia, are not written, they are *rewritten.*") He
wouldn't even talk to Vincent about preparing the production until the
script was "right."

In my eagerness to get the production going I'd do the rewrites
overnight. Although they were exactly what we'd discussed, the scenes
I brought Omar in the morning were never right. Never. He pounded
on his desk. From out of their pouches his old-sultan's eyes scorched
me with contempt. He had worked with the greatest film writers in the
world and none of them had had the nerve to bring him changes off
the top of their heads! I hadn't worked hard enough. "Go home and
work!" he bellowed.

One day his behavior changed completely. He confronted me
with a miserable face. He had undertaken our picture, he said feebly,
to aid and instruct inexperienced film makers (it was only our third
film), but the agony wasn't worth it. Dispiritedly, he slid my rewrites
back to me over the desk. Impossible! He had never had such trouble
with a writer in his life. For weeks, sleepless nights because of me, and
now he was constipated because of me.

My God, I thought as I walked home, the great, the celebrated,
the world-renowned Omar Lederman's lower colon is screwed up and
it's all my fault. It didn't enter my head that Omar's accusation implied
that I had a kind of power over him. Never having had any power I
wouldn't have recognized what feeling powerful was like anyway. I
reacted exactly as he meant me to by bending double under a ton of
guilt. Now you've done it, I scolded my hunched reflection in the shop
windows, now you've really upset him! I had been taught that one thing
a nice woman doesn't do, *mustn't* do, is upset a man. One does not
argue, pout, cry, appear too intelligent, burn dinner or forget where the
cuff links are—to which I could now add, or write fast.

I continued to make changes overnight while my discussions with
Omar were fresh in my head, but sometimes I waited two weeks before
submitting them. During those periods I got calls at random hours of
the day. *"Are you working?"* Omar would roar into the phone or, if he'd

78

called earlier and found me out, *"I know you are not working!"* For me, at least, 1984 had arrived.

He always loved the delayed new scenes. "You are a very fine writer," he would assure me. "We do more pictures together, you and me. I do not yet know about the husband," he'd add slyly.

"You finally do what I implore you!" he said the first time I supposedly took ten days to do it in. "You see how improved is the script?"

I nodded, although I couldn't see how improved was the script. I thought most of the changes were a horrible mistake. However, one doesn't start a row with a Legend, especially when no one else on earth wants to make the picture.

When his secretary appeared he handed her the scenes.

"Blue pages," he told her.

"What're blue pages?" I asked.

"You do not do blue pages when you work with the husband?"

"I don't know what they are."

"You are the most incredible know-nothing writer I ever meet. Blue pages, my dear Lucia, are final revisions."

"Vincent didn't care what color paper I used for final revisions."

"Perhaps he is a know-nothing director."

"He's brilliant! He's going to make this a brilliant picture!"

"We put that discussion on hold."

After the secretary left, Omar smiled at me.

"Everything functions now," he said.

"Functions?"

"Everything is okay."

"Everything in the script is okay?"

"Everything in the script needs work," he roared. *"My bowels are okay!"*

It hadn't been like that on our first picture. I made plenty of revisions in the script, instant rewrites sitting on the floor of a set or on the grass or on the platform of a train station—wherever Vincent was shooting. In those days no one in the world had the right to give us orders, or command us, or threaten us, or hobble us with scorn or sarcasm, because we and our friend Scott had raised all the money ourselves. We were doing what we had dreamed of doing. We were making a movie.

Long shot

It was worth everything, she thought, the way he looked that morning. As long as she lived she would remember his face rising like a moon, full and pale, as he straightened up from his crouch beside the camera dolly and into her sight line and said gently, and for the first time in his life, "Action." His face, incandescent with joy, would forever be a freeze-frame in her mind.

It was worth the wounds when the script was rejected by every studio.

It was worth the dismay when they found out it had never been read even by story editors, let alone executives who make decisions. It had been read by "readers" who handle the slush pile of scripts by unknowns. And not read. These lowly employees also covered books and wrote up synopses. "After I sent for the coverage," one reader told them, "I didn't have to read the script. Nobody could make a movie out of that little-nothing book."

It was worth the anger when one promoter offered to come up with the money if they'd put a rape in the script and make the masturbation scene explicit.

It was worth the disappointment when the rich play-backers whom Vincent knew said they were interested only in gambling on the theatre. "And besides, Vinnie dear, if you're so set on making a movie couldn't you find a more cheerful subject?"

It was worth all the horrors of money raising—the entrapment in endless dinners and cocktail hours with prospective investors. Within five minutes they could sense there'd be no money forthcoming, only opinions.

Who wants to go to a movie to see weirdos when you can see weirdos out on the streets?

You'll offend a lot of people with that scene where she's, you know, touching herself.

I wish it had more fun in it like that Jack Lemmon thing we saw the other night.

You've got to put in flashbacks to show what their lives were like before.

I bet you could get Paul Newman if you built up the role of that teacher.

The message I get from it is that we shouldn't care what other people think of us. If we didn't care what other people think of us we'd all act like barbarians.

It was worth not taking money for the wrong reason.

I'll make an investment if you'll let my nephew write the score.

My girl friend's an actress. Give her the part and I'll buy plenty of units.

It was worth taking some money for the wrong reason:

My accountant says I can make money this year by losing money.

I'll put in a couple of thousand because my wife hates the script. I'll back anything my wife hates.

Finally Vincent formed a partnership with Scott Fuller, a close friend since their summer-stock days when Vincent was a stage manager and Scott a set designer. In the years since then, Scott had worked on several East Coast films as art director. He loved the script, wanted to produce it and immediately brought in two large investments from members of his family. Lucia borrowed on all the stock she owned and turned over that money. The sale of units was slow and difficult even when they were split up so that shares could be bought for as little as $300. A year went by and they had only half the money they needed.

Scott tracked down a multimillionaire real estate developer who was interested in movies and after several strenuous sessions persuaded him to make the biggest investment of all. They were still many thousands short. At that point Scott emptied his bank account and bought the rest of the units. They were ready to make the movie.

As producer, Scott wrestled and pleaded with his friends at the lab and the equipment company to get deferments. He went after Local 52 and the teamsters, arguing that this was a first picture on a minuscule budget. The unions finally gave them a break. Scott haggled down every expenditure they had to make and found locations in a small city near New York where the cost of everything would be less.

He warned Vincent he had twenty-five days to shoot. They couldn't afford one day more.

They couldn't afford to rent a projection room either. When the first few days' rushes came back from the lab they showed them in the evening on a bedsheet tacked to the wall of their motel room. Lucia could hardly believe what she saw—the actors got up and sat down, they walked, they opened doors, they climbed stairs, they touched each other, they moved. And their lips moved—they spoke her words. It was a moving picture. A *movie!*

After Vincent fell asleep she lay beside him staring at the white sheet on the wall, replaying the images—the images he had chosen and worked out and directed. After a while she closed her eyes and put her arm around him, her love, her husband, her director.

6

Cal finished his two-week rewrite in four weeks. He left a note on my desk.

Sorry not to see you before I skeedadle (sp?). If you ever shake your habit (writing, ha, ha!) and turn into a plain little lady, give me a holler.

yr friend,
C.J.

P.S. Don't take any long walks on short docks.

Beneath the P.S. he had drawn the smile logo that was on his yellow bag.

From the platform I looked out over the auditorium filled with members of my union. These were my brothers and sisters—a mere sprinkling of sisters because the studios and networks and independents didn't hire many women. And now, whatever our sex, they were refusing us a fair minimum wage. They were refusing us cost-of-living protection, profit participation, rights in material, residuals in perpetuity and a long list of other benefits we were getting ready to strike for. We were writers, despised menials. Our curve peaked above all others on the Hollywood Misery Graph, and we were so lacking in clout we didn't even appear on the Power Graph. But no matter how they treated or resented us, they needed us. We were planning to quit writing to demonstrate how much.

For me and several others, however, there was a complication symbolically based on a hyphen. We were "hyphenates"—writer-producers, writer-directors, writer-actors. If there was to be a strike, the rules would forbid us to cross the picket lines. This meeting had been called to consider the problem of our nonwriting services. In my case "produce" had been a practically meaningless term, and I spent a few minutes explaining why and how. The audience was attentive—there were frequent nods and tight-lipped smiles. Almost everyone there had had his own Ernie Kaplan.

Civilians are apt to dismiss these accounts with a yawn and attempt to change the subject. But writers hang on them. It's as if with each picture we undertake a journey to some menacing place—like the Arctic Circle, for example—and we have this compulsion to share all the horrors with each other: the week I ate boiled boot straps, the day my toes fell off, the night the polar bear ambushed me. "So what?" civilians would ask. "No one's twisting your arm, no one's forcing you to write screenplays!" And then they'd come up with the most infuriating myth of all. "Anyway, you're getting damn well paid for it!" Last year the average income of a member of the Writers Guild was less than a studio maintenance worker's.

I was winding up my story. " . . . And so if I'm kept out of the studio and off the locations the picture will be handed over to Ernie Kaplan like a gift from my own union. He'll be rid of me, which is exactly what he wants. Fellow members of the Guild, I will never scab! If we strike, I will not write a single word! But allow me, at least, to fight back at one of our worst enemies. Allow me to cross the picket line and try to function as a producer."

There were immediate boos and shouts of "No! No! Never!" A man in the third row leapt to his feet, shaking his fist. "Cross that picket line and you'll never work out here again!" he screamed. Halfway back another man jumped up. "Cross that line and you're expelled from this Guild for life!" A woman jumped up. She curled her hands around her mouth like a megaphone. "Strikebreaker!" she shrieked. *"Strikebreaker!"* Everyone except the other hyphenates in the room applauded wildly.

"Where's your suit? Aren't you going to swim, darling?"
"Sssh—not out here. Haven't time to swim."
"What kept you?"
"Margo. Can't type a letter without a mistake."
"You ought to look for another secretary."
"It's the kid's first job. She'll shape up."
"Why are you pinching your face together like that?"
"I'm squinting—sun's in my eyes."
"Your lips are squinting too."

"What does that mean?"

"Isn't it odd how often we have to ask each other what we mean, as if we're speaking a different language?"

"*Lips* can't squint."

"I mean you look sort of—mopey."

"Got a table?"

"Over there, near the diving board."

I hadn't gone to my office that day, so Philip suggested he come to the hotel and take me to lunch at the pool. We skirted rows of oiled and reddened bodies supine on towel-covered chaises. The whole area looked like a huge glazed apricot tart.

Philip's mopiness vanished temporarily as he waved and smiled to more or less a dozen of what he would call his "close personal friends." He reminded me of Vincent in that respect. Neither of them had any plain friends or even acquaintances. I led him to a little table under a yellow pagoda-shaped umbrella where I had been sitting in my drag as his screenwriter, notebooks, script pages and pens spread out in front of me.

I pushed the clutter to one side. "Lunch'll be here any minute. Shrimp salad. Iced tea."

"Hell, I can't eat shrimp!"

"Darling, I mean Philip, you eat shrimp at Foo Chow's."

"Developed an allergy to them. They make my nose stuff up."

"Maybe it was something else."

"*I can't eat shrimp!*" He sounded almost hysterical. "Order me a chicken salad."

I leapt up and dashed to the phone at the other end of the pool. Room Service informed me that my first order was on the way, that they were very busy, that they couldn't say how long it would take to send out a chicken salad—and, the severe governessy voice added, they would have to charge for the two shrimp salads in any case.

When I got back to the table, lunch had arrived. The check was anchored under one glass of iced tea and Philip was morosely drinking the other.

"Go ahead," he said, "don't wait for me."

The shrimp were plump, pink and huge. "Delicious! A shame you have to give them up."

"I've had to give up many delicious things in my life." He added mysteriously, "And still do."

I handed him a brown envelope. "New scene. Can Margo retype it? Doesn't have to be perfect."

"She'll manage." He put the envelope aside.

"Aren't you going to read it?"

"Not now."

This was unlike him. He usually pounced upon every page. I pushed my dark glasses up on top of my head and peered at him.

"Philip, what *is* the matter?"

"I've got to talk to you."

"About what?"

"I don't know how to say it. . . ."

"Say it."

"I can't make love to you any more."

"You *physically* can't?"

He bridled. "Why the hell would you think that?"

"What *do* you mean?"

"I mean I've decided I'm not going to make love to you any more."

"You can but you won't?"

"I mean I'm married. I mean I don't want to bust up my marriage."

"I don't want you to. That's the last thing I want. What's the problem?"

"I've got three kids. I mean I've got responsibilities. . . ."

"Philip, could we please try talking without saying 'I mean?' It's driving me nuts." I put down my fork. "You've had dozens of affairs. What's different?"

"You're different. The others didn't matter to me, but if I go on making love to you I'm sure to fall *in* love with you and then—" He stopped and contemplated me. I hadn't seen that expression in anyone's eyes since high school. Calf eyes, we used to call them. "My life would be a shambles. I'd want to be with you all the time."

It was like saying, as Vincent used to do, If I eat one peanut I'll eat the whole jarful. Did that necessarily follow? I used to wonder. Now apparently I equaled one peanut to Philip. He intended, I assumed, to pay me a compliment. Was I, at last, a *femme fatale*? Would continuing to go to bed with me plunge this man into such insane rapture he would desert his wife of twenty-four years and his dependents? I half lowered my eyelids and concentrated on the Givenchy logo on his navy sports shirt, considering what it would be like to be with *him* all the time. Even though the soft focus provided by my eyelashes the prospect was not pleasing. I shuddered slightly. Philip noticed and misinterpreted it as an excess of emotion. He looked alarmed.

86

"You're not going to break down, are you?"

Conceited bastard. I smiled and widened my eyes so he could see they were clear and dry. "Why're you telling me this now? Today?"

"You're a very intense woman. I mean you need a very intense involvement. I mean I can't make a commitment. Scares hell out of me."

There was no point in reminding him that the first night we met he had announced that, thanks to EST, a commitment no longer scared him. Anyway, I hate the word commitment and try never to utter it.

"Has Janice said anything?" I asked.

"Janice is at La Costa for the week." He sounded annoyed. "It's my decision. I want us to be just—friends. I mean I've always stayed friends with my ex-mistresses."

"Whatever for?"

His eyes flickered but he decided not to answer. "Since you and I are going to be partners I foresee us having a very strong friendship."

"Careful." I grinned at him. "Strong means intense."

"You're not writing now! You don't have to show off your vocabulary!"

"Gee, you're in a bad humor."

"I'm hungry, damn it! Can't you call and hurry them up?"

I sat tight. "You call if you want to."

Just as he was looking at his watch and groaning, the chicken salad arrived with another check and without rolls and butter. The waiter explained that rolls and butter did not automatically accompany the salads; they had to be ordered. Philip ordered them. He put the new check on top of the first one under my iced tea glass. Either the food or the prospect of never going to bed with me again brightened him up.

"Soon as Rossen and Kramer get back from New York they want to meet with us—about giving us offices on the lot."

"How do they feel about it?"

"Very interested. They know your work."

He transferred the tomatoes and hard-boiled eggs from his plate to my plate. Tomatoes gave him heartburn and eggs are either full of cholesterol or cause it, I'm not sure which.

"I told them about the script, and I said we want to develop other projects. We'd better dream up some ideas before we see them."

"Let's do it Thursday night. Obviously, we'll have plenty of time."

"Oh, hell! You're taking what I said as a rejection."

"What should I take it as?"

"You've got to understand. I'm a man in a terrible bind."

He said this in such an incongruously complacent tone I realized an exchange of moods had taken place. Philip had arrived joyless and was now lighthearted while I had been feeling fine when he came and now felt less fine. I suppose when a man kicks you out of bed, no matter what your reservations are about him, your self-esteem is bound to take a dive.

Philip was gulping down his salad so our conversation rather came to a halt at that point, and a few minutes later he rushed off to "take a meeting."

After Philip left these things happened:

The waiter brought the rolls and butter along with another check.

I discovered I was stuck with all three checks, two of them astronomical.

A woman with an elaborately lacquered yellow coiffure, diamond earrings and brown doughy thighs arose from a mat, carefully lowered herself into the unoccupied pool and began a cautious breaststroke without splashing a drop of water on her hair.

A burned-almost-black young man with a halo of black curly hair on his head and a rug of it on his shoulders and chest hung up the phone in his cabana. I had noticed him continually dialing and talking, the instrument clenched between his chin and shoulder as if it grew there among the curls. He came out of the cabana and crossed to my table. He said the pool boy had told him who I was, but he was sure I didn't know who he was. He handed me his card. The card said "Burton Productions, International, Limited." He told me he was Burton and listed a string of "exploitation product" he had produced, none of which I had ever heard of. He said he'd have been mighty disappointed if a person with my kind of integrity had heard of them. He said he now felt ready to "make art," and he'd give anything if I'd write a script for him. Anything but money, apparently. He said he wasn't at all sure he could afford a writer like me. He revolved his lustrous black eyes from my head to my toes.

"With your list of wonderful product," he said, "I thought you'd be a little old lady and you're not."

"I'm not?"

"How about dinner at La Serre? Afterward we can have a nightcap at The London Club. That's my club."

It would have been a change from Foo Chow's and Baskin-Robbins but I could project the whole evening. First he'd talk about the crassness of Hollywood, where everything was measured by the buck.

Then he'd talk about how "really meaningful pictures" were possible if creative people took on the project as a labor of love. He'd give me that double-talk about how we could be partners and do something we believed in, and if I'd write a script he'd get a deal and of course we'd go halves on all the profits. Finally, sufficiently softened by drink and my recent "narcissistic mortification," as the shrink calls it, I would take on this new hairy waif (who could afford a cabana and probably a suite at the hotel) and write him a script for nothing—as if I had learned nothing.

I pleaded too much work and turned down the invitation.

"That's A-okay," Burton said. He looked lustfully at the notebooks and script pages on the table. "I'm interested in excellence, and when a person is as interested in excellence as I am he is prepared to wait." He returned to his cabana and picked up the phone.

I sat at the table for a while, watching the woman in the pool. She was keeping her head above water, which, when I thought about my current work life and love life, was a damn sight more than I was doing. The extra shrimp salad, so long in the heat, began to smell fishy. There was something fishy about that whole lunch with Philip.

Sitting across from me and Ernie in Ernie's office, Keith Ryan looked more like a hustler than a screenwriter—although the way things are in our industry, the difference is constantly narrowing. He was typically California—long straight hair sunstreaked to an unreal platinum, tanned cute face, as cute as it must have been in the third grade. He looked as though he'd never been out of the Pacific except to be born. Are those pearls that are his eyes? It was difficult to imagine him braving winter winds on the Princeton campus. He was wearing sandals and cut-offs and a V-neck cashmere sweater and a gold Cartier "love bracelet"—you can't get it off your wrist without the tiny vermeil screwdriver Cartier thoughtfully supplies with it. (Those eminent jewelers know more about love than most of us.) The script lay across his thighs. Below it his knees looked like big bronze doorknobs.

"Hal's speech on page twelve," he was saying, "where he tells Cecelia all about Andrew's background—his wife's death and the lost kids—it's just one big clump of obvious exposition. That's bad screenwriting, if you'll forgive me, Mrs. Wade."

"Ask Cal Jordan to forgive you. He wrote it."

"What I would do is disseminate these clues to the romantic irony of Andrew's character to achieve a kind of nonsophistic suspense. Thus we preserve Andrew's mystery for both Cecelia and the audience."

Ernie turned to me. "Fuckin' suspense—that's what we need!"

I shrugged. "I don't know what nonsophistic suspense is, but I had plain ordinary suspense in my original draft."

"The major problem is that there's nothing for Rosalind Young to play," Keith explained. "The role needs to be given dimension for Rosalind Young in order to take advantage of the extraordinary charisma Rosalind Young brings to the screen." He said "Rosalind Young" the way the rest of us say "Greta Garbo." "The way it's written now," Keith went on, "the character Rosalind Young plays is a ninny, if you'll forgive me, Mrs. Wade."

"Oh, sure." I made a vaguely priestlike gesture of absolution. "I'll forgive you."

"In other words, the character of Andrew has all the action and Cecelia merely reacts. Ontologically speaking, she simply isn't there."

"Uh-huh, uh-huh," Ernie said.

"There's an ideal place during the scene with the Indians when she could take action. She could also take action when Buck Barnes is defiling her—"

"When he's defiling her, okay, but not when he's raping her," Ernie said.

"This is a love story and there are no love scenes. We never see Andrew and Cecelia alone together. It was a mistake not to take time for two-scenes, if you'll forgive me, Mrs. Wade."

"I right now issue you a blanket forgiveness, Mr. Ryan."

"The minor characters sound like the same character, if you'll . . . there's no characterization of the minor characters."

"There was in my script—which I understand you read, Mr. Ryan."

He shook his head.

"Miss Young told us you'd read it."

"I didn't want to be influenced by it. I wanted to bring my own existential vision to this picture."

"So you knew you were going to work on it?"

"I knew Rosalind Young would want me if she took the role. I'm her—you might say, I'm her house writer."

"Can't imagine how you got the job," I said bitchily.

"What d'ya mean?" Ernie growled. "This kid can write!"

"Is that the reason you got the job?"

The pearls didn't blink. "The second reason," he said.

I liked him for that. I forgave him for saying he hadn't read my script when he had, for saying he'd gone to Princeton when he hadn't.

90

After our meeting Ernie sent him upstairs to settle into Cal's former office and start work.

On Thursday Philip called me at the office to say that Margo was typing my scene and that he thought it worked—for the most part.

"I'm not sure about the sequence in the self-service garage," he said. "Do you really think George would be fixing his own car?"

"That's the kind of guy he is! It's all set up in that earlier scene where he talks about working his way through school. He had a job in a garage, remember?"

"But, as Margo said, he has plenty of money now."

"*Margo?*"

"Don't get excited. She only mentioned it."

"Why don't you show the scene to your mail clerk? Maybe *he'd* find something to mention!"

"Maybe he damn well would!" Philip shouted. "Mail clerks grow up to be heads of studios!"

"What're you so angry about?"

"What're *you* angry about?"

"I think Margo's job is to type the scene, not to have an opinion."

"Why can't she have an opinion? She's a writer."

"Oh?"

"She showed me some of her poems. Boy, can that baby write!"

"Oh, really?"

There was a pause.

"Listen, I can't make it tonight," Philip said. "Rossen called from New York—he's supposed to be at that Film Center party. I've got to go in his place."

"I'm a member. I'll go with you."

"I'm taking Janice."

"I'll go by myself then."

"What for? It'll be a mob scene. I wish you'd stay in and work."

"But—"

"The sooner you finish the script, the sooner things'll happen for us."

"Okay."

"*Good girl!*"

After I hung up a wee alert buzzer went off in my head.

On Saturday I went to Gloria and Fred Gardner's for brunch and tennis. It was at their dinner party months before that I'd first met

91

Philip, and though I'd seen the Gardners frequently since then they'd hardly ever mentioned his name. This Sunday was different. As soon as the other four guests finished their coffee and went out onto the courts Gloria started to ask questions—how was Philip to work with, how was the script going, had he contributed any good ideas?

"D'you think he's bright?" Gloria asked. "He's got a reputation for being bright, hasn't he, Fred?"

"Smart businessman," Fred said.

"That's why I don't understand how he could do such a dumb thing!" Gloria offered me a basket of blueberry muffins. "Janice caught him in bed with some little cupcake." I studied the muffins and picked the one with the most blueberries. "She was supposed to get back from La Costa Friday, but instead she got back on Thursday night—and there they were!"

"Where?"

"The kids were at the beach house and they were in the Bel Air house. Can you imagine being dumb enough to do it in your own house?"

A piece of muffin had stuck in my throat. I washed it down with coffee. "Who told you?"

"Janice. She's hysterical. She's going to get a divorce."

"She's always threatening to get a divorce," Fred said. "Then she ends up looking the other way."

"You'd have to sprain your neck to look the other way when you find your own husband in your own bed with a cupcake you never saw before!"

"What difference would it make if Janice had seen her before?"

"Well, you know what I mean." Gloria turned to me. "So there you are! Write a movie about *that!*"

"Too cliché."

"And too *dumb!*" Gloria laughed. "Oh, well, Philip'll make a dandy extra man for dinner parties."

"Thought you were Janice's friend," Fred said.

"I *am* Janice's friend, but it's damn hard to find an attractive extra man in this town!"

"They'll get together again," Fred said. "They always do."

"Have they split up before?" I asked.

Gloria nodded. "But this time Janice is *really mad.*"

"Why more than usual?" Fred asked.

"Honestly, Fred—in her *own bed!*"

Fred shrugged. "Is it important whose bed it is?"

"Don't you understand? It's an invasion of her *personal space*. It's like being *raped*."

Fred put his coffee down. "A guy can't do anything these days without you calling it rape." He picked up his tennis racket and started across the lawn toward the tennis court.

"He doesn't understand what I'm talking about," Gloria said. "It's awful the way men have no feeling for that sort of thing."

"Who was the girl?"

"Janice doesn't know her name—his new secretary."

Later I played the best tennis I'd played since I'd come to California. Unleashed aggression. No guilt.

At the office I told Rita not to put Philip's calls through to me under any circumstances—to say I was incapacitated, in conference or in Inner Mongolia, for all I cared. The flash of dismay on Rita's face led me to believe she'd listened in on our conversations. Of all the talk that jammed the wires of Bungalow Five, ours was probably the closest to a sit-com. No doubt she'd gotten hooked.

I asked the switchboard operator at the Beverly Hills Hotel to screen my calls—a Mr. Philip Rowan was always, without exception, to be told I didn't answer. The operator yawned audibly. The superstud of the silver screen, the richest woman in the world, and a rock band which performed with a boa constrictor were registered in the hotel. She had bigger fish to fry.

Every morning I found telephone slips marked *Rowan* under my door. Some of the calls had come in at 2 A.M. and 3 A.M. In Tinsel Town where everyone was tucked into bed by ten o'clock ("This is a *working* town") Philip seemed to be keeping unusual hours in what was, I assumed, his bachelor pad. Insomnia had joined his heartburn and allergies. Early on the fourth day of this communication blackout I took a call from the Writers Guild. We were officially on strike. Every member was expected to serve on the picket lines now being set up in front of all production offices and studios. Any member who refused to picket, without a medical reason certified by a doctor, would be fined $100 a day. I was assigned, by coincidence, to report to the picket captain at the studio where I hadn't been allowed to do much work and was now not allowed to do any work at all.

All day long, six of us—five male writers and myself—marched back and forth in front of the studio gates brandishing our placards. It wasn't a fun thing to be doing. Our placards grew heavier each hour, we suffered under the blazing sun and we fulminated—exchanging stories about our brutal masters who were even then in air-conditioned offices busy with their evil pursuits. My kind of masochism is undependable; the pain of watching Ernie and Grant wave jauntily as they drove in every day did not metamorphose into pleasure. By the beginning of the second week I decided to phone the picket committee and plead for a transfer to another post.

That morning one of the male writers fainted from the heat and had to be sent home, and that afternoon Faye Siegal arrived to take his place. She was about my age, plump, with no-nonsense short straight hair and a knife-sharp nose. But the real blade was in her head. She had created, and was now the executive producer of, three long-running prime-time television series—breakthrough, tradition-busting shows that had turned the network bosses ashen-faced until they saw the ratings.

After the introductions she grabbed my arm. "Step on it," she said. "Got to take off twenty pounds." We trotted the distance in front of the studio gates twice without speaking. The male writers, inching along, looked at us as if we were insane. I forgot about a transfer and began to contemplate death from cardiac arrest. I slowed down to a shuffle.

"What's the matter?" Faye glanced over her shoulder. "You don't look out of condition. You don't look as much of a knucklehead as I thought you would either!"

I raced up alongside her. "Why'd you think I'd look like a knucklehead?"

"Read in the trades you hired Cal Jordan to rewrite your script."

"I did not! The studio hired him. Who is he? Do you know him?"

She cranked down her pace. "His first wife played the ingenue on a soap I wrote a hundred years ago. Poor Mary Sue—she hasn't been seen or heard of since."

"I've seen her. Cal has her tattooed on his arm."

"Right! He said he did it to prove the marriage was forever. The big fake! You must know what a big fake he is!"

"In what way?" I asked cautiously.

"He conned you! He's conned half the producers in town, but writers are supposed to be *smart!*" She looked at me and groaned. "How the hell've you stayed alive out here?"

"I'm not alive. I'm just walking back and forth and breathing."

When it was our turn for a break I dragged myself after Faye to the deli across the street and over a couple of cottage cheese salads she told me about Cal. He'd never been a cowboy. He'd probably never

94

seen a cow close up. He was just a guy from some godforsaken place in Pennsylvania who hitchhiked to Hollywood to make his fortune. He met Mary Sue when he came to the door of her house in Culver City and asked to cut the grass for a quarter. As Mary Sue watched him pushing the lawn mower in his filthy jeans and cowboy boots, he must've triggered off some mythic fantasy of the lone gunslinger in her. Either that or she was the kind of kid who freaked out on muscles and body odor.

Anyway, he moved in. One day he started reading the scripts she brought home and decided he could write scripts too. Mary Sue gave him the money to go to about a million Western movies and bought him a typewriter. His illiteracy worked for him—his dialogue sounded "real."

"The bottom line," Faye said, "is that he sold his very first script."

"And everything he's written he's swiped from other movies," I said dismally. "All he does is scramble it around."

"The macho stars and directors love him—he's got the same pig attitudes they've got. That's why he has a credit on half the Westerns that get produced."

"The real bottom line," I said, "is that he came to Hollywood to make his fortune and he did."

One day I told Faye about Philip.

"What the hell'd you expect?" she demanded. "You'll get your ass broken every time you write for love."

"I wrote scripts for my ex-husband for love."

"And he kicked you in the ass! So you turn around and do it again for another guy and now he's kicked you in the ass!"

"They're two entirely different situations. Besides, it wasn't love with Philip—it was sort of a cuckoo on-the-rebound kind of feeling." I loped along to keep up with her. "It's not that I want to be thanked," I gasped, "but I certainly didn't expect to be kicked."

"Oh, they'll *thank* you, all right, if you sew on their shirt buttons or make an apple pie like Mom's. But do something big for them, something they desperately need you to do—it's like you cut off their balls."

"My God, *why?*"

"They go through these head trips. First they start to suspect maybe they couldn't've done it without you. Next they realize how much they depended on you. Finally they loathe you for making them depend on you."

95

"I didn't *make* them!"

"I know that. You know that. But their little jock brains refuse to know it. So you're a candidate for a busted ass! I'm speaking from experience—I used to be as big a dunce as you are."

I glanced at her sharp-nosed stubborn profile. "That's hard to believe."

"Ah, listen, honeybunch, it's a woman thing. We were brought up to crawl around at their feet." Without slowing her trot, Faye mopped her face with her sleeve. "You can't win. Like when I stopped smoking, I got fat. When I quit playing squaw my husband quit coming home."

I stopped to breathe in great gulps of smoggy steam.

"What shall I do about Philip?"

"Do what I do. I don't put down one single goddamned word without being paid for it. Being paid for it changes everything."

I rushed along after her again, my shirt wilted, my hair matted and dusty.

"How does being paid change everything?"

She had taken to treating me as semiretarded. Her tone was patient. "They only respect what's hard to get. The more money it costs the more they respect it. In this town it's all about The Green."

"Philip will never pay me."

"Then feed the pages to a shredding machine. It's only half written, so you'll end up only half as stupid as you are."

I knew it would happen sooner or later. That evening when I got back from the picket line Philip waylaid me in the lobby of the hotel.

"You look like hell," he said. "I'm sorry. I'm very sorry."

"About the way I look?"

"About what—happened."

"D'you think *that's* why I look like hell?"

"I know you heard about it."

"I would not look like hell," I shouted, "if you screwed every secretary in every studio in town!" A couple of people checking in at the desk whirled around to gape at us. The desk clerk didn't look up. At the Beverly Hills Hotel the desk clerks have heard everything—over and over.

"For God's sake," Philip said, "lower your voice." He started to pull me away toward the empty couches near the fireplace where a fake fire flames from fake logs every day of the year. I struggled with him.

"I'm on strike!" My voice rang through the lobby. "I'm not supposed to talk to my *exploiters.*"

By this time a little knot of people on their way to the Polo Lounge had stopped to listen.

"You're going to talk to me," Philip said grimly. He pushed me down onto one of the couches and held me there.

"If the Writers Guild finds out about this, I'll be blackballed for life."

I heard someone ask, "Who is she?" Someone answered, "Who cares? Some writer," and the spectators went on their way.

"You've been avoiding me," Philip said in his private voice, the one he used when he called me from home. "You owe me a chance to explain."

I took out a cigarette.

"What happened is that I acted on impulse. That's my single worst failing—impulsiveness."

I lighted my cigarette.

"I get a notion and then I act on it."

I exhaled a long stream of cigarette smoke.

Philip averted his head to avoid my impurities. "I've decided to go to an analyst and work on my tendency to be impulsive."

A yawn started in the back of my throat. I stifled it. "You ought to work on your tendency to be stingy," I said. "You should've shelled out twenty bucks for a motel room."

"There's no such thing as a motel room for twenty bucks! *Forty* bucks is more like it! And the house was just sitting there—empty." His eyes focused somewhere across the lobby. "It was a big shock for Margo. Poor kid was traumatized."

"Traumas are good for poets. She can write a jingle about it."

He refocused his eyes back on me. "The only thing I feel okay about is that I leveled with you."

"*Leveled* with me!" God, I thought, his brain is a bowl of tapioca. "I understood Margo was your secretary."

"She was."

"But I assumed she did her touch typing on a *typewriter.*"

"The reason I made love to Margo was because I knew I could never fall *in* love with her."

I felt the yawn coming on again and gave in to it. "Excuse me." I took my hand away from my mouth. "Let's change the subject, Philip."

"Good! How's the script?"

"I'm not allowed to work on it during the strike."

"Sure you can. You're doing it for yourself. It's your script."

"I thought it was yours. You kept calling it yours."

"I'm not employing you."

"I want to be employed. I want you to pay me. When the strike's over I'll have my agent call you."

He bared his perfect teeth in an incredulous smile. "But you offered to do it for nothing!"

"An impulsive gesture—you know where impulsiveness leads."

"Lucia, we made an agreement with each other. Are you the kind of person who backs out on an agreement?"

"Yes, I am. I am the kind of person who backs out on an agreement." I tossed my cigarette onto the fake logs. For an instant there was a flare of authentic fire.

We took a long look into each other's eyes. For a moment I softened, waiting for "the schoolgirl who used to be me," as the song says. She didn't appear. She thought green was the color of myrtle or moss or yew trees or the sap in spring. Her stuffed-with-sonnets mind couldn't cope with The Green.

Philip had set his jaw. He stood up. I stood up too. I walked with him to the entrance of the hotel, not because there was any more to say but because I wanted it to end where it began. I liked the rounded-off feeling that gave me. It's an old device in the theatre and it's been used in films so often it's out of favor now—but I wasn't writing a film. I was living my life.

At the entrance I gave Philip a long piercing stare. "Consider yourself kissed good-bye," I said.

Faye didn't show up on the line the next day. The picket captain told me one of her sons had had a motorcycle accident and was in the hospital. The boy was going to be okay, Faye assured me when I called her, but there was no predicting when she'd be back. The strike negotiations were dragging. It was rumored a settlement might not be reached for months. I couldn't face picketing without Faye. The few New York-based members of the Guild were obviously not called upon to picket, so I decided to go back to my base in New York. When I put on a skirt to travel in, the waistline fell down around my hips. I was about to live, as Janice would have put it, closer to the bone.

And closer to the end of my allotted span—or so I was reminded by a couple of phone calls I got when I was back in New York. The first one was from the editor of a woman's magazine with an enormous circulation among nest-makers. In between the how-to articles—how to decorate with Japanese paper parasols, how to spackle-paint your kitchen floor—the magazine featured spunky pieces by women who had been battered by low blows of Fate. "Head-in-the-air stories," the editor called them. "With so many divorced younger women in the marriage market you probably won't have a chance to marry again," she said. "I want you to write a head-in-the-air story about the special problems of being divorced in mid-life."

"Like what?"

"Well, the difficulty of finding fulfillment for the emotional side of your nature."

"You mean sex?"

"I don't suppose the problem of *sex* arises very often at your age, but you could talk about your search for men *friends.*"

"I don't have to search. They come around by themselves to get me to write scripts for them."

"Of course you're a special case. Our readers can't identify with a writer so we'd like you to soft-pedal your profession. What we basically want to know is how you felt about being alone—the hurt, the heartbreak, the falling apart."

"I haven't fallen apart since I've been alone. I fell apart when I was married."

"Then you could tell how you put the pieces together again and went on to find a richer life."

"Poorer, financially speaking."

"I mean in terms of enhancing your own personhood—looking at sunsets, walking in the woods, putting up beach-plum jam, giving your bedroom a new look with Japanese paper parasols. . . ."

"You've already run that parasol piece, haven't you?"

"Tell us how you prop yourself up with meaningful relationships. Do you give charming little buffet suppers at home? You might let us have a menu or two and put in something amusing like how you learned to carve a roast or buy a bargain wine—all the things your ex-husband used to do for you."

"My ex-husband never, ever, bought a bargain wine."

"We have thousands of readers your story could impact on, thousands of readers who've been abandoned like you."

"I wasn't abandoned!"

I heard the editor gasp. "Oh, dear me! I'm sorry, I thought—"

"At least I don't look at it that way. The way I look at it the prick walked out."

I hung up with my head in the air.

The phone rang again. A pleasant male voice wondered if I could spare a minute to answer a few questions—he was doing marketing research for a well-known cosmetic product used by women.

"What's the product?" I asked.

"We'll get to that. First of all, are you between the ages of fifteen and twenty-five?"

"No."

"Between twenty-five and thirty-five?"

"No."

"Between thirty-five and forty-five?"

"No."

Click. The line went dead.

My ex-husband called. He commiserated with me about the strike. I commiserated with him about his last picture, which had bombed almost as badly as his next-to-last picture.

"If you believe your good reviews you've got to believe your bad ones," he said.

"Uh-huh."

There was a pause. I knew he was getting ready to tell me something unpleasant or to ask me to do something unpleasant, which was the only reason he ever called. True to form, he told me that he was not my ex-husband in the precise meaning of the prefix since his caper in the Dominican Republic might not hold up in court if it were challenged.

"Who'd ever challenge it?"

"We've got to get a divorce in New York."

"Don't you feel divorced *enough?*"

"Do you want to get the divorce or shall I?"

"I'm between San Marco and San Teodoro."

"What?"

"Venice. Don't you remember?"

"I'll get the divorce," he barked, irritated because I expected him to remember anything from our marriage, including the fact that I had written the scripts of our films. "I just wanted to let you know."

"Which is more than you did last time!" The memory flooded back and adrenaline flooded into my bloodstream with it. "It's my

100

turn," I said. "It'll be your turn next year and my turn the year after that—we'll keep doing it until Diana feels sure you're divorced."

"Diana has nothing to do with it," he assured me icily.

"By the way, you haven't asked how Tory is."

"How the hell is she?"

"Fine."

He banged down the phone.

Subjective pan

The release print of their movie was ready just in time to meet the deadline for entries in the Venice Film Festival, but not in time to get Italian subtitles made even if they'd had the money for them. They shipped a print to Venice anyway and waited for word. No word came. They sent urgent cables. Silence. Since they were already in debt —to the investors, the lab, the landlord, the market—what difference did the phone bill make? They telephoned again and again. The print hadn't arrived. The print was held up in customs. Customs had released the print but it hadn't been screened. The print had been screened and turned down. The woman at the other end of the line regretted it. Maybe because there were no subtitles, the other members of the Selection Committee had not understood. Her English was good, and she thought it was a beautiful little film.

Vincent flew to Venice. He waited outside the woman's office door for hours. He was alternately ignored or ordered to remove himself —it was too late to schedule the picture, the program was set. He cajoled, he argued, he pleaded, he flirted, he fell, he said later, to his knees and implored. After a week he called Lucia in New York. The film was in the Festival.

He met her at the airport and took her into Venice in a private motorboat. Incomparable Venice! It was more than all the paintings and the photographs. They stood holding hands as the boat moved through the Grand Canal past the arches and colonnades and balconies of the palaces, their muted colors seen twice, once on the facades rising from the banks and again in the rippling reflections in the water. Venice is a dream, she thought. Our film is in the Festival!

Overhead the sun blazed in sparkling sky.

This is the noon of my life.

That night they had drinks at Harry's Bar along with a mob of boisterous American tourists and the brooding ghost of Hemingway, dinner on the vine-arbored terrace of a *ristorante* near the Ponte di Rialto. *What news on the Rialto? Our film is in the Festival!* After dinner they promenaded around the basilica, staring up at the two granite columns, one holding the statue of the lion of San Marco, the other San Teodoro and his crocodile. The space between them, their guidebook explained, had once been used for executions, so when a Venetian says he is "between San Marco and San Teodoro" he means he is in a very tight spot. Between San Marco and San Teodoro! They used it from then on as part of their private language.

Finally they sat down at a table in the Piazza and ordered espresso and Sambuca. In deference to the tourists the little orchestra near them played old popular melodies from many countries. The Spaniards cheered when they played *Besame Mucho,* the Germans stamped their feet in time to *Oh, Mein Papa!* and the French wailed along with *Mon Homme.* For the Americans the selection that night was *Cheek to Cheek.* They got up and danced cheek to cheek, danced in the Piazza as if they were in an old RKO musical.

Later they strolled about under the constellations of summer. Lucia showed Vincent the four bright stars that make up the Great Square with Andromeda on one side (he admired her long wriggling legs) and the winged horse, Pegasus, on the other. She told him the story of the princess chained to a rock, left to the mercies of the sea monster (his stars were too faint that night, she couldn't find him), but just as the sea monster was about to swallow the princess, Perseus freed her and married her and the two of them rode off on Pegasus.

She hadn't told the story since her children were little and she couldn't remember the ending so she made it up. "And they lived happily ever after," she said.

The whole evening was as corny as an old Astaire and Rogers movie and it was the sweetest of evenings.

The next morning they explored the canals by gondola and, after lunch, window-shopped along the narrow passageways. Suddenly he announced he had an errand to do and told her to go ahead and find a table in front of Florian's. She bought a packet of maize on the way and sat in the sun feeding the pigeons and watching the tourists in their straw gondolier hats writing postcards.

She saw him coming toward her from the other end of the Piazza.

103

He was backlighted by the sun so that his figure and face were dark, his head splendidly wreathed in glowing curls. He's beautiful, she thought. Out of all the people in this square he's chosen me. He's coming toward *me*. When he got to the table he flung a chain down in front of her. It lay glinting on the table, not an ordinary chain—it was made of tiny flexible solid squares of gold. They toasted each other. They toasted their film. They toasted the marvel of being alive and together in Venice. When the bottle was empty, whirling clusters of pigeons escorted them to their hotel. Beaming and fuzzy, they went upstairs to bed and into each other's arms in the afternoon as the Venetians do. If they are lucky Venetians.

The screening was announced for the Volpi Room, a small theatre with about two hundred seats. The catastrophe was that it was scheduled for nine o'clock on the morning of the second day of the Festival. On the first night there was to be a big star-studded Italian film and afterward a lavish party that would certainly last till dawn. Who would get out of bed early the next morning to see an unknown film, directed and written by totally unknown Americans—a film that had no advance word of mouth, no posters, no publicity, no stories in the press and, worst of all, no subtitles?

Scott had arrived from New York. All day before the opening night the three of them trudged up and down the beaches on the Lido searching among the sunbathers and in the cabanas for anyone who looked friendly. They came on like political campaigners, introducing themselves, shaking hands and then in English, or in faltering French or Italian, telling about their film. The people they spoke to smiled and listened. "Please come," they begged. "Volpi Room, nine o'clock tomorrow morning." The smiles turned into disbelieving laughter. But everyone wished them well. *"In bócca al lupo,"* the Italians said. *"Bonne chance,"* the French said. "Good luck, chaps," the British said. "Huh?" the Americans said. "Nine o'clock? You guys crazy?" Nobody accepted their invitation except some free-lance journalists who weren't invited to the opening night festivities anyway.

By nine o'clock the next morning the Volpi Room was jammed. People were lined up along the side aisles and standing crowded behind the last row of seats. Most of them were film buffs who ignored the carnival aspects of the Festival and went to see everything on the program. This was the first time of dozens of times to come that they attended a public screening of their own film—a screening for an

104

audience of strangers. They were indeed between San Marco and San Teodoro as they stood in the back watching through waves of nausea and dizziness, their guts knotted, their ears tuned up to hear coughing or even yawning. For Lucia it was far worse than the Broadway opening of her play because of Vincent. About fifteen minutes into the first reel, two people got up and stalked out. They gaped at each other, horrified. Lucia hooked arms with Vincent and leaned against him, her knees weak. No one else left.

Her mouth was dry. Her skin was burning and yet she was shivering. She recognized the body signals that warned: danger get out of here, run! Oh, God, she thought, why are we here three thousand miles from home defenseless on that screen? Why did we leave that shot in? Why didn't we cut that scene? Why does that sequence play so tentatively? Shouldn't there be a close-up there? More coverage there? Too many dissolves. Too talky. Why did I write that dialogue? What does that line *mean?* How could I have written *that* line? If only we could do it all over again! If only we'd never done it! Why couldn't we live our lives with jobs from nine to five like everyone else? Why did we stumble into this *folie à deux?* We were crazy to make a movie! It was the opposite of childbirth, she thought, the labor pains were all pleasure and showing off the baby unmitigated pain. She closed her fingers around her gold chain and prayed.

But that's lovely, she thought, the way she moves toward him through the shadows and into the light. And he's playing that exactly right, just as Vincent directed him. And that scene is so honest, their faces, the way Vincent planned it and cut it. That one is funny. They're laughing! I hear the audience *laughing!* And there, the way the camera moves, and there, too, that encounter between them—could anyone have directed it with more sensitivity? I love this film, she thought.

Suddenly Italian voices in the projection booth shrieked through the theatre, drowning out the sound track. They pooled all their lire and Scott raced into the booth. Money calmed the argument. From then on all was quiet, and gradually they became aware that it was the concentrated silence of an audience involved with what was happening on the screen. The silence held until the last few minutes, when there were audible tears and nose-blowing. As soon as the image faded out the applause began and boomed all through the end titles. When the house lights came up the audience sprang to its feet, still clapping and cheering.

———

Vincent was an immediate star. He was on Italian television or radio almost every day. He was interviewed on film for American, British and French television. Journalists from every country stood in line with notebooks and recorders waiting to talk to him. He answered questions and told anecdotes about the making of the picture, intense, charming, dramatic, amusing—he became known around the Festival as a great interview. There were always several reporters and photographers at lunch and drinks and dinner, all faces turned toward Vincent. No one asked Scott or Lucia to join him during the interviews, nor did he suggest it—which disturbed Scott. Vincent told Lucia he couldn't help it if no one wanted to talk to the producer. Nobody cares about the producer of a film, he said.

No one cared much about the writer either. Europe was the home of the *auteur* theory—the director was the author of the film no matter who had written the script. It never occurred to Lucia that this wasn't an immutable truth, and anyway it fit the definition of "wife" she'd grown up with. She saw herself as Vincent's companion and helpmate—not beside him, a few steps behind him. A husband, she had been taught, was a necessary condition of her existence and she must live within his skin. If Vincent had a fever she took her temperature. If he was happy she lighted up like Giraudoux's chandelier. If he was defeated she was ready to fall on her sword. If he was attacked she wanted to kill. Her life was dependent on his life. His life.

During the Festival their film was screened three more times on demand, each time to a jammed theatre. On closing night when the prizes were announced, Vincent won the *Opera Prima*, best first work of a director.

But they couldn't sell the film. In spite of the enthusiastic reception and the prize and the wheeling and dealing on the Lido, no American distributor made them an offer. Scott returned to New York to try to hustle a deal. Vincent and Lucia had given up their apartment because they couldn't afford the rent. They went to Rome, where they could stretch the last of their money. Their hotel was shabby and unheated, the ancient marble floors held the cold, the water was always cold, but their room was hung with antique mirrors in gilded rococo frames and a cheerful little girl with a Della Robbia face and hands reddened with chilblains brought them morning coffee in bed. Once a day they ate pasta served on paper tablecloths at a neighborhood trattoria. Vincent bought a wide-brimmed black felt Fellini hat, Lucia bought a heavy woolen dress, they learned some Italian, explored the city, lighted candles in every church they passed and waited for the telephone to ring. A few weeks before Christmas it did, and they left for New York.

7

One day after I'd returned to New York I got a call from Linda, a college classmate of mine. Even though she lived in Shaker Heights and we hadn't seen each other often during that eternity since we graduated, she claimed she worried about me. She hadn't approved of my remarriage—she herself had married on Commencement Day and stayed married to Bob (almost a clone of my first husband), now the president of a large corporation in Cleveland. From what little I told her when she came to New York a couple of times a year she didn't approve of the "beaus" in my single life either. Linda still used the vocabulary of our school days—a man was a "beau" and a beau was either a "dreamboat" or a "crumb." The way she talked made me feel ancient. However, she meant well when she telephoned to insist I meet a dreamboat named Arnold Rivers. She gave him a great notice: brilliant industrial tycoon, dynamic, good-looking, separated and rich. "Besides," she said, "he's in his fifties. He's not a callow young man."

"Vincent wasn't callow. He was shallow."

"Arnold's *mature.*"

"Tell me what's wrong with him."

"Not one thing!"

"Come on, tell me."

She hesitated. "He's not very tall."

"How short is he?"

"Not *very* short. You won't even notice it, he has such a swell personality. And he's dying to call you!"

"Why?"

"He moved to New York a couple of months ago and he doesn't know any available women there."

"Available for what?"

"Gosh, you sound suspicious! I guess most of the men you go out with are only after One Thing?"

"On the contrary, alas."

"Arnold's looking for someone with substance. That's why he left his wife—she has no substance."

"How come?"

"She just stayed out there in Connecticut with the kids all the time. Arnold was all over the place, meeting top-level people at conventions in Houston, Tokyo, Paris, you name it, rushing down to Washington to see important government officials—he was on all sorts of panels and boards, speaking at seminars and universities. When he got home all his wife had to talk about was the PTA and the pediatrician."

"Poor woman."

"I'm not sorry for her. She didn't *grow*. She hasn't a darn thing to offer a man like Arnold. He needs someone who's *grown*—like you."

"Why do I need him?"

"To go out with! To have fun with!"

"I go out all the time. Once in a while I even have fun."

"Bob and I think you and Arnold would be a nifty combination! I must warn you, though, Arnold doesn't know a thing about show business."

"That's in his favor."

"But he saw that marvelous TV show you won the Emmy for and I told him you're a famous movie writer—"

"I'm not famous."

"For a person like Arnold you're a star! He's never known anybody who does creative writing!"

"I haven't had a blind date since we were freshmen. They were all awful."

"Good grief, what've you got to *lose?*" Linda demanded. "If you don't like him it's only *one evening* out of your life!"

When I got home from a dinner party that night my service said Mr. Arnold Rivers had called twice.

He called the next morning and talked about what a great gal Linda was and what a great fella Bob was and how when Bob was in the East they played golf at Arnold's club and when Arnold was in Cleveland they played golf at Bob's club and how they had spent a wonderful week in Palm Springs last winter playing thirty-six holes a day and taking a French lesson every night. The lessons were given by a retired professor who lives out there and tutors executives who do business in France and at least now Arnold knows, he said, how to tell *la fille de chambre* he wants a board in his bed because the worst thing about France is the beds and the next worst thing is the telephone. He prefers Switzerland. He is always happy to be hoteled in Switzerland where the maid puts a board in his bed and doesn't have her hand out all the time. This sort of free-association monologue went on without pause. I took it as a sign of nervousness. Finally Arnold got around to asking me out to dinner. We agreed upon a night and he said he'd come over directly from his office at six. He didn't ask if that hour was all right with me and I didn't tell him it was inconveniently early. I took it as a sign of eagerness.

When I opened the door for Arnold Rivers I saw a nice-looking man, his thick gray hair combed across his forehead in what we used to call a "dip." He was wearing an expensive-looking suit with a vest, tailored to his pear-shaped body, a tie that matched his handkerchief and the handkerchief too carefully arranged in his breast pocket. (My instinct said, vain.) He was indeed short, shorter than I. (My instinct said, watch it!) He bared what seemed to be ninety-two big teeth, his eyes crinkled, his nose wrinkled. He was exuding so much energy I thought he might blast off right there on my threshold. (My instinct said, counterfeit.) Although I could see perfectly well he was wearing shoes, probably my size, which is eight, why did my instinct say storm trooper boots? If I had listened to my instinct I'd have slammed the door. Stone deaf, as usual, I opened the door wider. Arnold Rivers stepped into my front hall and into my life and I lost far more than one evening. When we two clasped hands our neuroses meshed and clicked together like two finely wrought gears. The writer meets the wheeler-dealer! That was what it looked like. The loony girl with daisies in her hair meets the rudest little roughneck on the block was what it was.

Arnold's monologue on the phone had not been due to nervousness. Arnold, or "A.R.," as he told me to call him, liked to talk —to talk without stopping. Long ago, speaking of someone else, my shrink had remarked that compulsive talking is often an attempt to ward off aggression. But I was anything but aggressive that night— my dress was soft and silky and my jewelry unthreatening, a single black pearl suspended from a silver chain which Vincent had brought me when I was nominated for an Oscar. My behavior was gracious. I poured Arnold a weak scotch and soda as he requested and put a lemon twist in it. He didn't want a lemon twist. I fished it out with tongs. He tasted the drink and decided the twist had

110

left a lemon flavor. I took that scotch and soda back to the bar and poured him a fresh one. There was a Bee Gees album on the record player, fresh flowers on the coffee table and a marvelous paté with little squares of dark bread.

Tory pranced over and demonstrated her friendship by dropping her ball on his crotch, which is what she does to all my guests. When Arnold removed the ball and put it on a bookshelf out of her reach she seemed astonished but not aggressive. That night I couldn't imagine what Arnold was trying to ward off—although I know now.

"Hey!" he said. "You ought to learn what's in my folder. I'll put it in a nutshell for you."

His nutshell was as big as the Ritz. He began an account which lasted a full half hour without any interruptions from me because he wouldn't allow any interruptions. If I even tried to ask a question such as "What is a two-feather Indian?" he would freeze his toothy smile and hold up his hand in a blocking gesture. "Allow me to finish, L.W." No one had ever called me L.W. before. It conjured up a vision of myself as one of those brisk executives in corporate management. Instead of the jeans and cigarette-burned sweater I wore at the typewriter, I was in a sleek banker's-stripe gray suit and a silk shirt, with maybe a ruffle-edged collar to show there'd been no loss of femininity. Instead of sneakers I saw my feet in a sleek pair of shoes—medium-high heels with a T-strap, sexy but not *too* sexy as befits a woman who can cope with profit-and-loss statements. Later, during the mesmerizing flow of Arnold's discourse, I added more details: a corner office on a high floor, a desk imported from Abitare, a secretary for whom *I* made coffee. Although I was hardly a feminist heroine in real life I always made myself one in fantasy.

At no time did I have a chance to ask Arnold if he would like another drink, and when I stood up to freshen my own I sensed his irritation and backed up to the bar to keep my attentive face toward him. As a result I tripped over the bored-to-sleep Tory and sat down hard on the floor. When Arnold sprang to help me up I tried for a quick interpolation, like "What's a two-feather Indian?" but he set me on my feet without missing a word.

This is what I learned about him. Married thirty-three years to a woman he would always respect as the mother of his children. When he left he agreed to a financial settlement that made her the richest separated woman in Connecticut. Two beautiful daughters. One married to a broker, already a "two-feather Indian" in a big Wall Street firm; three beautiful children. The other daughter is "a wondrous kooky

111

gal" with a "strong goal orientation." She is apprenticed to a potter in Taos. Her goal is pots.

Arnold himself was active in worthy causes and on the boards of worthy organizations. He was right then president of the board of some college which was pioneering an experiment in education. The college had no campus, no buildings, no curriculum. It awarded degrees for life experience. It had already awarded Arnold a master's degree, and he intended to work for his doctorate as soon as he had the time. He also rattled off a list of philanthropies which included practically all the known diseases of the human race. He warned me he would ask for donations to some of them but I mustn't "hinge-head" him because true charity comes from the heart. (Heart, as I was to find out, was a word that popped up frequently in Arnold's discourses.) " 'Though I speak with the tongues of men and angels and have not charity, I am become as sounding brass,' " he quoted. "Bet you can't identify the source?" Before I could snap out "Corinthians," he held up his hand. "Ecclesiastes!" he said. I let it pass. Short of pouncing upon him and pressing my thumbs into his throat there was no way I could not let it pass.

Finally he got around to his business. Apexco Industries, Inc., was a conglomeration of companies, four in the States, one in Japan, one in France. They manufactured things like refrigerating equipment, plumbing fixtures, chemicals, crane equipment and a knickknack essential to jet engines. Arnold made it clear that even though he was on *Fortune* magazine's list of the highest-salaried corporate heads in America, he was not at heart one of them. Other tycoons were concerned with "profit maximization." Arnold's concern was "people maximization." When I knew him better I would realize how deeply he cared about people. At one of his plants there was already a sauna, a bowling alley and a fruit juice bar. At another factory, this one in Kansas, he had installed an organic-food cafeteria. All his executives were required to jog seven miles a day. In the jungle world of materialist values Arnold was considered a crackpot. He considered himself a visionary. A framed quotation hung in his office. " 'Vision is the art of seeing things invisible.' " He held up his hand again—needlessly, since I'd never heard of that one. "Jonathan Swift." There was a golden silence for seven seconds and I realized he had wound it up.

"Have I given you an information overload, L.W.?"

"I can handle it, A.R."

He bounced out of his chair. "Hey! What about dinner?"

"But it's only six thirty."

"My tummy's growling!"

The Bee Gees album had long since played itself out. I crossed the room to turn off the record player. Arnold followed me. "Got any Tony Bennett albums? I'm nuts about Tony Bennett."

"I think I've got some cassettes—haven't played them for a long time."

He was flipping through my collection, neatly lined up in a narrow box. He found four of Bennett's. "Let me have these," he said, "since you don't use them. I have a cassette thing in my car." I watched the cassettes disappearing into his pocket.

"You can pick the restaurant," he offered. "I'm not habituated to New York places."

"How about the Oyster Bar in the Plaza?"

"I can't eat anything that comes out of the sea."

"Russian Tea Room?"

"Cabbage soup? Cabbage is not a friend of my tummy. I'm a meat-and-potatoes fella!"

"It's awfully early but I suppose we could go to Elaine's."

"What's Elaine's?"

"They have everything. Wonderful steak and French fries—"

"I can't eat fried food. Could they bake me a potato?"

They did. They politely hid their reluctance to ruin a choice Boston strip steak by broiling it to a crisp the way he ordered it and they gave him a plate of plain sliced tomatoes (oil and vinegar were not friends). He was impressed. "Not a bad little place," he said. He surveyed the room full of empty tables. "Too bad they aren't doing any business."

"You can't get a table after eight thirty," I told him. "Half the night there're people waiting twenty deep at the bar." I tossed off a list of the regulars at Elaine's—everyone I could think of from Mike Nichols to Jackie Onassis, from Woody Allen to Lillian Hellman.

Arnold's eyes glowed. "I'll have to reeducate my tummy," he said, "so it won't growl until eight thirty."

I had expected that during dinner he'd ask me what was in *my* folder. Not a single question. Instead he showed me some magic tricks he performed with a coin. He held up a dime, made some hanky-panky gestures through the air and took the dime out of his nose or from behind his ear. Then he took it out of the neckline of my dress and from behind my ear. He was skillful at it but he didn't know when to stop. I saw Elaine watching him. She looked at me and revolved her

113

eyes toward the ceiling. Like the staff of the Beverly Hills Hotel, Elaine has seen almost everything—but coin tricks in her famous bistro was a first.

When our bill arrived the waiter informed Arnold that they didn't accept credit cards but would take a personal check. Arnold didn't have a check with him.

"I have a charge," I said. "I'll sign for it."

When the taxi stopped in front of my apartment Arnold instructed the driver to keep his flag up. Then he kissed me on the cheek and said he'd call me soon. When I got upstairs I looked at the clock. It was eight twenty.

The next morning I received one dozen red roses and an envelope. Inside was Arnold's card. Across it he had written, *Fond good wishes, Arnold Rivers.* There was no check in the envelope.

A few days later Linda called. I told her that I'd been out with Arnold and that it had been a spellbinding experience. After all, how often does a strange new man take off with four of your cassettes, get you home from Elaine's by eight twenty and assume you're paying for dinner? It had been a blind date made in psychoanalytic heaven. Already in thrall to the bully in him, I couldn't wait to see what would happen next.

Arnold "dated" me as if he were at a business convention and I was a hostess hired to run the Hospitality Suite. The hospitality was pretty much all mine. He explained that he had no friends in the city —presumably they were all in Connecticut staunchly buttressing his discarded wife. His corporate colleagues were strictly for business and his country club buddies were strictly for golf. I, it seemed, was strictly for leading him into the razzle-dazzle world of show business. I took him to Broadway opening night parties and backers' auditions and film preview parties and parties for books by actors. I took him to the Tony Awards and the Emmy Awards and the film festival at Lincoln Center. I introduced him to the stars of stage and screen and television, to writers, directors and producers. He was goggle-eyed.

He began to read *Variety.* Studio politics fascinated him—the jungle fighting, the power plays, the intrigues. "I should have gone into your business," he told me. "I'm a genius at manipulating people." (There it was—he laid it out in plain English—but who listened?) When he talked to theatre people he threw around terms like "the nut" and "ice" and "house-record." When he talked to movie people he

114

discussed "package deals" and "gross receipts" and "net receipts" and "cross-collateralization." He referred to Lauren Bacall as "Betty" and to Neil Simon as "Doc" and he learned how to tell a good table from a bad table at Elaine's (where I still signed the bills) and Sardi's (on credit cards, thank God!). One night I introduced him to Truman Capote. He was so zealous in his flattery that Truman invited him to sit down at his table. There was only room for one and since Arnold couldn't get rid of me he missed his chance to sup with Greatness. He did get two autographs from Telly Savalas, and one from Gene Shalit, for his grandchildren. I, who thought I had finally taken up with a civilian, found myself with a closet fan!

In between our public appearances Arnold came over for dinner quite often. After so many years with Vincent, who ate everything in sight, some of Philip Rowan's pickiness about food had startled me. They were nothing compared to the long list of non-friends of Arnold's tummy. I was reminded of those years when my children were little and lived on ground steak and rice pudding. Here I was, more than two decades later, serving up kid's food again to a fifty-five-year-old tycoon. But his tycoon-ness was the point. As a small girl I had observed that a businessman goes out into the big important real world and does big important real things while a woman stays home and does unreal things like matching the bedspreads to the draperies and lining the pantry shelves with scalloped paper. At night the businessman returns like a warrior, stretched limp and drained on his shield, and the woman tiptoes around with an ice bag and a perfectly mixed martini and speaks, if she speaks at all, soothing words in a modulated voice. Aside from the details that is what Arnold expected from me and, so strong were those early imprints, that is what he got—in spite of the fact that I had been marching in feminist parades carrying placards emblazoned with fierce slogans like GOOD-BYE TO ALL THAT! UP FROM THE KITCHEN FLOOR! OFF MY BACK! With Arnold I regressed to the age of eight because he made things out of steel and iron and chrome. *Real* things.

After dinner there was always the ritual sexual scuffle. As a separated man he seemed to think sex followed a meal somewhat like after-dinner mints. I had never served after-dinner mints in my life and I had no intention of serving myself either. Arnold was bewildered. Long before he left his wife, "gals" had thrown themselves at him. He told me about one of them. She was a professor of economics with two Ph.D.s whom he had met at a colloquium in Aspen. After the evening seminar they had strolled out onto the grounds of their hotel "to dialogue" about the American expansionary economic policy and whether its effect on weaker economies would eliminate international financial imbalances. Chilled by the Colorado mountain air they had suddenly embraced—on Arnold's part it was for the sake of warmth, he said, but the professor, feeling his arms around her, had suffered a misinformation overload. She began some "heavy necking."

"Takes two to neck," I said.

"Naturally, I was agreeable, but after about an hour I said good night. Then it was *hell* trying to get to sleep—"

"You were feeling horny?"

"Gee whiz, L.W., you talk like a fella!"

"Well, weren't you?"

"Not at all. I couldn't get to sleep because the maid forgot to put a board in my bed. No sooner *did* I get to sleep than the phone rang. The professor was on the line begging me to let her come to my room!"

"This woman had *two* Ph.D.s?"

"Aggressive gal! I told her to take a tranquilizer and hung up."

"That was hostile of you."

"Hostile?"

"Turning her on and rejecting her."

"I had to prioritize my options! I had a seminar at eight in the morning."

"Was she there?"

"She was there mooning at me in the morning seminar and then she was there mooning at me in the afternoon seminar."

"What'd you do?"

"Sandbagged her. Told her she'd have to reorient her goal because as far as I was concerned she was only a friend of my heart."

"Did she stop mooning at the evening seminar?"

"I didn't risk it." He shuddered. "I hopped on a plane and got out of there."

After a few kisses and a few firm pushes on my part he got out of my apartment too. I was the one who was prioritizing. I had to be in court for my divorce early the next morning.

My regular lawyer didn't handle divorces so he had sent me to a lawyer who did. That gentleman was appalled when he drove up and saw me waiting in front of my building. He opened the taxi door and leaned out.

"You're not going to court like that, are you?"

I was wearing pants and a white T-shirt with THE EXORCIST printed across it in big blue letters.

116

"What's wrong?"

"It's not the proper attire. It's not dignified. The judge won't like it."

"Too late to change now." I got into the taxi and we took off. A disapproving frost hovered over the back seat. "You're dressed for a picnic," my divorce lawyer said. "A divorce is not a picnic."

"Of course it's a picnic! It's cuts and scratches and spilled milk and burned fingers and a stomachache."

"Jokey shirt's all right for a kid. You're not a kid."

I knew what I was to him. When I came to his office for our first meeting he half closed his eyes with ennui and summed up my situation this way: "You're an older broad who's been left for a younger broad."

"Not that young. She's my husband's age."

"Younger than *you.*"

The way he said it made me feel like that hundred-and-four-year-old mother of the seventy-nine-year-old son in the yogurt commercial. He fiddled with the pens on his desk.

"Same old story," he said. "I've heard it a thousand times."

I resented his assumption that my divorce was no more interesting than a humdrum statistic and rummaged around in my head for some information that might force him to raise the hoods on his hooded eyes.

"She's a sculptor. In steel. And now she intends to write screenplays. Don't you find that bizarre? She wants my husband *and* my profession!"

He didn't answer. He moved the photograph of his grandchildren onto his blotter.

"What if she wants my dog? I have this fantasy that she'll kidnap my dog. I have this other fantasy that she'll buy my building and take over my apartment—for storing her steel planks."

He wet his finger and rubbed at a tarnish mark on the frame of the photograph.

"I have this recurrent nightmare. She's being served a *boeuf en croute* with my initials baked into the crust and she eats them. Gobbles up my initials! The aborigines in the Fiji Islands do that—they devour a symbol of a person and then the person sickens and dies." I leaned my head on my hand. "As a matter of fact, I don't feel very well right now."

The hoods lifted. "What're you so overwrought about?" he asked. "You're a broad who's been divorced before."

At least, he'd opened his eyes.

———

Since Vincent and I already had a separation agreement and we hadn't lived together for over two years, it was a no-fault divorce. The judge barely looked at me as he asked a few routine questions. It was all over in five minutes. When I got home I took off the Exorcist shirt and threw it down the incinerator. Then I put on a sweater and took Tory to the park.

That morning when I had gone into the courthouse I couldn't avoid seeing the city hall, but I hadn't allowed myself to think about it then. In the park I did—about our wedding and all the years after that. When did it begin to go wrong? I wondered. How did it happen? Why did it happen? What did I do? What did he do? Was there no way we could have stopped it from going so wrong? A line from a Hemingway story came back to me: "How could we have been such good friends and had such a lovely time and had it all turn out so badly?" A dozen games of ball with Tory and an hour later, I, like Hemingway's character, had no answers.

When we got home I called up my now-for-sure ex-husband.

"Relax," I said. "We're divorced in New York."

"Good."

"We won't have to do it again—our marriage is exorcized. I wore an Exorcist T-shirt."

"A *what* T-shirt?"

"From the movie. Billy Friedkin gave it to me one night in Elaine's."

"You wore it to the hearing?"

"That's right."

There was a silence. I waited. He's going to say something sweet or warm, I thought. He's going to say he remembers the lovely times too. He's going to say *something*.

"Jesus," he said, "what a terrific item for Rona Barrett!"

Tracking shot

The New York reviews were sensational.

They had a hit.

It was Venice all over again but bigger and better.

Night after night they stood in the snow and watched the lines outside the theatre, stretching down the street and around the block. They'd go inside during the film, lean against a wall halfway down the aisle and watch the audience. There were no coughs, no restlessness, no talking. The concentration was visible on the rows of faces. The laughter would come precisely where they had meant it to and later the glisten of tears at the places where their own eyes used to sting. They had made a movie to please themselves and it pleased all these strangers! They had reached these strangers! It was the headiest sensation of their lives.

Reporters came around to talk to them, to find out all about the film and who they were and how they did it. Scott's name rarely came up in these interviews and no one wrote pieces about him.

"We're the celebrities," Vincent said.

That seemed to mean their names were recognized. They were given good tables at restaurants and photographed at parties. There were items about where they'd been and whom they'd been with in the columns. The groups of freaky types who hung around first nights at the theatre and opening-night galas of films asked for their autographs.

They were celebrities on a continuous round of celebrations.

At the New Year's Eve party they went to that year Vincent got loaded long before twelve o'clock and had to lie down on their host's bed. Lucia stayed in the bedroom with him and watched the festivities on Times Square on the television set. After the lighted ball dropped at twelve o'clock she bent over to kiss him. "Happy New Year, darling," she said. He didn't answer. He had passed out.

They were celebrities.

Late one morning in March Sidney Powker arrived at their hotel. He was accompanied by two young agents from his office lugging a bottle of Dom Perignon in an ice bucket. They brought the breathtaking good news that Vincent had been nominated for an Oscar. At five o'clock in the afternoon they were back again with the refilled ice bucket and another bottle of Dom Perignon. Lucia had been nominated for an Oscar too.

"We didn't know about you this morning," Sidney explained. "All we got from the coast office was a list of the big stuff. They didn't call about the supporting players and set designers and writers and all that until a little while ago."

They drank the champagne. They assured each other that they wouldn't win and it didn't matter. The nominations were what mattered. To have been chosen by their peers was the real honor.

A few days before the awards ceremonies they flew to California and checked in at the Beverly Hills Hotel. Baskets of flowers and fruit were waiting for them in their suite. Five minutes after they arrived Vincent picked up the phone to make a call. "Welcome, Mr. Wade," the operator said. "May I help you, Mr. Wade?" It was the same when Lucia called Room Service. "May I help you, Mr. Wade?" Room Service asked. The next morning the waiter served their breakfast in the private patio opening off their sitting room, and they ate it under a palm tree surrounded by flowering hedges. After the cold rains and end-of-winter grime of New York it was, in spite of the male-oriented staff, a kind of paradise.

They spent the days sunning themselves at the pool. They had only to lift a finger to get an extra towel, suntan oil, a book left behind in the suite, Bloody Marys, more ice, a telephone for outgoing calls plugged in beside them. When their lunch arrived it was set up for them on a little table under a yellow umbrella. It seemed as if everyone around the pool had a famous face. The voices of the operators never stopped calling through the loudspeakers, paging famous names. All the sunbathers would look up and stare as the famous name, affecting annoyance at having been located, would amble toward the phone booths. One afternoon four male superstars were at the table next to them. "At a million dollars a picture," Vincent told Lucia, "you're looking at four million dollars." They rarely saw anyone but children go into the pool.

Opposite them on the other side of the pool was a row of cabanas, each with a changing room, table and chairs and a private telephone. They were mostly occupied by moguls, who sat under the awnings, their stomachs bulging over their shorts, smoking cigars and discussing deals. The wives sat in the sun in big straw hats and cover-ups, reading or doing needlepoint. Other moguls were with clusters of young girls in bikinis, all slender and long-legged, all with straight blond hair, all tanned. The girls lounged around on chaises in front of the cabanas talking with each other. The wives talked to no one. The moguls talked on the phone or to the other moguls, or they squinted at the trades or played gin rummy. The only time they talked to the women was at lunch.

Every night before dinner, from six to eight, sometimes till nine, they spent drinking in the Polo Lounge. It was the place to be so everybody was there. The booths were full of men of every age but the girls they were with all seemed to be one age—twenty-two. The men, most of them in the industry, talked with each other across their own tables and bantered with their counterparts at other tables. Whenever one of the girls said anything the man with her rarely answered. He nodded. All around the room girls were saying things and men were nodding at them but talking to each other. Shouts of male laughter ricocheted around the room but after the shouts, when they thought no one was watching, some of the men eyed some of the other men jealously or resentfully. At first Lucia thought it had to do with whose girls were more sensational-looking or sexier. By eavesdropping she learned it had nothing to do with girls. The men who did the eyeing were waiting for deals. The others had deals or were just back from shooting or were already editing their films.

One evening a man they didn't know congratulated them on their movie, introduced himself and sat down. He was wearing a filthy sheepskin vest, a wrinkled T-shirt with a multicolored rainbow printed on it and a chain around his neck with a pendant in the shape of a rainbow. There was stubble on his chin, and his frizzy hair stood out from his head in an electric shock effect. His eyes were wild. He looked as if he'd been wandering around Katmandu for six months, but he'd just come from a sneak where his first film, *Rainbow*, got a standing ovation. "I got a smash on my hands, man!" He told them he'd struggled for eight years to get the picture made because, although everyone thought the script was brilliant, no one wanted to let him direct it.

"Turned down half a million for it," he said.

"For the *script!*" Lucia exclaimed. "Wow!"

"Sold my house, sold my cars, hocked everything I owned, my wife divorced me, my kids had holes in their shoes. I lived on corn flakes. I slept in a basement without a toilet—had to shit in the goddamned *L.A. Times!* I paid my dues, man!"

The movie was about an orphan girl who discovers she has psychic powers so she goes to Vegas to play roulette. All she wants is to win enough money to set her boyfriend up in the fast-food business, but a gang of hoods kidnaps her and forces her to play roulette for them and there are shootings and car chases and it all ends up with a pot of gold for the orphan girl and her boyfriend.

"What it's got going for it is it makes an affirmative statement. I'm that girl, see? She's *me*. I'm a very affirmative man, man!"

He sounded even more excited about the deals he had for tie-ins. He had deals for Rainbow chains, Rainbow belt buckles, Rainbow mugs, Rainbow earrings, Rainbow money clips, Rainbow ashtrays, and Rainbow cocktail glasses. He had deals for Rainbow T-shirts, Rainbow tote bags, Rainbow pillows, Rainbow pennants. Somebody wanted him to license Rainbow fast-food joints and Rainbow milk shakes. "Who knows where it'll end, man!" Before he left he wrote down their address in New York so he could send Lucia a Rainbow tote bag and Vincent a Rainbow ashtray.

Most of the other people who sat down with them weren't as fascinating as this director-writer-producer, but they stayed on in the Polo Lounge because that was the place to be.

Vincent, Lucia and Scott were in the back seat of a big black limousine in what looked like an endless line of big black limousines inching along the boulevard to the theatre where the award ceremonies were to be held. It seemed more like a funeral cortege than a triumphant procession of nominees, stars and the Hollywood elite. Inside their car the atmosphere was certainly funereal. That day, when Scott had arrived, Vincent told him their partnership was over. Vincent intended to produce his next picture himself as well as direct it, and although he didn't put it in exactly those words, he made it clear to Scott that he wasn't needed any more. Lucia felt guilty and ashamed about the split. She knew they could never have made the first picture without Scott. There would have been no picture without him. And he had done far more than raise money and invest all of his own—he had nursed the project along every minute from shooting to post-production. The picture was as much his as theirs. Scott didn't say anything when he heard Vincent's decision. He seemed numb. He sat numbly now, on the other side of Lucia, not speaking.

As they finally approached the theatre they saw that the grandstands in front of it were jammed with fans. Overhead, powerful searchlights crisscrossed the sky. Other lights were focused directly onto a red carpet that led from the entrance to the curb where the limousines unloaded. The line waited as each car stopped and the chauffeur got out and opened the door. Immediately the passengers were blockaded by a phalanx of photographers and TV cameramen. After they were released, loudspeakers blared out their names as they proceeded up the red carpet.

When their own limousine drew up to the curb, Vincent opened the door himself. He leapt out, helped Lucia out and pulled her along after him. She looked back to see if Scott was following them but a crowd had already closed around them flashing bulbs and thrusting mikes into their faces. After they told the mikes how happy and excited they were, they headed up the carpet. Suddenly they heard their own names bellowing from the speakers and a racket of applause and whistles from the grandstands.

"Jesus, listen to that!" Vincent grinned and waved both arms at the fans. "They know who I am!"

They were escorted to their special seats in the theatre and didn't see Scott again until a few minutes later when he was shown to a seat beside them.

They didn't win the Oscars.

"Damn it, you made the wrong turn, driver!"

"I think this road'll run into Weybridge, sir, and from Weybridge I think I know how to get to Pine View."

"I was told to turn off at Laurel Drive. This isn't Laurel Drive!"

"I think this way is shorter, sir."

"I don't give a damn if it's shorter or longer. I want to get where I'm going."

"I'll get you there, sir."

"Christ, you just passed Bel Glen! You're supposed to take a right on Bel Glen!"

"A right would lead us back to Sunset, sir."

"How can it lead us *back* to Sunset when it's going up the hill *away* from Sunset?"

"All these roads up here curve around, sir. It's very confusing but—"

"*You're* the one who's confused. *I'm* not confused. I was told to take a right on Bel Glen."

"They must've said to take a right on Bel Grove. I think you misunderstood, sir."

"Never mind what you think! Turn this goddamn car around, go back to Bel Glen and take a right."

"Don't think that'll get us there, sir."

"What's your name, driver?"

"Joe, sir."

"I suggest you stop thinking, Joe. If you were a thinker you wouldn't be a chauffeur, would you?"

Joe didn't answer. He turned the car around, drove back to Bel Glen and took a right. In a few minutes they were on Sunset Boulevard. Joe didn't speak at all during the intricate winding drive back up into the hills. They got to the house on Pine View forty-five minutes late. When Lucia thanked Joe and said good-bye he simply stared over her head.

They climbed up through a rock garden along a twisting flagstone path. Around one curve was a Henry Moore sculpture, around another a Giacometti. Inside the house the view of Los Angeles twinkling like a mirror image of the Milky Way competed with the Kandinskys and Klees and Mondrians on the wall. One of Jacques Lipchitz's stone women guarded the fireplace. It was a small "A-list" party—twelve famous faces around the dinner table. Everyone there wanted to know all about how they'd made their movie. Vincent was charged up by the attention as he told one perils-of-Pauline anecdote after another. He improved on some of them, but it was worth it to hear the response and the laughter. Everyone said they'd always dreamed of doing the very same thing. They said they were fed up with the stinking Hollywood rat race and someday they'd tell the studios to go fuck themselves and then they were going to make their own small personal pictures —pictures about real human beings, pictures with heart. That's what it's all about, they said.

After dinner they adjourned to the projection room. At the touch of a button a huge Braque painting disappeared up into a ceiling niche and a movie screen slid down. When the projectionist signaled from his booth they stretched out on plump couches and watched a movie not yet in release. It was a horror-thriller full of rampaging madness, the cutting as dizzily violent as the story. One character was decapitated. They watched his head roll down a staircase, the blood leaving scarlet designs on the white carpet. "Action painting!" piped a voice. When the movie was over everyone agreed it was going to be a smash at the box office.

An eminently bankable middle-aged director gave them a lift back to the hotel in his Rolls. He was, he groaned, about to leave for eight months to shoot a star-studded epic in Dubrovnik, "tits and ass, Yugoslavian style." The budget was fifteen million dollars.

Vincent laughed. "My next one is under half a million."

"Oh, God, I envy you!" the director said.

"No stars, obviously."

"Oh, God, stars are a pain in the ass!"

"Doesn't matter anyhow, it's about young kids and how adults screw up the world for them."

"Oh, God, what a statement!"

"Eight-week shooting schedule."

"Oh, God, I'd love to change places with you!"

When they drove up to the hotel the director leaned over and grabbed Lucia's arm. "Take good care of that kid," he said. "Oh, God, that kid's got heart!"

In the Polo Lounge over a nightcap Lucia said, "I think he really would like to change places with you."

"He's full of bullshit. They're all full of bullshit. They wouldn't be caught dead making little pictures. Little pictures don't pay for paintings and screening rooms and Rolls-Royces." He signaled for another double scotch.

"Wouldn't you rather make our picture than the one we saw tonight?"

"Yeah, sure. It's got lotsa heart."

When he ordered his third drink Lucia left him there and went to bed. She lay awake wondering why she didn't feel happy when she had everything to be happy about.

The next day Vincent called the limousine service and told them to put an exorbitant tip for Joe on his bill. "I gave him a hard time," he explained to the dispatcher. "The money'll make it up to him."

"I'm certainly not going to sit here!"

"Sorry, Mr. Wade, everything else is reserved."

"I have a reservation. I called this morning."

"We've held this table for you, sir."

"Vincent, it's all right . . ."

"It's not all right. Tell me your name, captain."

"Claude, sir."

"Apparently you don't know who I am, Claude. I'm a film director. I was one of the Oscar nominees the other night."

"Congratulations, sir."

"You seat celebrities in the front room, don't you?"

"Vincent, please, let's—"

"Don't you, Claude?"

"There's nothing available in the front room, sir."

"Is the manager here? Is the owner here? Who can I talk to about this?"

"I'm afraid you have to talk to me, sir."

"You're well advised to be afraid, Claude, because I'm going to walk out and I'm never coming back and I'll see that none of my friends come back here either."

They ended up having dinner at Giancarlo's, an Italian joint in Westwood, where Giancarlo himself recognized Vincent's name and pumped his hand. After that they waited thirty minutes for a booth and another thirty minutes for their Scallopini Picatta. But several people came over to their table to say they'd seen them on television the night of the awards and had loved their movie.

They had dinner at Giancarlo's many times after that. They knew who Vincent was there.

". . . No, I do not want to be referred to another dentist. Dr. Hechlinger was recommended to me. I want to see Dr. Hechlinger. . . . I simply want a filling replaced. . . . When you tell him my name I'm sure he'll manage to fit me in. . . . Let *me* talk to Dr. Hechlinger. . . . No, you can't. I want to speak to him myself. Tell him to call me when he's finished, I'm at the Beverly Hills Hotel. . . . Why won't he? . . . But apparently you *can't* handle it, my dear. You don't seem to know who I am. . . ."

By the time they left California Lucia wasn't sure who he was either.

On a few occasions after my not-too-*intime* evenings with Arnold I received a dozen red roses the next day—but not, since the first time, with Arnold's card. These orders were phoned in to the florist by one of his secretaries, I assumed, as I read the florist's meandering downhill scrawl. The sentiments were always the same. *Fond good wishes, Arnold Rivers.* The use of the last name was rather formal, but what did the florist know? From the little I'd picked up about graphology the florist's handwriting indicated he was in low spirits, which must have affected his flowers—they were always dead within twelve hours. It's the thought that counts, my mother, everyone's mothers, used to say. That generation believed in so many things that weren't true.

Arnold sent me a dozen red roses for Christmas too. The florist was in worse shape. His handwriting was so shaky every letter had shirred outlines. I diagnos.. d it as acute holiday depression, an affliction I sometimes suffered from myself, and predicted it would pass by January second.

On New Year's Eve I took Arnold to the starriest party in town —three floors of stars in the Park Avenue triplex of a Broadway composer. The sight of all those theatre and television greats, all those super-famous writers and actors and musicians and "names" poured so much testosterone into Arnold's glands that when we got home there was no fighting him off. I had become irresistibly sexy-by-association.

Oh, why not? I thought. At least he's not going to want me to write a script for him. The scriptless fuck!

Arnold made love in the dark as if he were doing something sneaky like leaving a divot on the green, or juggling his tax returns, or snitching silverware. When he was finished he immediately had something to say. They were not honeyed words.

"I'm going to take a shower," he said.

"A shower? What for?"

"I feel like taking a shower."

"Right now? Why?"

He leapt up, grabbed his clothes and pattered down the hall to the guest bathroom. He pattered back again directly.

"No bath towels in there."

"I know."

"Get me one, will you?"

"Can't you take a shower when you get home?"

"Where's your linen closet? I'll get a towel myself."

I could dimly see his silhouette as he stood in the doorway clutching his clothes in front of him. "Oh, don't be silly," I said. "Come on back to bed."

"No, I've got to take a shower!" He sounded panicky, like a little kid who'd had an accident.

"Why?" I suspected why but I wanted to make him say it.

He wouldn't. He changed to a fake avuncular voice. "Come on, L.W." he cajoled, "be a good girl and get me a towel."

Our "dialoguing" was at an impasse. I got up and gave him a towel.

After he had showered and dressed he came back into the bedroom and bent over me.

"The nicest thing I can do for you now," he whispered, "is to let you sleep."

"I'm not at all sleepy!"

"Good night, L.W." His lips brushed my cheek. "I'll let myself out."

When I heard the front door close I turned on the light and looked over at the dresser. There was no money on it, but the way he'd behaved there might as well have been.

The next day was New Year's Day. The day after that the roses arrived. *Fond good wishes, Arnold Rivers.* He might have taken the trouble to think up a variation this time, I thought. "You are a three-feather Indian, Arnold Rivers." Actually, as far as that brief horizontal episode went I was a ten-feather Indian and he was a paleface. My prediction about the florist had been correct. His handwriting was strong and slanted upward on the card. He was feeling okay. I wasn't. Not particularly.

For the next few weeks there was an increase in the number of bath towels on my laundry list. If Arnold had been out of town he'd come directly to my apartment from the airport. If we were at a dinner party he'd send me smoldering glances across the table and hurry me home before brandy was served. His lovemaking remained furtive, but with my strong Pollyanna "orientation" I kept thinking it would change. It didn't change. It more or less stopped. However, the rest of his behavior changed. Along with carnal knowledge came a noticeable lack of what Colette called "conjugal courtesy." Often while we were talking he'd take a file out of his pocket and clean his nails. After dinner he'd produce a toothpick and pick his teeth in front of me. Also, the energy had drained out of him. Whenever I opened the door he'd be standing in the hall in what looked like a state of collapse, shoulders slumping, no toothy smiles any more, just lusterless eyes. His first words were always a panted "I'm exhausted." He'd drag himself inside, allow me to kiss his cheek, allow me to take his coat, allow me to pour him a weak scotch and soda. Most often he'd go straight to the phone and allow me to listen to a business discussion for ten, even twenty minutes. During dinner he'd act sulky and limp. When I first met him he'd never stopped talking; now he barely talked at all. It dawned on me finally that he was treating me very much as Vincent had treated me —like a wife. This must've been the way Arnold had treated his wife.

As soon as dinner was over he'd scoot out the door with the excuse that he expected a call from Tokyo or Kansas City or Nice. One night, out of boredom and resentment and just for the hell of it, I followed him down the hall and tapped him on the shoulder. When he turned I put my arms around him. He acted as if he had been engulfed by an octopus. He removed my arms and shook out his hands afterward with a funny little up-and-down gesture as if he'd gotten a viscous substance on his fingers.

"Hey!" he said. "What're you doing?"

"Making a pass at you."

"Gee whiz, L.W., I hope every time I come over you're not going to threaten me with sex!"

I giggled. "*Threaten* you?"

He made a little speech. Didn't I realize he was ready to drop with fatigue? Had I no conception of the pressures he was under? Need he remind me that he was responsible for the welfare of thousands of people? I didn't see the connection. How, I wondered, would his abstinence boost either the piece rate or the spirits of the peons on his assembly lines? Considering what he'd been like as a lover I didn't care whether we ever made it into the bedroom again, but I smothered an impulse to tell him so because that wouldn't have been gracious, kind, ladylike or ball-preserving—all the things my mother had programmed me to be. Good manners and this lunatic necessity to protect a man's ego at any cost forced me to feign vast disappointment. My *politesse* apparently went too far.

The next morning the phone rang. Without opening my eyes I fumbled for it on the bedside table and knocked it to the floor. When I leaned over to pick it up I heard Arnold shouting, "What's going on there?" Finally I got the earpiece to my ear.

"What's the matter with you, L.W.?"

I squinted one eye at the clock. "It's only seven thirty."

"I've got to see you right away."

"What is it? What's wrong?"

"I'll be right over."

Fifteen minutes later he rang the bell. His hair was still damp, he looked squeaky clean. God knew how many showers he'd taken. His face was grave.

He marched into the living room as I started toward the kitchen to put the coffee on.

"No coffee," he said. "You know I don't drink coffee."

"I'm going to be very fuzzy unless *I* have some coffee."

"Forget your addictions this morning. I don't have time."

He eased himself into a chair and put his shiny little shoes up on the ottoman. I sank down on the couch and yawned at him from behind a vase of yellow tulips I had bought myself.

"Move those." He gestured at the tulips. "I can't see you." I moved them to another part of the coffee table.

He stared at me. He opened his mouth and closed it again. My curiosity tripled.

Finally he said, "I don't like the way you're sprawled out there. I want to feel you're awake at least."

I straightened up and lifted my eyelids.

"Why are you smiling in that strange way?"

"What strange way? I'm just smiling."

"Why?"

I shrugged. "To look pleasant."

"I'm afraid what I have to say isn't very pleasant."

130

"For God's sake, Arnold, what is it?" I reached for a cigarette.

"I wish you wouldn't smoke. I can't stand the smell of cigarette smoke in the morning."

I dropped the cigarette. "Tell me why you're here at this hour."

"This is a perfectly civilized hour. Everyone on my team is at their desk at this hour."

"His." I corrected him to demonstrate that I wasn't on his team. "His desk."

"I'm here to discuss a certain facet of our relationship," he said. I nodded. "Why're you nodding? Do you know what it is?"

"You're mad because I haven't introduced you to Barbara Walters yet."

He gave me a sour look. "Cut out the wisecracks, L.W."

"No," I said. "I haven't a clue what it is."

"Then nodding your head is inappropriate, isn't it?"

The whole scene was inappropriate, not to say preposterous. What was this tiny tycoon doing in my living room at eight in the morning ordering me around and patronizing me as if I were some sniveling junior member of his team? Suddenly I saw Tory pointing her muzzle toward the terrace door. I jumped up and opened it for her.

Arnold groaned. "I'm only asking for three minutes of your undivided attention so I can say what I have to say."

"Say it, Arnold!"

His voice changed. It was his old flirtatious voice, which I hadn't heard for a long time. "You're a very lovely woman . . ."

"But?"

"Making love to you has been a very lovely experience . . ."

"But?"

"Cut out the interpolations and hear me out, L.W."

"Go ahead, A.R."

He came over to the couch and sat down beside me. He slid my hand between both of his and pressed it sympathetically as if he were making a condolence call. "Regrettably, I can't make love to you any more."

It *was* a condolence call!

"Is that all?" I asked, mentally thumbing my nose at my mother. Here we go again, I thought—those eight little words seemed to be a refrain running through my life in the past few years. What was it going to be this time? He'd have to be damn inventive to top the others.

"This isn't easy for me. I was up half the night worrying about how you'd feel."

How I felt was I was dying for a cigarette. I reached over to the coffee table to get one.

"Oh, well, go ahead." Arnold gave his permission expansively. "I've put you under a strain."

While I lighted up he explained that he'd been married to the same woman for thirty-three years, which I already knew, and that he'd left her only a few months ago, which I also already knew, and that he'd never been unfaithful to her except for horsing around at conventions, which I had certainly suspected. That didn't count, he said, but I did count—and he had this tremendous guilt about being unfaithful to his wife with me. This guilt was so tremendous he couldn't "ostrich" about it any longer.

"How come you didn't feel this tremendous guilt when you were doing your damnedest to get me into bed?"

"It was you who did your damnedest to get me into bed, L.W.!"

"As I remember it I fought you off for three months."

"That was your game plan, wasn't it? Challenging me to conquer you? I'm not the kind of fella who backs away from a challenge."

"I seduced you by fighting you off?" I felt lightheaded but it wasn't from the early morning intake of nicotine. "You're full of crap, Arnold."

He winced. "I wish you wouldn't use that word."

I could tell he was considering holding my hand again, but I had a cigarette in one of them and I promptly slipped the other beneath my thigh. "A certain amount of anxiety always goes along with a modification of policy," he said.

"Who's got anxiety?"

"I realize my problem is anomalous because I'm separated from my wife." He sighed. "Perhaps time will solve it. For the present, my dear L.W., I invite you to become a friend of my heart. Will you be a friend of my heart?" He fixed his beady blue eyes on me, only now, due to the sentiment of the request, they were soft beads.

"Like the professor you told me about?"

"Who?"

"At the colloquium in Aspen."

"Did I tell you about her? I must've been trying to make a point in the context of other material."

You made a point, I thought, but not the one you were trying to make.

Although I hadn't accepted his invitation, Arnold naturally assumed I had. He swung his feet to the floor. As he walked through the

132

hall there was a spring to his step that hadn't been there before. Tory had returned from the terrace, and he even gave her a lighthearted pat as he passed.

As soon as he was gone I raced into the kitchen to put the coffee on. Then I went into the living room and dropped down on all fours in front of Tory. "You're a friend of my heart, Tory!" I shouted. "You're a friend of my heart!" We roughhoused and shadowboxed and finally I grabbed her and we rolled over and over on the rug. The more I screamed with laughter, the louder she barked.

I didn't see as much of Arnold as I had before I was tapped to become a friend of his heart because I stopped inviting him to dinner or anywhere else. For a change the invitations, when they came, came from him. If we were going to the theatre he continued to ask me to pick up the tickets. If he wanted a limo he asked me to order one from the service where I had a charge account so the bills came to me.

"I'm not your secretary," I told him one day. "Ask your secretary to make your arrangements."

"What a hypocrite you are, L.W.!"

"Me?"

"You say you support women's lib, and women's lib says the boss mustn't ask his secretary to take care of personal stuff."

"Why's it all right to ask me?"

"What're friends for?"

By that time I figured he owed me roughly six hundred dollars, and although I reminded him about it occasionally, he never paid me back.

"This is Dr. Arnold Rivers' secretary," said a voice over the telephone.

"Who?"

"Dr. Arnold Rivers' secretary."

"You mean *Mr.* Arnold Rivers?"

"It is the identical individual," the voice explained patiently, "but since Dr. Rivers received his doctor's degree he has instructed all of us to call him doctor."

"Gotcha!"

"Dr. Rivers asked me to inform you that he'll be on the "On Target" show at seven thirty tonight along with Dr. Margaret Mead and Dr. David Susskind."

"I believe you mean Mr. David Susskind."

"Dr. Rivers is so fussy about titles," the voice wailed. "It's very confusing."

Later, Arnold himself called to clear up the confusion. His Ph.D. was, he told me, a recent honor bestowed upon him by his pet college in gratitude for "a considerable donation."

I watched the "On Target" show that evening. Dr. Rivers assured Dr. Mead and Mr. Susskind that he was deeply interested in a close-up look at the working conditions in the workplace. He planned, he said, to get a job on an assembly line for a month as soon as he had the time.

As soon as Hell freezes over, I thought.

Double exposure

"It's just as nerve-wracking the second time as the first time."

"Ghastly! Will it be this way the rest of our lives?"

"If we make movies the rest of our lives. Do you really, honestly, think it's good?"

"Yes, I do. Please don't order another drink."

"Don't tell me what to order. Do you think my work is good?"

"Yes."

"Yes *what?*"

"Your work is very good."

"But not great?"

"You did a great job."

"But *I'm* not great?"

"I think you're wonderful."

"But not a genius?"

"You may be."

"May be?"

"You are—to me."

"But not to other people?"

"Darling, how can I answer for other people? Who cares about other people?"

"Am I the most talented film director you've ever known?"

"You're the *only* one I've ever known."

"Don't be a wise-ass. I mean whose work you've seen."

"I adore your work."

"More than Bergman's? More than Fellini's or Truffaut's?"

"Oh, darling, that's a silly question—I mean . . ."

"I know what you mean."

"You're the best director I know."

"I want to be the best director in the world!"

"You're my favorite person in the world."

"You've got some reservations about the film, haven't you?"

"Not reservations, exactly . . ."

"What would you've cut?"

"Darling, let's not talk about it now. We've both been drinking. Let's go home."

"What would you have cut?"

"Well, I—I don't know—made it a little tighter maybe . . ."

"Tighter how?"

"Some of the scenes seem to be—they could be tighter. Just a bit, though. It really doesn't matter."

"Of course it matters! Which scenes?"

"I don't know—the playroom scene for one. . . ."

"God, are you *wrong!* That's the best scene in the picture."

"Where she opens the music box and it plays "The Campbells Are Coming"—I felt that part could have been shorter, just a few frames. After we hear the refrain once I'd've cut to him lying in the grass."

"But the music-box song is the key to her character! That's why I let the box play out each time she opens it. You wrote it that way, for God's sake!"

"No, I didn't mean—you're right, I did. It works. Darling, let's go. Don't have another—"

"Stop nagging, will you? What else? I suppose you hate the cocktail party scene."

"I told you I didn't like it in the rough cut, but—"

"What's *wrong* with it?"

"It—it doesn't seem to work. It's my fault—the dialogue isn't all that clever. I mean my lines are awfully soggy there, and we really don't need that scene."

"I think we need it."

"Well you know, from what the kids say the audience can imagine what the adults are like."

"From what the *kids* say, huh? The *kids* tell the audience, huh? I must be under an enormous misapprehension. I've been misguidedly thinking that the essence of film is to *show*, not *tell!"*

"I guess you're right."

"You *guess* I'm right? For your information I *am* right. I like the cocktail party scene. It's damn well directed, too."

"Good. Then I'm glad it's in the picture."

"Tell me what else you don't like."

"No, it just makes you angry. What's the point?"

"The point is I want the *truth!* If you won't tell me the truth no one will."

"The picture's locked up. Let's talk about something else, darling. Don't! Let go! That hurts!"

"Then tell me."

"I'm not absolutely crazy about the way Rick plays the opening sequence. He's too broad. In my opinion."

"He's funny! You laughed! Every time we screened it I heard you laugh."

"He is funny—but not in the right way."

"I see. So there's a right way to be funny."

"Kit's playing the comedy for real, out of her character, and he's playing it as farce."

"That's the way he wanted to play it and I agree with him. The lines are farcical. You don't think those lines can come out any other way, do you?"

"I did when I wrote them."

"I get it! Your dialogue is perfect and I misdirected the actor!"

"We'll get away with it."

"*We? I'm* the one who'll get clobbered!"

"I think it's a good picture and it'll be a success, and if it isn't we'll make another picture. We'll survive."

"Bet your ass *you'll* survive!"

"You will too. You're not going to quit, are you? You're not going off to sell buttons in Bloomingdale's, are you?"

"That's what you think I should be doing? Way down deep you don't think I should be a director?"

"Oh, stop it, you idiot! Please don't order another—"

"I'll order what I fucking please."

"You're smashed already."

"Get off my back!"

"Listen, I'm just as nervous as you are. My guts are knotted up too. I feel scared and everything you're feeling. Why take it out on each other? Let's hope people will like the picture. Let's hope for the best."

"Hope for the best? *Hope for the best?* The Campbells are coming, hurrah! Hurrah! Christ, you sound like your own fucking character!"

"Why not? I wrote her."

"Two bloody goddamn years of my life are in that picture. *Of my life! I'm* the one who's on the line!"

"Let go! You're hurting me!"

"I'm the one they'll ram in the balls, not you!"

"If I had any balls I'd offer to take your place."

"You've got 'em, my dear. A big collection. Mine too."

"Oh, Vincent, don't. I understand you're upset but—"

"Don't be so fucking understanding. Bores the ass off me."

"Come on, we're going home."

"I'm staying here. You go home."

"I want you to come with me."

"What for? So I can listen to you put down my movie? Tell me what a lousy director I am? Tell me how I've done in your fucking script?"

"Oh, God!"

"Not once during the shooting—not one time—did you ever come up to me and tell me something I did was great . . ."

"You're mad! I *did. All the time!*"

"Never paid me a compliment, never said a kind word . . ."

"You *are* mad!"

"I'm the one who's exposed on that screen—I'm the one who's *naked* up there. I'm the one who'll get zapped, not *you!* You've got a nice safe little cop-out—you can blame the director. It's a director's medium, blah, blah, blah. I wrote him this terrific script and then he —blah, blah, blah. Cut that out! People are looking at you. That's what you want, huh? Show everybody in the place what a monster I am?"

"Give me the key! Give me taxi fare! Right now! *Give it to me!*"

"With pleasure. Go home and cry. Go paddle around in your self-pity, poor little *writer!*"

The Campbells never came. There were no hurrahs. By midnight of the opening day they had all the New York reviews. Some were less terrible than others. Some mentioned good things in the film. The script got a share of the blame—not as big a share as the direction. Critics who had embraced them for their first picture unsheathed their machetes and hacked at their former opinions. There were several ominous mentions of "beginners' luck." When the magazine reviews came in, a few were fairly good. One was even enthusiastic. It didn't help. The picture bombed. After that Vincent didn't work. Lucia worked. She was hired to write treatments that never went to script. She was hired to write a script for the actress girl friend of a studio head. The love affair was over before the script was finished and the project was dropped. Finally her agent got her a job—a screenplay based on a thriller for a French director. She went to France for two months.

When she got back to New York Vincent told her he had a terrific idea for a television film based on a story he'd always loved—a famous story by Quentin Moore. He had already interested a network in the idea, but there was no assurance that Moore would let them make the film. Moore had announced in countless interviews that he didn't trust television people. However, they weren't television people and Moore's agent had admired their first film. She was willing to arrange a meeting for them. "The key is to get him to trust you with his beautiful story," she said.

9

The Writers Guild was still on strike when I "skyed out to the coast" as *Variety* would put it, to serve on the Grants Committee of the National Film Center. Before I left, Arnold told me he was going to be in Los Angeles part of that week too, that he'd be staying at the Beverly Wilshire Hotel, and perhaps we could get together over the weekend. He'd let me know.

While I was in Los Angeles I telephoned Ernie Kaplan to ask about the picture.

"Fuckin' sensational!" he crowed. "Come on over—I'll show you the rough cut."

"You know I can't cross the picket line."

"No pickets here after six P.M."

"It doesn't matter. I'm not allowed to go onto the lot."

"Who's to know?"

"The Guild's offered five thousand dollars to anyone who informs on a member who breaks the rules. You wouldn't squeal on me for five thousand dollars, would you, Ernie?"

"No, but I can't guarantee what the fuckin' projectionist'll do or the fuckin' cutter or whoever else sees you here."

"But *you* wouldn't?"

"What do I need a fuckin' five thou for?"

"In other words you'd do it for nothing?"

"Can't you take a joke?"

I could take a joke but not a chance. I never saw the rough cut.

When Gregory Stonorov invited me to a dinner party on Saturday night and told me to bring someone if I wanted to, I decided out of my innate generosity and asininity to ask Arnold. I called him, and because I was at the Film Center I made the call collect.

He came onto the wire like a tornado. "I don't accept collect calls!" he howled. "Anyone wants to talk to me can damn well pay for the call themselves! Why the hell're you calling me collect?"

Because I'm taking a Ph.D. in Numskullery. "I was going to invite you to a Hollywood A-list party."

"When is it?" he barked.

"Saturday night."

He also bit. "I'll have to break a date."

"Forget it," I said.

"Chances are I can duck out of my date."

Oh, sure you can. "Forget it, Arnold."

"First you invite me, then you tell me to forget it!"

Zing it to him. "Don't change your plans. I'll ask someone else."

"Can't you wait till I make some arrangements? I'll let you know Friday."

"Friday's too late."

"All right, all right, I'll go with you."

"You might be a little more gracious about it."

"How can I be gracious in the context of this material?"

"What fucking material are you talking about, Arnold?"

"I'm in a meeting!" He banged down the phone.

Gregory and Laura Stonorov were close friends of mine, a sophisticated, generous, lively couple who had built a stunning house on a cliff above the Pacific a few miles past Malibu. Spread out on the side away from the ocean were spacious gardens with tiled patios and fountains, an enormous swimming pool and tennis courts. Arnold was impressed as we drove up to the house and, once inside, impressed by the paintings and sculptures, the view and, most of all, the guests. There were prominent directors and producers whose names he recognized, actors and actresses whose movies he'd seen, various studio moguls and their wives and a sprinkling of big names from Washington.

After we got our drinks I steered Arnold through the party introducing him to the people I knew. Whenever I got caught up in a conversation, he wandered away. From the corner of my eye I saw him barreling up to the movie stars, one after another. "I know who you are!" I heard him say each time. "I'm Dr. Arnold Rivers." He didn't, thank God, ask for autographs.

At dinner he was seated between me and Betsy Croyden, a high-powered Washington journalist who wrote a syndicated political column. At one point she asked him what his medical specialty was.

"I'm not in medicine."

"I thought you said you were a doctor."

"I am. My doctorate's in economics."

"Oh?" She gave him a peculiar look. "Mine's in political science."

"So you're *Dr.* Croyden!" Arnold said in a welcome-to-the-club voice. "Why don't you use your title?"

"Isn't that a little *outré?*" She turned her back to him and began to talk to someone on her other side.

Arnold whipped around to me. "What's *outré?*"

"French for excessive."

He whipped around to Betsy again and gave her a firm knock on the shoulder. As he'd said himself, he wasn't the kind of fella to back away from a challenge.

After dinner a group of us were talking in the library when I saw Arnold beckoning to me from the doorway. Reluctantly, I stood up and went over to him.

"Let's go," he said.

"But it's early."

"I'm exhausted. Got to pack."

"Can't you pack in the morning?"

He had a breakfast meeting in the morning and, he reminded me, we still had an hour's drive back to Beverly Hills. When I explained to Gregory, he asked if we'd give Betsy Croyden a lift to the Beverly Wilshire. She'd flown in from London the day before and still had jet lag.

A little after eleven Arnold dropped me at my hotel.

When I called the Stonorovs the next morning Gregory came to the phone. I thanked him for the party.

"Thought you left early because your friend was exhausted," he said.

"That's why."

"He must've gotten a second wind. He stayed up in the Wilshire bar with Betsy till two o'clock."

"No kidding!"

"Bored the pants off her. She says she couldn't interrupt him long enough to get away—he never stopped talking."

"He does go on."

"What're you doing with him?"

"Not much."

"Is he great in the sack?"

"Awful."

"I've never understood why you're with the men you're with."

"Neither have I."

"This one's a killer!"

Suddenly the fit between Arnold's sadism and my masochism loosened and I felt a jolt as our gears flew apart.

"Stay away from that one, sweetie."

"I will."

Arnold called me from the airport around noon.

"Nice little gathering last night," he said.

"Sleep well?"

"Not—enough." His tone was cautious. There was a pause as he deployed his armored tanks.

"Betsy Croydon's fascinating, isn't she?"

"You know me—I'm hard to fascinate."

"So is Betsy. She told Gregory she was awfully bored in the Wilshire bar last night."

He tasted blood. His own this time. The tanks rolled. "What right've you got to check up on me?" he shrieked. "I'm a free agent! We're not engaged! We're not married! Gregory's got a hell of a nerve reporting to you! Next time I see him I'll tell him so."

"There won't be a next time. He didn't like you."

"The fella doesn't even know me! That's a rotten attitude to take."

"Not as rotten as hurrying me away from his party and dropping me off like a package."

"I had a couple of drinks with Betsy, not that I have to account to you."

"Speaking of accounts, I want a check for the six hundred dollars you owe me."

"I owe you! What for?"

"Theatre tickets, dinners, limos, all the things you said you'd pay me back for. I'll get the receipts together if you want to see them."

"So it's always the man who pays, isn't it?"

"In this case, it'll never be enough."

"You sure talk out of both sides of your mouth. You're no women's libber!"

143

"Suppose I start by liberating myself from you! I resign as a friend of your heart!"

A pause. "You don't seem like yourself, L.W."

"I am not myself! 'I am become as sounding brass!' " I shouted. "And I'll identify the source for you! *Corinthians!*"

I slammed down the phone.

When I returned to New York I found a note from Arnold along with a check for six hundred dollars.

Dear L. W.,

You may now call off your collection agencies, implications and direct threats. I may not do it immediately but I ultimately pay my debts. I trust we will continue to nourish a growing warm friendship.

Fond good wishes,
Arnold Rivers

Extreme close-up

The Great Writer had decided to trust them with his beautiful story! This announcement was made in a high-pitched voice with a Boston Brahmin accent as flawless as if he'd acquired it in his playpen. They were now entitled, the Great Writer implied, to participate in his greatness. The reason they knew he was a Great Writer was because he continually referred to himself that way. In the rarefied air of upper literary circles the pundits referred to him as "a lyrical craftsman" or "the possessor of a fragile poetic sensibility." His *Collected Stories* appeared on the syllabus of English courses all over the country. The blurbs on that book jacket used the word "great" but they were quotes from two of his former male lovers, also writers, and a dotty old grand dame of letters who, when he was very young, had employed him as her secretary. She was over seventy then and arthritic, so he had taken on the extra duty of brushing her hair. The nightly ritual of the silver tresses—he had written a beautiful story about that, but it was not the beautiful story they were interested in.

Excited now that his decision was made, the Great Writer leapt up from his Chippendale chair and crossed the room to a drink tray sitting on an open escritoire. His apartment was in a conventional building on Fifth Avenue, but everything had been done to the interior (including hand-blown glass in the sitting-room windows) to simulate a house on Beacon Hill. Not that the Great Writer had ever concealed the fact that he had been born into a shanty Irish family in South Boston. ("If I didn't eat in the soup kitchen the nuns ran, I didn't eat at all.") From the looks of him now in his late forties he had more than made up for those early days when poor equaled skinny. His belly swayed on his once-spindly frame like a soft melon. His head, another melon, sat directly on his torso as if his neck had

145

given up under the weight and sunk down between his shoulders. The upper melon was crowned by a fluff of yellow curls, the color so uniform it had to have come out of a bottle. Below the curls was the face of an overage lubricious choirboy: pug nose, dimples, blue eyes, roses in his cheeks. A closer look revealed the roses were spreading patches of broken capillaries. The Great Writer had a great craving for alcohol.

Many of his early stories dealt with his Dickensian childhood seen through a sentimental mist of memory but undeniably authentic. This background made him seem all the more exotic to his rich chums. Ever since the musical made from one of his novels had been a hit on Broadway he had no chums who weren't rich. He was a familiar figure to the staffs of stately homes and *palazzi* and to the crews of yachts preferably moored along the Côte d'Azur. His hostesses adored him because he traded fair. What they bought with their invitations was attention. He more than paid back in attention—to what they wore, their jewels, their coiffures, their servant problems, their marriage problems and most particularly their sex lives. No one's secrets were safe with him, but it didn't matter because he traded fair in delicious gossip too. If the details of any confidence were not up to his standards of outrageousness he would invent better ones. His motto was "never disappoint" and he never did. He was the darling of the New Society and, as he had explained on many television talk shows, the New Society was based on accomplishment, not on who one's father was.

The Great Writer's father was a hod carrier who appeared briefly in an early story called *Miss Cyrilla's Keepsake*. The core of the story was the intense relationship between a bright slum boy and a spinster librarian from an old New England family—the kind of family that spoke neither to the Cabots nor the Lowells. The story had first been published in a university quarterly and after that in countless anthologies. This was the beautiful story that the Great Writer was going to entrust to Vincent and, as an afterthought, to Lucia too.

Over his drink he talked about it on and on. His voice rose as if it were bouncing off a tightly tuned violin string. Plink! Plink! Plink! He had written this story, he said, in a single night while he was in Cuba staying on the Hemingways' finca. He was just out of Harvard then and Papa was madly in love with him and they had gotten very drunk, and Papa's wife served rice and black beans for dinner. Maybe it was the beans that reminded him of Boston, or maybe it was the way Papa looked at him that reminded him of Miss Cyrilla, who had been, as they knew from the story, madly in love with him too. Anyway, when

146

everyone was asleep he wrote the story and put it on Papa's desk, and when Papa got up at dawn he read it and he came into the Great Writer's room with wet eyes and of course, Papa being Papa, what he said was that it was written well and truly.

Since then this story had been called a masterpiece (a minor masterpiece) and he had to agree with the people who called it that (his publishers). For years other directors had begged to put this story on television. He had turned them down. He had not trusted them. He had vowed he would never allow this story to be violated—as it had to be when transferred to film. This story was not fiction, it was truth. It had a very deep personal meaning for him. But now that he had seen that divine movie Vincent had made he had no misgivings whatsoever. A director like Vincent would never violate the truth.

Lucia stole a glance at Vincent, whose gaze hadn't wavered from the Great Writer's face. His eyes were glistening with a film of moisture he seemed to be able to produce at will. They beamed fellow feeling—compassion, fondness, warmth. He is doing, she thought, his Eye Number. It was working. The Great Writer was staring back into those green pools and telling Vincent how completely he trusted him with this precious piece of his life, this piece of his beating heart.

As for the script—for the first time in twenty minutes the Great Writer's gaze shifted to Lucia. Of course, he trusted her too. However, her job would not be difficult. In that little eleven-page story there was plenty of material that would make the basis of scenes, and the parting scene on the bank of the Charles River was already there. That parting scene where Miss Cyrilla recites those lines from Yeats and breaks down and then the boy, Michael, finishes the poem for her—it made him weep salty tears whenever he thought about it. And after that, there was the plangent coda at the end. Really, all Lucia had to do was extrapolate the story.

"Extrapolate it, but not *violate* it." Vincent's voice was emphatic.

"Ninety minutes won't be hard to fill," the Great Writer assured Lucia, "if you mine my treasures."

"Seventy-six minutes," Lucia said, "because of the commercials."

The Great Writer's eyebrows shot up. Mother of God! He'd forgotten about the commercials. How could he bear it if some old bitch worried about her dentures or her ca-ca between the acts of his beautiful story? Vincent must get the network to cross its heart the commercials would be in good taste. Networks, Vincent informed him gloomily, don't have hearts. Well then, the Great Writer would not

147

sign the contract. He pushed out his lower lip. It was not as if he were being offered a princely sum for his beautiful story. The three of them sat in bleak silence for a moment.

Suddenly a sparkle reappeared in the Great Writer's eyes and the choirboy dimples reappeared in his cheeks. He had a very very naughty idea!

Last winter at a house party in Marrakech one of the guests was a man named Dodson Clarke, a big mogul of this very network. He was accompanied by his wife, a horsy type who gave the impression she was wearing spurs even when barefooted. The Great Writer had picked up teeny vibrations about that marriage. One of the teeny vibrations was that Dodson Clarke was not one hundred percent straight, ninety-nine percent, maybe, but not one hundred percent. Since the Clarkes weren't the most scintillating people you'd ever want to know, the Great Writer had not kept up the contact back in New York. What if he did it now? What if he invited Mr. Dodson Clarke to Chez Honorine for lunch and came on to him—nothing showy, just a teeny Irish jig to soup up his hormones? And then, toward dessert time, what if the Great Writer flat out stated his conditions about the commercials? Either they must be the *right* commercials or he'd blow the whole deal. He was positive it would work. Considering all the trash broadcast over his network, Mr. Dodson Clarke wouldn't be about to let a Great Writer get away. In more than one sense perhaps. He threw back his head and laughed. His laugh was surprisingly loud and deep in contrast to the ting-a-ling of his voice. Now wasn't that a *scrumptious* scheme?

It broke Vincent up. "Love it, love it, *love it!*" he howled.

They mustn't breathe it to a soul, the Great Writer warned. It was to be their own deep dark secret just among the three of them. He stood up, indicating the audience was over. Vincent and Lucia stood up too. The Great Writer's slippers pattered over the Tabriz rug to a butternut pedestal table covered with miniature carved jade figures. He picked one up and pressed it into Vincent's hand. "A keepsake," he said, "for my jade-eyed director!" Vincent stared at the little figure in his palm. Then he clasped the Great Writer in his arms. They looked, Lucia thought, like Papa Bear hugging Goldilocks.

Blithely, the Great Writer shepherded them to the door. "You two sweet people run along and think about everything we've talked about, and after I make goo-goo eyes at Mr. Dodson Clarke, I'll take *you* to lunch at Chez Honorine."

————

The Great Writer's name was Quentin Moore—"Q" to his intimates and the gossip columnists. At Chez Honorine, there was a table known as "Q's table." It was not in the so-called "right" section, a long narrow room lined with banquettes just beyond the entrance. It was in the far corner of the square back room, a location otherwise allotted to tourists and anyone wearing polyester. Quentin lunched or dined there several times a week. For his purpose, as much to hold court as to eat, his table was exactly the right table. His courtiers had to rise from their banquettes, promenade through the narrow room and weave their way around waiters and serving carts as they crossed the back room. There was little chance of these processions going unnoticed. With forks halfway to their mouths the other patrons constantly peered toward the commotion in Q's corner.

The first time Vincent and Lucia came to lunch Quentin was already at his table with Contessa Natalia Pigazzi. He'd told them about her on the phone. "Nat's my very best friend. We can talk about everything in front of her." The Contessa, well over forty, was very tall and angular for an Italian, with satiny black hair pulled back into a twist, black eyes and a slender arching nose. She wore a black dress, emeralds in her earlobes and a gold cross set with emeralds nestled at the base of her throat. She looked chic enough to be a model, which she had been, and imperious enough to be a contessa, which if Conte Pigazzi had anything to say about it, she would not be for long. A great deal of money was involved in the divorce, so their charges and counter-charges of international adulteries dotted the newspapers like a rash. Wherever she went, photographers leapt at her from their stakeouts in front of restaurants and clubs. Quentin appeared in these photographs with his arm thrust aggressively through hers, their hands entwined. He was always with her, he explained, because he had taken on the extra duty of bolstering her morale. He was simply the kind of person who took on extra duties—as witness the hair-brushing for the arthritic lady years ago.

While they were having their first drink the visitations from the banquettes began. Both Quentin and the Contessa seemed as delighted and astonished to see their chums as if they hadn't seen them the night before, as if they hadn't all talked on the phone that morning and revealed where they'd be at one o'clock. After the hugs and airy kisses, the visiting eyes slid curiously over the two strangers.

"You know these sweet people!" Quention assured them. Nobody did. "You must've seen that divine movie they made!" Blank faces.

These were not the kind of people who stood in movie lines on Third Avenue. "And now they're going to make my movie, my story *Miss Cyrilla's Keepsake!* You're all going to see it on television and it's going to be divine!" The faces lighted. These were not the kind of people who read Quentin's stories but they were aware he had written them. Enthusiastic congratulations all around.

After the first onslaught of table-hoppers left, Quentin signaled the captain for another round of drinks. Then he reached over and lifted the cross from the Contessa's throat. "You haven't said a word about Nat's emeralds," he whined. He tilted the stones to catch the light. "I chose them for her at Bulgari's the last time we were in Milano."

"Divine!" Vincent said.

Quentin glanced at him. "Vincent has emerald eyes today, hasn't he, Nat darling?"

The Contessa took Vincent's chin in her hand. She craned her long neck and peered at him. *"E vero."*

"The other day his eyes were jade. The very first time we met in my agent's office they were shamrocks." Quentin's dimples puckered. "That's the reason I trust him. He looks as Irish as Paddy's pig!"

"For God's sake, Q!" Vincent interrupted. "What happened with Dodson Clarke?"

"Oh, goody! Let's talk about Dodson Clarke!"

"What'd he say?"

"He said he'd pitch the show himself—to a dignified sponsor who wants to project a dignified corporate image."

"Sensational!"

"There won't be any commercials. Just before the show starts a voice will announce that the following program has been made possible by the X steel company or oil company or whatever. The voice will be a resonant baritone. I told him to get Richard Burton or I'd blow the deal!"

"You *are* naughty," Vincent said.

"And then at the very end the X company will deliver a restrained and lofty message to its customers. So"—Quentin grinned—"there you are!"

"You did it!" Vincent exulted. "You did it!"

"What I did, my dear, was give myself a hideous problem. Dodson's madly in love with me! I don't know what to do about it."

The Contessa giggled. "Since when you don't know what to do about love, *càro?*"

150

"He wants me to call him Dods. *Dods!*" Quentin rolled his eyes. "And that's not the worst of it—he invited me to play golf at the Beaver Hill Club!"

"Don't you play golf?" Lucia asked.

Vincent gave her a disdainful look. "Does anyone?"

"Golf is for *politicians,* sweetness," Quentin explained. "I got out of that but I'm stuck for Saturday night. He insisted I come to his house for dinner. That wife! If I pick up the wrong fork she'll slam me across the knuckles with her riding crop!"

"You never pick up the wrong fork, *càro.*"

"I might *revert.* You know how nervous I get when people are madly in love with me."

"But everyone is, *càro.*"

Quentin moaned. "*I* like to be the one who's madly in love." He winked at Lucia. "So do you, sweetness, I can tell."

"I like to be loved back, too."

"Two hearts that beat as one?" Quentin made a face. "Isn't that rather ranch-housey? All those little people groping each other on their J. C. Penney sheets!"

"I like Bill Blass sheets," the Contessa said.

Quentin patted Lucia's hand. "Writers are energized by *unrequited* love, sweetness. Always remember I told you that."

After lunch, while they were still having coffee, Quentin stood up. "*Andiamo,* Nat darling, we're late for Dr. Eickenberry. We're going to have our pores cleaned," he explained. He leaned toward Lucia. "Would you like to come along and have your pores cleaned?"

"My what?"

"Your *pores.* Dr. Eickenberry is the best dermatologist in the whole world!"

"Do I need my pores cleaned?"

"At your age, sweetness, it can't hurt."

"What about me?" Vincent asked.

"Oh, you—you're a *baby!* You've got a baby's skin!" Quentin took the Contessa's hand. "Now you two sweet people just sit here and finish your coffee. Everything's taken care of."

Vincent and Lucia watched them bustle off through the restaurant. "Q's very amusing, isn't he?" Vincent asked. His eyes, Lucia noticed, were peacock green.

A week later Quentin went to Italy with the Contessa. During the three months he was away he sent postcard pictures of churches from

151

Milan and Rome and Venice. He had, he wrote, lighted candles for the production in each of them. He also wrote he was bringing them two gold religious medals, one of St. Vincent de Paul and one of St. Lucy, the martyr of Syracuse. After he returned to New York it took time for him to get over his jet lag, open his fan mail, answer invitations and ferret out who had had breast lifts, thigh tucks, heart attacks, crabs, clap, tubes tied, who had gone round the bend and who had come out of the closet during his absence. Another month went by. By then, Vincent had a rough cut ready to show him.

Quentin and the Contessa came to see the rough cut along with a slim, olive-skinned, very young man with jet black bangs and eyes like melting licorice. His name was Patrizio. Quentin had found him at the Cinecitta Studios in Rome where he was apprenticed to a famous director—that is, he had been allowed to observe the maestro's cinematic techniques in exchange for driving him to and from the set, bringing his cups of espresso and other duties which Quentin did not describe. The most amusing thing about it all was that Patrizio had been born and brought up on Mulberry Street in lower Manhattan, so Quentin might just as easily have found him there except that Quentin had never been lower in Manhattan than Chez Honorine on East 52nd Street. Patrizio was into film and Quentin had persuaded him to return to his native turf and become a film writer. One of these days Lucia must take him under her wing and give him some pointers. She could become, in effect, Patrizio's Miss Loocheea. Life would not only imitate art. Life would imitate life.

Patrizio was wearing skinny jeans, an open-necked shirt, gold medallion glinting at his throat and an immaculate butter-colored chamois jacket which he couldn't keep his hands off of. He stroked and patted it constantly as Quentin explained how Patrizio had shown up at Chez Honorine without a jacket and Quentin had refused to let him wear the one the captain kept for such emergencies. Quentin would certainly not sit across the table from that sleazy old tweed thing, so they had skipped next door and bought a jacket he *could* sit across the table from. Chez Honorine had its standards and Quentin most certainly had his. Anyway, he'd only ordered one bottle of wine at lunch because they all wanted to be very alert for the screening. He didn't say how many drinks he'd ordered before lunch but from the sound of his slurred words it was several.

———

The five of them were alone in the projection room, Vincent and Lucia in the last row nervously watching the back of Quentin's head. It bobbed up and down with his deep loud laughter at one point. After that it told them nothing until halfway through the film, when it was suddenly smacked down on Patrizio's shoulder and stayed there. They tensed up, appalled by the same thought—the Great Writer had fallen asleep. After a moment they heard a sob and then a loud clack as the Contessa opened her alligator bag. She produced a handkerchief and leaned over to give it to Quentin. They relaxed as, muffled by the handkerchief, Quentin's sobs continued until the last image faded from the screen.

When the lights went on Patrizio leapt up scowling to examine the wet stain on his jacket. The Contessa helped Quentin to his feet. He flung his arms around Vincent and wept salty tears against his chest. Never mind, never mind—he shut off Vincent's apologies for the scratched work print, for the crudity of the assemblage still without titles or credits or music—never mind all that! There was his beautiful story exactly as he had lived it right up there on the silver screen! He thought he was going to faint. He hobbled shakily into the elevator, supported between the Contessa and Patrizio, and threw a dozen kisses with both of his pudgy hands until the doors closed.

"I'm doing the titles and credits tomorrow," Vincent said, "and I want to talk to you about something. First of all, dear heart, you did a marvelous job on the script. I love everything you did. Adding that classroom scene was a terrific idea, and that scene at her house where he doesn't know which fork to use is hilarious. God knows we needed some comedy! Don't you love my shot there, that three-hundred-and-sixty-degree pan around the table? And you were right about the ending —it's so much more cinematic than the ending of the story. It's shattering now. Ain't gonna be a dry eye in the house! We'll win every Emmy there is! But I have one teeny suggestion to make about the credits. Of course Q's name will be above the title, and I'm going to have a single frame for 'Based on the story by Quentin Moore' but— now don't say anything right away, think it over—how do you feel about giving Q co-credit on the screenplay too? The only reason I think we should do it is because you were so *true* to the story. I mean, after all there was no *huge* departure from the story—you did use almost everything in it. In a sense that makes him co-writer, doesn't it? And

153

it would be a—a sort of tribute. I wouldn't dream of suggesting it if I felt it would hurt you in any way. In my opinion it can only be *good* for you. It puts you right up there—to have your name bracketed with the name of a great writer like Quentin Moore. Don't you agree? That's great! I thought you would. And listen, dear heart, we—we have to give him first billing, don't you think? It would look sort of sleazy, wouldn't it, to put his name second to yours? He *is* the big gun in this project. We owe Q a hell of a lot, and this would be a very generous thank-you gesture on our part. Don't you feel it would? I'm glad! I counted on you to feel the same way I do."

About a month before the broadcast they started to do pre-publicity for the show. Every one of the reporters who came around to interview them wanted to know what it had been like to work with Quentin Moore.

"He was just beautiful!" Vincent said. "He's phenomenally imaginative—which won't come as a surprise to anybody. What really impressed me, though, was his intuitive understanding of what works on the screen. He was a powerhouse of ideas all during the production. And there were perks," he added with a charming wink. "When you work with Q you get to have some sensational lunches and to hear some sensational gossip!" The reporters laughed. "Seriously," Vincent continued, "and I'm sure Lucia will agree with me—it was a dream of a collaboration!"

The reporters turned to Lucia. "A dream!" she said.

Quentin never mentioned the credits to Lucia, but Vincent reported he'd been terribly pleased. After the broadcast *Miss Cyrilla's Keepsake* got excellent reviews all over the country, and later when the Emmy nominations were announced it won four—one for the actress who played Miss Cyrilla, one for the cinematographer and one for each of the writers. It was an incomprehensible blow that Vincent had been left out. Lucia thought it was the best work he'd ever done, and she felt wounded for him.

They were standing on the terrace of Quentin's Connecticut house watching Patrizio in his thong bikini play in the pool. He played like a lean mahogany-colored porpoise, emerging with a half-twist leap from the water, surface-diving again to show off his glistening buttocks. It drove Tory crazy. She raced from one side of the pool to the other, barking. When Patrizio splashed her she shook drops from her coat in

154

wriggles of ecstasy. Finally he pulled her into the pool and swam breaststroke beside her, two dark heads in the turquoise water.

"Great playmates, those big poodles!" Quentin said.

"And so intelligent," Lucia said. "They can be taught to do anything."

"Oh, sweetness, don't I know! Alexandra Prinz is never without a big poodle—she's worn out seven of them!"

"Worn them out? How?"

Quentin and Vincent exchanged looks. Then they whooped with laughter.

"What's so funny?" Patrizio shouted.

"None of your beeswax, my beauty!"

Patrizio went into a backstroke, his arms cutting rhythmic arcs through geysers of sparkling water, his teeth flashing.

"He *is* a beauty, isn't he?" Quentin said. "The older I get the younger I want them—like you, sweetness." He shrugged. "I have to have sex at least once a day or my complexion goes. My skin just dries up. It *shreds!*" He finished the last of his gin and tonic. "Come on inside," he said. "We've got to get to work."

The network had been persuaded by "Dods" to finance two more specials based on another two of the Great Writer's beautiful stories, and Quentin had invited them to his country house to make a selection. Lucia would choose the story she wanted to adapt and Quentin would choose the story he wanted to adapt and they'd share credits on both stories the way they did on *Miss Cyrilla's Keepsake.* That way everything would be all uniform and nice.

"But I don't see why—" Lucia stopped in mid-sentence. Vincent was giving her a warning stare. She checked to see if the ash on her cigarette was about to drop. It wasn't.

"Don't see why what, sweetness?"

"Never mind. Nothing."

"Lucia would love to do *Lady with Embroidery Hoop* if it's all right with you," Vincent said.

"It's all right with me, but I have a teeny notion something's not all right with her."

"No, no," Lucia said, "everything's fine."

"Don't be naughty. Tell me what's bothering you."

Lucia glanced toward Vincent. He was watching his finger stir the ice cubes around in his glass.

"Speak up, Loocheea!"

It was clear Quentin wasn't going to drop it. "Uniformity," she said. "I don't see why it's important."

"I didn't say it was important. I said it was nice."

Lucia took a deep breath. "What if we each put our names on our own scripts? Wouldn't that be better?"

"Better?"

"I—I don't think I should take credit for what you write."

"Don't let that worry you, sweetness. People have been swiping stuff from me all my life."

"Swiping isn't what I'm talking about, Quentin."

"They've even been swiping *me!* I was a character in thirteen novels last time I counted."

Lucia avoided looking at Vincent. "I think you should get credit for what you write and I should get credit for what I write."

"Oh, dear me, now everything's getting all confused," Quentin pouted. "I thought we three had something very, very special together and now I find out you've been *brooding* about the credits."

"I haven't been brooding."

"You *look* very broody today, Loocheea. Are you having your monthlies? Or are you in the change already? I *never* brood—it's very bad for the skin."

Vincent had crossed to the window. He was standing there looking out toward the pool. Lucia addressed his silent back. "It's not fair to share credits," she said stubbornly.

"You were all for it last time."

"Well, I—well, we thought it was something we ought to do."

"*I* thought it was something you ought to do."

"You didn't even know about it!"

"I beg your pardon, Loocheea." Quentin dimpled. "It was my idea! Didn't your scrumptious green-eyed husband tell you?"

Vincent turned. He glared at Lucia. "What the fuck's the matter with you? We had a long talk about it."

Quentin clopped sulkily across the room to the bar. "You see, sweetness, that's the way I wanted it last time—and if you don't want it that way this time we'll forget about our project and be friends. It's all the same to me. I've got hundreds of writers and directors begging for my beautiful stories." He mixed himself another gin and tonic. "Understand, Loocheea, I'm not going away. I'm going to stay right in town and work with you. I'll go over your draft and you'll go over my draft and by the time we get to the final drafts it'll *be* a collaboration. See what I mean, sweetness?"

156

"I see what you mean."

"So it's not going to be unfair, is it?"

"No."

"Now can we get to work?"

"Yes."

"Goody!"

After they had discussed the stories for a while, Quentin complained about the heat. "Why don't you two sweet people run upstairs and change and we'll all have a swim before lunch."

"I'll swim later," Vincent said. "I'm going for a walk." He set off across the lawn.

Lucia went up to the guest bedroom and flopped down on the bed. Through the open window she heard laughter and Patrizio and Quentin shouting teasingly to each other in Italian. Then a splash as Quentin dove into the pool, the sounds of swimming and Tory's frantic barking. She knew Vincent had gone for a walk because he wanted to put off being alone with her. He needn't have worried. She'd made up her mind downstairs never to mention that conversation to him. What the hell difference does it make, she thought, as long as we get the work?

She got up and started to undress. By the time she had her bathing suit on the playful raucousness at the pool had stopped. Everything was quiet. She looked out of the window. Tory was lying in the shade under a tree. Quentin and Patrizio were stretched out together on one of the mats in the sun. They were making love. She went back to the bed and lay down again. A few minutes later Quentin screamed. He sounded like one of those teakettles that signal when the water is boiling.

When Quentin read Lucia's script of *Lady with Embroidery Hoop* he loved it. He said there wasn't a teeny thing he'd change. A couple of weeks after that he sent them his own script based on *Delia's Despair*. They could tell from the style, the choice of words, the total ineptness of it that he couldn't possibly have written it. It was unusable. Lucia rewrote it from beginning to end. Quentin said he loved her version. He said it showed the difference between the talent of the artist who creates the primary material and the craft of the adapter. Lucia, he said, was a divine craftsman.

Since he had already been paid the twenty-five-thousand-dollar adaptation fee there was no money left in the *Delia's Despair* production budget to pay Lucia, so Vincent bought her a fur coat.

She wore it for the first time to the Emmy awards. Patrizio had a new coat too. It was leather on the outside, sheared opossum on the inside, with a big black seal collar to match his eyes. The Contessa wore sable. The hotel ballroom was jammed. They sat at a round table with the cast, the production designer and the cinematographer. During dinner Lucia kept repeating to herself the brief speech she'd make if she won the award. It was a tribute to Vincent's work.

At nine o'clock the master of ceremonies walked out onto the platform and the program began. Brilliant light swept the room as the cameras focused on the nominees and television celebrities. The writing award came up toward the end of the first hour. Lucia grabbed Vincent's hand. The envelope was opened. She heard Quentin's name and her own and the boom of applause. She leapt up, Vincent kissed her, and then she was hurrying after Quentin to the platform. On the platform she was kissed by a tall actress who put the golden Emmy statuette into her arms.

Quentin had gone directly to the microphone. She stood a little behind him, blinded by the lights, trying to find Vincent's face in the crowd. Suddenly the ballroom was ringing with cheers and applause and a production assistant was trying to lead her off the platform.

"Wait!" She pulled back. "It's my turn to—"

"Too late now, Mrs. Wade."

"But I've *got* to—"

"We're on a tight schedule, Mrs. Wade." The production assistant gestured toward the microphone. The clapping was dying down. The presenter of the next award was already in place. "Please come along," the production assistant said, "the photographers are waiting." He yanked her off the platform.

As they were being escorted through the ballroom Quentin rushed over to the Contessa. "Come on, Nat!" he piped. "I want you with me!" Clutching her arm he propelled her ahead of Lucia into an anteroom. The photographers stampeded toward the two of them. One loud-breathing, fiery-eyed giant gave Lucia a stiff push out of his way. Two more sprang in front of her; their bulky shoulder bags bumping and banging into her knocked her Emmy to the floor. She stooped to retrieve it. When she straightened up she saw Quentin, his arm tightly around the Contessa. They were smiling into a battery of lenses. The flashbulbs were flashing, the cameras clicking.

"One more! One more! Another one, please!" the photographers shouted. Their bodies in closed formation formed a solid barrier in front of Lucia. Gradually she pushed and edged her way around them.

She picked up the skirt of her long dress and took a giant step between the crouching backs. When Quentin saw her he gestured her away.

"Not now, sweetness—they're taking pictures!"

"But Quentin—"

"Please, sweetness, stand back!"

"But Quentin—"

Someone shouted, "Give him a big kiss, Countess!" The Contessa curved her long neck sideways and pressed her lips against Quentin's cheek. More clicks. More flashes. More shouting. "Again, Countess! One more, Countess!"

By this time Lucia had been elbowed several feet away. One of the security guards came up to her and asked for her autograph.

A photograph of the Contessa kissing Quentin was syndicated in papers around the world. A friend, traveling through the Far East sent it from Tokyo. Another friend sent it from Tel Aviv. But whether the story was printed from top to bottom or right to left, Lucia knew what it said. It said that Quentin Moore was being congratulated by Contessa Natalia Pigazzi on winning an Emmy for his television play *Miss Cyrilla's Keepsake*, directed by Vincent Wade. That was the way the story had appeared in the American press. At least it made Vincent feel better.

10

The Lady and the Robber turned out to be, as Cal Jordan would've put it, "bug juice." I saw it at a large preview screening in New York which I attended wearing dark glasses and my head wrapped in a scarf, the same disguise I'd worn when I went to *Deep Throat* with Philip Rowan. The audience shrieked and hooted as if they were obeying cue cards every five minutes, and I sank lower and lower in my seat. Much of the dialogue I recognized as Cal's, but Keith Ryan must've written those pawky lines between the two stars. "What is love?" Cecelia asks Andrew. "Love is two raindrops," he replies. "They come together and then they are one." Buck Barnes did indeed rape Cecelia. "No, no," she mewed, but she had been directed to have a "Yes, yes" expression on her face. After Andrew killed Buck in the hideous ballet Grant Ames had promised (those balls did quiver, man!), he carried Cecelia off to bed. She seemed as delighted and turned on as any creature in Ernie Kaplan's fantasies. Andrew did not die in the end as he had in every version of the script I'd written. Although he'd been shot to ribbons by the government agents who were chasing him, Cecelia helped him to his feet and, arms about each other, Andrew streaming with blood, they limped off into the wilderness. It would've taken all the surgeons in Cedars-Sinai Hospital to put Andrew back together again, but presumably in 1880 love cured all.

Afterward I was sneaking out in the midst of the crowd, minding my own business, when I felt two arms tighten around me from behind and heard Ernie Kaplan's voice close to my neck. "Fuckin' sensational, huh?" When I whirled about he kissed me on the mouth. So much for my disguise. So much for the germ theory of disease. The only thing I caught was the contemptuous eye of the *New Yorker* critic.

The picture bombed. The first wave of "popcorn munchers"

must've spread the word. The following waves bought their popcorn in other theatres. The reviews were terrible for everyone involved. As the nominal writer I cringed every time I opened a paper or magazine: "The script is a mess," "The script is brainless," "The film's dialogue is as numbing as its violence." A couple of the critics were nice to me. "The screenwriter we know can do very much better because she has done very much better" or "Judging from Lucia Wade's other credits there must have been a great deal of tampering with the script." Remarks like these lifted my spirits slightly but didn't do much for my status in the job market. Unlike everyone else that year I had no identity crisis. I knew exactly who I was. I was an unemployed screenwriter.

Reverse angle

Lucia put her arm around him, her hand on the warm hill of his belly, lopsided now, its biggest bulge resting against the bed. He didn't move. She drew her hand gently downward over the thick roll of extra flesh above his groin. He twitched irritably away.

"Don't."

"Why not?"

"I don't want you to."

"Why not?"

He uttered a short exasperated groan and jerked himself closer to his side of the bed. She waited. When he still didn't answer, she said, "We'll get somebody to make the picture. I know we will."

"If you *know* that makes everything all right, then."

"I know how awful you feel. . . ."

"If you know so much, leave me alone." He yanked the blanket up over his shoulder.

"It's not the end of the world—we've got each other and—"

"There you go!" His voice was muffled against the pillow. "You sound like a Hallmark card."

After a while when she thought he was asleep she moved cautiously closer to him and put her arm around him again as far as she could reach across his chest. She pressed her face against his hard smooth back. Suddenly he grabbed her arm and flung it away from him.

"Why'd you do that?"

"Christ!"

"If you'd only talk to me. . . ."

"What the fuck do you want me to talk about at two o'clock in the morning?"

"Why don't we ever make love any more?"

162

"I don't *know* why! *I'll think about it, okay? Now will you shut up?*" he demanded furiously. "Can I go to *sleep,* for Chrissake?"

She smoked a cigarette until his breathing was deep and rhythmic. He had turned onto his back and his arms were flung up on the pillow on either side of his head, palms upward, fingers curled. He looked so vulnerable when he slept. Not at all the way he was awake, walled up and smoldering. She turned on her bedside light and reached for a book. Tory got up from the floor at the bottom of the bed and put her muzzle over the blanket. Her eager black eyes caught the light and glowed.

"Down," Lucia whispered. "Go to sleep."

Tory backed away and took a running leap up onto the bed. Lucia glanced anxiously at Vincent. The impact hadn't awakened him. She began to stroke the dog's throat. Tory pointed her muzzle toward the ceiling, her eyes heavy-lidded with pleasure. After a while she licked Lucia's hand with her wet pink tongue.

"You're some great animal!" Lucia whispered.

After a while she fell asleep, pressed close to the furry body, her fingers clutching Tory's topknot.

The next night they were at home for dinner. There was no cocktail hour—Vincent was on a diet again and allowed only one glass of wine a day. A couple of minutes before seven he appeared in the dining room carrying the portable television set from Lucia's study. He put it down at one end of the table and swiveled it into position so that the glassy gray screen faced the china and candles and flowers.

"If you don't mind," Vincent said, "I'd like to watch the news." He was plugging the cord into a wall socket.

"Can't you watch the news at eleven o'clock?"

"I prefer to watch it now." He had snapped on the set and Walter Cronkite was reciting the usual list of international tensions.

"It's so damn rude," Lucia said.

The housekeeper came in from the kitchen. She glanced at the television set, tactfully showing no surprise, her expression serene. It was the same expression she wore on those mornings when she had found Vincent passed out in boozy sleep on his bathroom floor. She was sixty-four years old and nothing any man could do surprised her any more. She served the cups of consommé and went back into the kitchen.

Lucia picked up her soup spoon and looked at herself in it. For some reason, perhaps due to the curve of its bowl, her head was

163

refracted back to her upside down. Appropriate, she thought. They ate their consommé listening to a riot in the streets of some Middle Eastern city. The housekeeper removed the first course while a Washington correspondent was interviewing a senator. She brought in a platter of broiled lamb chops and green beans, passed the platter and left again.

Vincent sliced a piece of lamb off his chop, put it in his mouth and chewed slowly as the diet experts recommended. Then he took a long swallow of red wine. He put the glass down, belched loudly and turned his attention back to the television screen. Suddenly Lucia reached over and turned off the set. Vincent studied his plate. He speared a forkful of green beans and chewed them for a long time. After he swallowed, he said, "If you want to talk so much, let's talk."

"Darling, please don't use that tone with me."

"You asked me a question last night—"

"Never mind, let's forget about it."

"Oh, no! You *asked* it and I've been thinking and I think I know the answer."

Lucia braced herself. She waited for him to say that he was bored with her, that she was no longer sexy enough or attractive enough. He continued to eat. She suspected he was trying to compel her to ask him for the answer so that later he could, as usual, blame her for forcing him to say something nasty.

"What's the answer?"

"You can't have a baby."

This was so unexpected she froze for a moment. Then she laughed incredulously. "Because I can't have a baby?"

"That's why I don't make love to you any more."

"You mean every time you make love you want to have a baby?"

"The *possibility* has to be there."

She put her fork down, still smiling. "Are you serious?"

"Goddamn serious."

"You mean you—*want* a baby?"

"What I said was I want to know it's possible."

"But—but when you were begging me to marry you you insisted you *didn't* want children."

"I need to feel I could have them if I *did* want them."

"You've made all this up so you can blame me. Whatever it is, it's always got to be my fault."

He shrugged, that contemptuous drop-dead lift of one shoulder she knew so well. "If I don't feel horny with you, that's the reason."

164

"You know damn well I can still get pregnant."

He looked across the table at her, his eyes narrow slits of green. "Statistics are against you," he said. "Even if you did the kid might have a pointy head or something." He chewed up another piece of lamb. "You're too old to have a baby."

She gave him a blank look and pushed her chair back from the table. "Excuse me," she said politely.

As she walked out of the room she heard Vincent snap on the television set again. It was a sportscaster, this time, talking about the New York Jets.

She sat in her study, bent over the desk, her cheek lying flat on the blotter, arms folded across her stomach. After a few minutes, when she heard him coming down the hall, she straightened up, reached for a pen and pretended to be checking the script. He paused in the doorway.

"I'm going out."

She understood he only bothered to say so because he wanted her to ask him where. "Where?" she asked obediently.

"Out."

"To plant your little seed?"

"When I'm ready, maybe I will."

"Perhaps I can help you. It's rather like casting, isn't it? What does the role call for aside from youth?"

He said nothing, just stood there leaning against the doorframe, his eyes sullen. For the first time he looked absurd to her, like a fat man in a cartoon with crayoned-on red hair and beard, his droopy trousers belted somewhere below his paunch.

"How do you plan to hook her? Read Giraudoux? Sprinkle parsley on her eggs?" Please take it back, she pleaded with him silently, say you didn't mean it, say it's because you aren't allowed to eat or drink and you're scared you'll never make another picture, say anything, take one step into the room, erase that hateful green stare, take it back.

He walked away toward the foyer. She heard him getting his jacket out of the closet and then the sound of the door closing.

I should leave him, she thought.

She'd thought it before—every time he cut her down, wiped out her confidence, drew blood where she was the most undefended. But then, once he'd done that, she was without the strength to leave, was terrified of leaving. And after a while, when his mood changed, the flowers would arrive, the wonderful, original, surprising presents, the

165

sweet notes tacked to the board above her desk, the little silver bowls from Cartier engraved "Love always."

Kicks and kisses.

It was the mix that mixed her up.

She remembered the first time she'd watched him mixing the sound track of a film, standing before the board in the control room, turning knobs, pressing buttons, controlling everything.

My knobs, my buttons. That's how he controls me.

But she still couldn't admit, even to herself, that she'd been dreaming the wrong dream.

11

Sidney sent me a four-page autobiographical essay written by a schoolgirl named Emily Ann Converse who was born in Cincinnati, Ohio, in 1902 and died there during the flu epidemic in 1918. It was a well-known little piece much anthologized—I recalled it vaguely from a school English book. Norman Bernheim, the producer who intended to make a two-hour television drama out of it, was in town and wanted to meet with me.

Bernheim's specialty was family pictures: simple stories, simply told. Some critics found them simpleminded and simply schmaltz, but they were wildly profitable in those parts of America where families who go to a flick together stick together. Bernheim was much called upon to lecture at schools and churches and PTAs. His movies won a lot of prizes such as the Minnesota State Junior Chamber of Commerce medal and the Consolidated Schools Magazine Film-of-the-Month Award. He took his constituency seriously and he took himself seriously. A minute after I walked into his hotel suite (he was wearing California denims and beads, his thin black hair combed forward to hide a bald spot), I realized he was not a madcap personality.

"The first thing I want you to do," he said, "is to tell me why Norman Bernheim wants to produce a two-hour television drama about Emily Ann Converse."

"Well, uh—shouldn't you be telling me?"

"Let me explain the way I work with writers. I use a system designed to clear up the fuzziness and confusion in the writer's mind. The Socratic method."

That voice has depressed me before, but when did I hear it?

"Do you understand what I mean by the Socratic method?" I nodded. "Define it for me."

"Uh—asking questions."

"For what purpose?"

"Uh—to clear up the fuzziness and confusion in the writer's mind."

"To what end?"

"To, uh—I don't know."

"The answer is to establish a proposition. In this case the proposition is that Norman Bernheim wants to produce a two-hour television drama about Emily Ann Converse. First question: Why should Norman Bernheim want to produce a two-hour television drama about Emily Ann Converse?"

I stuck with the third person. "Because Norman Bernheim thinks he will make a lot of money, get high ratings and win an Emmy."

He looked extremely irritated. "You're off on the wrong track entirely! Let me rephrase the question: What makes Emily Ann Converse *significant* enough to be the subject of a two-hour television drama produced by Norman Bernheim?"

"Uh—because her little essay has lasted and been reprinted so often."

"Why has it lasted and been reprinted?"

"I guess it's—rather inspirational."

"In what way?"

"She tells how kind she is to animals and how she helps poor people and colored people, as she calls them."

Bernheim sniffed. "What would you suggest she call them?"

I skipped out of the trap. "Colored people is okay because she was writing in 1918."

"Does her charity work make her significant?"

"Well, she also collected tin and rubber for the war effort."

"Does her patriotism make her significant?"

I chewed nervously on a hangnail while I pondered whether to say "yes" when his frown indicated the answer might be "no."

"Let me put it another way. Why should we *care* about Emily Ann Converse?"

"Because we care about any young life that's snuffed out so early."

"Norman Bernheim is not doing a drama about *any* young life. Why should we care about *Emily Ann Converse?*"

"Why shouldn't we care about her?"

"I'm asking the questions. You come up with the answers, please."

I knew we were playing Socrates and student, but it felt like

168

principal and third grader. "Look, Mr. Bernheim," I said, "I think the answer is in the script. If the script is well written we *will* care about her."

"Since you don't know what makes Emily Ann Converse significant, how can the script be well written?"

"Because I'll be the writer."

"I don't share your self-confidence." He stood up and started across the room. I thought he might be going to get a ruler to rap my knuckles with but he was only after a cigarette. On the way back he stumbled and kicked me in the ankle.

"Ow!" I cried.

He didn't say anything.

"Excuse me," I said.

"Excuse you for what?"

"When the producer kicks the writer it's the writer who's supposed to say 'Excuse me.' "

My humble acknowledgment of the pecking order didn't distract him for an instant. "I feel the word 'significant' is confusing you," he said. "I'll select another word. What makes Emily Ann Converse *special?*"

How am I going to get out of here? "I don't know."

"You can't tell me why she's special?"

"Uh-uh."

He leaned his chin on his hand and narrowed his eyes at me. *Here come a hundred demerits.* There was another reprieve. "Then are you able to tell me what makes Emily Ann Converse a heroine?"

I've got to get out of here. "She's not a heroine."

"Say that again?"

Since I was pouring hemlock I filled the cup. "She comes across in those four pages as a self-serving little snot."

On the way home I told the cabdriver to go the long way through the park. When he asked me why he should go through the park I told him to shut up. It wasn't only that the question exasperated me, it was that I wanted to concentrate. I knew I'd never met Norman Bernheim before that day but I knew I'd heard his voice. Where had I heard his voice?

By the time the cab drew up to my building I had the answer. It was in that room next to mine months ago in the Beverly Hills Hotel. It was Norman Bernheim who'd been boasting about fucking someone in the fountain on Wilshire Boulevard.

So what? I thought. Just because his pictures get a G rating, he himself doesn't have to. It was merely a little snippet of what is called "human interest material."

Shortly after I flunked out of Emily Ann Converse I got two other jobs and was fired from both of them, something that had never happened to me before.

The first blow came from a very big star, an actress I adored for her talent and her determination to help women in the industry. She had been issuing strong statements to the press about how she intended to use her clout to put women to work behind the camera on her pictures—writers, cinematographers, production designers, crew—all the positions women were having such a difficult time getting hired for. She signed me to adapt a novel she had optioned for herself to star in and produce. I was so elated by our story conferences I wrote her a note telling her how much I admired her and how exciting I found our collaboration. She taped the note on the wall above her desk.

When I was only a few scenes into the screenplay she telephoned. She had, she exulted, gotten "an expression of interest" from a genius of a director, the very one she'd set her heart on. Alas, he didn't think I was "tough enough" for the material. If he were to direct the picture he wanted his own writer, "a tough young guy who'd write a tough script." The big star confessed she'd had sleepless nights since she'd heard this and she felt simply wretched about it but what could she do? "Get another director," I suggested. She fired me and within a week she was giving out interviews about how determined she was to hire as many women as et cetera et cetera. The experience did toughen me up, I guess, in the sense that afterward I no longer believed all women were my sisters.

I wasn't exactly fired but I parted by mutual agreement with another producer when I was halfway through a script about a divorced woman lawyer. He said I'd totally misunderstood his concept. He said he wanted to show the audience the awful toll a woman pays for being a successful professional person. He'd wanted the lawyer to be hated by her "neglected child," tripped up by her chauvinist male colleagues, unloved and lonely with no alternative when she wanted sex except to pick up a stud in a bar.

"The way you're writing her," he said, "she's happy and fulfilled. If she's happy and fulfilled what's the point of doing the show?"

170

Go to black

A couple of days before she was to join him in California she called Vincent at the Beverly Hills Hotel. He sounded low. No one liked *The Nearest Exit*. Some people did like it, he amended, but no one wanted to make it. He'd been trying everywhere. It was at Imperial now. Arthur Bauman had promised to get back to Sidney as soon as he'd read it. Aside from that, nothing new. He'd been seeing a lot of Gary Hogg, a screenwriter who, he said, had written a book called *Tootsie Roll*, brilliant, nutty and very sexy, sure to be a best seller.

"How's the new one going?" he asked.

"Slow. I don't know Italians well enough. I'm never sure how he'd act, what he'd do that would be typically Italian—"

"Wing it. Peter won't know the difference."

"But Mastroianni will. By the way, do you know where my Olivetti is?"

"Your what?"

"The typewriter I use for traveling. I can't find it."

"How the fuck would I know where it is?" He was suddenly incensed. "Buy another one or we'll rent one out here. Jesus Christ, is that why you called?"

"No, I called to talk to you."

"Okay, we've talked. *Okay?*"

"What're you so angry about?"

"See you Sunday," he said.

The next day, by coincidence, she found out why he was angry. It was the kind of freaky coincidence that wouldn't wash in a script. She'd racked her brains and spent days figuring out how to avoid coincidences when she wrote and, when she taught, commanded her students to avoid them. But these things happened, the kids would argue, they happened in real life! Almost every week she'd speak her piece about real life and reel life.

Real life brought her typewriter to the door the next day in the hand of a pale pretty girl in jeans and a lint-covered pea jacket, wispy strands of hair escaping from under her visored cap. When the girl heard Vincent was out of town she said to tell him Terry said thanks ever so much and that she was moving to Miami because she'd gotten a job in stock for the winter.

"You're an actress?"

"Yes, but I wanted to be a writer. I told Vincent I couldn't afford a typewriter so he brought this one up to Elaine's one night and gave it to me. He's a very giving person."

"Yes, he is."

"I don't think I ought to keep it because my writing didn't turn out. Tell him I hate writing!" She laughed. "I hate typing worse than I hate writing."

"I'll tell him."

"The ribbon's sort of tangled up."

"That's okay. Good luck in Miami."

What bothered her was not that he hadn't told her about the typewriter, Lucia assured herself, as she threaded in a new ribbon. He was always reluctant to tell her anything straight out unless he was drunk. If he had told her she'd probably have laughed—the gesture was so like him and she knew his penchant for struggling young actresses —and gone out and bought herself a new Olivetti. But why hadn't he bought Terry a new typewriter?

The name tag that had been fastened to the handle was gone. She strapped on another one, carried the typewriter into the bedroom and set it down beside her half-packed luggage. That's what bothered her, she thought, that he had given away *her* typewriter.

She walked into the suite, the bellhop wheeling his cart behind her. Vincent didn't even notice the Olivetti lying on top of her luggage. He was much more interested in the copy of *Tootsie Roll* under her arm.

"How'd you like it?"

"First thirty pages are kind of funny. The rest is sophomoric."

His face darkened. "You're the only person I know of who thinks it's sophomoric."

"Oh, Vincent, come on! It's not even good porn—it's a dirty little boy's book."

172

"Everyone out here thinks it's brilliant. You'd be well advised to shut up about it."

"Why?"

"Because you don't know what you're talking about!" He watched her unpacking for a moment. Then he said, "I'm going down to the Polo Lounge to have a drink with Gary. I trust you won't go through your put-down routine if you intend to join us."

"No, thank you." She banged a drawer shut. "What's the matter? I haven't been here five minutes and you act as if . . ."

"As if what?"

"As if you wish I hadn't come."

"Look, Gary's writing a screenplay based on that book—and I want to direct it."

"Do you really?"

"Don't worry, damn little chance I'll get it. Studio thinks I'm not *right* for it. Only thing I'm supposed to be *right* for is emotional drama, relationships, that kind of crap."

"The kind of crap I write?"

"Oh, Jesus!"

He put a couple of packs of cigarettes in his pocket and left. She heard him pounding through the sitting room and then the door slammed.

They were driving down from the hotel to the "flats" of Beverly Hills on their way to the Gilberts' Sunday night party.

"This is a test," he said. "I'm taking you to this party to test you."

"*Test* me?"

"I want to find out whether you dig the things I dig."

"After all these years you ought to know."

"You used to—but you don't any more."

"What makes you think so?"

"I—sense it."

"Sense *what?*"

"I don't know, recently you've spoiled things."

"What things?"

"I was at the Gilberts' last Sunday night and I thought it was terrific! They play opera records, they have these big bowls of spaghetti —you can *feel* the warmth over there." He stubbed out his cigarette and immediately lighted another. "I kept thinking if you'd been there you wouldn't've liked it. You'd've spoiled it for me."

"I like opera and spaghetti. I like warmth."

"It's those vibes you send out."

"What vibes?"

"The way you are about discos. It spoils all the fun."

"I never say anything. I act perfectly pleasant. I don't mope around."

"The point is you don't dig the kind of things that give me pleasure."

Like eating too much and drinking too much? she wanted to ask, but didn't.

"You really should get with it," he said. "Not on account of me. On account of that's where it's at."

She gave him a sharp sideways glance—the sulky bearded profile she knew so well, his hair long, almost to his shoulders now, shirt unbuttoned halfway to his waist, a gold chain and a string of jade and gold beads around his neck. She'd seen movie moguls twice his age in the Polo Lounge in the same getup. All trying to look like hippie kids.

"You've got an *attitude*," he said, "like a disapproving old lady. I wish you didn't have that *attitude*."

I wish you didn't dress like a hippie kid, she wanted to say and wouldn't have dreamed of saying. Hippie kids were where it was at. She changed the subject.

"What kind of car is this?"

"Don't you know a Mercedes when you see one?"

"I thought Stuart only rented Cadillacs."

"Cadillacs!" He hooted. "Who drives a goddamned Cadillac any more? I told Stuart if he wanted my business he'd have to get me a Mercedes."

Cars lined the Gilberts' street on both sides. They finally found a place to park around the corner and walked back.

"I warn you," he said, "this isn't your usual A-list Hollywood bash."

"You're the one who's crazy about those parties," she reminded him.

"That's where the deals are made in this town. It'd be a damn good thing for us if we got invited to more of them."

"Guess we haven't made the A list or even the B list?"

"Fuck 'em. Bunch of sycophants sucking up to the stars. Those people aren't real. This crowd you'll see at the Gilberts'—they aren't stars but they're *real*."

In the flats of Beverly Hills all the houses are miniature somethings—Moroccan villas, French chateaux, Tudor manors—all sitting among palm trees on small suburban lawns. He led her up the walk toward a white house, a portico spanning its width supported by a long row of white columns—a miniature Tara.

"What happens if I flunk?" she asked. "Do I get banished to the slave cabins out back?"

"What?"

"If I flunk your test?"

"That'll be sad. I'll feel very sad for you."

Frankly, my dear, I don't give a damn, she said to herself and wished she were Clark Gable disappearing into the night.

The Gilberts had been New York actors whom Vincent and Lucia used to see around the Actor's Studio and Downey's. They were enormously talented, mad about the theatre, and big draws at the box office. When they were on stage together there was a chemistry between them that could turn even a so-so play into a hit. But there began to be too many so-so plays. They got bored and discouraged and decided to move to the coast. Nick had landed a continuing role in a "sand and tits" series about the Foreign Legion. Emily had a few supporting parts in films and some leads in television specials, but as time went on and she got close to forty, it was clear she wasn't going to be a big star in Hollywood. In a recent interview she insisted she had no anxiety about getting older—she was ready now to be "the American Jeanne Moreau." This was the usual whistling-in-the-dark statement made by many screen actresses Emily's age. If Jeanne Moreau hadn't been making pictures, most of them would have given up and gone into interior decorating or real estate.

Emily met them at the door, a blond snow goddess. "Vinnie!" she shrieked. "You're too much! Those flowers are *fabulous!*" After she kissed Vincent she kissed Lucia. Then Nick was hugging them and leading them to the bar. On the way he introduced them to a few people, and a few whom they knew said hello. There were about thirty guests at the party, mostly actors and actresses, a few agents, a few self-styled producers, a couple of obscure directors. In this gathering Vincent and Lucia were the stars—or rather Vincent was. Directors cast pictures. He was immediately surrounded by actresses.

After a drink was pressed into her hand no one paid any attention to Lucia. She wandered around the room listening to *La Bohème* and stopped to admire a gigantic arrangement of flowers on the piano, Vincent's card wired to one of the stems. "There is so much love in your house," he had written. Trying to look bright-eyed and eager she lingered on the edge of a group of three men and two women. No one acknowledged her presence. They were absorbed in a conversation that had begun before she arrived.

". . . no surprise to me he got canned," one of the women was saying. "He's always been a hack."

"Ass-kissing hack," a man said. "He'll hustle himself another picture."

"Maybe Ken Kardon'll give him a picture. He's balling Ken's daughter."

"Depends how good he balls."

"Enid told me he's pretty good," the other woman said.

"Then why'd she split?"

"Because he got thrown off the picture. You know Enid!" The woman laughed. "Enid only fucks upward."

"Excuse me," Lucia murmured. She strolled toward an adjoining room where Nick and an actor named Randy Columbo were shooting pool. She stood in the doorway watching Nick absentmindedly chalk the end of his cue stick. His eyes were fixed on the phone on the window seat.

"Man, she's got to be at the airport by now," he said to Randy.

"Depends on the traffic, man."

"She promised to call me when she got to the airport."

"Call *here?* You got extensions in this house, man!"

"If someone else answers she'll hang up."

Nick crouched and squinted down his stick at the cue ball. "Listen to that fuckin' Puccini!" he said. "Man, between her and that fuckin' Puccini I feel like I'm getting an ulcer!"

Lucia turned and started across the living room toward Vincent. On the way a talent agent from Sidney Powker's Coast office grabbed her arm. "Lucia knows Carl," he said to the woman with him. "Lucia can tell you."

"Hello, Leon," Lucia said.

"Meet Joanne Marks. She's casting director for Lancer Productions."

Lucia shook hands with a birdlike woman made top-heavy by moon-shaped glasses and a full Afro hairdo. "What can I tell you?" she asked.

"That actor, Carl Rayne," Joanne said in a pugnacious voice. "Is he a fag or isn't he a fag?"

"Haven't the least idea."

176

"He was pretty faggy in that picture of yours."

"*I* didn't think so."

"Carl Rayne is bi," Leon said.

"To hear you talk, all your faggot clients are bi."

"No kidding, Joanne, he fucks girls."

"I don't give a shit if he fucks soccer shoes!" Joanne said. "He's too soft for the role."

"Excuse me," Lucia said.

Vincent was sitting with a striking-looking girl, probably still in her teens. She had a glowingly healthy tan, Christmas-tree-angel blond curls and huge dark eyes that seemed to take up half her face. Lucia had seen that face recently on the cover of *Vogue* or *Harper's Bazaar*. Her name was Cam Alcott. When Vincent introduced her she shook hands with barely a token glance at Lucia. Her attention whizzed back to Vincent.

"Cam is Porter Alcott's daughter," Vincent said. "Soon as she loses her baby fat she's going to be a big star like her daddy."

Cam gave Vincent a poke in the belly. "What about you losing your middle-aged fat?"

"Middle-aged? That hurts! I'm a young man!"

"You'd look like one if you flattened out your gut."

"First thing you got to learn, Cam baby, is not to get sassy with the director."

"Why not?"

"Because the director is God, that's why not. Now behave yourself or I won't let my wife fix up that scene for you."

"Fix up what scene?" Lucia asked.

"I forgot! I thought you were just a wife," Cam apologized. "Most of the wives out here are just, you know, wives." She gave Lucia a real look this time. "What's your sign?"

"Libra. Fix up what scene?" Lucia asked Vincent again.

"For Cam's screen test—"

"Plenty of directors want me without a test," Cam interrupted. "Why do I have to make a test for you?"

"You don't *have* to, Cam baby. We can forget the whole thing."

"Let me lay this on you right now. I'm not going to kill myself if you don't like the test." She fished an ice cube out of her glass and sucked it. "Being a big movie star is not my trip."

"What's your trip, Cam baby?"

"I want to get away from all the tinsel in this town."

"Which scene do you want me to fix?" Lucia asked.

Vincent was grinning at Cam. "Where do you want to get away to?"

"Somewhere where there's no tinsel. A ranch with chickens and goats and horses. And a swimming pool where the wild geese can rest on their way north."

"What'll you do there?"

"*Do?* Why does a person have to do anything? I'll just be. To *be* is the secret of happiness, as the Winnebago Indians can tell you." She plucked at her zigzag patterned poncho. "Like this?"

"Pretty dress," Vincent said.

"It's not a dress. It's a bedspread. My basic wardrobe is six bedspreads all handwoven by the Winnebago Indians. The Winnebago Indians don't believe in private property. They believe the world belongs to everybody, and so do I. Especially the beaches. The way my stepmother chases people off our beach is *gross.*"

"Which scene?" Lucia asked. Vincent gave her a blank look. "You said you wanted me to fix a scene."

"The Harriet scene. You'll have to change the references to her age and make her kid younger. Make him a baby. No, that won't work. Cut the kid."

"Sounds like a super movie," Cam said. "Who's going to play the old guy?"

"I didn't say he was an old guy. He's only forty-five!"

"That's my daddy's age."

"What if I talked to your daddy about it? Think he'd do it, Cam baby?"

"Bet your ass he'd do it. For seven hundred and fifty thou and ten percent of the gross!"

"Excuse me," Lucia said.

She crossed to the dining room where Emily had poured Bolognese sauce over a huge bowl of spaghetti. Lucia picked up two spoons and started to toss the spaghetti.

"Thanks." Emily came in with the grated cheese. "I don't know where Nick is. Bastard's never around when I need help."

After everyone was served Lucia took her plate into the living room. A tall gangly young man with aviator glasses and a short curly beard came up to her. She remembered his name was Paul something. "Will you have supper with me?" he asked. "I know a place where we can talk." He led her toward the room with the pool table. Nick was just hanging up the phone when they came in.

"Buon appetíto!" he cried out happily and left, singing *"Ah, Mimi, mia bella Mimi!"* along with the record.

Lucia and Paul sat down on the window seat.

"You and your husband making a picture out here?" he asked.

She shook her head. "Trying to hustle a deal for a picture."

"Your first one blew my mind. Second one didn't make it for me."

"I'm sorry." She wasn't sorry. She didn't give a damn what he thought, and now she was trapped with him while he would undoubtedly tell her what he thought.

"Second one had a wonderful script but I didn't like the direction. What was the slow-motion sequence all about? Looked like a goddamn shampoo commercial! Boy, is your husband a heavy-handed director." She gazed stonily down at her plate, twirling spaghetti around her fork. "Hope that doesn't offend you."

"How can it offend me coming from you?"

"That's a tough thing to say. You don't even know who I am."

"Who are you?"

"Director. Commercials so far."

"Shampoo commercials?"

"Two c's in a k. It's crap but I'm a wizard at it."

"What's two c's in a k?"

"Two cunts in a kitchen."

"That does offend me."

"Okay, we're even. Let's clean up our act and start over. I saw the picture you did for that French director. Surprised me—I mean that you wrote the script."

"Why?"

"Thought you were exclusive to your husband."

"We needed the money."

"I'm ready to move into features now myself."

"Lots of luck."

"I need luck. I also need a good writer. I've optioned a property that would be perfect for you."

"I'm not available."

"When will you be available?"

"Never."

"Blew it, didn't I?" He stared at her. "Had you sized up as a cut-through-all-the-bullshit person."

She scooped spaghetti into her mouth and ignored him.

"Okay, okay, I guess you love the guy. You don't have to be blind, deaf and dumb about it. He'd have a hard time making it without you."

She took her plate off her lap and stood up. Then she turned the plate upside down over his head. The spaghetti slithered along his forehead and hung like fringe from his glasses. She put the empty plate down on the window seat.

"Excuse me," she said.

She crossed the wide front hall to the downstairs powder room. The door was locked so she leaned against the wall, waiting. She heard voices inside and giggling and the long slow hissing of breaths deeply indrawn through the nose. After a while the door opened and a young couple came out. She could see a little film of white dust on the girl's upper lip. They swept past Lucia, bright-eyed and flushed and as if their feet were a yard above the carpet.

On the way to the car Vincent said, "I was right, wasn't I? I told you it would be a terrific party. Wasn't I right?"

"It was interesting."

"What's that word 'interesting'? What's that mean? What kind of word is *interesting?*"

"Terrific party," she lied.

In the car he fumbled for several moments with the ignition key.

"Want me to drive?"

"What for?" He giggled. "Scared I'm too loaded to drive?"

"No," she lied again.

"Yes, you are!" He had the key in the slot now and started the motor. "You're wrong," he said as he drove off, "dead wrong."

"I may be wrong. I don't want to be dead."

"Little Vinnie isn't going to smash you up."

"Turn on the headlights, little Vinnie."

When he made no move to put them on she leaned over to search for the button on the dashboard. He blocked her with his arms and shoved her roughly back against the seat. He didn't turn on the lights.

A couple of minutes later she said, "You went past a stop sign."

"I did not. Where'd I go past a stop sign? I didn't see a stop sign."

"Another one coming up—next corner."

"Cut out the co-pilot jazz, for Chrissake! I see it."

Sunset Boulevard was deserted. She didn't say anything more because she'd seen the patrol car coming up fast behind them and she knew the cops would say plenty. The cops told him he was driving on the wrong side of the street and without lights. They watched while he groped clumsily through his wallet for his driver's license. He

180

couldn't find it. He said it must be at the hotel. The cops allowed Lucia to turn the car around and drive the half block to the hotel while they followed.

Over coffee the next morning, she said, "Are you serious about testing Cam Alcott?"

"Sure, I'm serious."

"About testing her for Harriet? Why not for Molly?"

"She's too gorgeous to play Molly. Can you imagine her as a little high school baby-sitter in the sticks?"

"She's the wrong age for Harriet. She'll sound ridiculous reading those lines."

"That's why I want you to fix them."

"She's wrong, Vincent. She's much too young."

"Where is it written that Harriet has to be in her mid-thirties?"

"It's written in the *script*. She's got a nine-year-old kid, she's been Todd's mistress for years. The scene's about a woman with mileage. It's not about a model."

"Got something against models?" He raised an eyebrow. "Plenty of them make it as actresses—with the right director."

"But what's the point? We haven't even got a deal."

"We may never get a deal on that script, my dear— everybody thinks it's shit. By the way, Sidney called yesterday."

"Did he hear from Arthur Bauman?" Vincent nodded. "What'd he say?"

"Nothing to toss your sweaty nightcap in the air about." He took his time finishing his coffee. "Arthur said, and I quote, 'What the hell is this about and who the hell would want to make it?' " He stood up. "That winds it up for the studios."

"I still don't think it's hopeless. I don't think we ought to give up." She blinked back the prickling in her eyes as she watched him moving glumly around the room collecting magazines, a pen, a pad. "You don't think the script is shit, do you?"

"I never felt it was the perfect movie property, if you recall."

"I know I talked you into it—but you do like the script, don't you?"

"Where're my sunglasses?"

"Maybe in your jacket pocket." He crossed to the closet and got his sunglasses. "You do want to direct it, don't you?"

"Did you see my clipboard?"

She pointed to the coffee table. He took the clipboard out from under a pile of books.

"Gary's book isn't here. Where is it?"

"How do I know? Maybe you slept with it under your pillow!"

"Oh-oh, bitchy!" He laughed as he went into the bedroom. "And jealous!"

"Jealous? Of that crap?" she shouted after him.

He came out of the bedroom with the book. "I'm going down to the pool."

"Why didn't you tell me yesterday that Sidney called?"

"So you could stay happy for one more day. That's my function, isn't it? To keep you happy?"

He left the room. She heard him greeting someone in the hall, his voice high, full of energy. It was his other voice, the one he hardly ever used with her any more. "Keep me happy?" she asked the closed door. She forced herself over to the typewriter, sat down and started to reread what she had written the day before. It didn't work. It wasn't right. It was awful. She tore up the pages and tossed them into the wastebasket. She rolled a fresh sheet into her typewriter and stared at it.

The phone rang twice that morning. Both calls were for Vincent. The first one was from a woman who said her name was Iris McKenzie. Lucia told her Vincent wasn't in.

"Did he say he was going to the Polo Lounge?" Miss McKenzie asked. "I've been waiting in the Polo Lounge for almost an hour."

"I think he was going to the pool."

"Gee, he must've forgotten our breakfast date. Do you know if he's read my screenplay yet?"

"I'm sorry I don't. Why don't you look for him at the pool?"

The second call was from Cam. Lucia told her Vincent was at the pool.

"Have him paged—tell him I'm still out in Malibu so I'm going to be late."

"I'm working. You'd better call him yourself."

"But that'll hold me up," Cam wailed. "I'm ready to leave this minute."

"Okay." Lucia hung up. She didn't call the pool.

Vincent was drinking a Bloody Mary when she came down at one o'clock. He was sitting under an umbrella at one of the little tables with John Buckley, a director friend of theirs, and a pug-nosed young woman with a peeling sunburn who turned out to be Iris McKenzie. John got unsteadily to his feet to hug Lucia. She could feel the tremor in his arms and guessed he'd probably been out there drinking all morning.

"We need another chair," Vincent said. "This one's Cam's."

"She called to say she'd be late."

"She's here." He indicated the far end of the pool where Cam was just hoisting herself out of the water. She stood dripping in her bikini, her hair a bright helmet plastered to her head. She waved at Vincent when he got up to pull a chair over from another table.

"Isn't her tan sensational?" he asked.

Iris pushed her dark glasses onto the top of her head and squinted at Lucia. "I've been dying to meet you," she said. "You're my role model."

"That's very sweet, but why?"

"I want to be like you—write screenplays and marry a director."

"Will I do?" asked John.

She gave him a flirty look. "What've you directed?"

"For God's sake, Iris baby," Vincent said, "John's been directing terrific pictures for twenty years!"

John grinned. "Not terrific enough, apparently."

"I must've seen them," Iris apologized, "but I never paid any attention to names of directors until I decided to write screenplays." She pointed to the red-covered script in front of Vincent. "That's my first one in print."

"In *mimeo*, Iris baby. It's *mimeographed.*"

"You can read it after Vincent reads it. What's your sign?"

"Cancer."

"I'm Aries. Cancer and Aries are a fabulous combination! We could get together before you read my script if you want to."

"Not so fast, Iris baby," John said. "I haven't even left my wife yet."

"When do you start shooting?" Lucia asked him. He shrugged. "Don't you have a date after all this time?"

"Don't have a script."

"What happened to the one you were so high on?"

"Producer threw it out—got another writer and started over."

"But you loved that script! Didn't you fight back?" John shook his head. "Why not?"

"Because I don't give a hoot in hell any more." He signaled the waiter for another Bloody Mary.

"What if you don't like the new one?"

"I'll shoot it. It's like a job at a fast-food stand, Lucia baby. Pay me and I'll put all the crap you want on your bun. I don't have to eat it."

When Cam came over to the table, Vincent tossed her a towel. She put it over her head and rubbed vigorously. Then she lifted a corner and peered out at Lucia.

"Fixed my scene yet, Lucy?"

"Lucia. No, not yet."

"When's she going to fix it, Vinnie?"

"Ask her."

"When *are* you going to fix my scene, Lucy?"

"My name is Lucia. I'm busy with something else right now."

"You can do it in ten minutes," Vincent said.

"I don't think so. It needs a lot of—adjusting."

"Don't worry, Cam baby, I'll fix it myself."

"Are you an actress?" Iris asked Cam.

"I'm going to be in Vinnie's picture."

"Hold it," Vincent said. "We don't know about that yet, do we?"

"If I get the part, I'm going to give my entire fee to the Winnebago Indians." Cam wrinkled her brow. "How do you give money to the Indians? Do you just walk up to the chief with a check and say 'Here'?"

"You walk up to the chief and say, 'How'!"

"That is *not* funny." Cam picked up a menu and gave Vincent a sulky look over it. "You're perpetuating a stereotype."

"Why all this generosity to the red brothers?" John asked.

"They're not into tinsel like everybody else around here."

"Cam's a Thoreau type," Vincent said. "She's going to buy a ranch and build Walden Pool."

"That's one of my plans," Cam said. "Or else I want to get my career going and achieve a one-to-one. That's my alternate plan."

After the waiter took their orders, Lucia told him to send her salad to the room. She stood up. "Got a lot of work," she explained.

"That's right, Lucia baby," John said. "Fight back on your typing machine."

On her way through the lobby she stopped at the desk to see if there was any mail. The desk clerk handed her an envelope. Inside was a postcard reproduction of a painting by Magritte of a man and a woman kissing, white cloths wrapped over their faces and around their heads. On the other side Paul had scribbled, "Lady, I like your style!" When she got upstairs she propped the postcard up on her desk and started to type. After a few minutes she put the postcard in the desk drawer. About a half hour later before she started to copy-read the pages she took the postcard out of the drawer, tore it up and dropped the pieces into the wastebasket.

Vincent came in around five, his face, in spite of the oil, newly reddened from the sun. He told her he'd run into an English producer at the pool, a man named Roger Wheldon, who was a master at setting up English-American co-production deals. He'd made a dinner date—just himself and Wheldon—to talk about a co-production for *The Nearest Exit.*

"I told him the story. He sounded interested."

"If he does come up with half the money, where'll we get the other half?"

"We'll worry about that later."

"I'd like to go with you."

"What for?"

"I can be terribly persuasive about that script."

"Meaning *I* can't?"

"I don't mean that." She tried to think what she did mean. "I'm up here alone so much—I'd like to go out."

"Why don't you work tonight? We'll go out tomorrow night."

She was in bed reading, trying to read, when he came in around two thirty—smashed, a boozy grin flickering around his mouth.

"You're up late," he said.

"So're you."

He tossed his jacket toward a chair and missed. Then he walked carefully and deliberately, as if he were following a chalk line, toward the bathroom. When he came out he sat down on his bed and started to undress.

"Why're you up so late?"

"I've been waiting for you."

He giggled. "That's a mistake."

"I have a message for you. Roger Wheldon called."

"*Roger Wheldon.*" He pulled off his slacks and dropped them to the floor.

"He said he'd call back in the morning." She watched him drop his shirt on top of his slacks. "So I guess you weren't out with Roger Wheldon."

"You *guess?* You *know* I wasn't out with him!" He giggled again. "I was out with Gary."

"I thought you said Gary went to Acapulco."

"Did I? That was a mistake."

"Why'd you say you were going out with Roger Wheldon?"

"Why'd I say I was going out with Roger Wheldon?" He mimicked her voice. "That was a mistake."

"What'd you do all evening?"

"What'd I do all evening? Well now, let me *think*." He took on the baby-talk inflections of a four-year-old. "I dra-ank. I ay-ate. I smo-oked. I taw-awked. I did wee-wee."

"Fascinating. Where?"

"Where did I dri-ink and ee-eat and smo-oke and taw-awk and do wee-wee?" He cocked his head and rolled his eyes upward for an instant. "I dra-ank, I ay-ate, I smo-oked—"

"Cut it out, Vincent."

"I taw-awked and I did wee-wee. . . ." He stopped and gave her a silly clown grin. "I don't remember where I dra-ank and ay-ate and—"

"Stop that!"

He shrugged and stood up. His shorts were Egyptian cotton from Battistoni with a tiny monogram on one leg. With a small ache she remembered the cheap tattered ones he'd worn in the Village long ago. He unsnapped the shorts and let them fall to the floor. Dragging them along, caught on one of his feet, he shuffled to the Room Service table. Why did his ballooning belly look grotesque now when it used to look lovable? He picked up a glass, emptied it into a coffee cup and filled the glass with the last of the melting cubes in the ice bucket. He followed his chalk line again to the bottle of scotch on the dresser.

"Don't drink any more," she said.

He thrust out his lower lip. "Why not, Mommy? I wanna drink, Mommy!"

She knew she shouldn't talk to him. She knew she should shut up and go to sleep and ignore him—but she couldn't stop herself.

"Were you really out with Gary?"

"That's for me to know and you to find out."

"Who were you with?"

"I was out with Gary, Mommy."

"Listen," she said, "I don't give a damn whom you were with! I just want you to know I can't live the way people live out here. I don't like sitting in a room by myself while you're out on the town. I'm not a Hollywood wife."

"Christ, don't I *know!*"

186

He came back and sat on the edge of his bed holding his glass. "Why couldn't I go with you tonight?"

"Why couldn't you go with me tonight? I'll tell you why you couldn't go with me tonight." He took a long drink.

"Well, why?"

"You couldn't go with me tonight because I didn't want you to go with me tonight."

"Why?"

The dopey grin was back on his face. "I wanted to get away from *Mommy* tonight! That's why!" He made a plopping sound with his tongue—his verbal period. He put the glass down on the table between the beds, stretched out, turned his back to her and pulled the covers over his shoulders.

She put her book down, turned off the light and stared at the shadowy ceiling. There was no sound anywhere inside the room or outdoors. The hotel was asleep. Beverly Hills was asleep. She closed her eyes. . . .

She was running so desperately she couldn't catch her breath. Her chest ached. She didn't know where she was running. Wherever it was she wasn't getting anywhere. She couldn't see. She couldn't breathe. A cloth was wrapped around her head, muffling her. She could taste the dry stuff in her mouth, choking her. She clawed at it and when it finally ripped away she saw she was in a ring. She was some addled creature trapped in a ring, dashing back and forth, turning around and around, trying to find a way out. There was no way out. She was a panicky cow in a ring. Milked dry. Dried up. And Vincent was circling her, closer and closer, his banderillo poised.

Her eyes shuddered open. She threw back the covers and leapt up, terrified. There was no ring. She was in a hotel room. The room swung back and forth in a wide arc, back and forth like a pendulum. Her heart was pounding. She could feel it in her throat, in her temples. The dark unmoving bulk on the other bed whirled in front of her.

"Vincent!" she cried. Her mouth was so dry it came out like a croak. "Vincent, I'm sick! I don't feel well! Vincent, *please!*" Suddenly she threw herself onto his bed and huddled close to him. He didn't move.

"Please turn around," she begged, "please turn around." She crouched against his massive back, that solid wall of flesh, unyielding as stone. His stone fortress, barred to her and silent.

"Vincent, something's the matter with me! I can't work. I didn't

187

do any work. I did work but it's no good. I'm scared! I had a nightmare! I don't know what's wrong with me. *Turn around! Please turn around!"*

Oh, God, what am I doing? she thought. Have I no dignity? No, she had no dignity. Had she no pride? She used to be so proud when he loved her. Isn't she the same human being now as she was then? No, she's not even human any more—she's just a scared sick cow.

"Please, please, *please* turn around. Take my hand. You don't have to talk to me—you don't have to say anything."

If he did, he'd say something nasty. So cruel when he was drunk. *In vino veritas.* Was it true? Was the alcohol-sodden one the real man? That mean, lashing tongue of his—was that real? Or was the sober one real? The sober one wasn't so different from the drunken one any more. The sober one had turned mean too. *This is a test. I'm going to test you. Everyone out here thinks it's brilliant—shut up about it. Isn't her tan sensational? You spoil things. You spoil all the fun. Like a disapproving old lady. You really should get with it. You're too old to have a baby.*

She was eight years old, standing on the lawn watching her father, red-faced and seething, hurl his bags into the car and slam the car doors without a word for her, without a glance, as if she were no more alive than the whitewashed stones that edged the driveway. The car wheels spinning on the gravel had pitched back a handful of pebbles. One pebble struck her neck as her father drove away forever without even waving. It left a mark that faded a little every day and finally vanished. For a while, whenever she thought about her father, she put her finger where the mark had been. One day she realized it was just a place where a stupid piece of gravel had hit her. She forgot about it. Why was she suddenly remembering it now after what seemed like a million years? How did Vincent know where it was? How did he know, when he took aim with his banderillo, that it was the perfect target.

"Vincent!" she tried to shake his heavy shoulder. "Vincent!"

He was never going to answer. He was dead to the world. No, dead to her. When did he die to her? When was the first time? If she could remember the first time she might go back and freeze the frame and live everything over again, make it all turn out differently. Magical thinking! God, what difference did it make when the first time was? It had happened. And everything that had happened since had happened. *I wanted to get away from Mommy tonight!* Oh the prick! The *prick* for saying that! They say at first you see red. She saw red. She saw the color of his blood. Or was it her own blood flooding behind her eyes? They say your brain bursts. Her brain exploded—she watched the streaks, fiery dots and dashes, fanning out into the darkness. Then, they say, you go crazy.

She began to pound her fists on his back. It was like pummeling granite. Her fists beat against him faster, harder. She pounded him as if she were sinking into a swamp and only he could pull her free. She pounded him as if she were suffocating under an avalanche and only he could bring her air. She pounded him for her life.

"I'm not your fucking mother!" she screamed.

She heaved herself higher in the bed and with all her strength drummed her fists against his head. That woke him, all right! How swiftly his hands came up to cover his head. She pounded on his hands.

"I'm not your fucking mother!"

Suddenly he turned. He doubled up his leg and kneed her violently in the stomach. She fell on her back between the beds. She scrambled to her feet, panting, grabbed the bedside lamp and slung it down at him. The cord was too short. The lamp hit the edge of the bed and crashed to the floor. She raced to the Room Service table, snatched up a glass and threw it. It smashed against the headboard. She reached for the ice bucket. He was after her in an instant. His fingers crushed her wrist. She moaned and dropped the bucket. With her free hand clenched she struck at him. He grabbed her other wrist. They struggled back and forth until he put his foot out and tripped her. He started to drag her across the room. Her nightgown caught under her body and ripped. The carpet scraped her skin. He dragged her all the way into the bathroom, where she lay on the cold white tiles, weak and gasping. She heard him open the medicine chest. He was lifting her to her feet. She swayed dizzily and put her sore hands on the basin to steady herself. He was prying her mouth open. She felt the two pills on her tongue, then his fingers poking them to the back of her throat. She gagged convulsively as the pills went down. A gargoyle face grimaced at her from the mirror, blotched and puffy, the maniac eyes streaming, the nose streaming, hair plastered in tufts across her forehead, her torn nightgown hung below her breasts, her breasts streaked red with burns from the carpet. Ugly—she was ugly, so ugly! Then he was picking her up. She lay safe in his arms, her face warmed against his chest that was flesh again and not stone. Safe. She was safe. He carried her into the bedroom and dropped her down on the bed like a sack of potatoes.

The next afternoon after she was packed and ready to leave for the airport she put on dark glasses and went down to the pool. She squinted along the toasting bodies until she saw him finally at the end of the row. He was talking to Iris, who sat cross-legged on the mat next to him, a solemn, absorbed expression on her face. *The way I used to look when I listened to him,* she thought. He picked up a script, riffled through it and pointed to a page. Iris nodded and pushed her glasses up on top of her head. Then she was talking and he was listening. She looked exhilarated—kindled. *That's what he used to do to me. He was flame. When did it stop? When was the first time?*

The operator's voice came over the loudspeaker. "Mr. Vincent Wade, telephone please. Mr. Vincent Wade, telephone please." She watched him get to his feet, the familiar wriggle as he pulled up his trunks and ambled toward the telephone. The sunbathers on their mats turned their heads to watch him. He had a grumpy look on his face, playing, she knew, to the gallery, acting the preoccupied artist suffering this petty intrusion from the outside world.

On the way back from the phone he spotted her and came over. His dark glasses confronted her dark glasses.

"What're you doing lurking out here?"

"I'm not *lurking.* I came to tell you I'm going back to New York."

"Better go back to your shrink too."

"When a person is treated as if she's worthless," the shrink said, "she's bound to *feel* worthless."

"You're not grieving for him," the shrink said. "You're grieving for a dream you had."

"You're a romantic," the shrink said. "You had a romantic ideal —you thought you would live together and work together and be happy forever. You thought that if you did everything he wanted and gave him everything he wanted he would love you. That's not the way it works," the shrink said.

"Why do you keep blaming yourself?" the shrink asked. "Why do you keep saying, 'I should have'? Doesn't it occur to you that he *shouldn't* have? Why do you think everything is your fault?"

"Given the kind of man he is, given his problems, it was doomed from the beginning. No matter what you had done it would have ended the same way," the shrink said.

But it didn't end. Sidney found a producer who loved *The Nearest Exit* and wanted to make the film. His name was Omar Lederman.

12

My luck did not improve. During the next three months I got involved with three different producers who had absolutely nothing in common except that they each ate one meal at my apartment and departed, never to be heard from again. I mean *never*—not a phone call, not a note, not a message, not a peep—as if they'd vanished off the face of the earth.

The one who came for breakfast had bought the rights to a pop hit song. We discussed the story narrated in the lyrics and how to extend it for a feature film. He took notes on all my ideas, assured me that I was a "big talent," that he couldn't wait to work with me, and kissed me on both cheeks when he left. The one who came to lunch had bought a spy thriller. He stayed most of the afternoon while we talked about which scenes to lose and which to add and made a list of possible stars and directors and talked about what fun it was going to be to make because it had to be shot all over Europe. He gave me a bear hug when he left. The one who came for dinner had read *Mixed Blessing,* the script Vincent walked out on when he walked out on me. He thought it was "brilliant," he wanted only a few minor changes. He planned to fly to the coast the following week to take the script to a star—he named an actress I'd dreamed about. It was definitely his next project, he promised.

"Call up Studio Duplicating Service and order another fifty copies. Gold cover, because you and I are going to mine gold with that brilliant script."

When he left he both hugged and kissed me.

Aside from these weird memories, what I have left over from the three of them is fifty copies of *Mixed Blessing* in gold covers and my canceled check to Studio Duplicating Service for five hundred dollars.

Could it have been the food?

One day looking at that pile of scripts, so new, so ready, so pristine, so "brilliant," I decided to do something about *Mixed Blessing* myself. It wasn't a flat-out obviously commercial script, but it could be a very special movie. One of the drawbacks was that the pivotal character was a twelve-year-old boy, but the boy's mother was a showy role for an actress—the character was theatrical, sensual, eccentric, spirited. Vincent had said the studio objected to the downbeat ending but I saw a way to fix it. I put in a call to Alden Cates at World-Wide (the studio that had turned it down). I wanted to convince Alden to read the script again. It was eleven in the morning California time, but like every person one telephones on the coast at any hour Alden had just "taken a meeting." He got back to me in a few hours.

"Remember that script I wrote called *Mixed Blessing?*" I asked him.

"I remember the title."

"Vincent told me you didn't like it, but I can fix it. I've thought of a new ending and—"

"Hold it! I didn't like the script?"

"Maybe you don't remember—it's almost three years now. We had a deal with you to make it, and Vincent blew the deal to make *The Comet.*"

"That bomb! I had a hell of a time with your husband over that one!"

"We're separated."

"He's some smooth operator, your husband!"

"We aren't together any more."

"I never saw a movie in that book! I only let your husband go ahead because of *Somersault.*"

"Listen, about *Mixed Blessing*—would you read the script again?"

"I never did read it."

"Maybe you've forgotten—"

"Your husband said the script was no good. He said he didn't want to make it so I didn't read it."

"Help me get this straight, Alden. Vincent told you the script was no good?"

"Right."

"So you never read it and therefore you couldn't have told him you didn't like it?"

"Right."

"Would you read it now?"

"Sure. Send me a copy."

I hung up. There were no more cigarettes on my desk. I walked into the living room to get one. There they were in the silver porringer with his bloody initials on it and the marks of his bloody serpent's teeth on it. I snatched up the porringer, rushed outside and hurled it over the terrace. It clanged on the pavement fourteen floors below. Christ, what a childish thing to do! What if I'd hit someone? Two minutes later I was down in the street expecting to see a crowd, expecting to hear an ambulance coming for the body and a police car coming for me.

There was no body. There was no porringer either. I must have looked like some crazed person walking around, eyes fixed on the curbs, dodging traffic, stooping to peer under parked cars. A man stopped and watched me. "May I be of assistance?" he called. He had a thick middle-European accent.

"I'm looking for a little silver bowl. . . ."

He doubled up to bend down and search with me, spotted the porringer before I did and crawled under a car to reach it. When he handed it to me I helped him brush off his suit.

"So kind of you," I said. "I'm very grateful."

We looked at each other in the late afternoon light. He had a morose, unusual face, long jaw, long nose, basset-hound eyes with little mournful pouches under them. I imagined him fleeing through a birch forest in the snow or lying flat on the floor of a car speeding across some forbidden frontier. The fugitive mileage on his face was intriguing and I thought of asking him up for a drink. Then I thought, What's happening to me, ready to pick up a strange man on the street? But they had all been strange men, the ones with proper introductions. Even so, I snatched the porringer out of his hands and raced into the door of my building.

Fade-in

Omar Lederman had a rotund face with a gray mustache and a short pointed beard, flawlessly clipped, like an upside-down triangle pasted on his chin. He wore rimless glasses over which his black eyebrows flared in two more triangles. Behind the glasses his eyes were black, slightly slanted, piercingly shrewd. The only hair left on his head hung in a curly fringe around the back so that his forehead seemed to go on forever. He sat behind an enormous desk, a sultan, flanked by two attending young Turks—a just-out-of-college eager beaver named Floyd Parker and a dour slack-mouthed type around thirty named Leo Brandt. On the wall behind the desk hung dozens of framed cinema awards and citations, photographs of international movie stars, various inhabitants of the White House, serene highnesses and deposed kings. The camera had captured them hugging Omar or presenting him with silver cups or statuettes or simply grinning beside him in the gardens of his great white villa near Kusadasi on the Aegean coast.

When they entered the office, Omar hoisted his considerable bulk out of his chair and came around the desk in an invisible mist of cologne. He bent low to kiss Lucia's hand. Oh, boy! she thought. Then he shook Vincent's hand and gave him a fatherly clap on the shoulder. He waved one of the Young Turks forward to light their cigarettes.

The Young Turks were marked in their deference to their sovereign. They leapt at the battery of phones on the desk the instant one buzzed and relayed messages in low voices directly into his ear. They produced with agility ashtrays, notes, phone numbers, a calendar. Omar opened a silver humidor engraved with his praises. They sprang forward with clippers and lighter.

"I have your permission to smoke a cigar, my dear Lucia?"

"Of course," Lucia said. "Please do."

194

Once Omar had a glow on his cigar the Young Turks sat down again and turned toward Vincent and Lucia. Their faces were as impassive as those of the gold Oscars marching along the windowsill thirty-three stories above Central Park.

Omar began by telling them how impressed he was with the script. It needed work but he had never seen a script in all his decades of making movies that didn't need work. This was a creative enterprise that he would discuss with dear Lucia in the hope that she would allow him to contribute some constructive suggestions. She must not fear he is like the producer in the old lemonade joke. They know the old lemonade joke about the two producers driving across the desert who run out of gas? They do not know it? These two producers get out of their car and start to walk. The sun beats down on them like fires of hell. After a few hours they are fainting. They are dying of thirst. Suddenly they see a shimmering object in the distance. With their last strength they stagger toward it. When they get close they find it is a huge cooler of frosty lemonade, beside it are two glasses. One of the producers reaches out a shaking hand and fills the glasses. Just as they are about to drink the lemonade the other producer says, "Wait a minute, Marty, first we pee in it to make it better."

In the midst of their laughter one of the phones rang. The younger Young Turk answered it and whispered in Omar's ear. "Will you excuse me, dear peoples?" Omar asked. He flipped a switch and instantly the room was filled with crackling static and the blurry voice of a man shouting for Omar and cursing the bad connection in French. The static and the screeches continued during the conversation as Omar barked questions in French into the speakerphone. He was asking about the grosses of one of his epics which had recently opened in Paris. The Frenchman rattled off the figures for three different theatres. There was a short discussion of the advertising and publicity campaign. Omar shouted out a list of commands. Then his voice changed. It became low and caressing as he inquired about someone he referred to as *ma petite*. Several times he asked, *"Elle est triste? Elle pense à moi?"* and each time the Frenchman would respond, *"Oui, Oui, Elle est très triste. Elle est moitié folle parce que vous n'êtes pas là."* Omar's face softened. He relayed a message to his *petite* that he missed her very much and would call her at the usual time. Then he flipped off the switch and returned his attention to the script.

They had chosen, he told them, a profound subject, a significant subject, one not often explored in film. He had many friends similar to their character, Todd—men who reach a certain age to

195

find their lives in ruins. *Cherchez la femme,* he said mournfully. He had had such a moment in his own life. *Cherchez la femme,* he repeated. *La femme* was not exactly pertinent to the reason for Todd's devastation in the script, but no one mentioned that. Omar sent a cloud of expensive cigar smoke out into the air. He was, he said, the namesake of a poet who had put it very well. " 'Ah, Love, could you and I with Fate conspire,' " he recited, " 'to grasp this sorry scheme of things entire, would not we shatter it to bits and then—remold it nearer to the heart's desire?' "

Omar Khayyam's question was not exactly pertinent to the script either, but then it was not exactly impertinent. Omar Lederman went on to explain that although the pictures that made him famous were huge high-budget epics, he was deeply attracted to modesty and simplicity. He welcomed this opportunity to make an East Coast low-budget film without, he sighed gratefully as he said it, without movie stars. *No movie stars,* he repeated. Instead, if dear Vincent agreed, they would look for the best New York actors together. He predicted that they would make a film "to break barriers"—an art film and a commercial success too. Why not, he asked, since he would be sponsoring two talented peoples? He leaned back in his chair, puffing and beaming. The beams radiating from him finally lighted the faces of the Young Turks. They beamed too.

Looking at Omar's congratulatory expression Lucia was struck by the thunderbolt effect of instant attraction. He was intelligent, he was cultivated, he had that aura of romantic *Weltschmerz* that Americans never achieve. And he vibrated power, the sexiest quality of all. Much later, looking back on their whole Omar Lederman period, Lucia thought it had been, for her, very like a love affair. There was the initial high during which anything jarring or disagreeable was resolutely ignored. There was the awful day when lucidity took over from lunacy, and after that the long dizzying roller-coaster ride until she hit bottom the morning Vincent was fired from the picture.

As this first meeting was about to end a stooped, middle-aged man, drawn and gray-skinned, stopped in. He was introduced as Omar's story editor. It was he who had first read the script and passed it on to his employer with an enthusiastic recommendation.

"What I particularly liked," he said to Lucia, "was the fragmented style you chose to—"

"We are not now discussing style," Omar interrupted sharply.

"—to show Todd's disorientation," the story editor went on. "I love the way you combine his fantasy with the reality which—"

"We are not discussing these subjects!" Omar shouted. "Why do you come in here and bring up these subjects?"

"I just wanted to tell Mrs. Wade that—"

"*I* tell Mrs. Wade what she is told," Omar roared. "Mrs. Wade is not *your* business. She is *my* business!" His face had turned purple. "Kindly return to your own business."

Lucia stared at the patterns on the oriental rug as the story editor left the room. Omar's complexion and voice returned to normal.

"So now we put everything on hold while my lawyers and your agent discuss our contracts," he said. "After that, we go to work." He came around the desk and kissed Lucia's hand again. Then one of the Young Turks showed them to the door.

The contracts stated that the picture was not to cost more than a half million dollars and their own fees, Vincent's as director and co-producer (Leo Brandt was the other co-producer) and Lucia's as writer, were set at an extremely modest figure, as befits a low-budget project. Otherwise they were the usual Lederman Productions contracts. Omar Lederman was to be executive producer but he had the right to remove his name from the picture if he wanted to. Lederman Productions owned the original story and screenplay. Lederman Productions had script approval, casting approval and final cut. Lederman Productions had, as is customary in Hollywood contracts, the right to replace the writer and the director. It was startling to realize that upon signing they would become disposable employees on a film they had initiated and developed, gambled their time and their own money on. They rationalized the startlement away. Was not Omar one of the "greats," a legendary film-maker who had assured them his intentions for the picture were the same as theirs? If he didn't make the picture nobody would.

They signed the contracts.

Lucia was requested to come to a story conference. "Without the husband," Omar specified. "We work alone." They weren't exactly alone. The Young Turks were there too. Lucia listened for several minutes while the three of them went through a sort of warm-up routine.

"Making pictures is like making war," Omar said. "We charge at danger, we risk our ass, we fight for our life!"

"Our lives are always on the line, Omar," Leo said.

"Once we embark we never retreat. We *advance!* We march

through the mud, we freeze, we burn, we starve, we suffer, we bleed. . . ."

"We always bleed, Omar."

"We make our picture and we *kill* them! Or they kill us. . . ."

"When they don't line up at the box office we're dead, sir," Floyd said.

"If they don't buy tickets, Omar, we've lost the war."

"Maybe they buy tickets but they do not buy *enough* tickets. Then we are cripples! We have maybe one leg left to stand on. Next time we fight them it is twice as hard to kill them."

"We've got to kill them before they kill us, Omar."

"Every time, sir."

It was like a skit, Lucia thought. She wanted to laugh but gradually, in spite of herself, she felt a kind of energy flowing through her.

"So!" Omar folded his hands over his stomach. "Can we kill them with a picture that confuses them?"

"No way, Omar."

"No, sir."

"Lederman Law Number One: We do not confuse the audience. Lederman Law Number Two: We tell the audience what to think so they will think right."

"If we let them think on their own," Leo said, "they will think wrong."

"The audience expects to root for our hero. In my pictures we do not frustrate this expectation. That's Lederman Law Number Two."

"Number Three, sir."

"Lederman Law Number Three."

Leo nodded. "We lose the war if there's ambivalence."

Omar's face turned purple. "I am not now talking about ambivalence!" he shouted. "I am talking about *ambiguity!* Why do you not listen when I talk? What did I just say?"

"Ambiguity, Omar."

"Take my picture *The Emperor*. The Emperor orders his wife to be assassinated, he poisons his seven mistresses, he exiles his sons to Siberia—but the audience roots for him. Why? Because we *tell* them to! We show them the Emperor is a sympathetic man who has his good reasons."

"Everyone laughed when Mr. Lederman announced he'd make *The Emperor*."

"In the end Omar did the laughing—all the way to the bank."

"That picture grossed eighty million worldwide. So can you not say, my dear Lucia, that as a picture-maker I know what I am doing?"

"I would say you were born knowing, Mr. Lederman."

"What is this 'Mr. Lederman?' We are friends and colleagues. You can pay me the compliment of calling me Omar."

"You were born knowing, Omar."

Omar opened the silver humidor. "The smell of my cigar does not offend you?"

"No, no, not at all. I love it."

The clippers and lighter were produced. Omar snorted as he puffed. "What means that 'love'? You Americans love apples, you love oranges, you love baseball, you love sunshine, you love kitty-cats, you love everything! Why do you not keep this word for your lover?"

"I don't have a lover."

"Perhaps that is why you do not write love scenes very well."

"But Omar, there are no love scenes in this script."

"No, there are hate scenes. What your character Harriet says to your character Todd is a terrible thing. She slices his balls."

"It's her revenge."

"You say that to a man?"

"No, never."

"Your character Harriet says it for you. Now we know what you think!"

"I am not Harriet."

"In my country for that a woman is killed. In this country a woman is paid!" Omar puffed on his cigar for a moment. "Never mind. We put that on hold. It is not the subject of this meeting. The subject of this meeting is confusion. I am confused about your character Todd."

"Omar doesn't feel Todd is sympathetic," Leo said.

"My dear Lucia, Todd has no job, no money, his wife is gone, his children are gone. He has no home. He is a loser. You expect me to root for a loser?"

Lucia leaned forward and grasped the edge of the desk. "You're supposed to care about him, you're supposed to be moved by him—in the end you're supposed to feel heartbroken for him."

"What means this *you?*" Omar demanded. "This *you* is not *me.*"

"But Omar—"

"Do you want to hear what I say or do you want to interrupt?" Omar shouted. "I work with the greatest screenwriters in the world—they all are courteous not to interrupt!"

"Sorry."

Lucia saw that the blood had drained out of her knuckles. She took

199

her hands off the desk. "Your character Todd, my dear Lucia, he is crazy. Why does he say to everyone he is going home when he has no home to go to?"

"That's the point," Lucia said. "I—I'm afraid you're missing the—"

"I am not missing the point!" Omar roared. "If I am missing the point, the audience is missing the point! Is your character Todd crazy or is he not crazy?"

"He's—he's disoriented."

"What means this disoriented?"

"He wants so much to have his life the way it was when he was happy that he has convinced himself it *is* the way it was, that nothing has changed."

"So you describe to me a crazy man! We begin this film and this crazy man is walking down a road. Where from has he come? Insane asylum?"

"No. That is, we don't know. I—I don't think we have to know."

"That's where you're wrong," Floyd said.

Omar turned on him. "Who asks you?" he shouted. "I do not ask your opinion. The screenwriter does not ask your opinion! *You* are the one who is wrong! We do not need to know from where he is coming. We need to know *who he is. How can we know who is this man, Todd?*"

"We need a lot more exposition, Omar," Leo said.

Omar leaned back in his chair and contemplated Lucia over his cigar. "Why do you have such a puzzle look on your face, my dear Lucia? Exposition is an English word, is it not?"

"Omar asked you to meet with me alone," Leo explained a few days later, "because he feels I've licked the problem of exposition." He indicated a large sheet of graph paper spread on his desk. Across it he had drawn a line that zigzagged up and down in triangular peaks. Each peak bore a label in tiny handwriting. The drawing looked rather like an electrocardiogram of a healthy heart. But when Lucia bent closer to read the notations she saw that, for the film, it was a diagram of disaster. Leo explained that each little peak indicated a scene with a person from Todd's past life whom he would run into on his way home: an old army buddy to reveal his army life, a former college chum to reveal his college life, a former boss to reveal his career life, a schoolteacher to reveal his childhood and an old lady who had once been his baby nurse to reveal his babyhood.

"So far this is all off the top of my head," Leo said, "but by the

200

time you write those scenes the audience'll sure as hell know who Todd is."

"Uh-huh."

"For instance, his old nurse could say something about how his folks never paid any attention to him. And then his old college chum could recall how Todd always had to get the best grades, be the best at sports, lay the most girls because he had this intense desire to get attention—the attention he never got from his folks."

"Uh-huh."

"The way you've written it we don't know anything that's happened in his early life—so what I've done is make up a back story for you."

"Mmmm."

"It solves any confusion the audience might have about Todd, the way he is now."

"Mmmmm."

"I've some ideas about how we can make the audience care about him too but they aren't totally formulated yet. Try this on for size: Todd runs into his banker. His banker says, 'Look here, Todd, you've overdrawn your account again. This is the third time!' Everybody in the audience has done it or is scared of doing it. Makes him sympathetic."

"Uh-huh."

"What would you say to a dog?"

"A *dog?*"

"What if some stray mongrel starts to follow him and when he crosses the highway it follows him and gets hit by a car?"

"Killed?"

"Wait—so when Todd sees this he runs right back out in the traffic between all these speeding cars and picks up the dog. Then maybe the dog dies in his arms at the side of the highway."

"Oh."

"It sure as hell would make him sympathetic—when he risks his life to rescue that dog."

Late that afternoon Omar phoned. "I hear your discussion with Leo does not go well," he told Lucia.

"Was that a discussion? I don't remember having a discussion."

"How is it possible a discussion when you march out of his office? That is not very polite."

"Politer than punching him in the nose."

"What means this punching? Leo cannot make suggestions without threats?"

"He's a stupid idiot! I refuse to talk to him ever again!"

"That is difficult—he is co-producing this film."

"I don't want him to have anything to do with the script!"

"What about what *I* want?"

"I'll work on it with my husband."

"No."

"I've got to. He's the director!"

"Not the husband. You work with *me.*"

When the lights went up in the screening room, Omar turned around to Vincent.

"I despise these tests," he announced. "Not one girl is right to play Molly."

"I thought Claire Bosworth was good," Vincent said. "She's an excellent actress. She got rave notices for—"

"I despise her. She's ugly!"

"But Omar!" Lucia was shocked. "She's lovely looking!"

Omar made a face. "She looks like what you put in the garden to scare cows."

"Crows, sir," Floyd said. "You mean a scarecrow, sir."

"The two brunettes were prettier," Leo said.

Vincent shook his head. "The first one comes off as too urbane, and I'm not sure the other one can cut it. Her lack of experience showed."

"If she has no experience why do you waste our time to test her? Anyway she is not pretty." Omar frowned at Leo. "A flat chest—like central Anatolia." His polished nails drummed on the back of his seat. "I am not looking for pretty in this role. I am looking for *beautiful*— so it takes your breath. I am looking for a girl from another planet."

"But Omar—" Lucia was about to say something but his face stopped her.

"With you it is always 'But Omar'! I begin to think my name is But-Omar! Can you say what you want to say, my dear Lucia, without saying But-Omar?"

"Molly is supposed to be a typical small-town girl, seventeen years old. The kind of girl who baby-sits for the neighbors, helps her mother with the supper dishes. If she's too beautiful she won't be believable."

Omar snorted and turned to Vincent. "Stop to waste money," he instructed. "No more girl tests until you find me a girl from another planet."

"I am happy you approve of Claudia Manning," Omar said.

"Vincent's crazy about her. He says she's perfect for Harriet."

"You do not meet her?"

Lucia shook her head. "I've seen her in a couple of plays. It's a wonderful suggestion."

"If it is not a wonderful suggestion, I would not suggest it," Omar said grandly. "However, I want your opinion."

"If Vincent thinks she's right, I think she's right."

"So. Like the sun rises in the east you think what the husband thinks?"

"Most of the time."

"What means this—you American wives? You do not come out of the wedding with the husband, you come out with the Siamese twin! Joined at the hip! Everything must be together: breakfast, dinner, holidays, gin rummy, tennis, bank accounts. I have an American wife once—she insists on the orgasm together. Very difficult even when you are *not* joined at the hip. For my divorce I need a surgeon more than a lawyer. Do not smile so fast, my dear Lucia, you will too." He grinned. "When the time comes I recommend a talented man in Rio. Does not leave scars."

"I don't mind scars."

"Scars are ugly. Think of your lover!"

"I'm not sure I'll have a lover."

"I have already one in mind for you—a Turk also."

"God forbid!"

Omar chuckled. "I have a sense of humor so I am not insulted." He leafed through the script. "Now we have a Harriet, we attack the Harriet scene. I want you to make it longer and more fulsome."

"But—"

"Never do I work with such a writer! You object before I say anything!"

"Sorry."

"What I want to say is this Harriet scene is an excellent place for more exposition about your character Todd. Why do you look disagreeable?"

"That word 'exposition'! I hate it ever since my meeting with Leo."

"Forget Leo! What has Leo to do with us?" Omar shouted. His face began to turn purple.

Lucia felt her usual seasick feeling when Omar threatened to have a tantrum. It was, she thought, like riding in a canoe with a hippopotamus. She started to talk nice-hippopotamus talk. "You're right," she said quickly. "I already did use that scene to explain some things."

"Not *enough*. You never tell how your character Todd breaks off with your character Harriet."

"I—I guess I didn't think it was—necessary."

"It *is* necessary. We need it to motive that terrible thing she says to him when he comes to her house—how many years later?"

"About a year."

"You put no motive for her to say such a terrible thing. Now if he breaks off with her in a mean-bastard way she has a motive."

"I'll think about it."

"You do not have to think. *I* have thought. I tell you a story you can use. This is *entre nous* but you will run and tell the husband. You are the kind of woman who tells the husband everything. The husband, I promise, does not tell *you* everything." He gave her a long appraising look. "Why do you smoke too many cigarettes? Are you a tense person?"

"No. I don't know."

"*I* know."

"Tell me the story, Omar."

"You do not want to discuss that you are a tense person? We put that on hold." Omar hoisted himself out of his chair and crossed to the window. He looked down at the autumn-colored tree tops. Then he looked up at the sky. "The story is about my Bulgarian mistress," he said. "Your character Harriet reminds me." He seemed to be studying the cloud formations. "I see her now. So beautiful, so devoted, so understanding when I must be with my wife. I am married to my Swedish wife at the time." One of the Oscars on the sill was out of line. He straightened it. "My Bulgarian mistress does not care when she has the orgasm or if she does not have one, but *I* must have one. Bulgars are like that—they are used to Turkish rule." He seemed lost in memory for a moment. Then he sighed, walked heavily back to his chair and sat down. "My Bulgarian mistress does not allow me to give her presents. She does not want diamonds or sables or a Ferrari. Why, do you think, my dear Lucia?"

"She loved you for yourself alone!"

Omar smiled. "You are the most incredible unsophisticated person I meet in my life! Nothing to do with love! I am with her for three years and finally I figure out what she wants."

"What?"

"Like your character Harriet wants to marry your character Todd, my Bulgarian mistress wants *marriage.* Bulgars are like that too, always making territorial claims. I never marry a Bulgar—they are enemies of my people since 1396. I make a decision to break it off. Now arrives the part of the story you can use. Are you listening?"

"All ears, Omar."

"I invite her to lunch—to the most fashionable, most elegant, most expensive restaurant in New York. That year was a great Bordeaux. I order it. Château-Lafite Rothschild, 1961. Over the first glass I tell her it is finished."

"Just like that? What'd she do?"

"She talks pleasantly. Her new dress comes from her dressmaker, she regrets I never see her in it. Tonight she bakes an eggplant with yogurt. She regrets she never serve it to me. I order a splendid lunch. We eat it. Before coffee I leave—an important meeting, I tell her. At the door of the restaurant I wave. She waves back."

"And then what?"

"That is it. That is my story."

"I don't quite understand," Lucia said carefully, "how it applies to Todd and Harriet."

"This is what Todd does. He takes Harriet to an elegant restaurant and tells her it is finished."

"Why an elegant restaurant?"

Omar groaned. "You are the most incredible square-witted person I meet in my life! A mistress is not secure to cry tears, to scream, to make a big noise in a restaurant filled with elegant people. The man can get the whole thing over with and no fuss at all!"

"After three years? What a dirty trick!"

"*Of course* it is dirty! So we make Todd do a dirty trick and then, my dear Lucia, *then* Harriet has the motive to say that terrible thing —that he is bad in bed." Omar stood up chuckling and came around to kiss Lucia's hand. "Go home, my dear Lucia, and write that story into the scene."

"Dear peoples, I beg you, do not say one more time this actor is your character Todd." Omar implored them. "I see the test. I despise it. What is this sensitive? What is this vulnerable? This actor is ugly! No blood in him, too skinny, the face a bone, the body a bone. This actor is a skull and a bone! What audience looks at this man for two hours? This man I *know* is bad in bed. Your character Harriet does not need to make up that terrible thing to hurt him—for this actor it is true! Do not tell me one more time he is the best actor in America. I say he is the worst actor in America for this picture. I see it in my eyes! I smell it in my nose! The two other tests do not speak about. You waste our time, my dear Vincent, with useless tests. Maybe you prefer to make tests, not movies? Now you look at me like I cut off the heads of your mothers. I do it! I cut off the heads of your mothers to keep these actors out of our picture. With these actors our picture goes down the toilet. I see these tests two weeks ago. Torture in my stomach for two weeks. My stomach says we cannot make this picture without a movie star. No movie star—they kill us at the box office! A movie star means a movie star budget. I am willing! I have faith! Forget one half million. We spend maybe three–four million more and we kill them at the box office! I have exchanged my mind from our first meeting, dear peoples. I am wrong. When I am wrong I say I am wrong."

The October sunlight slanted through the windows and flashed on the row of gold Oscars that Omar had won, Lucia thought, for not being wrong.

"When I go to Hollywood for the first time," Omar said, "I hear all peoples talking about the couch for casting—this actress, that actress, she gets the role on the couch for casting. I am an immigrant. My English is not good. I look up this couch in the dictionary. It says a furniture to sit on. When I cast my first picture, I do not sit the actress on the chair. I sit her on the couch, the American way. I want to be very American in those days. Then I tell all peoples this actress, that actress, she got the role on the couch for casting. One day I wake up famous. I am a big scandal for sex with actresses. I am innocent! It is all a mistake with my English! You understand?" Vincent and Lucia nodded. "You understand this girl I now show you is not for sex, is my protégée?" They nodded again. "I never," Omar said, "I *never* mix my pleasure with my movie!" He glared at them and waited.

"Of course not," Lucia said.

"It can be very bad for the movie," Vincent said.

"This is a girl for your character Molly. This is a girl to take your breath—a girl from another planet!" Omar pressed a button, the door opened and one of his secretaries showed in a young woman. Omar came around his desk, kissed her hand and introduced her. Her name was Denise Gilmore. Beauty is in the eye of the beholder, as everyone

206

knows, but she took Lucia's breath away for other reasons. She was not from another planet, but the instant she spoke it was clear she was from another country. She wore a cream-colored silk dress with a tight gold belt. Above the belt in the front and below it in the back were lush curvy bulges. Her skin was so deeply tanned it almost matched her black curly hair, and while it was possible she could play seventeen it was more possible she could play twenty-seven or thirty-four. Vincent and Lucia avoided each other's eyes as they talked with her. Yes, New York pleased her, it was her first visit. Yes, the sun pleased her, she had spent the summer on the Mediterranean. No, she had not studied acting but she had acted in three French films—all by the same director, a French name they had never heard. The films were about young people who danced and swam and drove cars very fast. In one film she was broken in a car crash. Very sad. They used little sacks of *teinte rouge* for blood. Very amusing. Movies pleased her. Her favorite actress was Elizabeth Taylor. Very sexy. Richard Burton did not please her. Holes in his skin.

After a few minutes Omar signaled her to leave the room. There was silence. Lucia studied the patterns in the rug, which by this time she knew by heart. Vincent stroked his beard and stared thoughtfully out of the window. After a moment he said, "Her accent worries me, Omar."

"She speaks perfect English. Her father is English!"

"Her accent is French."

"You can teach her the American accent."

"I don't know—it would take a long time."

"This girl is bright. She learns fast."

"She's a little too—rounded, don't you think?"

"What means this rounded?" Vincent gestured a circle. "But she has a tiny waist, tiny bones!" Omar cried eagerly. "She can lose many pounds in one weekend. I know her to do it."

"It's—it's too bad she let herself get so dark," Lucia said.

"We get the best makeup man. The best makeup man fixes her." He turned to Vincent. "You teach her American for two weeks. After that you test her."

When they were out on the street Lucia said, "Maybe it's a joke. Maybe he's putting us on."

They walked the rest of the way home in silence.

Over drinks she asked, "Did you believe him? That casting couch story?"

"He's always screwed actresses—everybody knows that."

207

"Know what I think? I think when he sees the test he'll see how ridiculous it is."

"Who says I'm going to do the test?"

"Shall we quit?"

"And hand the picture over to him? That what you want?"

"Do you?"

"And then what? We aren't exactly being overwhelmed with offers."

"I'll finish the Mastroianni script."

"The Mastroianni script!" He threw back his head and laughed. It was an imitation of laughter. "Is that how you think of it? How the hell do you know Mastroianni'll want to do that script?"

"Peter said he would. If he likes it."

"If he likes it. If Peter can get him. If he'll accept me as director! If! If! If!"

"Peter said he'd accept you."

"Peter doesn't know his ass!" He crossed to the bar to pour himself another drink. "I'll do the fucking goddamn test! Jesus Christ, what else can I do?"

He refused to eat dinner. Around midnight he went into the kitchen and made sandwiches—melted cheese with chicken and ham, anything he could find. He brought one to her in bed. No parsley. There might not have been any in the refrigerator. In any case, he'd dropped that kind of panache with her a long time ago. Her stomach turned over as she contemplated the sandwich, two inches thick, the fried bread dripping with butter. She felt she might gag if she took a single bite.

"Looks delicious, darling," she said.

"Today let us have no But-Omar until I tell you what is on my mind. Give your word on the heads of your children?"

"All right."

"What is on my mind is the ending."

"The ending of the *film?*"

"I do not speak about the ending of the world or the ending of this lunch. How is your wine?"

"Delicious."

"You never, I believe, have a wine like this."

"What is it?"

"I tell you—you run out and buy it for the husband, so I do not tell you. You must not run out so much for the husband."

208

"Why?"

"You smile when I give marriage advice. You do not smile when I give writing advice. You hate it."

"Will I hate it today?"

"Of course. You forget I know more about movies than you do."

"What about the ending of the film, Omar?"

"It is not happy. They kill us at the box office for this not-happy ending."

"But Omar—"

"The heads of your children! Now listen to me. The audience is full of bad marriages, bad love affairs, bad stomachs, bad bowels. Their life is bad. They feel bad. They come to the movies to feel good. We must make them feel good."

"Oh, God!"

"We do not fade out with your character Todd at the door of his empty house. We draw back. We see your character Harriet in her car—"

"Oh, God!"

"Be quiet! She drives up the driveway. She gets out of her car. She walks toward your character Todd. *Then* we fade out."

"Impossible!"

"Put down your glass. The captain waits to fill it."

"The whole picture has been leading up to that moment at the empty house."

"I do not take out the empty house. I put in Harriet. Very simple. Happy ending."

"She would never come after him and take him back. *Never!"*

"Why not, if it makes the audience feel good?"

"It's out of character. It ruins the picture."

"Do not make yourself ugly wrinkles in your face like that. I despise wrinkles."

"You *mustn't* change the ending!"

"It is my picture. I do what I want. Taste the paté. You never, I believe, have a paté like this."

"The ending was there in the script when you read it. It was there when you bought it, it's *always* been there. Why do you want to change it now?"

"Now the picture costs three and a half million dollars. Unhappy is not a three-and-a-half-million-dollar ending."

"Promise me you won't change the ending or I'll throw a fit right here! I am not your Bulgarian mistress!"

"No, you are the husband's Bulgarian mistress."

"*What?* What do you mean?"

"You do not show your teeth with the husband. Only with me."

"Promise me, Omar!"

"I despise loud women, so I promise."

"I don't trust you."

"You are right not to trust me. Here is our poached bass. You have never, I believe. . . ."

Denise Gilmore's test was not a success and Omar, being a smart man, admitted he'd been wrong. From then on the casting was left to Vincent—except for Todd. Omar took the script and flew to California by himself to sign a star. He came back with a *coup*. John Matheson was available and had agreed to do the film. Matheson was a big draw, talented, handsome and the right age. His price was three quarters of a million dollars.

When Matheson arrived in New York, Vincent and Lucia were immediately attracted to him. He was low-keyed, gracious and crazy about the project. He had imaginative concepts about the character of Todd that sparked fresh ideas in both of them. The atmosphere of happy creativity around the rehearsals, fully reported by Leo, upset Omar. He called Vincent and Lucia into his office just before he left to spend the summer at his villa on the Aegean coast. He told them he planned to fly back every few weeks to see rushes and he would keep in touch with his "representative," Leo, by telephone almost every day. In the meantime he had orders for them. They were to have nothing to do with Matheson socially— no drinks, no dinners.

"Old Turkish proverb: 'You cannot jump into throat of a man with who you eat Imam Bayildi.' "

"We won't serve Imam Bayildi," Lucia said.

"It amuses you to show your little teeth?" Omar shrugged. "Amuse yourself." He turned to Vincent. "You do not permit Matheson into rushes."

Vincent's mouth dropped open. "How can I keep him out? What shall I tell him?"

"Nothing. I tell him!"

"But he's been making films for twenty years! He produced his last five films!"

"To me he is nothing but an employee. You peoples are nothing

210

but employees. I forbid decisions about money or script changes without my representative, Leo. Then Leo consults me."

A few days later the hippopotamus lumbered out of their canoe and left for Kusadasi.

13

I open one of the morning newspapers and find on a page devoted to food—surprise!—an article by Vincent Wade telling how, by sheer determination and true grit, he has lost sixty pounds! I close my eyes and superimpose Vincent's head on his body, minus sixty pounds. He looks, in my imagination, the way he looked after he left the London Clinic, but even thinner. I lift his beard and see that he has a neck again. I greet his neck. I put my arms around his waist and my hands meet behind him. I can even lace my fingers together. His middle is lean and hard. I congratulate him. I welcome back his lost cheekbones and admire the interesting hollows in his cheeks.

Vincent's never written any other pieces that I know of, and I wonder how he's come to write this one. I open my eyes and read on. He's telling all the poor fat slobs how he did it so they can do it too. He did it, he says, by sticking to a well-balanced diet, cutting out alcohol and riding his bicycle in the park. How on earth has he become so *sensible?* I read on. The real reason for his triumph, he writes, is that he has learned to like himself. He goes on with this for a while and becomes, I feel, a little mushy about it. He sounds like a man with a crush on his shaving mirror, a man who has become, in effect, his own best friend. But that can't be, I tell myself, the real reason for this metamorphosis. In all the years I knew him he always was his own best friend, and he was fat.

In the last paragraph I find the *real* real reason. "If you are fortunate enough to find someone who really cares for you as I did," he writes, "what better way to celebrate them than staying thin?" *Dear ex-husband, you have watched your weight, now please start watching your grammar!* I put down the paper, pick up my coffee cup and settle back against the pillows. For the next five minutes I project onto the white wall opposite my bed a movie called *Living with a Fat Man.*

I am projecting this movie at twenty-four frames a second but I pretend I've shot it at sixteen frames a second—it is undercranked in order to compress ten years into five minutes. As a result the two lead characters, Vincent and I, whiz about crazily in fast motion, all our movements jumpy and jerky. We are in restaurants, in dining rooms, on beaches, on grass, on boats, beside pools, in airplanes, in beds, at roadside stands, at street stalls, at tables—four or five thousand tables —and he is eating. My God, how he is eating! His spoons swoop from bowls to mouth. His forks zoom from plates to mouth. Sometimes his fork zooms from my plate to his mouth. Sometimes there is no spoon or fork, just his cupped hand full of mixed nuts or potato chips or buttered rolls or canapés. Sometimes there are two hands whizzing sandwiches across the screen. Because of the undercranking the sound track is garbled, squeaking and quacking like a flock of Donald Ducks. My voice is squeaking, "Please don't eat any more, darling, please don't order that, please don't have another helping, please don't finish mine, please don't cook anything at this hour, it's too early to eat, darling, it's too late to eat, darling, please let me throw it out, please don't open that jar, I love you, I want you to be well, I want you to be healthy, I don't want you to gain any more, please, please, please!" His voice is quacking, "Don't be a nag, don't be a bore, don't be a killjoy, don't be a shrew, leave me alone, I'm hungry, I want it, I'm starving, I want it, I want, I want, I want!"

I cut to other times. We are at home. We don't invite people over for dinner. We don't go out anywhere for dinner. He has psyched himself up to go on a diet—but it must be a crash diet. He insists on instantaneous weight loss. I squeak, "Crash diets aren't good for you. I'm afraid you'll get sick, please don't!" He quacks, "Why're you trying to keep me from losing weight? Why're you so hostile? Why're you such a bitch?"

The sound track stops. No more dialogue. I go on the diets with him to demonstrate I am a true helpmate, to prove I am not hostile, to prove I am loyal and a good person. We go on the safflower oil diet to the point of throwing up, we go on the meat-and-water diet to the point of fainting and nausea. We go on the Air Force diet, on the Mayo diet, on the Atkins diet, on the rice diet, on the calories-don't-count diet, on the grapefruit diet, on the banana-and-cottage-cheese diet, on the grapes-and-lettuce diet, we go on every diet there is. The deprivation gets to him. His eyes turn acid green. He is snappish and bad-tempered. He is depressed. He sleeps a lot. Finally he goes on the ultimate diet. I cut to a hospital. He is there for two weeks, fasting. He loses twenty pounds. The day he is discharged he makes a reservation at the best Italian restaurant in town. Cut to Italian restaurant. We are at our table at eight o'clock and he is deciding between *cannellóni alla Giorgio* and *fettucíne vérdi e bianchi.* The sound track starts up again. We squeak and quack but not about food or eating. On the subjects of food and eating there is nothing more to squeak and quack about. FADE TO BLACK. Cut off the projector.

I cared! Oh, how I cared! But apparently he feels I didn't *really* care.

I turn to the other morning paper and see an ad. "JEANE DIXON'S HOROSCOPES BY PHONE. Just dial the number for your sign (listed below) and hear a daily forecast prepared by the world-famous astrologer." I dial the number for my sign.

A jolly upbeat female voice peals in my ear. "Hello, Libra! Good luck is coming your way! Do not turn down dinner invitations from friends. Consult with a professional—it will pay off in the career department."

I was already consulting with a professional—Sidney Powker. His office was on a high floor of a glass skyscraper: leather couches, thick rugs, lots of chrome, colorful graphics on the walls. Sidney's office was not a bad place to spend time in, but most of the time I spent there was taken up with Sidney giving and me receiving bad news—they don't want you for the project at Imperial, they want a male writer; they don't want you for the project at Rogers-Fanner, they want a young writer; there's a lot of resistance to you at New Directions Productions, they want a hot writer; World-Wide already has a writer on that project; Stars International hasn't assigned a writer to that project yet but they don't think you're right for it—and so on and so on. I wasn't "right" for anything I hadn't done before, and the reason I hadn't done it before was that no one would hire me to do anything I hadn't done before.

According to Sidney I had two giant problems. One was *The Lady and the Robber:* "You're as good as your last picture." The second was that I lived on the East Coast and my absence from the West Coast made no one's heart grow fonder.

"I can fly out there in a few hours as I've always done."

"They fly you out it costs money, it's sort of a commitment. They wanna writer who can get to the studio on a half hour's notice and take a meeting. It's all how good you are at taking meetings. You take a good

214

meeting you get the job. If you were on the Coast my office out there'd have you up to your eyeballs in meetings. Move to the Coast," Sidney urged.

I was at the window looking at the glass skyscrapers glittering in the sun. Over the roofs of the smaller buildings nearby I could see the roof of my own building and my own small, snug apartment on top of it.

"Outta sight outta mind, honey."

"I'd never see a llama walking down the street at midnight in Beverly Hills."

"Say that again?"

"A man had a llama on a lead rein on Central Park South last night."

"A *llama?*"

"All the hookers took turns sitting on it while the man photographed them with a Polaroid flash camera. Three bucks a picture."

"He coulda got ten."

"I will never move to California," I said, just as California (black-haired version) walked into the room. Roy DeMarco was twenty-eight or -nine and good-looking enough to be an actor, if matinee idols were still in style—tall and fit with a tennis-every-day tan that looked twice as dark in the same room with the pallor of Sidney and me, a cleft dead center in his chin and super teeth. He was Philip Rowan twenty-five years ago except that he had already produced several movies for television. He was now "into" developing projects for the Big Screen and he wanted me for one of them, which was why I was in Sidney's office on that particular day.

The meeting started with the usual flimflam minuet. Roy lied and told me he'd seen all my pictures and loved them. I lied and told Roy I had seen all his pictures and loved them. Then he lied and told me we had met before in Beverly Hills.

"At Ma Maison," he said. "You and your husband-at-the-time were having dinner with Dusty."

"Right!" We had never had dinner with Dusty. Ma Maison didn't open until after we were divorced.

"No! It was at the Bistro. It wasn't Dusty, it was Jack. I was with Sue and we stopped at your table to say hello to Jack and he introduced us to you and your husband-at-the-time."

"Right!" We had never had dinner with Jack either, but I understood that Roy had to fade in on an establishing shot of his location on the A list and in the "in" restaurants.

"Know what I foresaw that night? I foresaw that someday that writer-person was going to split from that director-person and I'd grab her to write me a script."

"Your foresight was inaccurate. The director-person split from me."

"Asshole!"

I glanced at Sidney. "You shouldn't talk that way about one of Sidney's clients."

"He's very hot right now," Sidney said.

"*Hot!* Where's he hot?" Roy demanded. "He just made a couple of bombs!"

"I'm about to close a very big deal for him."

"Oh, good!" I said. "Now that he's taken care of you can close a big deal for me!"

"Hope you're not going to price yourself out of my budget," Roy said.

"She's expensive, Roy! Everyone's after her! She's got a big project going right now and five–six more stacked up."

Roy looked surprised. "I thought you said she was available."

"What I said was if she likes your project she can *become* available. We can stall the other things, can't we, honey?"

"You're doing fine, Sidney."

"If she's crazy about your project I give you my word she'll be available," Sidney said. It was about the only completely true thing that had been said in the room so far.

Roy gave me a long winsome look from under his Robert Taylor eyebrows. "You're a very attractive lady."

"Thank you."

"I've always had what you might call a European attitude toward older women."

"Oh?"

"If I didn't already have a mother I'd wish you were my mother."

"Are you looking for a writer or a mother?" My voice was only medium cool—after all, I hadn't heard what the project was yet.

"I'm looking for a writer who *is* a mother."

"Lucia's got two sensational kids," Sidney chimed in. Things were indeed bad, I thought, when my children had to be added to my credits.

"The reason is," Roy said, "this project you're so right for is about mother love, which is the most unselfish love there is. There's nothing a mother wouldn't do for her children, going all the way back to the Bible."

216

"Medea killed hers—going all the way back to the Greeks."

"Jesus! Never know where you're at with Greeks, do you?"

"Didn't you say you had a modern American story?" Sidney asked.

Roy nodded. "I'm going to tell it to you in total confidence. If it goes beyond this room you can just bet somebody'll rip it off."

"Loose lips sink ships," Sidney cautioned me.

Roy leapt out of his chair. "Think better on my feet," he explained. He paced the length of the room several times. "Okay! Sixteen-year-old chick. Sweet, simple cheerleader type. Bakes brownies. Wears boyfriend's letter sweater. Real down-home chick. Gets in with bunch of rotten kids. Peer pressure. Bunch of rotten kids goes shoplifting. Chick's only one caught with goods. Busted! In prison chick's terrified! Lonely! Okay! Tough twenty-year-old dyke. Pretends to be chick's friend. Hands out candy, cigarettes, sets hair, moves into same cell. Persuades chick to have sex. I want to show that scene but I want to show it with style and good taste." He whirled around to face me. "Can you live with it?"

"She can live with it," Sidney said, "can't you, honey?"

Roy paced another couple of lengths. "Okay! Chick gets sprung. Goes home. Guilt and shame! Fails in school. Guilt and shame! No social life. Guilt and shame! Breaks up with boyfriend. Guilt and shame! Writes note. Can't go on living. Runs up to attic. Hangs herself. I want to show that scene with style and good taste too. Pan around her old toys—dollhouse, teddy bear, rocking horse. Innocence! Pan up to chick dangling from rafter. *Lost* innocence!" Roy stopped in front of me. "You could write the hell out of that scene, Mrs. Wade!"

"You could write the hell out of it, honey!"

Roy changed direction and covered the width of the room, back and forth. "Okay! Cut to chick's mother. Fantastic part for Jane Fonda! Fonda swears revenge on dyke. Eye for eye. Vows to kill dyke who despoiled daughter. Now get this: Fonda deliberately commits crime! Gets herself into same prison—"

"Is that possible?" I asked. "Can you pick a prison the way you pick a hotel?"

"Dramatic license! Okay! Fonda in prison waiting for chance to get dyke. Cut to group-encounter thing run by prison psychologist. Dyke tells life story—what a load of shit she's taken from men so's it's turned her gay."

"As I understand it," I said, "that isn't the basic reason why a woman becomes homosexual."

217

"Dramatic license! Fonda hears dyke-who-despoiled-her-daughter's story. Feels sympathy. Heart softens. Vow to kill fades. Fonda takes dyke under wing, gives out bushels of mother love. Restores dyke's faith in good guys. Finally dyke is sprung. We know she's turned straight."

"How do we know that?"

"Astute question! Okay, when dyke gets out of slammer, Fonda introduces her to dead chick's boyfriend. They make it. Happy ending!" Roy flung himself into a chair and radiated a boyish smile meant to be irresistible to a woman of my age. I resisted it.

"Not necessarily a happy ending," I said.

"Why not?"

"Most lesbians don't want to be straight, so it wouldn't be a happy ending for lesbians."

Roy snorted. "How many tickets do *they* buy?"

I looked over at Sidney, who had his head down and was doodling on his desk pad. "I got a gut feeling it's commercial," he said.

"Bet your ass it's commercial."

"Why is it commercial?"

"There's a trend. Everybody's looking for lesbian stories. Just sold a script about a divorced woman in the suburbs who has an affair with another divorced woman in the suburbs."

"It isn't just out there," Roy said, "it's *everywhere!*"

"Was there any particular reason?" I asked Sidney. "I mean, why didn't the divorced woman in the suburbs have an affair with a divorced man in the suburbs?"

Roy groaned. "What a cliché!"

Sidney continued to avoid my eyes. "Why don't you mull the story over and we'll get back to Roy?"

"You do that," Roy said. "See if you can live with it."

I went home. "I can't live with it," I told Tory.

But how were we going to pay for the Alpo and the vet and the groomer and the ice cream bars we devoured in the park?

Alden Cates called. He said he was crazy about the script of *Mixed Blessing* ("brilliant!") but he wasn't all that crazy about it as a movie. The story was too offbeat, the kind of black comedy they do so well in Europe, take to festivals and win all the prizes. Then they bring it over here with subtitles, get rave reviews and give out a lot of interviews about cinema as an art form. That was Alden's major reservation—too many art values, too few commercial values. He remembered now that he had some fairly big doubts about it when he first read the "coverage" of the novel, but Vincent and I used to make those offbeat properties work and we were both so enthusiastic he'd gone along with us.

"And don't forget, you two were hot then—just off a hit."

"I'm not hot enough now?"

"You're only as good as your last picture, chum."

"Isn't that pretty silly? Why aren't I as good as my second last picture?"

"*Somersault* was a while ago. The feeling gets around that you're out of touch."

"But I'm writing better now than I ever did!"

"Also you don't have a director any more."

"What if I got one—without marrying him, of course?"

"He'd have to be big and bankable." Alden sounded tentative. "He'd have to be dynamite."

To keep my spirits up I let Sidney take me to lunch to discuss "dynamite" directors. When we sat down I could tell he was depressed. Weather talk usually cheered him, but even though we spent five minutes discussing the pouring rain outdoors he kept on his long face. Over the Bloody Marys I tried to find out why.

"I shouldn't dump it on you, honey." He sighed. "Your ex-husband shafted me."

"Why attach him to me?" I quibbled. "Why don't you say your hot client shafted you?"

"I got a letter from him this morning. He's not going to renew his contract with us. He's going with Kirkwood International."

"People go from one agency to another all the time. What's so terrible about it?"

"I really did close a big deal for him last week—that's what so terrible about it."

"Did you expect gratitude as well as ten percent?"

"Worked my tail off for months on that deal. I'm hoarse from arguing with all the people I had to argue with. Producer didn't want him. Studio didn't want him. Toughest negotiation I've ever been through. Then this letter comes. I couldn't believe my eyes."

"Believe your eyes." I let myself grin. "Guess you won't mind what I say about him from now on."

"I minded because you're a lady, honey. I don't like to hear that language from a lady."

"You've got to get over two delusions, Sidney. First of all that I'm a lady. Just before lunch I saw two guys flag down a cab. I ran like hell, jumped into it from the street side and rode off."

"Oh, well, it was raining."

"Your other delusion is that Vincent is a gentleman."

"Oh, well, I guess he's got his problems."

I reminded myself that it's impossible for an agent to speak ill of a former client—there's always the chance that he might come "home" some day. Agents are fond of referring to their agencies as the client's home, trying to trigger some atavistic yearning for hearth and hot soup and being tucked in for the night. Since my own early life contained none of those—I was pulled madly apart by divorcing parents mad at each other—I always shuddered at contract-renewal time. "Just sign here," Sidney said. "This is your home. I am your family."

After we ordered, Sidney produced a yellow pad and poised his pen above it. There weren't more than a half dozen big bankable directors at the time, and he knew what each one was working on and what he was committed to do afterward. It sounded as if they were all busy for the next five years. The pad remained blank. Then Sidney announced that he, himself, had some dynamite director-clients. My heart crumpled as I read the names he scribbled on the pad. These guys were comers, Sidney said, a couple of them were working on pictures that were guaranteed (another delusion) to be smash hits! He assured me Alden would accept them if Alden knew anything about talent. He also had some actress-clients he thought would be superb for the mother. All through lunch he put together these packages made up of his clients, and all through lunch I knew it was a futile exercise. It is also impossible to dampen the enthusiasm of an agent about to present a package to a studio and, he hopes, collect a package fee. After we left the restaurant Sidney was the one who was singin' in the rain. I was the one with the long face.

It had been, at the very least, convenient, I reflected, to have one's own package right at home. As long as I was working with Vincent I'd had no idea how frustrating the search for a director could be. So many things had to fit into place. And stay in place. It was like working out a jigsaw puzzle while jogging. The director had to like the script enough to devote one or two years of his life to it. He had to be available. He had to be willing to work at a certain studio with a certain producer, often with a certain star. And everyone involved in the project had to be willing to accept him. All sorts of animosities turned up. Some of the negatives were spoken: hate his pictures, heavy-handed, left-footed, an idiot, no talent, temperamental, drinks, won't listen to anyone, always stoned, always over budget, crazy. God knows what the unspoken ones were.

When Vincent and I had gone to see Omar Lederman about *The Nearest Exit*, Vincent was the director and I was the writer. That was a "given" for the project—or so we thought at the time.

Fade-out

They rented a house in the country near the locations. It came with a housekeeper and a gardener to run it, a pool and a high-ceilinged separate studio, perfect for screening rushes. It was the first place they had lived where Lucia could imagine raising a puppy. They studied the ads in the local paper and, on the Sunday before shooting, set out to visit kennels.

The owner of the first kennel they went to, an obese woman in a tight cotton dress, carried two standard poodle puppies outdoors in her arms. They looked like black furry balls decorating her huge breasts. The male sent out beseeching, seductive buy-me signals. The female's gaze was noncommittal and reserved. After a few seconds she turned her head and stared into the distance. Even when Lucia spoke coaxingly to her she would not look at them again. She stayed in silent profile while her brother yipped and squirmed, struggling to get down. The kennel owner put both puppies on the grass. They played, cuffing each other and shadowboxing. Then the male raced around in circles demonstrating how adorable he was on his unsteady six-week-old legs. Love me, he barked, love me! The female stood still, too proud to put on such a beggar act, but when Lucia picked her up the small body was shivering and Lucia could feel the small heart racing under her hand.

"I want this one," Lucia said.

"Wait a minute, she's a standard!"

"All we've got are standards right now," the kennel owner said.

"She's a female," Vincent objected. "We said we'd get a male."

"I know."

"She's going to grow up to be a very big dog."

"I don't care."

"That can be damned inconvenient in the city."

"I don't care."

"But this is the first place we've looked!"

"I want her."

"Let's go have some coffee and talk about it."

In the end he was a pushover. He wrapped the puppy in his sweater and she rode home curled up on Lucia's lap. As he drove, Vincent continually reached over to fondle her. She almost disappeared under his big gentle hand.

"Let's call her Victoire," Lucia said.

"That's appropriate!"

Lucia thought so too—for a different reason.

They called her "Tory" for short. That summer she spent her days trotting around the locations at Lucia's heels or in their trailer. She spent her nights on the newspaper-covered floor of their bathroom. Early in the morning she watched patiently while Vincent shaved and showered but as soon as he picked up a towel she seized a corner of it in her teeth. They played a tug-of-war game, Tory rumbling with fake-fierce growls, Vincent laughing the way Lucia hadn't heard him laugh for a long time.

Later they would go downstairs and out onto the terrace for breakfast. Lucia watched them from the bedroom window—Vincent drinking coffee and making notes on the shooting script, Tory at his feet, sitting up straight and bright-eyed, not begging, simply available in case there might be donations of toast. Beyond them Lucia could see the mirror-smooth surface of the pool, blue as the clear blue sky and the little diamond flashes of dew on the grass and flowers. It was like the beginning of the world at that hour, so unspoiled and peaceful. She felt almost happy again.

The first several days of shooting went smoothly. Everyone on the crew came over after the day's work to have a couple of drinks and watch rushes. When Vincent reported to John Matheson that the rushes looked great the news was received coldly. Sometime during the second week Matheson exploded.

"Too goddamned bad you're so goddamned insecure!"

Vincent looked bewildered. "What d'you mean?"

"Why else do I have to keep out of rushes?"

"What makes you think that's the reason?"

"Omar told me."

From then on Matheson was invited to come to rushes whenever he wanted to.

On a morning of the third week while Lucia was still at home, Omar's "representative," Leo, and two teamsters drove up to the house in a truck. By the time Lucia got outside the teamsters were already carrying the projector out of the studio. She raced across the lawn, Tory bounding after her, to confront Leo.

"We're taking the projector to our motel," he told her. "From now on we'll see rushes there."

"That's ridiculous. Why?"

"More convenient."

"But everyone likes coming here. Besides, they'd have to pay for their drinks at the motel." She watched the teamsters load the projector onto the truck. "Did you ask Vincent if you could do it?"

Leo smiled. "I don't have to ask Vincent anything."

"I'll call the police! I'll have you arrested for breaking and entering!" The teamsters went back into the studio to get the screen. "Omar told you to do this, didn't he?" Leo smiled again. "Go get him, Tory!" Lucia ordered.

The ten-week-old puppy was rolling around in the grass scratching her back, but even so Leo got into the truck and rolled up the window.

"I heard what you said about me!" he shouted. "Omar had his speakerphone on so I could hear every word!"

Toward the end of the month Vincent shot the Harriet scene. Everyone was excited when they saw the rushes and watched the sexual chemistry between Matheson and Claudia Manning ignite the screen. Beyond that, the two actors also projected a haunting feeling of loss and sorrow as two messed-up people who had almost made it together. There was applause in the screening room. Even Leo was enthusiastic. He rushed to the phone to call Kusadasi.

In midsummer, Omar flew back to run the rushes. He rumbled with discontent during the first half hour, then he began to rant about everything: direction, camera angles, coverage, acting. He worked himself up to the loudest, longest tantrum of all when he saw the Harriet scene. He was infuriated by the first shot in which Claudia Manning without makeup had a bath towel wrapped around her head like a turban. "She looks ugly! Ugly! I despise ugly women!" No amount of arguing could convince him that a woman not expecting anyone to call on her would have put her wet hair up in a towel after taking a shower. His representative Leo wiped the egg off his face and promptly denounced the towel. A few minutes later Omar shouted "Too shrill! She says that terrible thing to him in a too-shrill voice!" He turned his fiery

224

eyes on Vincent. "Bad enough she says it! You guarantee the whole neighborhood hears it!"

A few weeks after the wrap, Omar flew back again to see the first assemblage. After the screening he announced there must be no discussion. Everyone must think for forty-eight hours. At the end of forty-eight hours they were informed that Omar had gone back to Kusadasi "to think." The print was never returned to the cutting room.

It took Omar six weeks to think. When he reappeared in New York and summoned them to hear the results it was soon clear that he had not only been thinking, he had been traveling. He had decided, he said, that four scenes and the ending did not work. John Matheson felt the same way but would not be available again until midwinter so the reshooting would have to be done in California. Omar had gone out there himself and found locations without palm trees. Most important of all, he had been wrong about Claudia Manning. She did not have the "right quality." He had signed Mimi Knowlton, prettier and sexier, to replace her. He also wanted the Harriet scene lengthened by ten minutes and other changes he would discuss with Lucia when they all got to California. He added, as if it were an afterthought, that Ellis Taylor had agreed to interrupt preparations on his next film and direct the reshooting. However Omar would be pleased if Vincent came along to California "to supervise."

Vincent refused to go. Lucia refused to go. They walked out of the office and off the picture.

There was nothing their agent or lawyer could do. They had signed the contract. The picture belonged to Omar. They decided Lucia would go back to work on the "Mastroianni script." After a half-dozen tries they finally reached Peter Carr in Spain, where he was producing a Western. His offer stood, he said. If Lucia would write the first draft on spec he would do everything he could to put the project together with Vincent as director. He was sorry he couldn't pay Lucia anything at this stage, but he offered them his apartment in London if they'd like to get away.

They couldn't take Tory into England. They arranged to board her in the country and leave for London at the end of the week.

Omar called Lucia every day. Each time he had a different reason why she must come with him to California. The picture was her baby —she mustn't desert it. The picture would suffer if he had to get another writer. If she came to California everyone would understand it was still a picture by the Wades. He had a project he wanted to talk to her about, very big, very important, his next picture, perfect for her to write. He began to call her twice a day. He would not take no for an answer. A few hours before they were to go to the airport Lucia went to see him.

"So! You are here to tell me you come to California!"

"I'm here to tell you what I think of you."

"You waste your time, my dear Lucia."

"Why did you fire Vincent? I want to know *why!*"

"Simple answer. The husband makes a bad picture."

"*You* made it bad! You made the script bad! You made the shooting bad! You tore down his work, demoralized him. You're reshooting some of his best scenes!"

"Somebody bleeds. Somebody gets killed. Is how you make a success."

"You're peeing in the picture."

"Never mind your little bites. I know why they come. We put them on hold."

"You're going to ruin it, Omar!"

"Come to California and save it."

"I've told you and told you I won't do that to Vincent!"

"Rescue the picture from my black heart and bloody dagger."

"You'd never understand in a million years."

"I understand for the husband you are a tigress. For the picture you are a little mouse who runs away. Your mistake, my dear Lucia, is to who you are loyal. Very few peoples in the world deserves. The husband is not one."

"Good-bye, Omar."

"Sit down. I do not finish with you. *Sit down, I said!* Two minutes, then I hope we never see each other again. You exhaust me. I despise women with opinions. I prefer young girls. They have no opinions. Now I tell you something—"

"I don't want to hear it."

"*You listen to me!* What if I exchange the tables? I fire you. Does the husband leave the picture?"

"You know the answer to that—"

"Of course I know! The husband leaves *you.* He does not leave the picture."

"That's what you think!"

"You are the most incredible cabbagehead I meet in my life! You are an American *naif.* I am a smart old Turk. I tell you the husband leaves *you!*"

"I don't have to listen to this!"

"*Listen! Learn something!* I, Omar Lederman, I lie to make my pictures. I steal, I kill to make my pictures. No woman on the earth keeps me from my pictures. Maybe I faint with love one day, the next day I go to my picture, the woman is toilet paper!"

"I certainly believe you."

"I know the husband, my dear Lucia, I smell he is my brother the first day I see him. The husband and me, we are twin brothers! I smell it with my big sharp scimitar of a nose!"

"Good-bye, Omar."

Lying in bed in the London Clinic, Vincent explained it to her. After that the two specialists explained it to her.

She understood what they said. They used words like "lipids" and "endocardium" and "lumen" and "subclavian." She understood about the overweight, the incessant smoking, the drinking—those, the doctors said, they could be sure about. Stress was probably a factor and there might be other causes they couldn't be sure about. But he was young and strong and the damage was very slight. He would recover, they promised her, he would be completely well again. Of course he would have to stop mistreating his body—no more cigarettes, only two ounces of alcohol a day, a restricted diet, exercise. Eventually, they said, he'd be in great shape, healthier than he'd ever been. She listened carefully and she understood.

What she also understood was that after all the false alarms it had actually happened. She remembered the pseudo-attack on the ship crossing the Atlantic one year, the pseudo-attack in the car driving through France another year, the sudden terrors in New York—shortness of breath walking down the street, chest pains in the middle of the night. This time it was real.

He was vulnerable.

She bought a book and examined the color plate of the heart. It looked like a Leger painting. The hollow tubes of the veins and arteries were lilac, the atria were copper-colored, the ventricles were orange, the oxygenated blood was red, the deoxygenated blood was blue.

He was vulnerable.

They kept the attack a secret because later Vincent might be considered a "bad risk," the film insurance companies could refuse to insure him, he'd be prevented from working as a director. She wrote home that he was ill with hepatitis. She told their few friends in London he had hepatitis. The rare occasions when she accepted a dinner invitation she left the phone number with the service and checked with the operator every hour. Wherever she went someone had a hepatitis story to tell. Oh, yes, she agreed, Vincent had an unbearably high temperature too. Yes, the pain. All of him was yellow, she lied, even his eyeballs, even his fingernails. The aftereffects go on for months, her friends told her, it's a ghastly disease. She agreed.

At first she stayed in Peter's apartment and tried to work. It didn't go well. Peter's lame farcical idea about an inept Italian hood bungling a caper in New York with three American girls seemed more unfunny than ever. She'd never liked it and now she couldn't keep it in her mind. It had no right there. She had to concentrate on the oxygenated blood and the deoxygenated blood. Her mind had to keep them flowing, red and blue.

He is vulnerable.

Once a day she walked a couple of miles across London to see him, taking flowers and papers and magazines and clean pajamas. He seemed turned inward, withdrawn and very pale, but the doctor said that was natural. One rainy day, she came in, dripping, to find him asleep. She stood beside the bed watching him and suddenly his chest seemed utterly still. She started to put out her hand, to hold it in front of his nose, drew it back and fled from the room to call a sister. When they rushed in his eyes were open.

"Where's the cat?" he asked.

"The cat?"

"You look like something the cat dragged in."

The sister laughed. "Cheeky little devil, isn't he?"

She didn't tell him she'd quit working on the script. She spent the days walking. She bought a map and figured out how far she could go and return within an hour—as if an hour were a magic span during which nothing could happen to him. She'd stay beside the phone for another hour and then go out again. During the first several days she sometimes felt a sharp twinge of dread on the street and would dash into the traffic to flag a cab and get home to check with the service. Wherever she wandered she seemed to go into trancelike fantasies triggered by the names of the places she happened onto. In Fitzroy Square she was suddenly Ottoline foolishly scanning the street for Lytton Strachey. In Wimpole Street she was Elizabeth Barrett at the window with Flush in her arms, yearning for Robert Browning. At Victoria Station she was Celia Johnson, her face upturned while Trevor

Howard probed for the soot in her eye. The discomfort was so real, her eye watered and tears ran down her cheeks. One day in Harrods she got off the escalator onto a floor of grand pianos. As she wandered among them she became Anne Bancroft in *The Pumpkin Eater* having a nervous breakdown in Harrods' piano department. She felt faint and dizzy, slumped toward a bench, missed and fell to the floor. The salespeople were very kind. One of them led her to the infirmary, made her lie down on a cot and put an icebag on her forehead. Later, a porter was called to escort her to the street and find her a cab. After that she stopped roaming around and went out only to see Vincent or to buy groceries or books.

One day during his third week in the hospital she found him in the corridor, a robe tied tightly around his almost-flat stomach. He had had a barber in—his hair and beard were newly clipped. Above his beard were cheekbones she'd never seen before. The sisters said he was getting well because he was complaining about the food and the rules and cutting up and, they giggled, imitating their accents. They said they felt sorry for Lucia having to put up with him when he got home and advised her to drop him off at the nearest jumble stall. Vincent said that now he knew for sure the nurse in *A Farewell to Arms* was a fiction because not one of them was nearly so beautiful or sexy as she was. Cheeky little devil, the sisters laughed.

At the end of the fourth week he was discharged and told not to travel for another month. At the apartment he read and slept and watched television. If the weather was dry they'd go out into the little square at the bottom of their street. No matter how warm the sun was he insisted on wearing a coat and a long woolen scarf wrapped around his neck. He looked so fragile and frightened, he walked so slowly it broke her heart.

For weeks after they were back in New York if she was out walking Tory or running errands and heard the scream of an ambulance siren, she'd panic and race to a phone booth to call home. When Vincent answered she made up a reason for the call or hung up. Twice in their neighborhood she saw a cluster of people gathered around a body on the sidewalk. Both times she pushed savagely past them to find a stranger lying there. Once it was a drunk cursing the crowd. The other time an epileptic, a police officer taking care of him. When she moved away her legs were shaking. During the night she'd wake up to listen to Vincent breathe or put her hand on his chest to feel him breathe.

Her head was filled with red and blue.

He was vulnerable.

She read a novel called *Somersault* written by a talented New York writer. She thought it was both significant and entertaining, with great roles for two actors and an actress, and that it would make a marvelous movie. The night Vincent finished the book he clapped it shut and tossed it to the floor.

"Same old story—middle-class adultery!" he scoffed. "Who wants to see that again?"

"It's not the same old story. It's a witty portrait of a marriage. Millions of marriages are like that today. And I'd change the ending. I don't want her to leave her lover and go back to her husband. I want her to leave them both."

"And then what?"

"She's alone. Fadeout."

"What the hell kind of ending is that?"

"A contemporary ending. It's not really an ending. It's just where the picture stops. Maybe in the last shot she's striding down Fifth Avenue and the sun is shining and the flags are flying and the doormen tip their hats to her and she's holding her head high and she's smiling. Maybe freeze frame under end credits—a close-up of her looking directly into the camera, half terrified, half triumphant, welcoming her new life."

He scowled. "I don't want to make a feminist-message picture— even if anyone'll let me."

"It's a *story!* It's a story about one woman today. *Please*, let's buy the book. I know how to write the script! I'm dying to write the script! *Please* call the agent."

The agent said other producers were after the book and named a price they couldn't possibly pay. They took the author to lunch. Vincent told her the book was a witty portrait of millions of marriages. He told her that if he made the movie he'd have the wife leave both husband and lover. That was a much more contemporary ending, wasn't it? He described how he saw the last shot and the freeze frame under end credits. The author was thrilled. He complimented her writing and quoted some of her best lines back to her, laughing uproariously. He was seductive and vigorous. The author was bewitched. Over dessert he offered her less money in front and a bigger share of the profits.

The book was theirs.

He's wonderful, Lucia thought gratefully. He's his old self again.

14

A messenger delivers a note from Vincent. He writes to inform me he is going to marry Diana and he hopes I will wish them well. Since he didn't bother to inform me when he was divorcing me I don't understand why he bothers to inform me he is marrying her. Perhaps his manners have improved, certainly his opinion of marriage. The state of matrimony has, it seems, become "viable." When anyone gets married these days I have the same reaction I had when the astronauts walked on the moon—something I wouldn't dream of doing myself but I wish them well. "The wedding," Vincent writes, "will be on Sunday, May 9th." *May ninth!* That's the date he married me!

What does it mean? Why did he choose the same date? If Diana chose it why didn't he tell her to change it? Can he have forgotten we were married on May ninth, after all the fuss we used to make, about the number 9? It was "our number" at the roulette table, at the races, for setting combination locks, for license plates, for the number of long-stemmed roses he used to send me, the ninth of any month for the commencement of shooting.

On Sunday I send him a telegram. MAY 9 MUST BE YOUR LUCKY DAY. IN BOCCA AL LUPO.

As Jeane Dixon had instructed I was accepting dinner invitations from friends or, by my definition, acquaintances. One of them was a man named Hart Weiler, who could be described, if one was lenient, as a man of letters. If one was not lenient he was a half-assed writer. He wrote little pieces on arcane subjects for little magazines, liner notes for esoteric records and travel articles. The low pay for this sort of work didn't matter since he had, as they say, independent means. Hart sent me Xeroxes of everything he wrote. His stuff fluttered out of my letter

231

box every few days along with announcements of *expositions des sculptures* addressed to my ex-husband. Diana had steered him to some pretty fancy galleries during that first rendezvous in Paris when he still thought his address was my address and not her address. These oversize shiny postcards kept dropping on me along with Hart's tearsheets on "Flemish Attitudes Toward Bigamy in the Twelfth Century" and "The Desultory Delights of the Dingle Peninsula." Junk mail.

Hart liked expensive French restaurants, the kind that employ sommeliers with whom he could have lengthy discussions in French to show off his knowledge of wines. In the sense of that statement by Edith Wharton, "If you make up your mind not to be happy, you can have a fairly good time," I had a fairly good time—eating and drinking, that is. The most boring thing about Hart was his obsessive need to talk about his ex-mistress, Cornelia. Unlike her Roman namesake, Cornelia had only one child, a ten-year-old boy. Hart didn't like children. He said he hadn't even liked children when *he* was a child. After an altercation, the last in a long series, about his refusal to play touch football in the park, Cornelia packed up her son and split. In every other way the relationship had been ideal. When they could park the boy with Cornelia's ex-husband they had traveled all over the world together, which presumably accounted for the delights of the Dingle Peninsula and of places like Maastricht and Vaduz.

One evening we got all the way to the *café filtre* without a single mention of Cornelia. At that point, he reached for my hand. He didn't take it or grasp it, he kind of smuggled it into his own. In my experience when a man treats your hand like contraband as, for example, Arnold Rivers had done, he is about to tell you something which he had decided will make you unhappy.

"This is a farewell dinner," Hart said.

"Oh? Where're you off to?"

"Cornelia and I have decided to try it again."

"Wonderful! I know how much you want that!"

"You're being an awfully good sport about it." His tone was aggrieved. "I'm not sure it'll work out."

"Of course it will!"

"What I'd like to do," he said earnestly, "is keep you on standby until I see how it goes."

I removed my hand, picked up my bag, got to my feet and left the restaurant. Once on the street I breathed in great gulps of awful, wonderful New York air and walked briskly over to Rizzoli's Fifth Avenue bookshop—open every night till midnight. I was on my way to visit my secret love, my perfect love, one of its charms being that it couldn't talk. It was a huge volume of glorious photographs of Italy and I stopped in to see it often, usually during my evening walks with Tory. I could have bought it and taken it home but I knew by then that love is lost in the act of domestication.

I was dreaming over a lyrical shot of Assisi, pink and gray, on a distant hilltop when I glanced up and into the face of the man who had helped me find the porringer weeks before. He spoke to me in fluent Italian. When I tried to answer in Italian it came out, "I am beside myself with joy to see you!" He laughed happily—the first and almost the last time I was ever to hear him laugh. We switched to English.

"Why do you have such sad eyes?" I asked.

"I'm a Hungarian," he said.

We strolled over to the Plaza for a drink. His name was Istvan Mahler. He had been born in Budapest, fled to Argentina as an adolescent during the war and finally got to America. He was now an American citizen attached to the World Health Organization. Before that, since he spoke a dozen languages, he had worked for various multinational corporations. While he told me this, clouds of middle-European angst hung in the air over our table. My circumstances at the time had made me into an aficionado of angst, so when he asked if he might take me to dinner at the end of the week, I accepted.

We went to an Hungarian restaurant in the East Eighties that advertised a Gypsy Ensemble. Istvan ordered a red *egri bikaver* (bull's blood, he said) without any discussion with the waiter about it. I liked him for that. When one of the musicians came over to us Istvan requested a csardas, "They Have Stolen the Song from My Lips," and while it was played he sang the lyric in Hungarian. The violinist bent low over our table, his bow swooped back and forth, skimming our chicken paprikas, his heavily fringed black eyes filled with tears. When the song was over Istvan put his head down on my shoulder and wept. I patted his cheek and felt my own eyes moistening. It was all, I thought, very Old World—we were characters in a Lubitsch movie. On other nights he took me to assorted Slavic restaurants and to the opera and ballet and I took him to screenings and parties. By this time I was calling him Pista, short for Istvan, and he was calling me "duck" or *"mon ange."*

Like almost all the men I've known, Pista was chronically depressed and he suffered from those old standbys, back pain and insom-

233

nia. But he never arrived to pick me up without a present—a bottle of Polish vodka he had himself treated with peppercorns, the first pineapple of the season, a recording of *Die Fledermaus*, a porcelain duck.

I was having a fairly good time.

Harvey Paul was a fiftyish entrepreneur who had gotten extremely rich on chains of shoe stores, which naturally prepared him to become a movie mogul. He was looking for a writer for an original story idea of his own, and guess who popped into Sidney's head first? So there I was back in Sidney's office listening to this guy carry on about all the "sickie celluloid" that was being ground out in Hollywood and how he was going to turn that all around with "a good old-fashioned love story like they used to make."

"What I'm aiming for is the kind of heart tug that was in *Another Sunrise*. You see that picture?"

"The one about the two paraplegics?" I shook my head.

"Grossed sixty million worldwide! How come you didn't see it?"

"I'm not mad about movies about paralyzed people."

"Paralyzed people got as much right to love as you do." Harvey gave me a distrustful glare. "Got anything against disfigurement?"

"Disfigurement?"

"How do you feel about third-degree burns?"

"Not great."

"What's the matter? You used to write heart-tug pictures yourself."

"Not with scabs."

That turned Harvey off me, for which I didn't blame him a bit, but Sidney covered up and coaxed and finally he told us his idea. The title was "Masks." "Catchy," Sidney said. The boy was a world-famous plastic surgeon. The girl was brought into his hospital with a face like a roasted marshmallow. Thanks to the wonders of modern medicine the doctor makes her a new face. When he's finished she's so gorgeous he falls madly in love with her "and wants to jump on her bones."

"Kind of a Pygmalion story," Sidney said. "Can't beat that!"

Harvey did though. He beat it to death. The girl "didn't want to be balled" because of her beautiful face, she wanted to be balled because of her "beautiful inner soul." She runs away and the doctor sets out to find her and anything you can think of that might happen from then on couldn't be as loony as Harvey's plot. The bottom line is that they both explore each other's beautiful inner souls and then they live

234

happily ever after jumping on each other's bones. Without masks.

After twenty minutes of this Harvey leaned back in his chair. "How's that for a love story about a meaningful relationship?"

I lighted a cigarette, crossed to the window and stared down at my apartment a few blocks away. *Oh, God, give me wings!*

"Catchy premise," Sidney said. "What d'you think, honey?"

"Too many scabs."

"The scabs are only in the first reel!" Harvey cried. "After that, it's all skin grafts!"

After Harvey left I implored Sidney not to ask me over to his office to hear any stories that had to do with burns, skin grafts, goiters, bowlegs, paralysis, hysterectomies, herpes, lower back pain, asthma, the lame, the halt or the blind.

Several days later I was reading a copy of *Daily Variety* when I saw that World-Wide had bought a novel called *Parnella* by Derek Northshield, "a sweeping firestorm of a story about a woman's soaring passion in a world of scarlet pleasures." *Parnella* had been on the best-seller list for thirty-seven weeks so far. I hadn't read it or anything else by Northshield, but all his books had been bought by movie companies and made into terribly successful, terrible movies. "Made" was the operative word. I rushed to the phone and rang up Alden, who miraculously was not taking a meeting. He was taking lunch.

While I waited for him to call me back I dialed Jeane Dixon again. "Hello, Libra! Superiors might be willing to grant favors today. If you have been hoping for a reasonable request to be answered this might be the day to make your pitch. The situation at home needs attention."

When Alden called I made my pitch.

"Yeah, we bought the book," he said wearily.

"I want to write the screenplay."

"Have you read the book?"

"No, but I'm dying to write the screenplay."

"You're not right for it."

"Please Alden, grant me this favor. It's a reasonable request."

"It's not your kind of thing. We want the script to follow the book exactly."

"I'll follow the book exactly."

"I know you! You'll start changing it around and putting your own ideas into it and your own integrity into it—"

"No, I won't. I won't put any integrity into it."

"What'd you say? This is a terrible connection."

235

"Alden," I shouted, "can you hear me now?" There was a framed photograph of Colette on my desk. I reached over and covered her ear. "Alden!" I screamed. *"I promise you! I promise you I won't put any integrity into it!"*

"What's the matter with you? Cracking up?"

"Selling out."

"I'm not buying, chum." He hung up.

The situation at home certainly needed attention.

The phone rang. It was Sidney, whom I hadn't heard from in a while.

"I've had an inquiry about you," he said. "These people want you for a property called *One Day and Forever.*"

"I'll do it!"

"Wait a minute, it's about—now don't hang up on me—it's about a leper colony."

"That's all right. Leprosy wasn't on my list."

"The nurse is a leper, the guy's a defrocked priest."

"Two alienated outcasts who discover love and a reason to go on living?"

"Like that."

"Make the deal."

"They're considering some other writers. . . ."

"You just said they wanted me."

"I've got to do a snow job for you. I've got to really push you, considering—"

"Push me."

"I always work my tail off for you, honey."

"Maybe I should get ten percent and you should get the writer's fee, Sidney."

"Enzo Columbo owns the book."

"Enzo Columbo? Doesn't he write film scores?"

"The man's a musical genius. Four Oscars. It'll be his first time out as a director."

"Okay, I've been on that trip."

"His American partner wants to produce. First film for both of them."

"Good! They can show me the ropes."

Enzo Columbo's *mamma* had done a job on him. He was a forty-five-year-old Italian male, which means he was five years old. Any woman over thirty automatically became his *mamma* too. At lunch in

236

the Russian Tea Room there were two of us over thirty, I and the waitress. I lost track of the demands he made on her—more caviar, more toast, more chopped eggs, another knife, another napkin, another pat of butter. He demanded her attention and he got it because he was so adorable with his funny accent and wild Latin gestures. The waitress would have liked to cuddle him against her big breasts, which of course was what he really wanted. His partner, Kurt Newman, was in the record business and had produced all of Enzo's albums. He was a roly-poly man with thick glasses and a half-moon smile which he lavished constantly on the musical genius. It was clear Enzo had cast him as the proud *papa*. I decided to stay firmly in my role as *scrittrice*.

By that time I had read *One Day and Forever* in English translation from the Italian. It was indeed set in a leper colony. The nurse's disease had run its course when the story began. She was what is known as a burnt-out case. The priest was a burnt-out case spiritually. There were many discussions about sin and the loss of God's grace between these two. All that was to be cut, Enzo said. He was interested only in the love story.

"In my movie the world is a leper colony," he explained, "and we are all diseased, mutilated, without fingers, without toes, our sores oozing into each other's faces. Only when we are in love are we not lepers. Okay?"

"Sure," I said, "it's okay with me."

Enzo stopped talking. His eyes had collided with the body conformation of a very young woman who was being seated at the next table. I watched him age to puberty, all glands engorged with hot Italian blood. Kurt turned his half-moon smile on me and winked. We waited for Enzo's detumescence, which took quite a while. The restaurant was filling up with stunning young dancers straight from their classes in Carnegie Hall. At this rate, I thought, our lunch could last till dinnertime.

Enzo turned back to me. "And when my characters fill up with emotions too deep for words they will sing what is in their hearts!"

"*Sing?*"

"Sing what they dare not speak!"

"You want to make a musical about a leper colony?"

Enzo pouted at my tone of incredulity. "I am a composer. It is a natural idea."

It was an idea only a *mamma* could love but I, thank God, was not his *mamma*.

Enzo raised his voice. "My musical is like no other musical ever

237

made! My musical is about the victory of love in the leper colony of the world!"

At the next table the young woman's head revolved on her dancer's long neck. She oozed at Enzo.

He leapt up. "Tomorrow we have another story conference!" He raised my hand, brushed his lips above it, dropped it and with a half pirouette sat down at the next table.

Kurt and I stirred the sour cream around in our bowls of borscht and ate in silence. Then Kurt said sadly, "You're not going to write it, are you?"

"I'm sorry. But you won't have any trouble getting another writer."

"I wanted you. I wanted to find out where you're coming from."

"Coming from?"

"Where you're at."

"Oh. I'm nowhere in particular."

"I'm fifty-four years old and I have a potbelly," Kurt said. He paused. He seemed to be waiting for something. His eyes behind the thick glasses were waiting.

"That's all right," I said. "That's okay."

"Would you like to have dinner and go to the movies some night?"

"After Labor Day—when I get back from East Hampton."

"No afflictions of any kind whatsoever ever again," I told Sidney. "Don't even bother to call me."

"What do you want to write about, honey?"

"About life."

"Go on."

"That's it."

"You can't tell The Money you wanna write a movie about life! Now if you say you wanna write a movie about *life on Mars*—that sounds commercial!"

"Life on earth, Sidney. About decent human beings with decent emotions."

His brow wrinkled. "That word decent—it's got overtones."

"Overtones of what, for God's sake?"

"Doesn't sound commercial. You'd never get it made. What good's it gonna do you to write a movie that doesn't get made?"

238

Dissolve

The wife, they say, is always the last to know. Or had she known without *knowing*, as they also say? Or had she not known but should have known, should have been aware enough, observant enough, should have received it on the radar of the special intuition women are supposed to have about such matters? If she hadn't known, if she hadn't even *imagined*, why hadn't she? If no scrap of thought about it had ever entered her head, why hadn't it?

Enter Diana! Lucia found herself a character in an antiquated film —"a three-hanky picture for the femmes," as *Variety* used to put it ages ago, when they dealt with the laughably Victorian plot point of adultery, instead of incest or child porn or gang rapes, all the subjects that make going to the movies so much fun today. So here she is mixed up in this fusty situation, a story she'd rather die than write, let alone live. How had she managed it? She hadn't managed it. The Husband and the Other Woman had managed it for her. They were forced to cast her as the Wife Who Is Always the Last to Know. Also, she was useful as a device for intrigue, for a comfortable soupçon of guilt, for the partings and comings together that make an affair so deliciously hazardous for married lovers—each married to someone else. There was that time, for example, in the hotel on the Côte d'Azur when, once seated in the dining room, the Husband and the Other Woman discovered two friends of the Husband and the Wife at the next table. What a charade that dinner must have been—no holding hands across the table, no blatantly melting glances over the rims of glasses—and yet how titillating to be caught out in this romantic seaport, the Wife's favorite place in the world! They had felt compelled to vanish early the next morning, but that was delicious too.

The Other Woman's Husband is also in the cast, but what his role

239

is or how he plays it is unknown to Lucia. No three of the four characters in this story are ever on camera at the same time. The whole damn thing is a series of two-scenes—except at the beginning, which Lucia didn't know was the beginning.

A dinner party on a large terrace overlooking the East River. Diana enters. Diana the Huntress, Goddess of the Chase. (This is hindsight.) She is wearing a short white tunic, a quiver of golden arrows hangs from her left shoulder and she carries a bow made of gold. No. Actually, Diana enters wearing a sleeveless white dress and carrying a little gold-mesh evening bag. Those well-developed muscles in her arms —the result of constantly drawing her bow? No. Diana is a sculptor who works with metal and the muscles are the result of wrestling with huge planks of steel. Not beautiful, not plain, she smiles a lot even when there is nothing particular to smile about—an ingenuous, disarming (who is armed?) smile. Her light brown hair is cut like a gamine's but she doesn't look like a gamine. She looks like Diana the Huntress, Goddess of the Chase. She is the kind of woman whose eyes, when one is introduced, rest fleetingly on one's face, then sweep over one's necklace, one's dress, one's shoes—a three-second checkout of designer origins. This appraising glance seems to serve the same purpose for some women as the special handclasp of secret male societies. But what is the secret? That they belong to the same charge accounts? Lucia doesn't feel any such bond with Diana. She doesn't feel anything about Diana at all. She is too busy figuring out the minimum number of hours the evening will last. It is that kind of party.

There are two tables at dinner. Diana sits next to Vincent at one of them, and the hostess, rigidly balancing things out, places Lucia next to Diana's husband at the other one. Diana's husband is very amiable, very courteous. During the first course he divides his attention between Lucia and the woman on his other side. With Lucia he talks about his country place where he raises quarter horses and jumpers. He talks about his three young daughters, who have been winning ribbons at horse shows since they were old enough to ride. When he turns away, the man on the other side of Lucia informs her that he is an investment counselor. He is a conservative person, he says, but he's got to admit the market is bullish. Interest rates are rising but not so steeply, he cautions, that they'll throw prices into a tailspin.

Lucia can hear Vincent's voice racketing through the air from the other table, excited and too loud. He is "on." He is telling amusing stories—all of which Lucia has already heard in their various forms but

240

which Diana, of course, has never heard. Appreciative gusts of laughter from Diana. He is relating an anecdote about a nutty mix-up of rooms in Palm Springs last winter, but the way he tells it he was there alone. He rarely uses the first person plural any more.

While they are having the main course, Diana's husband complains about nannies. They need someone competent because Diana works in her Soho loft every day. They have had nothing but trouble with nannies, he says, of all nationalities. The top floor of their house, where the servants sleep, has been a miniature U.N.

The man on the other side of Lucia discovers she's a writer. "Where do you get your inspiration?" he asks. "How many hours do you spend at your typewriter? How many carbons do you make?"

Salad and cheese are being served, and Vincent is talking about his great-aunt's ormolu-mounted marquetry corner cabinet. It is his most treasured possession and he frequently tells the story of how he came to own it—a story which can be condensed or expanded accord ing to the response of his audience. On this particular evening Lucia is sure it will last through to the last forkful of dessert. She hears Vincent explaining how he spotted its special beauty and coveted it when he was twelve years old or six years old—his age at the time also depends on the audience. At any rate, a couple of years ago his aunt was widowed, moved from a large house to an apartment and through some oversight the ormolu-mounted marquetry corner cabinet was sent with a load of other stuff to a Salvation Army shop. Vincent rushed over there and bought it back for a hundred dollars, or sometimes for fifty dollars. He had no idea how valuable it was until he had it appraised by an expert from Parke-Bernet who pronounced it (during this account) fifteenth-century, Louis Onze.

Wow! Lucia thinks. The ormolu-mounted marquetry corner cabinet had started out being Louis Quinze. Around 1770 was the Parke-Bernet man's estimate. But Louis Onze? Isn't that improving it too much? Did they even make marquetry in the fifteenth century? Whether Diana knows the answer or not she wisely keeps her eyes open and her mouth shut. Vincent is explaining that there are not more than a half dozen such cabinets left in the world. He believes the Vienna Rothschilds have one and there may be one in the Vatican.

The September night is soft and windless, the sky brilliant. Lucia rolls her eyes upward and spots Aldebaran, fifty-four light years away. After that it is easy to find what she is looking for—Taurus, the Bull.

"How wide are your margins?" asks the man beside her.

When they get downstairs after the party Diana and her husband have a car and driver waiting and offer them a lift home. A few minutes later they part with the usual flattering and hypocritical (Lucia thinks) assurances that they must see each other again soon.

Going up in their own elevator, Vincent says, "Interesting couple."

"I sat next to him at dinner but I never found out what he does."

"He doesn't *do* anything!" Vincent laughs. "They're both stinking rich!" His eyes are greenback green.

They walk down the hall to their door.

"Terrific evening!" Vincent says as he unlocks it.

Two days later Vincent tosses a note onto Lucia's desk. "Dear Vinnie," Diana writes, "this is just to tell you how much I enjoyed talking with you the other night. It was a real pleasure, and I hope we get a chance to do it soon again."

Lucia laughs and hands the note back to him. "Funny note!"

"What's funny about it?"

"I can't imagine writing a note like that to a married man without at least mentioning his wife as a—as a matter of manners."

That was the trouble with Lucia. She had, in this case, a failure of imagination. Dumbbell that she was, she didn't once imagine Vincent phoning Diana to give her another shot of real pleasure. And to make a lunch date.

About a month later they were invited to Diana's house for dinner. It was a five-story town house in the East Sixties, set off from its neighbors by a starkly modern facade and a Mondrianlike wrought-iron gate guarding the entrance. From the sidewalk they could see into the kitchen, where a Chinese chef in a white coat and apron was presiding over the stove.

"Oh, good!" Lucia said. "Chinese food!"

In the marble foyer a houseman took their coats and led them up a curving stairway and into the living room. The walls were blinding white, the few pieces of furniture black leather and heavy chrome, the floors terrazzo. Ceiling spots were trained on three huge steel sculptures, all painted a brilliant red, the color of blood or the Aegean Sea at sunset. Diana and her husband were waiting for them. Diana was wearing a draped white dress fastened on one shoulder with a gold clasp. She checked out Lucia's black de la Renta and Jourdan sandals but the gold chain stumped her. After her eyes had returned to it a couple of times Lucia came to her rescue.

"From a little shop near the Piazza San Marco," Lucia said. "Vincent gave it to me when we were there for the Venice Film Festival."

Diana reached over and picked part of the chain off Lucia's bosom. A few inches of it glittered across her hard palm.

"Venice Film Festival," she murmured.

With drinks in hand they toured the sculptures. The huge metal planks were beautifully welded and balanced against each other. To Lucia the first one looked like heaps of giant jackstraws abandoned by giant jackstraw players.

"Extraordinary!" Vincent exclaimed. "Like jackstraws!"

Diana was delighted with his percipience. The sculpture was called "Slanting Rain" but she immediately renamed it "Jackstraws." The other two were called "Gordian Knot" and "Red Shadows."

"They must weigh a ton," Vincent said. "I don't know how you do it, Diana."

"I'm more powerful than I look," Diana said.

They descended the stairs again to a dining room that faced a floodlit garden. Another sculpture stood in front of the glass doors. This one was unpainted, the shining steel planks resting against one perpendicular plank. It's name, Diana said, was "Hecate." *Hecate of Hell,* Lucia thought, *hark, hark, her hounds are baying!* She was seated with her back to the sculpture and kept glancing apprehensively over her shoulder, wondering what would happen if it collapsed. What would happen, she decided, was that she would be killed. Having determined the worst, she left the matter to the Fates and concentrated on the dinner.

The menu was not Chinese. It was Italian.

"Isn't this *cannellóni* terrific?" Vincent asked.

Lucia agreed. *Cannellóni*, she told Diana, was mixed into all her memories of the months they'd holed up in Rome before they sold their first film. They used to have dinner in the same trattoria every night because it was cheap and served such good *cannellóni*. It was Vincent's favorite pasta in the world.

"What a coincidence!" Lucia said.

They went back upstairs to the library for coffee. Diana took a book off a shelf and handed it to Vincent. "Read it right away," she ordered. "I think it would make a viable film. I need it back as soon as Vinnie's finished," she told Lucia, "so I'm afraid I can't ask you to read it."

"In my opinion it's not very well written," Diana's husband said.

"Vinnie says well-written books don't make good movies. If Vinnie thinks it's viable, I want to get an option on it and write the screenplay."

"Write the screenplay?" Diana's husband looked surprised.

"Why not?" Vincent said. "She's an artist! She has a fantastic visual sense!"

"But she doesn't know how to write a screenplay."

"I can learn!" Diana snapped back at him. "You had to learn, didn't you?" she challenged Lucia. "You'd never written a script before you wrote your first script, had you?" Lucia shook her head. "Of course you had Vinnie right there to help. . . ."

"He was a big help."

"Aren't there books that explain the techniques? Which ones did you use?"

"Best way to learn is to go to a lot of movies."

"What about the shots—all the camera stuff?"

"Don't bother with it. That's up to the director."

"So all you do is write dialogue?"

"It's a lot more complicated than that but—"

"Don't make it into a big deal," Vincent interrupted. "Anyone can get the hang of it from reading a few scripts."

He promised Diana he'd send some scripts over to her the next day, and then she asked him how one goes about optioning a book and the two of them talked about that while Diana's husband told Lucia about his latest venture—a building for public squash courts in the midtown area. "Squash has been an establishment game for too long," he said. "I'd like to see the streets filled with people carrying squash rackets instead of switchblades."

After a while he talked about some movie studio stock he owned and Vincent told him why that investment was nothing to toss his sweaty nightcap in the air about. All four of them discussed the film industry while they drank their last drink. Vincent recited the story about the two producers in the desert who wanted to pee in it to make it better, and Diana and her husband doubled up with laughter.

It was another terrific evening.

———

Although they had played bridge once in a while, in their nearly ten years of marriage Lucia had never known Vincent to play poker, but one day he said their lawyer, Don Chapin, had invited him to join a game. He planned to have dinner with Don before the game to get his advice about the publicity and ad campaign for *Somersault.* It became a regular thing. Vincent had dinner with Don and played poker every Thursday night.

A few weeks before the opening of *Somersault* they planned a private screening and a supper party at The Four Seasons afterward. There were only fifty seats in the screening room, which made it difficult to include everyone they wanted. Vincent crossed several old friends off the list to make room for so-called "opinion makers," but their new friends, Diana and her husband, remained on the list.

The public relations firm they had hired to help with the publicity for *Somersault* booked Vincent onto several network talk shows just before the opening. Since *Somersault* was about an ill-matched husband and wife, one of the hosts involved his panel in a discussion of marriage. Lucia sat in front of the television screen and watched Vincent announce to forty million people that he no longer believed in that kind of relationship, that marriage was simply "not a viable way of life." (He was using the word "viable" quite often in those days.) The telephone immediately began to ring. She told everyone he'd only been teasing, he'd gotten carried away, he'd tried to be amusing—it was just a joke that misfired.

When Vincent came in he laughed the whole thing off. He said he'd been fidgety and nervous, and before the show he'd had a few drinks; he said lots of people make frivolous remarks when they're on TV with a bunch of talking heads.

The next time Lucia saw the public relations people she asked why she was never used to go on television to promote the film.

"You're not our client," they said. "Your husband's our client. He made that very clear to us when he signed the contract."

Although they often went to art galleries and museums when they were in Europe, Lucia couldn't remember Vincent ever wanting to in New York. Suddenly he did want to, and that's what they did every Saturday afternoon. On weekdays he apparently continued his rounds.

"You ought to get yourself up to the Met," he'd say offhandedly, "before the Marini show closes. Talk about traditionalism combined with primitivism! Talk about phallic imagery!" or "Why don't you run over to MOMA and look at the Pollocks? And remember they're not called drip paintings. The correct term is poured paintings." "Marlborough's showing Oldenburg," he said one day. "God, what that guy can do with fiberglass and bronze!"

The catalogs he brought back piled up on his desk.

How wide are my margins?

He is in love.

"Love happens," Graham Greene wrote somewhere. "One is kidnapped by mistake." (Not always by *mistake!*) In any case Vincent was kidnapped, and there was no way to ransom him because he didn't want to be ransomed. What good would it do to mount a surprise attack with ball-point pens and typewriter along with a custom-staled familiar face, the banality of more than ten intimate years? The abductor has the most potent weapon of all: she is new to him. Her reactions to his celebrity, his screenings, his charm, his routines, his anecdotes, his jokes, his presents, his parsley are all new to him. Unknown, unpredictable and therefore inflaming.

My fault, Lucia thought. I don't respond to his tricks any more. How can I gasp as he pulls seventeen silk scarves out of his sleeve when I know how he does it? His Roman candles and catherine wheels and sparklers no longer dazzle me. There are blind spots on my retinas from watching them too often. Besides, I'm too straight for him, too ordinary and organized. I pay the bills on time and buy the Christmas presents and tip the building staff. I write thank-you notes and fill out the form for Tory's license. I'm polite to waiters. I apologize to limo drivers for their long waits. I never make a fuss in restaurants or send the frozen crabmeat back to the kitchen. I sit at the typewriter. I meet the deadlines. I order the slipcovers. I store the winter clothes in mothproof bags. I'm sensible. I'm tame. I bore him.

He adores theatrics. He grooves on spectacles. How much more alluring I'd be if I had a gift for creating Events—if I plunged naked into the fountain at Rockefeller Center waving a bottle of Romanee-Conti, if I shoplifted diamonds in Cartier to pay for a coke habit. How much more intriguing if I swallowed thirty sleeping pills so he could play savior with the ambulance and stomach pump. Perhaps I could hook his attention if I seduced the doorman or joined the Moonies or withdrew all the money in our joint account and ran off to Fez with a Swedish actress. Best of all, if I went crazy he'd be crazy about me

246

for my craziness. He'd come to Silver Hill on visiting days with nine long-stemmed roses and nine jars of fresh caviar and his eyes would mist over and he'd be into his Eye Number.

Maybe it was to foil his goddamned Eye Number that she stayed sane.

So he was in love.

And *Somersault* opened to rave reviews and became their biggest hit.

He should have been a happy man, but he didn't seem happy while he was shooting in Dublin. He was having trouble with the actors who were having trouble with their friend's script, and then he had Lucia rewriting it, and then he had trouble with their friend.

After three weeks Vincent told Lucia to stop rewriting. He reminded the actors that they had signed to do the script as written and he insisted that he was going to shoot the script as written. He told Lucia to go back to work on *Mixed Blessing*.

15

The newspaper again. The food page again. Vincent again. There is a large photograph of him wearing a chef's apron but I can't see his new shape because he's mostly hidden by a huge stove on which is a huge pot into which he is plunging a huge spoon. His beard, I notice, is brushing Diana's cheek as she stands very close to him smiling into the pot. Around this photograph are smaller shots of people captured in the act of tossing salads, pouring sauces, slicing patés and plucking goodies from a loaded buffet table. "Guests Bring Own Specialties and Recipes," the headline says and underneath, "Unique Buffet Supper at the Vincent Wades." A few years ago the Vincent Wades gave the identical supper party with almost the identical coverage. At the time, needless to say, there was a different Mrs. Wade.

As I glance through the text, I see, as is to be expected, that the recipes are different too. A few years ago there were directions for making "Vincent and Lucia Wade's *Mousse de Foie Gras*"—about 1,000 calories per portion. This year it is "Vincent and Diana Wade's Breast of Duckling with Fresh Figs." The figs, I read, are stewed in wine plus artificial sweetener and the ingredients in the sauce include non-fat dry milk, low-fat cottage cheese and low-fat yogurt. Sounds delicious. I clip it out and pin it up on the corkboard in my kitchen. It appears that my life with Vincent is being, as they say on television, rerun. He's had the identical parties for opinion makers after the private screenings of his films, only now Diana is the hostess. When one of the films was accepted by the Venice Festival, Diana went to Venice. In a recent magazine piece about men who cook there was a photograph of him kneading dough for a *boeuf en croûte* in Diana's kitchen.

"Happy families are all alike," Tolstoy said. Are they ever! At least in the early years.

Sidney is screaming at me, something he's never done before. *"It is not an affliction!"* he screams. *"It's a dysfunction!"*

"I'm not gonna let you say no to this one," he screams, "because this one's gonna get *made!*"

"The money's big bucks!" he screams.

"Get off your ass and go to that fuckin' meeting!" he screams. He's never used four-letter words with me before either.

"One question, Sidney. Why don't they get a male writer?"

"Male writers don't wanna touch it!"

"Why?"

"If a guy writes it everyone's gonna think he's got it."

"So what?"

"This is a very delicate subject!" Sidney screams. "A man can't handle this subject!"

I go to the meeting.

Gil Harrison, the handsome top-level network executive in charge of the project, seems like a nice guy. They all seem nice at the first meeting. He is flanked by two younger associates. They are all always flanked by two younger associates. I've never figured out why. Is it to avoid loneliness at the top? Is it to have witnesses to these world-shaking discussions? Is it to intimidate the writer? The associates have the same faces as Omar Lederman's Young Turks—stony and impassive. They rise as Gil comes around an enormous glass table-desk to shake hands with me. When we're all seated Gil points out that my blue-and-white striped shirt is exactly like his blue-and-white striped shirt. His is from André Olivier. Mine's from Dorso's in Beverly Hills. Gil tells me the latest Beverly Hills funny story about the couple out there who has everything: mansion, pool, Jacuzzi, Picassos, Rolls-Royce, etc. "Darling," the husband says one day, "if I lost it all would you still love me?" *"Of course* I'd love you!" the wife replies. "I'd *miss* you but I'd love you!" We laugh. Even the two associates, who've probably heard it several times, laugh. Maybe that's what they're there for.

Finally Gil gets down to business and lays out the concept. What he wants is a two-hour teleplay about a happily married couple ("Let's call them Jim and Nancy Marshall") in their early thirties. Suddenly

Jim develops this sexual dysfunction every time he makes love to Nancy. It gets so bad he's afraid even to try. He turns off. The marriage is on the verge of ruin. In desperation Jim consults a therapist who specializes in problems like his. The major part of the drama will show him in treatment learning what it is that caused his problem and the techniques he and his wife can use to help him get over it. I must've looked puzzled then, because Gil assured me that the research has already been done and they would give me all the books when I left. The bottom line of the story is that Jim Marshall is cured and the marriage is saved.

The story, Gil said, could go along any way I wanted it to within the limits of good taste. "There'll be lots of things you can't really get into," he tells me. "You'll have to cut away in the physical scenes and be sort of subtle about what's going on—but not too subtle. My Aunt Norma's got to understand it. Two minutes after she turns on her set my Aunt Norma's got to dig exactly what Jim's trouble is."

A little while later I stagger up Sixth Avenue under a load of oversized books. Their titles can be read from twenty feet away: *Sex Therapy Today, Male Sexuality, Sexual Behavior in the Human Male, The Sensuous Man, Illustrated Manual of Sex Therapy*. No one on the street gives me a second look.

This is New York.

A few days later contracts are drawn up and I find myself hired to write a two-hour film for television about premature ejaculation.

I decide to write the television script in East Hampton, where I've rented a house for the summer. My daughter, Jane, is going to stay with me. She is writing something, she won't say what, but it is definitely not a screenplay. ("I could never be a total doormat like you.") We move into the house with our typewriters and our dogs (Jane's is a Cairn named Daisy) and plan to have a productive summer: work during the week, fun and guests on the weekends. I invite Pista, whom Jane has never met, out for the Fourth of July weekend.

On Friday evening I drive to the station to meet the train. It arrives at six from New York and is rather archly known as the "Daddy Train." The platform is crowded with mothers and children. Most of the mothers have vertical lines in their foreheads, as if they have spent the week frowning. They have tight mouths too. I suspect they've also spent the week hoarding up grievances for Friday night.

There are many people like me meeting weekend guests. I notice a handsome, slender woman in an immaculate white jump suit. Her

250

ash-blond hair is drawn back and tied with a blue ribbon. Her tan is the color of apricots. I see her in a flash of film clips—perfect backhand on the tennis court, perfect crawl in the pool, in the candlelight over a perfectly grilled lobster, gold hoops in her perfect earlobes. The train is chugging toward us. The children dash to the edge of the platform. The mothers yank them back. The handsome blonde lights a cigarette and gazes dreamily up the tracks. Or is it sensuously?

I see Pista before he sees me. He's wearing gray flannels and a gold-buttoned blazer, a polished leather suitcase large enough to take him around the world in his hand. He looks elegant in contrast to the daddies in their wrinkled seersucker suits with tattered newspapers under their arms. The shrieking children mount an assault. The daddies put on phony daddy smiles. Pista smiles too—his genuine gloomy smile —and, wincing with back pain, hands me his suitcase.

The blonde is talking to a muscular bronzed man with fans of squint lines around his eyes. He joins her in my film clip on the deck of a yacht racing in first for the America's Cup. As we pass them I hear the blonde snarl wrathfully ". . . because I had your phone bugged, you prick!" It seems the movies in my head are as phantasmagorical as the ones on the screen.

On the way home Pista tells me he has been to three doctors this week. One says he has a slipped disk, one says it's a pinched nerve, the third doesn't say what it is but recommends traction. He goes on about the doctors until we drive up to the house. Then he steps out of the car and hurries toward the door. I bump into Jane as I struggle inside with his suitcase.

"Why didn't you call me to do that?" she asks. Then in a lower voice. "He's very *European,* isn't he?"

Melissa, a friend of Jane's who dropped out of college, joins us for dinner. She has been living at the beach for a year with a local youth named Doug and her Irish setter named Red. In the winters she reads. In the summers she works for a caterer helping to make and sell delicacies to the summer people. She says she is content with her life. Her only complaints are about the Public.

"The Public," she tells us as we sit around with our drinks, "was extremely cranky today."

"You mean rude?"

"They're rude every day. This was on a different level. They were dreadfully nerved up."

"What is it, nerved up?" Pista asks.

251

"They behaved like miserable sons of bitches," I explain.

Pista nods. "Fortunate people are spoiled people."

"They were pleading for barbecued ducks and chocolate chiffon cake. They were practically down on their knees for smoked salmon at twenty dollars a pound." Melissa looks shocked. "They held out trembling hands imploring us to put paté into them."

What is left of a pound of the aforementioned paté is on a platter on the coffee table. Pista makes an imperious gesture toward me and for about the fifth time I spread some for him on a triangle of bread, ignoring Jane's dark look.

"What's wrong with the Public is that it's a holiday weekend," I tell Melissa, "and everybody has houseguests."

"And they suddenly realize what hell it's going to be until Monday night," Jane says. How can she tell? I wonder. Pista's only been in the house an hour.

"If people feel that way, why do they invite guests?" Melissa asks.

"There are a number of reasons," Jane murmurs mysteriously.

"This paté is delicious," Pista says.

The following morning I am making coffee in the kitchen which is next to the first-floor guest room when Pista comes in. He kisses my hand.

"How'd you sleep?" I ask, an automatic hostess question and a mistake.

"Like a rock—"

"Oh, good!"

"Only until two in the morning. Then the dogs barked and woke me up."

"Must've been when Jane came in from that party."

"I tossed and turned. I could not get back to sleep."

"I'm sorry."

"I crept upstairs and knocked at your door but you wouldn't let me in."

"I didn't hear you."

"So I came back downstairs. It was five thirty before I got to sleep but then I slept until twenty to nine." He takes the glass of orange juice I hand him. "You, I know, slept well."

"Eight hours," I answer meanly.

He sighs. "You are a fortunate woman." He drains the glass and puts it down on the table. Then he grasps my shoulders and kisses me.

I kiss him back because I feel guilty about not answering last night when I heard him knock.

We're having a heat wave. I'm sitting at the typewriter in my bedroom dripping with sweat, suffocating in the hot heavy air. And I'm blocked. I can't write. I can't get with the badly timed disorder in Jim Marshall's private parts. The network's division of Standards and Practices, I've been told, will go along with the term "private parts" but not with any specific anatomical words. I shall have to become a master of euphemism and turn out 120 pages of script on the penis without mentioning the penis.

Part of the trouble is that I'm impatient with Jim Marshall. Why doesn't the poor bastard stop agonizing about it? Why does he make it into a federal case? How come his entire male self-image depends on the procrastination of a little muscular spasm? Why doesn't he run away from Nancy or enter a monastery or, for God's sake, give up sex —which sounds like a super idea on a day like this. In fact it's sounded like a super idea to me personally ever since I began to write about Jim. Like him, I am turned off. It has led to some misunderstanding with Pista, even though I've explained that this kind of thing happens to writers. "I am Madame Bovary," said Flaubert. "I am Jim Marshall," say I. Oh, God!

I squint out at the pool where Pista is doing a breaststroke which is good for his back. The dogs, half crazed from the heat, bark at him when he reaches the end of the pool. Then they gallop groggily back to the other end and wait to bark at him again. I know they torment him, but short of penning them up there is no way to stop them.

From Jane's room I hear a flurry on her typewriter. Sunk in Jim's despondency I whimper back on my own. Jane continues typing *con brío*. A sexy neighbor makes a pass at Jim. I type *con agitazióne*. We continue this nutty duet until a car drives up to the house and Jane runs downstairs. A minute later I hear voices below my back window. Jane's is indignant. Melissa's is hysterical. I rush out to the terrace to find out what's wrong.

Melissa's story tumbles out. The bottom line is that Doug has fallen in love with a fifteen-year-old girl he met on the beach. Melissa's thin shoulders hunch with pain. "He says he prefers younger women and he smiles all the time. He says he can't help smiling because he's so happy." She grinds her cigarette out among the fallen apples. "He keeps telling me he wants to be free."

"You can't go on living with him," Jane says.

"You and Red move in with us," I tell Melissa. When she throws herself into my arms I feel I'm embracing a part of myself.

Later I explain to Pista what Doug is like. "A handsome beach bum with a totally blank mind. Never reads a book—barely got through high school. He hires out for odd jobs around here."

"Why does Melissa love him?"

"Why does anybody love anybody?"

"And she is bringing her dog?" He sighs. "How you love dogs!"

I nod. "You don't?"

"I was fleeing for my life during my youth. I was not fortunate enough to be a normal boy with a dog."

It's six o'clock. As they did yesterday, Jane, Melissa and Pista are going to the beach. As I did yesterday I refuse to go with them.

"Put yourself in the sea," Pista coaxes. "It feels different from the pool."

I shake my head. I know how it feels.

"You haven't been to the beach since we moved out here," Jane says.

"I've been everywhere, duck. This is the most beautiful beach in the world."

I know how it looks. A ten-minute walk on the white sand and we came to a spill of slippery black rocks stretching out into the water. Up on the cliff opposite the rocks is a flagpole and behind it a rambling gray-shingled cottage. At the base of the cliff there's a natural sandy hollow in the dune grass. Loaded with a blanket, towels, a hamper, Vincent and I used to trudge up there every day, Tory frisking ahead of us. That was the summer Vincent was cutting *Somersault* and we'd rented a big house with a glassed-in sun-room large enough to hold his movieola and editing tables. He worked all morning with the editors and then we'd go to the beach for lunch. We swam and drank wine and read and slept. I remember Tory dashing into the surf for her ball and then back to us and that shower of icy drops when she shook herself. I don't remember what we talked about or thought about. We were just there—like the sea and the sun and the sand.

"If you change your mind drive over and join us," Pista says. I watch them pile into Melissa's car with the three dogs. After they're gone I walk out onto the terrace with a drink. Deliberately, I choose a chair under the apple tree. Maybe an apple will drop on my head and, as an apple did for Newton, knock a bright idea into it. Namely, that if I want to stay away from all the beaches in this world where I was happy or unhappy with Vincent I'll have to establish residence in Patagonia.

The three of us have come back from a dinner party a little smashed. Pista sits down at the piano. Like all pianos in rented houses it is out of tune, and Pista plays by ear. All the same we like his schmaltzy repertoire. Melissa and I swoop around the room to "The Blue Danube Waltz." Pista changes to something from *Die Fledermaus*. *"Klange der Heimat,"* he says, "Sounds of the Homeland." We improvise a csardas until we are out of breath. When he switches to a bossa nova we dance to that. He plays on and on. The girls wander off to the kitchen to fix nightcaps. I fling myself down on the sofa to rest.

Pista returns to *Die Fledermaus*. *"Rosalinde, meine teuerste Rosalinde."* His voice throbs and quavers. I peer around the back of the sofa and see him look up from the keyboard. He can't see me stretched out flat on the cushions. His face darkens with chagrin when he thinks he is abandoned. But he's not quite abandoned. The three dogs are sitting attentively beside the piano stool, their muzzles twitching in the air, their glittering eyes fixed on him. He glares daggers at them. Suddenly he stops in the middle of a chord and slams down the empty music stand. He rises and spreads his arms wide in a grand-opera gesture of despair.

"La commèdia," he shouts at the dogs, *"la commèdia è finita!"*

On Sunday morning Pista is at the pool doing his back exercises. I am having breakfast on the terrace when Jane and Melissa and the dogs come back from the village with *The New York Times*. Jane puts the paper down on the table. Melissa takes the leashes off the dogs, and Daisy and Red dash off toward the pool to bark at Pista. Tory stays because she sees I'm eating. The two girls, faces flushed from the heat, draw up chairs and I pour coffee for them.

"What's new on Main Street?" I ask.

"Better ask what's new at the end of our lane," Jane answers. Her voice, I reflect, has been ominous all weekend.

"What's new at the end of our lane?"

"Your most recent ex-husband is living there." I stir my eggs around on my plate. "It's the first time I've seen him since his transformation," Jane says.

I give up on the eggs and burn my mouth on a swallow of hot coffee. "How does he look?"

"He looks . . ." She stops to pinpoint the exact word. *"Suburban."*

"His wife," Melissa says, "was riding up and down in front of the house on her bike. She smiled at us. She smiled the whole time we were standing there."

"What did Tory do when she saw Vincent?"

"Nothing whatsoever. Ignored him."

"Are you saying that to please me?"

"Mother," Jane says, "it pleases me to please you but I never lie to please you."

"Didn't she wag her tail?"

"She didn't even glance at him. She stared into the distance."

I lean over and hug Tory. Annoyed, she dodges away from me and refastens her avid eyes on my plate. I give her a strip of bacon. "What did Vincent do?"

"He sort of held out his hand, but before he could touch her his wife said, 'Don't do that—you'll stir up her old memories.' "

"God! She tells him how to behave with his dog!"

"Tory hasn't been his dog for years. Any more than you've been his wife."

"He certainly isn't the man you were married to," Melissa says. "He doesn't look like him or sound like him."

"Or apparently smell like him." I put my plate down on the flagstones, and we watch Tory clean up the rest of the eggs with noisy wolfish gulps.

"That's the only time she seems like a dog," I say. "When she eats."

"She's a dog," Jane says, "but a dog with *integrity.* "

That evening I go along to the beach. After our swim we take the dogs for a walk past the spill of black rocks and the flagpole. The little crescent carved out of the bottom of the cliff is still there. The dune grass is still there. From the corner of my eye I see on the sand a torn bathing cap and a couple of empty beer bottles glowing red in the reflection of the sunset. I walk past the place without any feeling at all. It's just an anonymous sandy hollow like a thousand others up and down the beach. That's all it is.

"If only I'd never tried to unlock Doug's brain," Melissa moans.

"Does he have a brain?" Jane asks.

"If only I hadn't forced him to read *Wuthering Heights!*"

We are eating corn on the cob and waiting for dark to go to a beach party and watch fireworks.

"After he read it he started to think of himself as a Heathcliff type." Jane and I pop eyes at each other. "Now you may remember the last name of the girl Heathcliff falls in love with is Earnshaw—which happens to be Doug's girl friend's last name, only it's spelled differently."

"Which doesn't matter," Jane says, "because Doug can't spell."

"My deduction is that the book gave Doug dangerous ideas."

"Are you agreeing with the Nazis?" Pista demands belligerently. "Are you saying books should be burned?"

I can't bear his literal-mindedness. When I say so his feelings are hurt. We exchange a few unkind words and glower at each other over our corncobs.

Pista puts his down and pushes his plate away. " 'It is bleak,' " he says, " 'it is dark. Nothing lies ahead.' "

"Oh, stop that."

"I am quoting Dostoyevsky. I would not expect you to understand—you and your fortunate life." He frowns at the girls. "Nor you two—*jeunesse dorée.*"

"*Jeunesse dorée!*" Melissa bursts into tears and runs out of the room.

Jane reaches for the butter. "I like that quote. I'm going to use it as an epigraph for my autobiography."

"You can't use it," Pista tells her. "For you life is not a tragedy."

"Not yet," Jane agrees, "but soon, I hope."

When we get home after the fireworks Pista pointedly does not kiss me good night but hurries down the hall to his room. As I switch off the lamp I see that one of the dogs made a mistake on the floor. Pista must have stepped on it because the little pad is squashed flat. Should I get a paper towel and clean his shoe? I get a paper towel and clean the floor instead. As I climb the stairs to my room I decide that deep down I am a petty-minded person.

On Monday Melissa comes home from work with a bruise on her cheek and a holiday weekend horror story. She tells us that a woman sped up to the caterer's in a Mercedes and rushed inside just as Melissa was selling the last of the ziti salad. The woman's eyes swiveled frantically back and forth from the tray to the container Melissa was packing.

"Bitch!" she screamed. "You aren't saving me even one little noodle!" Then she pitched her keys into Melissa's face.

In spite of this injustice Melissa looks uncharacteristically happy. She has heard from Doug. She hasn't exactly heard from him but she saw him when he came to the caterers to collect the garbage. "He brought me a strawberry," she tells us. "Without a word, he put this strawberry into my hand and went away. I take it as a reason for optimism," she says. "I take it as a message of love."

An hour later I'm sitting on a bench in the village with Pista waiting for the jitney that will take him back to New York. His expression is even more melancholy than usual—not because the jitney is late but because there are now certain tensions between us.

I crane my neck. "Where can it be?"

"Please don't wait. You have far better things to do."

"No, it's just that I hate long good-byes."

"The ultimate long good-bye is death," Pista says. "I saw the movie."

At that moment the jitney careens around the corner and stops in front of us.

Pista kisses me on each cheek.

"I'll call you tomorrow morning," he says, "and let you know how I slept." Just before he boards he presses a clump of Kleenex into my hand. I wave good-bye.

La commèdia è finita!

I open the Kleenex and find a strawberry.

Is it ever finished?

Final cut

"If we can stay friends," Vincent said, "it would please me very much."

He'd toss his sweaty nightcap in the air!

"No reason not to be sensible about the situation."

That's what brought me down. Being sensible.

"We can leave the details to lawyers and separate like civilized people."

And assure our dog that each of us will love her just as much as ever.

"I'll always consider what we had together as a very precious chapter."

His life is a book.

"We opened an important parenthesis and now we're closing it."

I am punctuation.

"Nothing lasts forever. Everything has to end."

Was he always so pompous?

"So let's resolve the whole thing with good taste."

Which means I silently fade away.

"Too boring," Lucia said.

"Beg your pardon?"

"Suppose I wrote a scene about a husband and wife splitting up? If the characters did it with good taste the audience would cough. They'd run out to buy candy bars or go to the bathroom."

"This isn't a film, my dear."

"How do you know?"

"Come on! If you're not going to discuss it like a rational person I'd better go."

"If you go I could have the splitting-up scene take place off camera

259

and perhaps substitute a confrontation scene between the Wife and the Other Woman."

"I hope you're not suggesting—I hope you don't intend to—it wouldn't be at all in good taste for you to confront Diana."

"What is your brand-new obsession with good taste?"

"That's exactly the kind of rancorous remark I wanted us to avoid."

"Why? Can't my dialogue be at least half as lively as movie dialogue?"

"Forget about the movies, will you? You're not writing a scene."

"You're not directing one either."

The solution came to Lucia a few days later. Not in the middle of the night when, according to the mystique, writers are supposed to get their best ideas. "Where do you get your inspiration?" The man at the terrace dinner party had stumped her with that question. Now she could give him an answer. This one came to her in broad daylight in Herman's Sports Shop where she was looking for a warm-up suit to send to her son. She would create an Event. She would write a movie ending to her life with Vincent. And she would cast it, direct it and produce it as well. With this one scene she would become an *auteur* at last. Since Vincent was so turned on by spectacles it would be her farewell present to him, the last thing she would ever do to please him.

When she got home she went straight to the phone and rang up Diana. She explained her idea. "It's a contest," she said. "With action, with visuals, without dialogue. Pure cinema."

Diana didn't see the point at first. "Why should we have a contest?" she objected. "I've won him already. He's here."

"The outcome won't change anything. You'll win him all over again."

"Why should I do it twice?"

"Because this is drama, Diana! Bigger than life! You'll win him fair and square this time. You'll demonstrate your superiority in public and show everyone you deserve him much more than I do."

That appealed to Diana. Gradually, she became enthusiastic, and in another two minutes she was urging Lucia to go ahead and rent a school gymnasium on a Saturday. They began to discuss details.

"We can buy suction-rubber-tipped arrows at Herman's Sports Shop," Lucia said, "but even so Vincent should wear a fencer's mask and a fencer's padded jacket for protection. He can draw a target on the jacket."

"Great idea! I'll buy him a red Magic Marker."

"I plan to wear a black leotard—like Masha, I'll be in mourning for my life—and tennis shoes."

"Topsiders or Adidas?"

"My old ones."

"That's okay," Diana said graciously. "You must start economizing. I assume you won't ask Vincent for alimony. I'm not asking my husband for alimony. I've already told Vincent that I would never ask *him* for alimony."

"Odd that you discussed it."

"The rich are different!" Diana snapped out the line without attribution.

"To get back to the subject, Diana, I suggest you wear a short white tunic—"

"And my gold sandals laced around my legs with gold thongs."

"Nice touch. My cheerleaders will be in black with black pom-poms. Yours should be in white with white pom-poms."

"My fans can sit on benches along one wall and your fans can sit on benches along the opposite wall."

"The entire Event won't take more than twenty minutes. There'll be plenty of time afterward for people to go on to art galleries or bicycle around the park."

"Hold on a minute," Diana said. Lucia could hear her telling Vincent about their conversation. He came to the phone himself.

"I'll take care of the publicity!" He sounded excited. "I'll call Rona Barrett! I'll get *Variety* to cover it! I'll feed Liz Smith some items! I'll invite a top-notch photographer from Magnum!"

Diana got back on the line. "Who's going to referee?"

"Referee?"

"I don't trust your eyesight and I'm sure you don't trust mine." Lucia's shrink would have said Diana was projecting. "You've got to find an objective person with perfect vision to referee."

Lucia thought for a moment. "I'll put an ad in the personal column of *The New York Review of Books.*"

Vincent grabbed the phone. "I'll have flyers printed up and hire a couple of kids to hand them out in front of Bloomingdale's!"

"But," Lucia objected, "do we want just anyone?"

"If we get a crowd the networks will cover it! We'll be on the six o'clock news!"

When the next issue of *The New York Review of Books* appeared on the stands, Lucia's ad was in it between "Warm, vibrant woman seeks erotic interval with warm vibrant man, Jewish preferred" and "Lonely professor desires cheerful nymph for sharing roses and Mozart, wine and Ovid." Lucia's ad said, "Wanted: referee for competitive event. No experience necessary. Applicant must have perfect eyesight. Call 212-555-7598." She hired the first person who phoned, a man who swore he had 20/20 vision. She gave him the particulars of time and place and fee and requested that he appear in a dark suit. He sounded hesitant about that. He had, he admitted, one dark suit but he wore it only once a year on—"Make it twice," Lucia interrupted and cut him off because she was in a hurry to collect her fans.

These calls did not go well. A pronounced the whole idea sick and refused to attend. B was allergic to the smell of sweat socks and loathed anything that took place in a gym. C thought it sounded depressing and she was already on four Equanils a day. D thought it sounded amusing but she had to stay home and wait for her pillow furniture to be delivered. E had a deadline for her *New York Magazine* piece on angel-dust pastries. F had to be at his country house to install a butcher-block kitchen counter with built-in disposal. G had an appointment at the vet's—her declawed cat had developed a severe biting problem. H always spent Saturday with his daughters. He was afraid his ex-wife would cancel his visitation rights if he took them to anything gory.

"There won't be any blood. The arrows are rubber."

"I don't want my girls to get the idea that the way to win a man is to be good at archery."

"Is there a better way?"

"The whole man-woman thing's a crap shoot," H said. But he wouldn't come.

Lucia didn't invite her shrink because her shrink would want to know why Lucia considered everything in her life primarily as material for a film script and in that way avoided really experiencing her experiences. "Film is truth at twenty-four frames a second" did not cut any ice with her shrink. All the talk would cost money that Lucia wouldn't have after renting the gym, paying the referee and her cheerleaders and buying a bow and three arrows at Herman's Sports Shop.

On the day of the Event Lucia arrived with Tory but without fans. After their initial consternation her cheerleaders rallied and performed as planned. "Give us an L! Give us a U! Give us a C! Give us an I! Give us an A!" Tory dropped her ball and barked. The cheerleaders shouted "Lucia!," leapt into the air and shook their pom-poms. The photographer from Magnum ignored them all. They were not his clients, and besides that chapter was closed.

On Diana's side of the gym the stands were jammed and the ambiance was festive. Some people had brought wicker hampers and were unpacking smoked Scottish salmon sandwiches and iced vodka. Many of the others were popping champagne corks and passing the wine around in plastic glasses. There were several couples with picnic baskets packed by Lutece and Chez Honorine. One balding man with a dark-skinned curly-haired young girl had a silver platter on his lap. The two of them seemed to be sharing a poached bass. *A poached bass?* Lucia put on her glasses. It was Omar and Denise Gilmore! As she scanned the rows she recognized more faces. She saw the Contessa Pigazzi and, by standing on her toes and stretching her neck, she could just barely get a glimpse of Quentin Moore's yellow locks. There was a whole planeload of people there from California, the Gilberts and Paul what's-his-name and Cam Alcott and Iris McKenzie. John Buckley sat at the end of their row swigging drinks from a flask. Lucia was surprised to see the nurses Vincent had had in London—perhaps they had come on Laker Airlines. There were also dozens of strangers stuffing popcorn into their mouths. The Public, Lucia thought, the people who had happened to be in front of Bloomingdale's at the right time.

The referee turned up in a dark suit with a rose in his buttonhole. He was a middle-sized man with a leprechaun's face. Lucia stared at him for so long he asked if something was wrong.

"Your eyes are green!"

"You didn't specify a color."

"I ought to fire you!"

"My eyes are gray," he assured her quickly, "with flecks of blue and yellow that *appear* green."

Fast talker, she thought. She could tell he needed the job—his suit was too small for him, shiny at the elbows and knees. Anyway, it was too late to fire him. She thrust a whistle into his hand.

"I've brought along a tape measure," he told her. "It's marked out in millimeters."

"That was unnecessary," she said coldly.

They were interrupted by the White cheerleaders, who were screaming like crazy. Diana had appeared in a tunic of shining white satin wearing her gold sandals and quiver. The photographer's camera flashed as she strode back and forth in front of the cheering crowd, glacial and perfect and unconcerned. Suddenly there was another huge burst of applause and all eyes were on Vincent making an entrance in his mask and padded jacket. Instead of a target on the jacket he had drawn a large heart and filled it in with red. He removed the mask to pose for the photographer, his teeth gleaming in the ginger nest of his beard.

When everything had quieted down he took his place at one end of the gym. Diana and Lucia walked to the center of the floor and shook hands. Diana's eyes slid along Lucia's Danskin leotard downward.

"Black legs and white feet! You look like Mickey Mouse."

"We agreed on no dialogue. Remember, Diana?"

"Vinnie says audiences get off on noble characters of exalted stature."

It sounded more like Aristotle than Vincent, but Lucia kept to their agreement and said nothing.

The referee was blowing his whistle. Diana stepped up to the white line first. Exuding a kind of drop-dead hauteur she drew her bow. Her arrow flashed through the air, struck the center of the red heart and stayed there, its feathers quivering. Vincent's body had trembled under the impact like the trembling of lovemaking. The fans screeched with joy. The referee shouted "Bull's-eye!" and ran up to grasp the arrow. It made a loud rubbery *plop* as he removed it.

Lucia stepped up to the white line. When she took aim the heart on Vincent's jacket faded out of focus and instantly the color plate she had pored over in London was superimposed. There's been a misunderstanding, she thought, I didn't order any special effects. Nevertheless there they were—the atria and the ventricles, the oxygenated and deoxygenated blood, the red and the blue. She squeezed her eyes shut to blot them out and released her arrow. It arched ceilingward, glanced off the basketball backboard, plummeted down and slithered along the floor. Laughter and groans from the crowd. Quentin Moore climbed up onto his bench.

"Should've had your pores cleaned, sweetness!" he shrieked.

The referee crawled under a trampoline to recover the arrow.

Diana's second arrow struck the bull's-eye again and again the same business. Vincent trembled. Cheers and whistles. The referee did his job.

Lucia squinted along her second arrow. The Magic Marker heart remained in focus but the sound track was out of sync. Against the background murmur and rustle she could hear Vincent's voice in her ear. "God, you're going to be dynamite at fifty!" He sounded ten years younger and far away as if he were on the other side of the planet. It was a rotten job of dubbing because she could see his lips weren't moving. "I'll love you even more at fifty!" he said. She let fly her arrow to shut him up. The arrow sped sideways, fortunately toward her own empty benches, and ricocheted from one to the other, plopping and clattering.

Omar stood up in the stands. *"Why you do not put yourself on hold?"* he roared at her.

The arrow came to rest at Tory's feet. Tory snatched it up in her teeth and stood irresolute, not knowing whether to take it to Vincent, who had taught her to retrieve sticks, or to Lucia, who fed her and brushed her and ordered her bones from the market. A broken family, Lucia thought, and its divided loyalties! She was wondering if Tory would have a nervous breakdown when suddenly she realized that according to their preset rules (two out of three) the Event was over. The fans were mobbing Diana. Vincent raised her to his shoulders and started to bear her triumphantly around the gym. Everyone else streamed off the benches and fell in behind, joggling and kicking in a sort of frenzied conga line. At its tail end was a little man with little shiny shoes. "That woman is a star!" he was howling. "I want that star's autograph!"

As the line zigzagged back and forth a tanned man with corrugated waves of silver hair bared his perfect teeth at Lucia. "You don't know beans about archery," he shouted, "but you can write a script for me!" After he'd been swept along for several yards he twisted his head around to look back at her. *"On spec!"* he screamed. Someone grabbed Lucia's arm and gave her a swift push. "Get the fuck outta the way!" a voice squawked. She whirled around to see a mingy-looking man with a toasted bald head. He was staggering under a hand-held camera rig, its lens pointed at the dancing celebrants.

"What d'you think you're doing?" Lucia demanded.

"Stealing footage."

"What for?"

"I'm a producer! I steal anything!"

He rotated the camera and pointed it at her.

"You'll find out when you get to the fuckin' coast!"

Lucia put her hands up to block the lens and backed away. Then she turned and fled toward the locker room. My God, she thought, the clowns who walk past Bloomingdale's!

When the referee came into the locker room she was stretched out on a bench smoking a cigarette. He sat down on another bench and watched Tory licking the salty sweat from her face.

"Nolo contendere," he said.

"Obviously."

"You didn't tone up your muscles. You didn't wear your glasses."

"No."

"You didn't even give up smoking."

Suddenly Lucia scowled. "Why did you come in here? The scene is over."

"What about me?"

"I can X you out on my typewriter."

"Or add another scene for just the two of us."

"Why should I?"

"A writer's job is to write." The referee smiled. "I must, of course, say anything you want me to say."

"I have no idea what I want you to say."

"Let me start talking. It'll come."

"Okay, start."

"A question. When was the last time you drew a bow?"

"When I was a little girl at camp. I won a red ribbon, third place for Brownies."

"Brownies?"

"It was a Girl Scout camp."

"Diana is the sister of Apollo, daughter of Zeus, huntsman-in-chief to the gods. There never was any hope for you."

"I know."

"Why'd you do it?"

"Not to be ordinary at the very end. Not to be soothing and polite about it."

"How come the gentleman target was decked out like a valentine?"

"That's how he sees himself—as a valentine but no longer addressed to me." She stubbed out her cigarette. "When I was in the sixth grade I received forty-two valentines addressed to me."

"You were loved."

"I thought I would grow up to be loved too. There was no reason to think otherwise then."

"And now?"

"It never lasts."

"Successore nova vincitur omnis amor. If your Latin is as rusty as

266

your archery, that means, 'All love is vanquished by succeeding love.' "

"I know who you are!" Lucia pushed Tory away and sat up. "You're 'Lonely professor desires cheerful nymph for sharing!' "

"Would you like to?"

"Don't be ridiculous. I'm not cheerful."

"We'll work on it."

"I'm too old to be a nymph."

"Age is irrelevant."

"I've been conned that way before. Anyhow, I'm through with the whole wine-and-roses trip."

"You wouldn't have answered my ad?"

"I haven't been a professor-in-a-seedy-suit groupie since I left college."

"My apologies for the suit. I only wear it on Commencement Day under a robe. Usually I wear Irish tweeds."

"In my sophomore year I had a heart-shattering experience with a professor in Irish tweeds."

"But I'm a totally different person!"

"Thank heavens, so am I."

Tory ran over to the referee and dropped her ball on his lap. Lucia reached for her bag and took out a white envelope.

"Your check. I'm sorry the job wasn't more of a challenge."

"I'm not." The referee threw the ball to the other end of the locker room for Tory. "I can barely see without bifocals."

"But you swore that—"

"I wanted to meet you."

"You're a liar with green eyes!"

"Can you forgive me?"

"It's a combination I was once fiercely attracted to."

"May I invite you to tea at least?"

"First I've got to go home and take a shower. I've got to feed my dog."

They had tea in the Palm Court at the Plaza sitting at a little table under a palm. The referee did all the talking while Lucia forced herself to stare into his green eyes. She was trying to cure her phobia the way a woman who was terrified of germs might cure herself by deliberately eating a hot dog she found in the street.

The referee lied and lied. He told her that true love may be around any corner and that middle age is a time of passion and pleasure. Worthy adventures are always the risky ones, he said, and only nitwits

267

manage to sidestep banana peels or duck pies in the face. Parsley, he said, is a hocus-pocus decoration meant to make whatever is served up look better than it is. He said there is no shame in being excessive in feeling and that anger is a short madness. *Ira furor brevis est,* he said.

In the center of the court under another clump of palms, a string trio played their own archaic lies: "I'll Always Be in Love with You," "You're My Everything," "Our Love Is Here to Stay." When they came up with an honest song and launched into the first few bars of "Just One of Those Things" it was time to leave.

Before they parted, Lucia thanked the referee. "You lie beautifully," she said. "It's been a lovely afternoon."

"You're about to have many of them," he told her. "Lovely nights too."

As she watched him skip away into the twilight she felt remarkably cheerful.

Who me?

16

How can you sleep beside a man for over ten years and then, three years later, look straight into his face and not have a notion who he is? I'm sure it's possible because it happened to me. If I'd heard it happened to someone else I'd have insisted it is impossible. All I can say is that Elaine's Restaurant is dark and makes everyone's eyes look dark.

This stranger is holding out his hand. "Thought I'd come over and say hello."

"Hello." I shake his hand. *Who is he?*

Then he is shaking my friend's hand and I hear her saying, "Nice to see you, Vincent."

Vincent!

"Vincent!" I shout. I leap up and stand there gaping at him. He's *thin.*

"Vincent, you look terrific!"

"You didn't even recognize me," he says, gleeful.

His beard and mustache are gone. I see a mouth I never saw naked before, and a chin. I'm instantly in mourning for his ginger-red beard and mustache. *What's happened to his hair? It's all cut off and combed forward in front like bangs.*

"Just terrific," I repeat, "but . . ."

"But what?"

"But now you—you look like everybody else." I mean only that he doesn't look like himself to me. He's furious. I've seen *that* expression before.

"That may be," he says icily, "but I feel wonderful!" He stalks off toward Diana sitting several tables away.

I sit down again. "How in the world did you recognize him?" I demand of my friend.

"He's very changed—but he's still Vincent."

"I didn't know who he was! I can't believe it! *I did not know who he was!*"

I'm unsettled for the rest of the evening. After we finish dinner I don't want to sit around drinking brandy, I just want to go home.

When I walk in, Tory greets me wagging her tail and we do what we do every night—go out into the long apartment corridor to play ball. After I throw the ball about two dozen times I put Tory out on the terrace, then I give her a bowl of milk and a dog biscuit. This is our nightly routine. Nothing is different. *Something is different.*

Later I'm in bed reading. Tory is asleep near my feet. I put the book down and lean over to stroke her head. "Hey!" I whisper. "Know what? Daddy Dog is dead."

The first call on Monday morning is from Kurt Newman. We make a date to have dinner and go to a movie. In discussing restaurants I discover that Kurt has no food allergies, there are no enemies of his stomach. He is bringing me, he says, a big load of record albums, which leads me to believe he has a strong back. It is autumn in New York and things are looking up.

The second call on Monday morning is from Sidney Powker. He has read my script over the weekend. He loves it. He says it's brilliant. Gil Harrison and his associates have read it too. They love it. They say it's brilliant.

"Great scenes, honey!" Sidney chortles. "I laughed! I cried! I couldn't put it down."

"Gee, Sidney."

"This show's dynamite. This show's gonna get a fifty share! Maybe even a sixty share!"

"You think people'll watch it?"

"When White Bread America digs what you're dealing with ain't nobody gonna turn that dial!"

"Not even Aunt Norma?"

"So a few old ladies—who cares? This one's gonna put you right up there, honey! You're gonna be so hot after this one you'll be fighting your way through the offers! And your price—sky's the limit!"

"Gee, Sidney."

"See how right I was? I had to bully you into doing it and I'm proud I did. I'm always looking out for you, honey. We're like a family."

"Bless you, Sidney."

270

"Gil and the guys wanna get together with you this week and discuss revisions."

"You said they loved it—"

"You know how it is. Contractually, you owe them a rewrite. They got some ideas, little things here and there, a few minor changes, honey, you know."

"I know. Blue pages."